BIOHAZARD

TIM CURRAN

www.severedpress.com

This novel is a work of fiction. Names, characters, places and incidents are the product of the author's imagination, or are used fictitiously. Any resemblance to actual events, locales or persons, living or dead, is purely coincidental.

ISBN: 978-0-9806065-8-4.

PROLOGUE

When the world ended on Thursday, October 17th, everyone ran blind and screaming with panic that it had finally happened, that Armageddon had finally been visited upon the sons and daughters of man. The optimistic were shocked; the pessimistic vindicated. The religious said it was the time of the Rapture. So as they waited for Jesus to call them home, the rest of us concentrated on staying alive.

No easy thing with the fallout.

The marauding militias.

The roving gangs.

The National Guard and special police units whose job it was to put them both down. Martial Law was declared country-wide. People were gunned down in the streets. Raped. Murdered. Assaulted. It went on and on.

And if all of that wasn't bad enough, by the end of the first week—seven days shy of Halloween—nuclear winter descended just as the theorists had always predicted. So much dust and debris had been tossed up into the atmosphere that the sun did not come out for almost a month. It was sheer blackness during that time and bitter subzero cold. And snow. It snowed for weeks on end. Nobody would ever know how many were killed off in those dire freezing weeks.

In the Midwest, the survivors—hardy northern types—dealt with it the way they dealt with it every winter. They burned wood. They scavenged pellet stoves, kerosene heaters, anything to keep them warm.

Then the sun came out again.

Just a ghost of it for the first few weeks. But then as the debris rained back to earth, much of it charged with deadly fallout, the sun assumed its ordinary cycles and though it was still cold, it was much warmer than it had been. And at least it wasn't pitch black twenty-four/seven.

Towards the end of December, a weird heat wave spread across the country and the snow melted and the rains came. Disease, which had been kept in check for the most part by the cold, went absolutely viral, raging in every population, creating pandemics and plagues and the already teetering civilian populations began to die off in numbers.

But some of us stayed alive.

And this is how we did it.

YOUNGSTOWN OHIO

1

When I close my eyes, I can still smell Youngstown.

Isn't that funny? I grew up there, played high school football there—go Blue Devils—and worked there, got married there...but now after all that, I can only remember the stink.

That invasive smell of rot and refuse.

It crawled up your nose and down into your belly, so that even with your eyes closed you knew you were in the city—rotting garbage and burning wood, fuel oil and the unburied dead. I figured, back then, that I should've bottled it, kept it on a shelf somewhere so that if the world ever started turning again, then I could pop the cork anytime I was feeling low and take a whiff. Then I could say to myself, yeah, maybe your life sucks, but it don't smell like Youngstown.

2

My wife had the gruesome twosome: radiation sickness and cholera. She got the former from the fallout coming down in the rains that swept the city for weeks, flooding the streets and backing up sewers and washing infected waste into yards and homes. She got the latter because like so many others she was weak from radiation sickness and the fact that the city's water supply was absolutely contaminated.

There was no point in bringing her to the hospital because they were vastly overcrowded with the sick and dying, corridors packed with people waiting for treatment, hospital incinerators blazing like blast furnaces as contaminated dressings, waste products, body fluids, and *corpses* were fed to the flames. The medical health system of Ohio, like the rest of the country, was inadequate as the infected and sick inundated it. It simply couldn't handle the sheer numbers.

It wasn't prepared.

And as drugs and medical supplies stopped coming in—factories around the country shutting down, commerce grinding to a halt—there wasn't enough to go around. Somewhere during the process, the staffs themselves sickened.

You get the picture.

Anyway, the fallout had already made Shelly pretty sick, but it was the cholera that hammered the final nail in her coffin. I washed her, medicated her, fed her, held her through many long nights.

Cholera is a nasty business.

Vomiting and diarrhea, painful cramping and dehydration, fevers and delusions. It's not pretty. I treated her the way the hospital told me to and with what they gave me. I made sure she drank lots of fluids. I dissolved packets of sodium, potassium, glucose, and chloride in her water, made sure she got it down. Gave her injections of antibiotics—tetracycline, ampicillin, chloramphenicol—but mostly I just held her and soothed her while something inside, maybe hope and faith, withered and went black like flower petals on a crypt floor.

It was horrible.

I kept remembering that in August we'd vacationed at Chesapeake Bay on Smith Island and things had been good, very good. The sun had been bright and the water had been sparkling and I rubbed suntan oil on her back. She was bronze in the sun and her eyes were a deep Caribbean blue. We made love at night and beach-bummed during the day and ate clams in the evening.

And six months later she died trembling in my arms.

I kept watch over her corpse for days.

It was some kind of twisted wake, I guess. I lit candles and talked to her, alternately crying and screaming out her name, but mostly drinking whiskey in some numb alcoholic stupor, my mind sucked into a whirlpooling psychosis of grief and guilt and denial.

Down below, in the streets, the corpse wagons rolled and the crazies rioted and what was left of the police put them down in a grisly baptismal of blood and then were themselves put down.

"They won't get you, Shelly," I told her. "I won't let them."

It was getting worse day by day.

Four months now. Four months and I was still in Youngstown, hoping, maybe, that humanity would regroup and that we'd be able to put Humpty Dumpty back together again. But it wasn't going to happen and what was spread out on the couch was testament to that.

I knew I should have gotten out.

I should have gotten both of us out of the city—maybe across the state line into PA, my sister in Newcastle—but I kept holding onto some crazy and utterly fucked-up idea that the end of the world was going to pass like a bout of the flu. Civilization had shit its pants and vomited its guts out, but it would pass. The fever would run its course.

That's how deep in denial I was. For when those bombs fell...and baby, they came down like rice at a wedding...the world ripped the seat right out of its pants like a fat lady bending over and there was no seamstress that could hope to stitch it back up again.

And now Shelly was dead.

Dead.

She was pale as bleached stone, her body shriveled and ghastly in death. Outside, a fearsome gonging rolled through the neighborhood. The bell of St. Mark's: *Bong, bong, bong, bring out yer dead!*

But I wasn't about to.

Not Shelly. I'd never let them get her. I'd never let them burn her in one of those terrible pits with the others. The idea was just grotesque to the extreme and I could not allow it to happen. But I couldn't sit with her day after day. Not only because it was seriously demented, but because eventually *they* would come for her. There had to be something I could do. Then I got the idea of burying her in secret. Such a thing was unlawful, it was banned. If people saw you they would report you and if the police and civil authorities caught you they would shoot you. But that only made it all that much more necessary.

I was going to bury my wife, have a little service over her grave.

That's what I was going to do and I coldly planned on murdering any asshole that got in my way. So, that godawful church bell gonging in my ears, I got my shit together, smoothed out the rough spots, and got down to it. For the first time in weeks I smiled, taking a secret, warped joy in the fact that I would bury my wife illegally. It was my way of raising my middle finger to the state. Fuck them. Fuck authority. Fuck those that had created this nightmare in the first place. Those evil, fucked-up minds, all part of the same corrupt bureaucracy that had killed the world.

I took a white satin coverlet that Shelly had loved and wrapped her up in it, kissed her cold dead lips once last time and stitched it shut. Outside, the trucks were getting closer. I could hear them rumbling, see their flashing lights arcing in the dark sky. Out on the streets there were voices.

They were coming.

Bring out yer dead.

3

Following nuclear winter, there was one nasty epidemic after another. People were dying in droves and the traditional mortuaries simply could not deal with it.

So the church bells rang.

They rang throughout the day and night and it wasn't because somebody was going to get married in the chapel of love. No, they rang because the corpse wagons were coming to collect the dead. Dumptrucks, flatbeds, it didn't matter. If it had a hopper it was converted to a corpse-collector. And given that radio, TV, and the internet had broken down, the city fathers decided to go with the oldest form of communication in cities and villages: the church bell. Churches were spread across Youngstown and most neighborhoods had one or two so when the wagons were rolling, the bells rang.

All you had to do was throw your loved ones' body out on the curb with your recycling and they'd grab it for you.

Civic action. Made a guy feel good.

Bong-bong-bong-BONG! The wagons are a rolling, brothers and sisters, so let's forget about care and decency and respect and get completely fucking Medieval on your ass. Uncle Joe vomited his guts out in bloody coils last night? Mom has drowned in a sea of her own collected waste? Little Cathy burst open with black, pustulating sores? The little missus got the spores and ulcers ate her down to a flux of cool, white jelly? No problem, my friend. Wrap him or her or it in a tarp or put what's left in a Hefty bag, box it, bag it, but please don't tag it, and we'll take care of the rest! Not quite dead but damn near? Cash 'em in anyway, no sense infecting the entire neighborhood. And while we're on the subject, you got some ugly dig-dogged looking boils on yer face, son, better jump up in the wagon before you start shitting out the red worms and pissing yellow slime and yer eyes fill with blood and explode out of yer head and stain the new sofa.

It was ugly.

It was degrading.

It was inhuman.

But it was also quite necessary, you see.

There were corpses everywhere in the city, rotting in the gutters and piled up on the sidewalks like garbage. There was radiation sickness, of course, from the clouds of fallout drifting west from New York and east from Chicago, but poor sanitation had led to rampant outbreaks of cholera, typhoid, diphtheria, and the plague. New forms of influenza and pneumonia were making the rounds as well as a mutant strain of hemorrhagic fever that was devastating what was left of certain eastern cities like Philadelphia and Pittsburgh and, according to survivor rumor, eating its way through Akron.

In Youngstown the bodies were burned, but after awhile there were just so many that people started throwing them out into yards and dumping them on sidewalks. And all those rotting stiffs, well, they became disease vectors bringing in the rats and the flies which further spread the pestilence. The pathogens were in the water, blown on the air, and people continued to die.

It was insane.

It was hopeless.

And it had only just begun.

4

As I plotted the secret burial of my wife, there was a knock at the door.

I wasn't going to answer it...but I knew if I didn't, the men from the corpse wagons would kick it down, come thundering forth in their white decon suits and take Shelly away before I could sneak off with her.

"Who is it?"

"It's me," a voice whispered. "It's Bill."

Bill Hermes lived down the hall. He was okay. An old railroad man and widower, we'd had him over for dinner dozens of time. Shelly was always fussing over him, making him cookies and bars and all that. A nice old guy.

I sighed. "What do you want?"

"Rick...need to talk to you."

I opened the door a crack. "What is it, Bill?"

He swallowed. "Rick, I'm here about Shelly. Nobody's seen her in weeks. People are starting to talk."

"Fuck 'em."

"Son...the wagons are coming."

"I don't have anything for 'em."

Bill wiped his teary eyes with a hankie. "Not saying you do. I'm hoping you don't. But...but I overheard a couple boys downstairs. They're saying that Shelly's on the list. *On that fucking list.* You know what that means."

That meant somebody had ratted us out, told the health department that Shelly was dying. Probably the hospital. Radiation sickness coupled with cholera...it was only a matter of time. The clean-up workers would come for her or at least demand proof that she was still breathing.

The trucks were getting closer.

"Thanks, Bill," I said, shutting the door.

Time to move.

Cradling Shelly in my arms and making sure the corridor was empty, I slipped downstairs using the back steps. Out in the alley, I carried her around the rear of the building and cut through the little field back there. I was sweating, shaking, feeling like some convict who had just gone over the wall at Sing Sing. Shelly hardly weighed anything. I could have run for miles with her. I was almost across the field when somebody shouted: *"There! There he is!"*

They were coming and I was running.

Men with flashlights were entering the field. I cut through a little thicket, snagging Shelly's shroud on blackberry thorns. I fought my way through, hands and face scratched. I fell only once but got right up again, kept going. When I made it out of the thicket, white-suited men were converging and trucks with spotlights were coming up the street.

I was trapped.

I started this way and that, but it was no good. The trucks were bearing down and the men with flashlights were closing in through the thicket. They were everywhere. Nowhere to run. It was perfectly surreal and completely unreal. The men chasing me. The flashlights. The trucks. The stink of death from the gutters. The stagnant mist creeping in off the river. The stars overhead blotted out by a dirty smudge of black smoke rising from the body pits outside the city where they burned the corpses.

I made a mad dash out into the street and one of the trucks nearly ran me down. Warning shots were fired, bullets zipping around. Spotlights found me and held me, blinding me there on the wet pavement.

A truck rolled to a stop and four men in white containment suits that were not so white anymore took hold of me while I fought and clawed and screamed. They stank of corpse-slime. I shouted at them and took a rifle butt to the temple that sent me sprawling. I was out for a moment or two after that, then I got back up again, fought my way through a tangle of men, hitting and being hit, knocking them aside in my wild flight. When I got around the back of the truck, I saw Shelly up there atop a moldering heap of corpses. Her shroud had burst, one chalk-white arm hanging out. I could smell the putrescence and hear the buzzing meat flies. Some of the corpses were rotten and green, writhing with worms.

Shelly. Oh dear God. *Shelly.*

The men grabbed at me, but I went loco. I hit and kicked and got free.

They fell back, not wanting to rupture their dirty suits. I jumped up amongst the carrion and nobody came after me. I was sweating and bleeding, head pounding like a drum, mind filled with shadows and screaming voices. It was insane, totally insane, but I just couldn't let Shelly be up there. Not with the others, not with those *dead ones.* And there were dozens and dozens of them in the back of the dump truck. Just a great shivering mass of carrion infested with crawling and squirming things. As I tried to climb up there my hands sank through spongy bellies that let out clouds of gagging yellow corpse gas. Out of my mind with grief, I crawled and clawed through a noisome sea of putrefaction. My fingers penetrated pulpy faces, scraping over skulls for purchase.

And then scant inches from Shelly's shroud...I collapsed.

Revolted, sickened, just beside myself, all the energy ran out of me. I slid down that heap of corpses, face netted with buzzing flies, rank meat packed beneath my fingernails.

"You ready to come down now, son?" one of the men asked.

I slid out of the back and they knocked me to the pavement, kicking the shit out of me until I lost consciousness. When I woke, a few hours later, I was lying in the grass where they'd thrown me. A dog was licking the filth from my fingers. My breath was fuming out in cold white clouds, the face of the moon above stained with a black trail of smoke from the ever-blazing body pits.

This is what it had come to.

God bless America.

5

All I wanted after that was to be alone, to brood and break down in private with a bottle of whiskey in one hand, but Bill Hermes found me and wouldn't let that happen.

"She's dead now," he said. "Shelly's gone and she's at peace. Don't profane her memory by destroying yourself."

Sage advice. I knew it made perfect sense just as I knew I would not follow it. All I wanted now was destruction, cool white oblivion. Maybe Bill sensed that too, because he boiled water on his woodstove and drew a bath and made me clean up. And when that was done, he made me some food. It was canned like everything else these days, but at least it was something to put in my stomach.

As I ate, picking at corned beef hash and powdered eggs, he watched me. Watched me very closely. He pulled a Winston out of a crumpled red pack, snapped off the filter and lit up, blowing smoke out of his nostrils. And never once did he take his eyes off of me.

"Well, go ahead, Bill," I said. "You got something to say, so say it."

He chuckled. "I'm thinking it's time you pack up your old kit bag and move on. Nothing here for you now. City's getting worse by the day. Get out. Get out into the country where a man has a chance."

"We lived here. This was our neighborhood."

"That's all past now, son. Nothing but memories. Get out for chrissake. Get out now."

"You coming?"

"For what? Ain't nothing out there for me. I'm too damn old to start again."

I set my fork down. "Nothing here but memories for you, too, Bill."

"When you get my age," he said, blowing out a cloud of smoke, "there ain't much else."

He turned away and looked out the curtains to the streets below. Just shook his head. "Goddamn cesspool, Rick. That's what. Been wanting to get out for a long time. Would've, too, if Ellen hadn't loved it here so much. She grew up two streets away. Even after she passed...I don't know...something held me."

"Something's holding me, too."

"Bullshit." Bill coughed into his hand and for maybe the first time, I noticed how blotchy his face looked. A funny yellow sheen to it. "Bullshit, I say. You need to go before it gets worse. Right goddamn now, Rick. I'm too old to go with you. You pull an old tree up by the roots, its dies. But a young one...you can replant it and it'll bear leaf. You following me?"

I was. "I'll think it over."

Bill looked like he was about to read me the riot act, but then the wind went out of him and he broke into a coughing fit. The cigarette fell from his fingers and he held himself up by the countertop.

I was on my feet. "Bill..."

He waved me away. "I'm all right. Just old. Just smoking too much for too long. That's all."

But I wasn't believing that. The coughing. The weakness. The blotchy face. No, this was something else entirely. And he had it good.

"Rick, get the hell out," he said, pulling himself up, standing erect with great exertion that left him gasping. "Ellen and I...oh, Jesus in heaven...we loved you and Shelly to death. Never had kids of our own. Always thought if we did, they might be like you two. So do an old man a favor and get out of the city."

"Bill, I..."

"Please, Rick."

There was no doubt about it at all then: Bill Hermes had radiation sickness.

A week later he was dead.

6

Bill Hermes was a good man. A wise man seasoned by time and experience. Did I listen to his advice? Of course not. I stayed. God help me, but I did.

Food and water were the biggest problems. For so long I had been mainly concerned with nursing Shelly back to health and in doing so, I had let everything else go to shit. Mother Hubbard's cupboard was bare as Miss July's thigh so I took to the streets with the rest of the gutter rats, scavenging anything I could find.

When Shelly's deterioration began, the city had been running a series of aid stations with fresh water, food, and medical supplies. But in the many weeks since these had all been closed up and boarded down. Other than the Army out patrolling there was little order, state and local government having collapsed on just about every conceivable level.

So gun in hand, I hunted.

And was hunted.

I had a 9mm Browning Hi-Power I'd taken from Bill Hermes' apartment. I'd never killed a man in my life and never truly wanted to, but I knew the time was coming. I'd jacked a few rounds over the heads of some bad boys that had been coming after me, but never anything more.

Then, about three or four days after Bill died, some old guy came up to me in the street, wanted a cigarette. Poor bastard was shot through with acute radiation sickness: teeth all gone, hair fallen out, face covered with ulcers.

But I wasn't taking any chances.

I put the gun on him, told him to stay back. With so many dying of infectious disease in the city, I had a real horror of all the nasty germs floating around out there and what they could do. The radiation did something to those germs, made bigger, badder, more virulent bugs out of them. Some were the same old bugs, but others were much deadlier than they once were. And I'd already been exposed to cholera by then and God knew what else. My number was going to come up sooner or later.

The old man attempted a smile. "Just want one of them cigarettes. That's all." He broke up into a coughing fit, spewing blood and bile to the sidewalk. "Gimme one, friend. Gimme one and I'll tell you where there's food. I ain't got but a day or two left. It won't do me no good."

I threw him a pack and a book of matches. "Keep 'em. I got more."

He was nearly orgasmic as he smoked that cigarette. Such is the nature of addiction. Something I knew well. I had quit smoking three years before...but after the bombs came down, what with the stress I started again. After he got a few drags down, he told me where there was a deli. Canned food that had barely been touched. I was welcome to it.

I scouted down a few streets, found the back door to the deli like the old guy said. And like he said, the deli had a storeroom with boxes and boxes of canned and dried goods. Like a kid in a candy store, I filled my sack with canned pasta, vegetables, tinned milk, mac and cheese. I was pretty happy about it all. I was doing real good. Too good, I soon learned.

When I tried to leave, a woman came stumbling out of the front of the store. She was wearing an old fur coat with nothing on beneath. Her flesh was pitted with spreading sores and flaking scabs. There was some crusty fungal growth coming out of her nose and she was entirely bald. She looked at me with glassy, fixed eyes and grinned with a mouth of graying, broken teeth.

"Mine," she said, holding out her filthy hands. *"It's all mine!"*

I put the Browning on her. "Get the fuck away from me."

"Mine!" she said, yellow foam running down her chin like she was rabid. *"Give it to me, pretty boy! It's all mine!"*

She launched herself forward and I didn't even get a shot off.

I brought the gun up, yes, but like most people that weren't used to killing, I hesitated. And that split second of hesitation was all she needed. She threw herself at me, knocking me flat, knocking the gun right out of my hand. I hit the floor and then she was on top of me, pinning me down. Her stench was gagging, sickening: like warm rotting fruit, a fermenting and moist odor. She had her scabby hands around my throat, squeezing the life out of me. My guts heaved. I needed badly to vomit. And it wasn't just her stink or the rot of her face or the foul slime that dripped from her mouth...it was what she was doing.

Gyrating.

Dry-humping me, rubbing her infested crotch against me with greasy violent gyrations.

"Pretty boy! Pretty boy! Pretty, pretty, pretty boy!" the hag kept saying, ribbons of slime hanging from her mouth. *"I'm fucking the pretty boy!"*

It was this more than anything that gave me the strength to fight back: pure, unreasoning physical revulsion. I hit her in the face three, four times, her head rocking back each time. And then I clawed at her eyes. Her ulcerated flesh was so soft with rot that my fingers slid right into her cheek and scraped against the skull beneath. And somewhere during the process, I hooked my knee under her and threw her off.

Then I dove for the gun and she scrambled after me on all fours like some obscene, fleshy spider. The Browning in my fist, I let out a savage screaming war cry and pulled the trigger.

The bullet caught her right in the belly and she went down to her knees, pressing scabby hands to the wound. Blood juiced out between her fingers.

"Ohhhhhhhh! Look what you did, pretty boy! Look what you did!"

When she came at me again, I shot her in the head. Brain matter and blood sprayed against the wall in an oily pattern. She hit the floor, mouth still opening and closing like a fish gulping for air. She trembled and flopped around and then jerked into stillness. In death, there was a mucid hissing and something like a gray clotted slime flooded out from between her legs.

Rotting fish. It smelled like rotting fish.

I threw up. The vomit came out in a warm spray and kept coming until I was shuddering with dry heaves. And when it was over I wondered if I hadn't just been purging my stomach contents, but maybe something more ethereal and necessary like my soul.

Anyway, I backed away from her corpse, into the store, made to run and there were two more: a man and a woman. Both bald. Both foaming at the mouth. Both with sores on their faces and those crazy eyes.

I shot both of them.

Kept shooting even when they were down.

This was my first altercation with the *Scabs,* as they were known. After that, after what that hideous woman had done to me which I likened almost to rape, I shot those ugly, infected bastards on sight without hesitation.

That was my first taste of blood. I had popped my cherry. It got real easy after that.

There were crazies everywhere. But, oddly enough, good people, too. People that would warn you against dangerous neighborhoods, places where night-things lay in wait, areas where the National Guard would shoot you on sight. One day, being chased by a gang of Scabs, a guy with a long black hillbilly beard came to my aid with a shotgun. He seemed all right. Afterwards, we had soup in his barren basement apartment. He never spoke and would only grunt when I asked him things. There were two shrouded forms stretched out on the floor.

"Those are my daughters," he finally said. "I killed 'em. I killed both of 'em. They was starting to change."

"Change?"

The guy put black fierce eyes on me. "Into them *others.* The ones with the glowing eyes. They only come out at night. Better watch yourself."

I got out of there, thinking the guy was as crazy as the rest. It wasn't until two days later that I knew he wasn't. You see, that's when I saw one of them.

One of the Children.

7

It was getting dark and I was far from home. That alone was trouble. With everything I'd seen by that point, I should have known better. But I lived by scavenging and I had to go where the best pickings were. On the corner of Mahoning Avenue and South Glenellen there was a St. Vinnie's depot where they stockpiled food for the needy. I had given a guy a .38 pistol for the information. He was leaving the city, he didn't care about the food.

So there I was.

I went into the depot by breaking a window in the alley. I slipped through, found the food with no problem. There were no crazies or mutants about so it was easy pickings. I loaded my bag with canned food, boxes of pasta, tins of deviled ham, the works.

My sack was full and I was a happy little gutter rat. I had just bought myself a few more weeks of life.

When I came out the sun was going down.

And when the sun goes down, all the night things slink out, all the predators and meat-eaters, headhunters and bone-collectors and bloodsuckers. On the sidewalk was a dog. It was just sitting there. A mangy, dirty golden retriever that was missing half an ear. His coat was crusty with dried blood. He looked up at me, laid back his ears and growled.

I could have shot him.

Maybe if I had instead of playing good Samaritan, I would have been home before the trouble started. But I felt sorry for that dog. He wasn't rabid. I could see that. Nor did he look infected with anything or mutated. I took a chance. I talked to him in very soothing tones. He calmed down right away. He wagged his tail and made a whining sound in his throat. And those eyes...Jesus...if you've ever had a retriever you know how they can look at you with the saddest eyes in creation, arching their eyebrows and looking so human you could cry.

That's what this fella did.

"It's okay, boy," I told him. "I won't hurt you. Maybe you can come live with me, eh? We can take care of each other."

He wagged his tail, still watching me. He was a good dog. I was willing to bet he'd been a family pet. Retrievers are great dogs...gentle, easy with kids, incredibly patient and loyal. I knew this old warhound had been of that variety. I got down on my knees by him and made a peace offering: a Slim Jim. One of those processed beef sticks. You know the kind. The dog loved it. He gobbled it right down so I gave him a second and a third and I had a friend for life. I could have cried because I had finally found someone—or something—to care about that I knew would care for me, too. That's the thing about a dog. You can love men and women, but the human breed is a selfish one and they'll hurt you if they get the chance. But not a dog. You feed them and care for them and they'll love you to death, follow you straight into hell without question, and tear the balls off anyone that threatens you. That's loyalty. Try and find that in a human being. Good luck.

So I had myself a pal.

But it was getting dark. Time to boogie. I walked away down the sidewalk, knowing I had about four blocks to go, but the dog didn't follow me. He just sat there on the sidewalk looking forlorn, destitute, and unhappy. "Well, come on!" I said, slapping my leg. He bolted after me, rubbing his snout against my leg, leaping around with the sort of pure joy only a dog knows.

We had a few more Slim Jims. I scratched his ears. I chatted with him. Then, as the shadows grew long, we both got very quiet as we stalked through what was very much enemy territory. The dog was hearing things, smelling things, sensing things. I felt more invulnerable than ever with him by my side: nothing can sneak up on a retriever when they're wide-eyed and bushy-tailed.

About two blocks from my building, the dog stopped.

He perked up his ears...well, one of them anyway...and cocked his head. He began sniffing the ground. He made a low growling sound of alarm in his throat. He had caught wind of something and he did not like it.

I urged him on and there, standing on the sidewalk in a pool of moonlight, was a little girl. She was just a little slip of a thing with pigtails and the filthy remains of a blue jumper. I figured she was maybe eight years old, something like that. The dog went wild, snapping and howling, just beside myself.

"Quiet," I told him. I looked to the girl. "Honey, what are you doing out this late? It's not safe...it's..."

That's about as far as I got. For right then I got a good look at her and something in my guts pulled up in fear. This was no little girl. Her eyes were bright and yellow, luminous, and her face was a seamed and corded fright mask, an awful grayish-blue in color. She held up hands to me, her mouth opening and revealing a set of tiny hooked teeth of the sort that were designed to seize prey and hold onto it. Steam was rising from her and there was a sound of crackling energy like static electricity in a blanket.

A shrill piping noise came from her mouth, growing in volume until it was nearly hypersonic, painful to hear. She drifted forward, a low pulsating glow enveloping her, sparking with nuclear waste. She did not walk, she *drifted,* hot radioactive steam boiling from her, leaving a flickering misty trail in her wake.

She would have had me.

I fell back and fired twice and missed with both rounds. But the dog wasn't about to let her get me, God bless him. He howled and charged, leaping right at her with jaws wide for attack. She enfolded him in her arms and he let out a wild, shrieking whine of pain. The dog literally burned up in her arms. It blazed with a cool blue fire, smoking and blistering, shriveling down to a blackened, smoldering thing right before my eyes. There was a hot, violent stink of cremated dog...then he fell from her arms, burning bones and blowing gray ash.

By then I was running. She did not come after me and by the time I got home and into my building I was shaking so badly I couldn't even hold the glass of whiskey I tried to pour down my throat. That poor dog. I would never forget him...what he did for me and what that irradiated wraith did to *him.*

After that, whenever I saw a dog that wasn't rabid, infected, or mutated, I gave him food, water, anything I could. And also after that, I shot the Children on sight. For if there are ghouls haunting the graveyard of this world, then they are the Children.

8

One thing I got used to very quickly were the corpses.

Because they were literally everywhere. The city itself wasn't much more than a blasted, broken corpse itself. There had been so much fighting between the National Guard and private militias that entire neighborhoods were burned out, buildings collapsed from heavy firepower. Avenues were congested with rubble and the blackened carapaces of vehicles. Telephone poles had been knocked over and lay tangled in the knotted mesh of their own wires.

And everywhere in the urban graveyard...bodies.

By April, the corpse wagon system had broken down entirely and the dead were left wherever they had fallen or were thrown.

They were the only raw materials the city had left and they were in abundance. In whole and in part. Some rotted down skeletons, others burned to blackened husks, and many more swollen up green in the sun, clouds of meatflies rising and descending, feeding and laying their eggs. It wasn't unusual to see the dead moving, shivering, because they were so infested with maggots. Many corpses had been gnawed upon. Probably rats. But other things, too, that only came out when the sun went down.

The heavy snows that had buried Youngstown had melted almost overnight, leaving standing pools of water throughout the city in which waterlogged bodies floated. The heavy rains had washed them into yards and doorways, created rivers of them that lapped up against storefronts. And what amazed me the most—and maybe frightened me, too—was that I and the other survivors paid the heaped human remains very little attention. We scavenged amongst them and hopped over them and kicked them aside, and the only time they were avoided was because of the disease vectors they might be carrying.

After awhile, you got used to anything.

So given that the city was inundated with the unburied dead in every possible stage of decomposition, it really was no surprise that nature in her endless creativity had now spawned mutants that took advantage of all the carrion.

A few blocks from my apartment house there was a 7-11. Back in the day I used to stop there for Slurpies and chili dogs, but within two months of Shelly's death it had been converted into a body dump for some insane reason. There were hundreds of bodies there broiling in the sun, exhaling clouds of flies and a hot, gaseous stench that would put you right down to your knees.

Word had it that even the incinerators and burning pits couldn't handle all the dead, so they were stored in alternate locations throughout the city. So the corpse wagons just dumped them in the parking lot.

I passed by it almost daily, paid little mind to the piled dead. The entire city stank like a sunwashed cadaver by that point, but it was particularly concentrated at the 7-11 so I always wore a neckerchief over my mouth. The only thing that intrigued me was the idea that there might be food in the 7-11 that nobody had scavenged. But even the idea of that couldn't get me to brave the carrion field. The flies were so thick in the air that it looked like a churning cloud of soot rising above the corpses which were heaped in dozens of mounds that had decayed into rank, oozing masses.

One day I found a box of untouched canned food at another Salvation Army depot and I had to pass the body dump on my way home. As I did, I saw that the bodies were moving.

They were actually *moving*.

I thought at first it was the gas making them writhe and shudder, but that's not what it was at all. Curious, I stood there with my box of goodies, the hot stink blowing over me, the flies buzzing madly.

And that's when I saw my first corpse-worm.

It burst from the mouth of a stiff...thick as a man's wrist, segmented, slick with something slimy like snot. It was flattened out like a tapeworm. It rose right up and hovered there like a cobra preparing to strike. Now it didn't have any eyes that I could see, but I was almost certain with a rising aversion that it was *looking* right at me. There was sort of a bulb where its mouth should have been and it kept opening and closing like it was breathing, the whole time dripping a black fluid like India ink.

I just stared, perplexed, revolted.

I dropped my box of food, cans of beans and Spaghettios rolling around the sidewalk.

That worm just hovered there like it was daring me to intervene. Then another worm slid out of a dead woman's green belly and another forced itself free from the eye socket of a fleshy skull. Pretty soon they were all coming out like they needed to sun themselves, like nightcrawlers drawn out by the rain. Some of them were no bigger around than fingers, but others were as thick as a human leg. They came out of nostrils and eye sockets and assholes, slithering forth and rising up, all of them slimy and corpse-belly white.

I had seen things by that point, things created by fallout that would have driven me mad a year before, but nothing like those worms.

They soon tired of me, however, having no interest whatsoever in living flesh, and went back to work. They started to eat, tunneling through that heaped carrion, sucking and slurping and chewing. Once they burrowed their way into a body, the buffet was open. That bulb or mouth or whatever in the Christ it was, would squirt some of that black juice into the corpse and the innards would liquefy. That juice was some sort of digestive enzyme, like what spiders inject into their prey—they'd squirt it in and then suck up the dissolved liquid.

It was sickening.

But what was even worse was that I saw a dozen worms slide up out of bodies and wrap themselves together in a fleshy helix. They coiled together like that, making some weird trilling sound, vibrating, a watery mucus enveloping them.

This is what made me run.

For I knew, you see, that they were breeding. And that horrible trilling sounded positively orgasmic, pleasurable...like the worms were getting off.

And this was but another component of the world I inherited.

9

By the time May rolled around it had reached the point where I simply had had enough. I was tired of scratching out my meager existence. Tired of the bullshit and the stress and the gnawing anxiety of survival. For after all: what exactly was I surviving *for?*

Depressed, weary, broken, I thought it over and came to what I thought was the only reasonable solution: I would kill myself. So one dreary night I got a knife and made ready to lay my wrists open.

Believe me, I didn't do this lightly. But I was exhausted. I just couldn't go on. You had to be an animal to survive and it just wasn't in me to do it day after fucking day. The world was dying one day at a time and my wife was gone. What was the point of trying to go on, trying to survive? Warmongers and politicians had torn the guts right out of everything and now it was all over. The American dream had become a global nightmare and gone was the green perfection of high summer and the cool white kiss of low winter and all the Saturdays and baseball games and Fourth of July's and crisp Autumn days and children's voices singing Christmas carols. All fucking gone. All wadded up like a piss-stained newspaper and thrown into the trash.

What was left was a lunatic asylum without boundaries.

Weather patterns went to hell. Freak storms swept the globe.

The water was contaminated.

Crops left rotting in the fields.

What remained of the human race was rioting, insane, or dying.

Diseases we had thought very little of in our enlightened age of antibiotics, and had long since been kicked to the curb, came knocking on the door with a fresh bloom of death in their cheeks: cholera, typhoid fever, bubonic plague, diphtheria, infectious influenza. A dozen mutated forms that were never even properly categorized.

Fallout came down in deadly clouds, in sweeping dust storms, in the rain that fell from the sky.

Rats and flies and mosquitoes and every form of vermin imaginable—and some *un*imaginable—were breeding in numbers that were unthinkable.

Gangs ran wild in the streets looting and raping and murdering.

There were bloody encounters between private militias and the army.

Bodies were piled on the sidewalks.

Entire neighborhoods were being "sterilized" to slow the spread of disease.

Corpses were burned in black smoldering pits.

This was the final inheritance of the nation and the world. While the TV and radio stations were still broadcasting and the internet was still active, I saw it all and was sickened and horrified like everyone else, pushed down into some dark quarter of my mind where I could scream in silence. And when all mass communication and mass media failed...I saw it out my window, in the streets below. There was no point in surviving. No point in seeing what a year would bring or ten of them. It had all been wiped clean. Just like they had always said about nuclear war: five minutes from the rocket age to the Stone Age.

I did not want to see what would come next.

So, alone and beaten, completely hollow inside, I pressed a knife to my wrist. And as I did so I heard a hissing sound like a gas valve left open. And a voice, a clear and authoritative voice, said in my ear, *"Do you want to live?"*

I dropped the knife first and then slid out of my chair like my bones were made of rubber. I was numb. I couldn't move, I couldn't talk, I couldn't even fucking breathe. I hit the floor, senseless and terrified, shaking so badly my teeth chattered. That voice, that awful voice—

"Do you want to live?"

"Yes," I said when my breath came back. I wasn't honestly sure if I wanted to or not, but I was so scared I was afraid to say anything else.

"Will you come unto me?" the voice said in a cool glacial hiss. *"Through me there is deliverance, there is survival. Expiation. I demand atonement. Bring unto me the burnt offerings selected by thy hand. They shall be blessed by fire.*

"Sacrifice..."

That was The Shape.

It never showed itself and maybe I was too unclean to look upon it. It told me how it had to happen, how it all had to come down. I had a benefactor. I didn't know what it was or what it wanted at that point, but it kept talking to me, whispering in my head, always pointing me in the right direction, keeping me alive. It terrified me. It intrigued me. I felt special. I felt damned. Months later, I could not be sure I really heard it. Maybe it wasn't a voice at all, maybe it was some warped subjective impression. And maybe I was just insane. But that's how it began. That's how I sold my soul to stay alive.

That's how I got into the business of condemning people to death.

But I didn't know about that part. Not then.

10

After that, I lived like a spider.

After The Shape had whispered to me—alluding to things I must do but never naming them—I hunted the city, seeking out damp, dark corners and crevices where I could secrete myself, webby and lightless places where the roving gangs of scavengers and the packs of wild dogs couldn't find me. I became good at hiding and stalking mainly because The Shape was always in my head, telling me where to find food and shelter, which damp and dripping cellars were safe and free of rabid rat colonies.

Then one day while out searching for weapons, I got drafted.

The Army or what was left of it found me.

I came out of an alley and I saw two men in white biosuits. They carried tactical carbines and were pointing them right in my face. There was no point in running; they would have cut me down in ten feet. So I just stood there, dumbly, the Browning Hi-Power at my waist and my scavenger bag thrown over one shoulder. I suppose by that point I looked like any other ragbag...unwashed, ragged, eyes crazy and desperate.

They kept their rifles on me.

"Listen," I finally said, holding my hands up, "I don't want any trouble. I was just trying to find something to eat. I'll just back away and go my own way. Okay?"

The two men just looked at each other through the plexiglass shields of their white helmets.

I started backing away.

And as I did so, the one on the left sprayed the alley wall with his carbine. 9mm rounds chewed into the brick just above my head. I went down on my knees, hands still up. "Jesus...take it easy, guys...just...take...it...easy..."

"You ain't going nowhere, fuckhead," one of them said. He looked at his partner. "Check him."

The guy charged over and knocked me on my ass. He stripped the Browning away and the scavenger bag, took my knife, everything but the clothes I wore. Then he made me lay spreadeagle in the alley, facedown in a dirty puddle. He ran a Geiger Counter over me, checked for sores, ulcers.

"Looks clean," the soldier said.

"Get up, fuckhead," the other guy said. "Congratulations, you've been drafted."

I looked up at him. "Hell are you talking about?"

But the guy just laughed as I was handcuffed and led to an olive drab tactical van down the street. They shoved and kicked me all the way. And when they asked me how I liked the Army, I told them to go fuck their mothers. Which got me a rifle butt to the back of the head and a ticket to la-la land.

Drafted.

That's what those assholes called it.

I was part of a clean-up crew, me and a bunch of other idiots that had been likewise "drafted."

There was nothing remotely military about the job. We simply had to pick up bodies. Decked out in white biosuits, we tooled around in garbage trucks collecting the dead which were a serious health threat.

That was how I met Specs, this skinny little guy with oversized glasses that the soldiers liked to pick on. Me, Specs, two others guys named Paulson and Jackoby made up the collection crew. Of course, the sergeant in charge—some hardballed lifer named Weeks—collectively called us his "Shitheads." He also had pet names for us: I was "Fuckhead," Specs was "Mama's Boy," Jackoby was "Shit-fer-Brains," and Paulson was "Mr. Fucking Useless."

It was quite a scene.

The corpses were gathered, then tossed into the hoppers like Monday's trash. The first time I saw Paulson pull the lever and cycle the bodies through, the hydraulic ram crushing and compacting the bodies, I threw up. Right in the street. My stomach was already bad from handling all that green meat, but the *sound* of it, those blades scooping the bodies into the main bin and smashing them to a pulp...it was just too much. I went down on my knees and stripped my mask off, blowing my guts right on the pavement.

The soldiers burst out laughing.

Weeks said, "You don't like that shit, Fuckhead? Maybe next I'll throw your ass in there, you fucking pussy."

Specs helped me to my feet. "You get used to it, man. It's fucked up, but you do."

No draftee in any war went through worse shit than we did.

You stood there in those hot suits, flies buzzing around you and maggots dropping from your gloves, just filthy with all the revolting shit that oozed from the bodies. And that was bad enough, but what was worse was *hearing* those cadavers compact. Even our helmets couldn't muffle the sound of dozens of putrefying corpses being crushed, bones snapping and flesh being squished to mush. Every time a load was cycled through, black muddy ooze would run from the bottom of the hopper and rain to the street, squeezed from the corpses like pulp from tomatoes.

And the smell of it...dear God, it was unspeakable.

But we had no choice.

While I and the other poor bastards tossed bodies in the hopper, the soldiers would keep their guns on us. If you tried to break out, tried to run, they'd cut you right down, throw you in the back with the stiffs.

When the honeybuckets were full, we drove them outside the city to the dump, emptying the hoppers into the immense body pits where the corpses were burned. A mile from the dump, you could see clouds of black smoke rising into the sky, smell the cremated flesh and burning hair. It was like standing downwind from the ovens at Treblinka.

If there was truly a hell on earth, then this was it.

II

Weeks was not only a psychotic who shot anything that moved, he was deluded and paranoid and should have been in a loony bin somewhere. I never learned what his deal was, whether he was born nuts or if Doomsday had totally unhinged him, but he did not believe that the United States had been decimated by nuclear weapons. At least, not the kind fired by *people*. He was certain that aliens from outer space were responsible and that even now, they were spreading disease and pestilence and were hiding out in human form.

"Tell me where you came from," he said to me one day.

"Youngstown."

"Oh, you think you're funny? You think this is a fucking joke?"

"You asked me, I told you."

He put his carbine on me. "And how am I supposed to know you ain't one of *them?* You ain't an Outsider?"

That's what Weeks called them: *Outsiders*. He never once used the word "alien" but then he did not have to. Everyone knew.

I didn't even know what the guy looked like. He never, ever took off his biosuit. He even slept in it. Even back at the barracks he wore it religiously because he had no intention of any Outsider bugs getting him and changing him into some *thing*. He liked to toy with us, his Shitheads, trying to scare us by threatening to throw us into the hoppers. That worked at first. But after handling the cold cuts day in and day out, it took a lot to ruffle our feathers.

The truth was, Weeks was terrified.

He was afraid of everybody and everything.

He was particularly scared of Paulson because he thought Paulson was an Outsider and he hadn't made his mind up about Specs just yet. So whenever he talked to them, he kept his distance and when he wanted to throw them a beating, he always made his bullyboy soldiers do it. I found out just how afraid he was one day when he slipped on some corpse slime leaking out of the back of the truck and I grabbed him before he fell down.

He screamed.

Screamed bloody murder.

He was so petrified that he brought up his carbine, fully intending to waste me right then and there, only he was hyperventilating so bad and his hands were shaking so wildly that he couldn't even hold onto the gun. He finally dropped it and crawled away.

"Unclean! Filthy! Dirty!" he cried out. *"You put those dirty filthy rotten hands on me! You're infested like all the rest!"*

He finally got to his feet and jumped in the cab where, no doubt, he was spraying himself down with antiseptics.

One of soldiers came over and put the barrel of his carbine right into my face. "I oughta fucking kill you right now, you stupid asshole!"

I felt no fear. Death was hardly a threat by that point. "Go ahead."

"What?"

"I said, *go ahead.*"

The soldier looked to his comrades and didn't know exactly how to handle this. The other soldiers just stood there, feeling awkward and no doubt stupid in their white biosuits. I did not back down. For after being on the collection team for over a month I knew the score. Lately, Weeks hadn't been able to draft anyone. Word had gotten around about what the Army was up to and people hid out when the vans came around. Only the diseased, the crazy, and the Scabs came out, but they were of no use.

Weeks needed me. He needed all of us.

That's why the soldier didn't kill me.

That's why he was *afraid* to kill me. Because the way things were, we were short-handed and if I died it meant one of the soldiers would take my place. Weeks would insist upon it. He threatened his boys with it all the time. And whoever pulled the trigger and killed his Shithead would get the job.

"I'm not kidding," the soldier said.

I stepped forward until the barrel of the carbine was so close I could smell the burnt cordite in the barrel. "So kill me, asshole. Do it. Go ahead. Then you can take your turn handling the meat."

The soldier stepped back, then shouted out something and clubbed me with his rifle. Under the circumstances, it was his only option. He couldn't kill me, but on the other hand he couldn't just walk away from such open disobedience. I mean, shit, what would the Army be if people stopped following orders and actually began thinking for themselves?

I pulled myself up, spit out some blood and grinned. "You raise that rifle to me again, sonny, and I'll ram it so far up your ass it'll tickle your tonsils."

He brought it up again as I knew he would in a typical threat response. *"You're dead! You're fucking dead! You hear me? You're fucking dead!"*

"So pull the trigger, you goddamn pussy."

He hesitated. I stepped forward. He backed up.

The other soldiers were watching closely, very closely.

"You ain't got the balls for it," I told him.

And there the confrontation ended. After what I'd been through, that little bully boy was pathetic. He was terrified of taking my place. He knew it. I knew it. There was always the chance that he'd lose it and gun me down, but that was no real threat either. So what? Shoveling corpses for a living doesn't exactly put you on the road to a brighter future. What I had done—and what my intention had been from the start—was to symbolically emasculate that little pushbutton jarhead in front of everyone. And I had. From that point on, as far as we were concerned, he wore a fucking skirt.

I had sown the seeds of open rebellion and the big one was coming.

The showdown.

I think all us shitheads were ready for it, hungry for it even. I knew it was coming because The Shape had already told me. Just like he/she/it had told me that it was going to work out in my favor.

12

When we weren't out collecting corpses for the common good, Weeks and his bully boys were based out of the National Guard Armory over in Austintown. It had once housed elements of the 838th Military Police Company. There was a bunkroom that looked like a hospital ward in an old movie. That's where we shitheads slept. They locked us in at night and let us out in the morning. It was quite a life. We'd come in after a day of handling the cold cuts, just filthy and stinking of decay, and they'd stick us in that room, make us sleep in our own filth.

At night, Specs would have awful nightmares. He'd be crying out or sobbing in his sleep which pissed the other guys off because they needed their rest. He'd be in the bunk next to mine and I'd have to shake him awake.

"Specs, Specs," I'd say. "Knock it off for chrissake."

He'd lay there in the darkness, face shiny with sweat, just blinking. He was all messed-up from Doomsday and who wasn't?

One night as I sat there sharing a smoke with him, he said, "You know what, Nash? I believe in omens and portents. I think the future's already written if you can figure out how to read it."

"No shit?" I said.

"Really, Nash, I'm not kidding."

I pulled off my smoke. "Specs, what difference would it make? The future is fucking black. You don't wanna know about it."

"Oh yes you do. If you read the signs they can keep you alive, keep you safe. If I had some Tarot cards I could show you your life path. What's gonna happen."

"I don't wanna know what's gonna happen."

Specs went on and on about all that whacky new age shit he was into. They could call it what they wanted, but it all sounded like fairground gypsy fortune telling to me. But Specs loved it, loved talking in great detail about everything from pyramid power to the energy of crystals.

After about twenty minutes of that, Paulson said, "Why don't you girls go get a room? I'm trying to fucking sleep here."

Specs was excited, though. "But, Nash, listen—"

"Go to sleep," I told him. I shut my eyes, thinking about all that crazy shit and remembering my wife. That night I had my own nightmares. I dreamed that rats were eating Shelly.

13

The showdown, the endgame as it were, came not three days later.

We were making the rounds, collecting the dead, and Weeks got a call over the radio that there were a bunch of corpses dirtying up the parking lot over at the Southern Park Mall. Couldn't have that. In a city inundated in the unburied dead, what remained of the civic authority wanted that goddamn mall parking lot cleaned up. Couldn't have all the friendly tourists that came to American Eagle or Victoria's Secret or Build-A-Bear Workshop seeing all the carrion out there. What would they think? Didn't matter that the mall was in ruins now and what tourists usually showed up were either crazy or burning with fallout.

Outside Sears, there was a heap of bodies pretty much on the order of what I had seen at the 7-11. One big stinking ugly mess. When we pulled up in the truck, we could already hear the flies buzzing. A flock of gulls and crows took to the air.

We shitheads jumped off the back of the truck, looked at each other, and just shook our heads. The stink was bad enough to put a maggot off meat. Just a great, flyblown heap of corpses that had to number in the hundreds. The scavengers had been at them and had dragged bits and pieces off in every direction.

"Okay, Fuckhead," Weeks said. "Take Shit-fer-Brains with you and wade in. Ain't gonna smell any better ten minutes from now."

"This is ridiculous," Specs said. "They're all soft...we'll need shovels."

"Shut the fuck up, Mama's Boy. Get in there. You, too, Mr. Fucking Useless. Load that hopper. Let's go!"

When we didn't move fast enough, one of the soldiers cracked a few shots over our heads. But even that only made us drag ourselves forward. When we got to the perimeter of the heap, staring at all those rotting husks and bird-pecked faces and trailing limbs, the rest of the crew just looked at me. Lately, they'd been looking at me a lot. I guess I was the leader of the revolt that we all knew was coming. And I could feel it gathering momentum...electric with potential, just waiting to explode. I think they could, too. We were waiting for a catalyst to light the fuse and it was coming, God yes, it was certainly coming.

"Let's do it," I told them. "Let's load that fucking hopper. Then we'll see."

We went at it.

It was revolting even by the standards set by other such jobs. The corpses were so ripe they pulled apart like boiled chicken. Arms came off, legs came off, moldering flesh pulled right off the bones beneath. We backed the truck up close as we could because this rank, evil-smelling mess had to be thrown in the hopper piecemeal. It took hours. We sweated in our filthy biosuits, enveloped in a gagging cloud of flies and grave-stench.

Somewhere during the process, Specs lost it.

He usually didn't so much as clear his throat around the soldiers, but today was different. Maybe he, too, was feeding off that potential. He was all assholes and elbows, crouched over and digging into the cold cuts, just lost in his work. Sinking his gloved hands deep into that seething, crawling rot, firing it behind him, arms pinwheeling, letting it fly into the hopper. A corpse-worm slid out of the remains of a child and he stomped it to white mush before it could do so much as writhe in the sunlight.

"That's it!" Weeks told him, keeping his distance, his carbine balanced over one shoulder. "That's the way, Mama's Boy! Get that shit in the hopper! Got to it, you sonofabitch!"

This spurred Specs into greater feats of corpse clearing. He dug into the mess, letting limbs and bones and globs of offal fly, almost knocking me on my ass with a stray femur. Then he happened upon a head. The head of a teenage girl. The face was nothing but fungus and corpse jelly oozing from the white skull beneath...but it stopped him dead.

He held up that head and it had long red hair hanging from the scalp. Hair that was greasy and clotted with filth, but red all the same.

"Fuck you doing, Mama's Boy?" one of the soldiers asked.

And everyone was kind of wondering the same.

Specs stood there, trembling, holding that decayed head up. Slime dripped from it and loathsome black beetles crawled over the backs of his hands and up his arms.

With a gagging, strangled cry, he dropped it.

It hit the pavement like a moist, soft pumpkin and broke right apart at his feet. Beetles poured from the shattered skull, a crawling flood of them.

Weeks stepped back even further, of course.

Specs kept making that gagging sound.

The head was the catalyst we were waiting for.

I stood up from the carrion pile. My white biosuit was smeared gray and black with corpse waste. I brushed some stray maggots off my sleeve. "Hey? You okay, Specs...*Specs?* You okay, man?"

"Get to work!" Weeks shouted.

But we were ignoring him. Specs was having an episode and maybe we were filthy with decaying flesh and corpse slime and maybe we spent our days juggling human remains at gunpoint, but all this bonded us together. Made us stronger. Made us care for each other and in the process, made us a little more human than the drones with the guns.

"I said, get to fucking work!" Weeks called out, popping a few rounds into the air.

"Go fuck yourself," Paulson told him.

Weeks took two trembling steps forward, ejecting the magazine from his tactical carbine and slapping a fresh one in place. "Hell did he just say to me?" he asked his soldiers.

"Told you—" one of them began, suppressing a mad desire to giggle "—told you to go fuck yourself...*sir.*"

Weeks raged but we paid him no mind. We were clustered around Specs, touching him, reassuring him, while he went on in a whining voice about his sister, about Darlene. Darlene and her beautiful red hair and how she rotted away in her bed of typhoid fever.

About this time, we realized that Weeks was shouting at us. We turned and he had his weapon on us, his hands shaking on it. He was either scared to death or so pissed off he could've passed nails.

"Mr. Fucking Useless!" he cried. "Step away from those Shitheads! Do it! Do it! Do it! *You better goddamn well do it right fucking now, you miserable ass-sucking squeeze of shit! I'll drop you where you stand! Yer a fucking walking dead man!*"

Paulson pulled off his helmet and threw it at Weeks who nearly jumped right out of his suit trying to avoid the filthy thing. It hit the ground and rolled across the parking lot.

"No," he said. "I refuse."

"No? No? No? *Fuck you mean, you refuse?*" Weeks said, his voice very dry like all the spit had just dried on his tongue. "*You can't refuse me! You can't fucking well refuse me! Are you out of yer fucking mind? Are you? Well...ARE YOU?*"

"Yes sir, believe so," Paulson said.

Specs, Jakoby, and me stood tight with him, ringing him in so that Weeks would have to shoot through us to get at him.

"Step away from him!" Weeks ordered us. "Get away from him or I'll cap every one of you!"

"Go ahead!" Specs shouted. "Go right ahead!"

Weeks moved in still closer and so did his soldiers and I was figuring this was it, this was how it ended and what a goddamn revolting way to go, standing there knee deep in human remains in filthy suits with flies buzzing all over us.

Weeks was going to shoot, there was no doubt of it, but then Specs reached into the hopper and grabbed an arm that was bloated white. "Hungry, asshole? How about a wing?" he threw the arm and it hit one of the soldiers with a moist thud that put him on his ass. He screamed.

We started laughing.

"How about a thigh?" Jakoby said and heaved a maggoty leg.

"Got me a breast here," Paulson said, gathering up a withered trunk. "At least I think it's a breast..." He let it fly.

Then all of us just went mad with the idea.

Limbs and bones, entrails and mucid clots of flesh started flying, raining down on the soldiers, making them jump and duck as they were spattered with carrion and maggots. Weeks tried to dart back, but I tossed a head that broke apart and splattered him with wormy gray matter.

He, of course, screamed.

Screamed and went right down on his ass.

One of the soldiers said, "Screw this," and turned, jogging across the parking lot.

"Get back here!" Weeks called out to him. "*You're deserting your post!*"

But the guy didn't listen and Weeks shot him, dropped him right there.

After that, it was sheer pandemonium.

One of the soldiers shot Jakoby as he tossed handfuls of grave matter at him. And about the time he went down—staggering, bullet-ridden, but managing to crash into the guy who had shot him—I threw a loop of bowels at Weeks and they struck him right in the chest leaving a gray, snaking stain on his white biosuit. He screamed and tossed his rifle.

"I'm contaminated! I'm unclean! I'm filthy! Dirty! Dirty! Dirty!" he shrieked out from inside his helmet, rolling around on the pavement, maybe trying to wipe the putrescence off himself.

The other soldier had gotten tangled up in Jakoby and finally succeeded in shoving him aside. He brought up his rifle as Paulson rushed him with a rotting body in his arms. He shot him. Gave him two three-round volleys and Paulson fell at his feet, hitting the pavement with the corpse that just simply exploded on impact.

The soldier would have had us, too, had fate not intervened at that moment.

Temporarily blinded from a spray of rancid flesh, his plexiglass helmet bubble was black and dripping with juice and bits of meat. He stripped his helmet off and threw it aside. And at that precise moment, one of the corpse-worms slid out of the belly of the cadaver that Paulson had dropped.

It was one of the biggest I had ever seen.

At first, I thought it was a section of swollen bowel spilling out from the corpse's belly, but then it *moved,* it coiled over the pavement, threading in and out of the stiff like rubbery white yarn. It was huge, flattened-out and segmented, shining with slime and drainage. It was making an almost angry humming sound that was high and strident.

The soldier saw it about the time it rose up from the corpse's belly with a juicy, succulent noise. It didn't have eyes that anyone could see, but it seemed to know where he was. That humming grew positively ear-shattering in its intensity. The worm's body swelled-up, thickening, growing bulbous like some impossibly fleshy penis. The bulb or head inflated, too.

The soldier brought his carbine to bear.

But the worm struck first: it shot an inky stream of juice into his face and the effect was instantaneous. He screamed and fell to his knees, his hands clutching his face...only his face was no longer a face as such, but something soft and pulpy that was squirting out between his fingers.

As the worm retreated, me and Specs went over to Weeks.

He was still whining and crying out in a high girlish voice about being unclean, crawling about on all fours. We just looked down on him, then we started kicking him. And we kept kicking him until he went limp.

Then we dragged his inert form over to the hopper.

We stripped his suit off.

And threw his ass in.

Then we started tossing bodies and body parts on top of him, everything we could find until he was buried in entrails and torsos and limbs, shivering beneath a blanket of carrion and graveworms. Somewhere during the process, he came awake, fighting and screaming, trying to free himself from the putrefying flesh and greening meat. He screamed and clawed.

And Specs, giggling, pulled the lever and the blades came scooping down.

Before Weeks disappeared, we saw him in there tangled in bowels and husks, his arm wedged into a slimy ribcage. And we also saw a fat white corpse-worm slide from a body and investigate his face.

Then the blades pushed him into the bin with the rest and the ram compacted it all with a crunching, pulping noise and fetid juice ran from the drain holes at the bottom of the truck.

That was it.

Specs and I tossed aside our suits, lit cigarettes like workmen after a hard day on the job, and walked away from it all. We went looking for a car. We were going to Cleveland.

CLEVELAND OHIO

1

Cleveland had a real bad rat problem, even worse than Youngstown. At night, hordes of them would come up out of the sewers and cellars and take to the streets in massive swarms like driver ants, devouring anything in their path. They were all rabid and incredibly vicious. By moonlight, you could see them down there, so many greasy gray bodies that you could have crossed the street walking on their backs and never once touched pavement. I saw them take down dog packs and street gangs, leave nothing but bones behind.

Cleveland, as it turned out, also had Red Rains.

2

I woke that first night in the city to the sound of Specs screaming. We were crashed out in a big Cadillac El Dorado we found parked in an empty lot over in Fairfax, just off Cedar Avenue on East 86th. Looked like it had been a pimp's car once...leopard seats with hot-red plush carpeting and tinted windows. Specs slept in the back; I took the front. Next morning, he woke up screaming.

I panicked and pulled my gun, wiping sleep from my eyes. All I had was a little five-shot snub-nosed .38 belly gun I'd taken off the mangled corpse of a cop in Ravenna a few days before. "What? What? What?" I said, looking for a target, anything.

Specs was breathing hard in the backseat. "Just had a dream...did I cry out?"

"Yeah, you fucking cried out, asshole. I thought you were being murdered."

"Oh, I'm sorry, Nash. Sometimes I get these bad dreams. Just corpses everywhere, you know? Sometimes I dream about my sister, about Darlene."

Poor Specs. I didn't want to get him going on his dead sister again. In those days I still had a watch on my wrist—a nice Indiglo Timex that Shelly had given me for my birthday—and I hadn't gone native yet and started clocking the time by the position of the sun. Watch said it was ten in the morning...but inside the car it was pretty dark. I thought maybe it was the tinted windows, but it wasn't that at all.

The windows, all the windows, of the Cadillac were covered in something dark. I didn't get it. I pulled off some tepid water I had in a bottle, tried to clear my head.

"What's all over the windows?" Specs asked me and I could already hear the paranoia creeping into his voice. Poor guy. Specs was a good person in most ways, but he was paranoid as hell. He saw the boogeyman around every corner and who could really blame him?

"I don't know," I said.

The Caddy had old-style crank windows. A huge vehicle back when they'd rolled them off the assembly lines in Detroit with plenty of leg room. I tried the windows and so did Specs, but they were jammed up. So I did what I didn't really want to do: I opened my door.

The world was red.

The streets, the buildings, even the trees and stoplight were fucking red like they'd been dipped in red ink. It was insane. Specs and I got out and walked around. Everything was covered in that crusty red film. I had never seen anything like it. It looked like the sky had rained blood during the night. I walked over to a spreading oak tree and, sure enough, a few drops of red were still dripping from the branches.

"It's blood, Nash. Jesus Christ, it's blood," Specs said, clinging so close to me I thought he was going to kiss me.

I shoved him away. "It ain't blood. It was some weird rain. Like an acid rain or something."

But I wasn't even sure that I believed it. Something inside me clenched tight as we walked those blood red streets. There was no life or movement anywhere. Just that hazy sky above and the graveyard stillness and all that red. It was like some kind of expressionistic painting or something and it made me go cold inside.

"You know what this is, don't you?" Specs said.

"No, I don't. But you're gonna tell me, I'm sure."

"It's an omen," Specs said. "It's a bad omen, Nash. Real bad."

And on that point, I believed him.

3

We walked for a good hour. After a time the red was just gone. Either the sun dried it up or it had only rained like that in particular parts of the city. I didn't know and I really didn't *want* to know. So we walked and Specs jabbered on non-stop as was his way. We didn't see anyone on Cedar Avenue, just desertion and devastation. Why I thought Cleveland would be any better than Youngstown, I did not know.

"Too bad we couldn't have kept the Caddy," Specs said. "That was one sweet ride."

"Sure," I said, scoping out the streets ahead of us, "one sweet ride with two flat tires and a dead engine."

"Well, it was sweet. You know it was. Would have been cool to tool around the city in that."

"Sure, we could've picked up some chicks," I said.

The city was dead. At least what we'd seen of it. Another graveyard. The rusted hulks of abandoned cars were everywhere: at the curbs, pulled up onto sidewalks, flipped over in the roads, smashed-up. I figured someone was around—or had been—because a lot of tires had been scavenged. Most likely for fires. Nothing burned like a tire.

What I saw of Cleveland was intact. I saw some neighborhoods that had burned or were fire-scarred, but not like in Youngstown. Entire sections of the city had been fire bombed to wipe out the infections and those that carried them. This did not look so systematic. Just ordinary fires, I thought.

Still, there was destruction. Buildings had collapsed into heaps of rubble that blocked thoroughfares. Houses had been burned flat. There were open cellars everywhere flooded with water and leaves, the homes and buildings that had once sat upon them nowhere to be seen. Weeds were growing up in the sidewalks. Telephone poles had fallen, some only standing because their wires held them up. Storefronts were fire damaged, plate glass windows shattered, brick facades riddled with bullet holes.

There were skeletons everywhere. Sprawled in yards, tossed in gutters, some still sitting behind the wheels of cars fully articulated. But all of them bird-pecked and gleaming white. Not just human skeletons either, but those of dogs and cats and rats and more than a few that were so unnatural looking I couldn't be sure what they were from. Bones were the only true raw material of the brave new world and they were in abundance.

After awhile, Specs and I took a break.

We pushed a heap of remains from a peeling bench and took a break. I had an olive drab Army knapsack that I used for scavenging. We each had a can of cold Dinty Moore Beef Stew and washed it down with warm Mountain Dew Code Red. That was our lunch.

I pulled off my Dew. "We gotta get us some wheels, Specs," I told him, because The Shape had whispered in my head that we had to keep moving west. And I wasn't about to walk.

"Yeah, too bad about that Caddy."

"We don't need a pimpmobile," I told him. "We need something rugged. A four-wheel drive or something. Roads are going to be bad now."

We'd driven motorcycles into Cleveland from Youngstown. Then we'd abandoned them in Garfield Heights after some big birds swooped down on us and stole Specs' hat. I don't know what they were. Looked like ravens. But huge, mutated. We decided after that we needed something with a roof over our heads.

"You ever wonder where we're going to be in a year from now, Nash?"

"No, I don't. I got enough problems here and now."

"I think about it sometimes. I wonder if maybe out there somewhere there's still cities with real people in 'em."

I didn't even bother speculating on that. I finished my stew and threw the can in the street. We survivors were terrible litterbugs. I smoked and sipped off my Dew. We'd looted the Dew from a deli in Garfield Heights. Everything was long rotten in there, but the canned stuff and soda was still good. Civilization may fall, but the Dew goes on forever.

"Why do you figure west, Nash? Why not south?"

He'd been thinking about asking me that for a long time. So I told him about The Shape. I didn't want to because he was too wrapped up in all that occult shit and I knew he'd make it into something supernatural. And he did, of course. But I had to tell him and I did.

After that, all he thought about was The Shape.

4

It was getting on dark and we still hadn't found a ride and I was getting sick to death of Specs speculating about The Shape—he was convinced it was an old pagan god that had resurfaced now that Christianity had bottomed out—and asking me fifty questions about it.

"Listen," I finally said. "What I told you was a secret and we're not going to talk about it, okay? Just let it lay."

We had other things to worry about.

I knew well enough from Youngtown that you didn't want to be caught out in the open after dark. We had to find a place to lay low. We were down along the Cuyahoga River. There wasn't much but a lot of industrial sites, many of which looked long abandoned, and the usual assortment of neighborhoods and storefronts that spring up around places like that. Lots of bars and lunch counters and not much else. We needed the right place. Something defensible.

As I looked around, Specs tugged on my elbow. "Nash," he said. "Oh boy, Nash. Look."

Shit. Scabs. About five or six of them just up the street sitting atop a pile of rubble, half-naked and moon-fleshed and filthy, like birds of prey on their high perches looking for tasty rodents. I wasn't entirely convinced that they'd even seen us. One of them, a woman in a black motorcycle jacket and nothing else, was staring intently in the direction we'd just come from. The others were staring dumbly at their own feet.

I carefully slipped the .38 from my jacket pocket.

Specs and I moved very slowly towards a run of ruined buildings about twenty feet away. I was very aware of how debris crunched under our boots. I think I held my breath the entire way. It was the longest twenty feet of my life. We ducked through a massive hole in the brick façade of a bar. It looked like it had been hit by an anti-tank round and it probably had been.

We made it.

"Hey, not bad—" Specs started to say.

"Shut up," I told him. "They're not fucking deaf."

I peaked around the corner. They hadn't moved. Holding my finger to my lips, I led Specs farther into the bar room. Whatever had blasted through that wall had kept going and blew out a good portion of the rear wall, taking out most of the bathroom. We climbed free of the building into a little alley paved in bricks. The shadows were starting to get long. The alley was a cul-de-sac whose entry was blocked by more rubble. We climbed through a missing window into another building and we soon saw that it was gutted inside. The upper floors were nearly gone. You could see the sky through a jagged chasm in the roof.

"What the hell happened here?" Specs asked.

"Must've been some kind of battle. Looks like this place took an airstrike or an artillery barrage."

A great section of the floor was missing, having fallen into the cellar below. We moved around this carefully, found a door, and on the other side, it was even worse. What we were looking at was like London after the blitz: heaps of rubble, buildings that were entirely gutted and reduced to debris. Roofs were gone, windows blasted out, entire walls missing. And floors? There were no floors. Just huge pits that looked down into the cellars below that were dark and ominous, choked with debris and flooded with black water. There was only a skeletal framework of joists to walk on. It would be risky.

"Oh, I don't know about this, Nash," Specs said. "I don't like this at all."

But we really didn't have a choice. Behind us, I could hear a lot of shouting and screaming. More Scabs had shown up. Going back that way wasn't an option.

"You can do it," I told him. "The joists are an easy foot across. Just don't look down."

We moved over to the edge of the pit, kicking up clouds of brick dust. I started out on one of the joists and it wasn't so bad. Plenty of room to walk. The trick was not to look down. It wasn't that it was a deep drop...probably eight feet or so, but eight feet into rubble and twisted metal, that rank-smelling water and who knew what kind of things lay right beneath the surface that would impale you?

"Come on," I told him. "Don't look down."

Hesitantly, he started across. He moved like a turtle at first, but once he got his feet under him it was no problem. We crossed the joists, ducked through a jagged archway and found ourselves in another building lacking a floor. I noticed that a cobwebbed rocking chair hung from the floor above by a section of electrical wiring. It swayed back and forth. The water below us was caked with leaves. A few plastic bottles bobbed.

I was about two-thirds of the way across on the center joist when I heard a muted splashing. Maybe not a splashing exactly, but sort of a slopping sound. I looked back and Specs was still coming, offering me a goofy smile. He hadn't heard it.

"This ain't so bad," he said. "Like walking curbs when you're a kid."

I nodded, smiling thinly. I heard that slopping again and looked back. This time I saw something. Something that froze me up and made my heart start hammering. Cool sweat ran down my face. Near to where Specs was I saw...thought I saw...a puckered white face pull down beneath the leaves and water.

I made it across.

"Something wrong, Nash?" Specs asked me.

"No, it's cool," I told him, just waiting for a pair of white, mottled hands to reach up and pull him into the flooded stygian depths. But it didn't happen. He made it across and we darted through a missing wall. Before us was a solid expanse of brick with no egress. Instead of going forward, I feared, we had somehow gotten turned sideways and were moving lengthwise through the buildings. We'd have been at it quite a while at that rate. I compensated, led us around some huge heaps of shattered brick, through a near-collapsed doorway, and into the utter darkness. In the distance I could see a patch of light.

We were in some kind of warehouse, I thought.

Boxes and barrels were stacked around us. It was very gloomy in there. There were roughly a million places for unfriendlies to hide and about the same amount of ways to die. The floor was concrete and unbroken.

I led Specs forward and he clung to me, pulling at the back of my jacket, bumping into me, grabbing me by the arm. It was like going through a carnival spookhouse with your badly frightened kid brother. The .38 in hand, I moved us along, trying not to trip over anything. We were not alone in there. I heard a scratching once and a dragging sound another time.

When the patch of light—a missing door—was about fifteen feet away, Specs pulled me to a stop.

"Listen," he said.

I heard it right away: a sort of low, coarse breathing in the darkness. Behind us, I could swear I saw grotesque forms threading through the shadows. Whatever was in there was closing in on us. I grabbed Specs and raced him to the door and out into the blinding light.

Nothing followed us.

The sky above looked odd, I thought. Kind of roiling with bloated pinkish clouds that started to look less and less pink and more brilliantly red by the moment. A drop of rain splatted at my foot. Another ran down the windshield of a wrecked pickup truck. Except it wasn't rain...it wasn't water. It was red. Like blood.

"Shit," I heard Specs say.

I turned to find the nearest shelter and there was a big guy with a pump shotgun in his hands. He looked mean. "Where do you assholes want it?" he said. "In the belly or in the head?"

5

I had my .38 out, but I honestly felt impotent with it next to that killing iron in the big man's hands. He was about 6'3, had to go in at an easy 250 if not more. His hair was short and choppy, but his beard was long and tangled. It reached right down to his chest. He wore a tattered jean vest with lots of patches on it. He was a biker. This guy was a fucking biker.

"We're not Scabs," Specs told him. "We're not infected."

"I know that, little man. You were Scabs, you wouldn't be alive right now. I was looking for some normal people and I suppose you two scrubs'll do." He was standing under the wide awning outside a shoe store, one eye cocked to the sky. A few more drops of blood fell. "You boys better get over here. You don't wanna get caught in a red rain."

We got under the awning with him. I lit a cigarette, explained who we were, where we had come from, how we were looking for some wheels to head west with. He nodded, didn't seem like he gave a shit. His bare arms were massive, set with tattoos and I could see right away that those tattoos symbolized something, all those snakes and deathheads and names and places. He wasn't just some wannabe punk or yuppy that thought some inking would make him into a real man. He was the genuine article: an outlaw biker.

"Name's McKree, Sean McKree. Friends call me 'Chang'," he told us, watching the sky. He did not look happy. "Fucking weather."

"Nice to meet you, Chang," Specs said.

"You can call me, *Sean,* little man," he said. "My friends are all dead."

More drops of red fell out in the streets, plopping onto the hoods of cars. Then the downpour began, an absolute curtain of what looked like blood. But not just liquid, but unidentifiable chunks of matter that thudded and splattered everywhere. It lasted about ten minutes and the stink of it was acrid. It reamed your nose right out. But that, too, faded in time. Out in the streets the liquid was drying up, leaving that sticky red film I had seen that morning. I looked closer and there was no mistaking it: there were bones in the street. Not human bones, I didn't think, but animal bones. Most of them quite small. They had not been there before.

"It is blood!" Specs said. "Bones, too!"

"Can't be blood," I told him. "That doesn't make any sense. It's acid rain or something."

"You're both right."

We looked at Sean. "You heard me," he said. "There's acid in that shit and it'll burn the soles off your boots and sting your skin if you get caught out in it. But it's mostly blood and run-off. See, there was a slaughterhouse on the Cuyahoga. Back in the day they used to release their by-products straight into the river and the river would turn red in the summer. But the EPA made 'em clean up their act," he explained to us. "So what they did is they built two gigantic steel rendering tanks that were like fifty feet deep and sixty feet across. They pumped all their by-products in there: blood, bones, fat, you name it. The tanks were full of acid..."

He told us that the tanks were open air so that evaporation would remove the liquid. Then the world puked out and those two full tanks of remains, acid, and run-off were just sitting there. He couldn't be sure, but now and again something like a wind-spout brewed up off the big lake and traveled down river, sucking up just about anything that wasn't tied down. For some reason, it sucked up what was in those tanks nearly every time. The tanks never dried out because the rain filled them up and the wind-spouts stirred them like cauldrons, scraping all the goodies from the bottom.

"I've seen the tanks," he said. "You can smell 'em for a mile. My guess is that in the plant there are other storage vats full of blood and slime, probably gravity-fed. Sooner or later, the rendering tanks'll dry up and run out of remains. But it hasn't happened yet."

We stood under the awning, smoking and chatting. Sean said we had to wait until the rain had completely dried or it would eat holes in our boots. So we waited and he told us about his life as an outlaw biker. He'd been a sergeant-at-arms for the Warlocks motorcycle gang out of New Jersey, which meant he was an enforcer that knocked heads together and killed people when the club ordered it. On the back of his vest there was a flaming skull. Above it, a rocker read: WARLOCKS MC. Below it, BAYONNE, NJ.

"You're a long way from Bayonne," I said.

"Yeah, I am, brother. Came here to straighten out some shit. It's what I do," he told me. "See...just before they dropped them fucking bombs, I was sent here to straighten out some business. It was club business. Private. But since there ain't no more law, no more feds, and no more clubs, I'll tell you. Here in Cleveland, there was a Hell's Angels charter, a clubhouse. One of their people—Ray Coombs, called him 'Ratbait'—got hisself killed. A couple hitters from the Blood Brothers did him in Newark. Blood Brothers were a bunch of kill-happy maggots that were trying hard to impress the Outlaws out of Detroit, so they started offing Angels. Hell's Angels and Outlaws were the big two in bike gangs then, you see, and they hated each other. Lots of killing on both sides, lots of retaliation and turf wars. I rode with the Warlocks. We were tight with the Angels. Word came out of Oakland, C-A, that they wanted these Blood Brothers done. They were hiding out in Cleveland, over in Stockyards. I got the job."

Specs was wide-eyed. "You mean you're a hit man? You mean you came to kill those bikers?"

"No, I came to fucking dance with 'em," Sean said. He looked over at me. "Something wrong with this guy?"

"No, he's just been through a lot."

Sean shrugged. "I got one of those dirt bags, then the bombs fell and I been here since. I was shacked up with an Angel called Dirty Sanchez and his old lady, Long Tall Sally. A couple weeks ago the Trogs got 'em. I been hunting Trogs since." He told us the Trogs lived underground, were real bad news, barely human. "When I'm not killing Trogs, I waste Scabs. But they're like shooting ducks. Easy. Trogs takes skill. There's sport involved."

Out in the streets, the rain had dried up, leaving a world that was stained red. Night was coming on fast. We needed a place to crash for the night where we didn't have to worry about getting our throats slit.

I heard a squeaking sound and saw a rat. I made to shoot it and Sean stayed my hand. Pretty soon there were seven or eight of them, big, ugly things with red eyes and those weird growths popping through their threadbare hides. They paid no attention to us. They went after the bones and within minutes there were no bones left. The rats were gone.

"You know where there's any good rides?" I asked.

Sean nodded. "Sure. I can get you anything you want. But not tonight. Heard a rumor from a ragbag this morning that the Hatchet Clans are pushing in from the north. You don't want to be out in the streets tonight."

"Hell are the Hatchet Clans?" I asked.

He laughed. "Brother, you don't wanna know."

6

"I puked out my last year of high school and stole a couple cars," Sean told us later in his heavily-fortified basement apartment while we ate pork and beans and drank warm beer. "They sent me to Juvie. I got out and stole another car, led the State Police on a merry chase. Judge said join the Army or do time. I joined the Army. I was a scout with the 4th Cavalry. I did my bit over in Iraq during Desert Storm, first one. Soon as I got out, I hooked up with my old friends and we started a bike club called the Dirty Dozen. Problem was, man, there were only four of us. Then we got six and the other clubs called us the Dirty *Half-Dozen.* They gave us lots of shit. By the time there were thirty of us and we backed down from no one, they stopped giving us shit. The Pagans and the Warlocks wanted to charter us, bring us in with them. Even the Outlaws and Angels were looking at us. We liked the Warlocks because they were fucking crazy like the Mongols out in California. That's how I got where I am. I'm leaving out the time I did and the drugs I pushed, the mothers I beat and all the bodies I got out there, but what's it matter now?"

"We're going west," Specs told him. "You should go with us."

"Fuck I wanna go west for?"

"Because that's where it's at. That's where it's gonna happen."

I caught Specs eye and let him know that we weren't going to be discussing The Shape. Not at this time. And maybe not ever again and sure as hell not with this thug. Sean seemed okay, but he was a very bad boy and I wasn't exactly comfortable with turning my back on him.

Sean stretched out on the couch. We were on the floor in sleeping bags. There was a locked green metal gun cabinet that I wanted badly to loot. There were all kinds of Army surplus around: food, clothing, tools, medical equipment, you name it. I figured Sean had been real busy at the local Army base or National Guard Armory. I stared at the flickering flame of a Primus stove, listening to him talk.

"Yeah, I got me some good prospects for tomorrow, my brothers," he said, staring up into the darkness. "There's a nest of Trogs not two blocks from here, over near where I found you boys. There's gotta be a sewer grating or manhole cover around there that I haven't found. They're down there somewhere, brothers. I'll get 'em. Fuck yes, I'll get 'em. Nothing finer than Trog-hunting. You boys oughta pitch in with me. I'll show you how it's done."

"We need a car," Specs said.

"Maybe I can help you with that tomorrow. First you gotta help me kill some Trogs." He laughed. "We better get some sleep. Trog-hunting is hard work. Nash, kill that stove. Let's rack out."

7

The next morning we ate good. Better than I had in many, many weeks. Sean's larder was far superior to our usual fair of cold Spaghettios and tins of deviled ham. He had lots of Army MREs and we ate scrambled eggs and bacon, crackers and jelly, and had some peach cobbler for dessert.

"Fill yourselves, my brothers," Sean told us. "You'll need your strength."

As it turned out, he was right. And that was something I learned to remember later: Sean was very often right.

Well, he armed us and led us out on a Trog hunt. He gave me a Beretta 9mm handgun and a 30.06 Savage. He gave Specs a bluesteel .357 Smith and told him not to blow his fucking foot off with it. He also made us wear yellow miner's hardhats with lights on them. Batteries being scarce, we weren't allowed to turn them on without his say so.

He showed me two white phosphorus grenades he had.

"For Trogs?" I said.

"If you get a pack of 'em, these'll sort 'em out. Hope I get to use them."

Christ.

Why did we go along with him? I don't know. There was no threat intended or implied. We could have walked—sans the guns—anytime we wanted, but we really didn't want to. I was amazed by Sean. He was a cool head that never lost his temper. Deadly as they came, but honest and loyal in his own way. And resourceful. Jesus, he was resourceful. Wasn't much he didn't know about guns and ammunition and fighting. He knew how to stay alive, that was for sure.

A few hours after breakfast—which was served at the crack of noon—we were back in the same vicinity where Sean had found us. He led us into a collapsing building down near the river. Most of the windows were boarded up and there was graffiti all over it. I figured it had been derelict long before Doomsday. Inside, it was dusty and dirty, cobwebs hanging down like party streamers. There were offices, storage rooms, and a big garage in the back. It looked kind of like an old fire hall. Light came in through missing boards in the windows and holes in the walls, but not a lot of it.

We moved through the dimness, past rotting cardboard boxes of ancient ledgers and file folders, water-damaged crates of rusting machine parts.

"What was this place?" Specs asked.

"Hell if I know," Sean told him. "Come on."

He directed us through the heaped wreckage, pawing through cobwebbed corridors. The masonry was crumbling around us. There were rat droppings everywhere. Sean found a human skull, kicked it, and laughed when it bounced off the wall and dropped neatly into a garbage can.

"Two points," he said.

A few bats were disturbed from their daytime sleep and winged angrily over our heads.

"Gah," Specs said. "I really hate bats."

"Least they're normal bats," Sean said. "Ain't the size of condors and got teeth like jaguars, laugh like hyenas. Seen a colony of 'em like that over in Detroit-Shoreway. Enough to give you fucking nightmares for a month."

He brought us through the garage and into a smaller room just off it. The ceiling was arched, fallen masonry on the floor. It not only smelled damp and fusty, but like warm decay and the reason for that soon became apparent.

There was the corpse of a woman in there.

"Oh God," Specs said.

The corpse was hung by the feet with rope, tied off to a beam above. It was just as white as boiled bone, looked like the blood had been drained from it drop by drop. It had been opened from belly to crotch and what had been inside was scooped free, leaving a great hollow. It looked like a side of beef in a slaughterhouse.

Sean waved the flies away from it with the barrel of his shotgun.

He stood there, nodding, intrigued by what he was seeing. He had a .44 magnum in a green Army-style web belt at his waist. There was a big Marine K-bar knife on the other hip, as well as a big hatchet and an empty white potato sack. I didn't want to know what that was for and he wasn't saying.

"See here?" he said. "She's been eaten on. Here and here. See the teeth marks?"

I saw them. The corpse was riddled with gouges and scratches. It looked like something had taken a bite out of her shoulder. Her vagina was missing.

"They like private parts, them Trogs," Sean explained. "Don't ask me why. Guts first, then the privates. I hung her up here yesterday morning and they must've went at her last night."

"You did this?" Specs said.

"She was dead already, little man. I just used her as bait."

It was sickening. He was obsessed with those things. The world had ground to a halt and he was carefree and happy hunting mutants. There was something very disturbing about that.

"They're not still around, are they?" I said.

Sean told me we had nothing to worry about. He had a theory that the underdwellers only came out at night like B-movie vampires because they had been living under the streets for so long, hiding in cellars and drainage ditches and sewers, that their eyes couldn't take the sunlight anymore. Like burrowing worms or moles or bats. It was a good theory, I thought, and it made sense. For the underdwellers—or *Trogs* as we called them—were essentially nocturnal like cave-dwellers, troglodytes. The radiation had started it; the darkness took care of the rest.

"They only come out at night," he said and I had absolutely no reason to dispute what he said.

I went over closer to the body. It was as revolting as any corpse and by that point I'd seen so many—especially after working on that clean-up crew—that it took quite a bit to gross me out. It smelled pretty bad, but it wasn't the decay I was smelling but something sharp and acrid, almost like cat pee mixed with ammonia if you can imagine that.

"Smell it, don't ya?" Sean said. "You know what that is, brother?"

I told him I didn't.

"That's Trog piss. Once you get a smell of it, you never forget it. See, Trogs like eating dead things. They ain't against taking you or me down and eating our 'nads on a stick, but what they like is something kind of soft, rotten...seasoned up, so to speak. They mark their goodies by pissing on 'em kind of like dogs marking territory." He showed me his wrist. There was old scar tissue there. "See that burn? Trog piss. Had one of 'em piss on me once. Shit burns."

Specs wouldn't come by the corpse. Even with working the clean-up crew, he was looking a little green. And that was mostly Sean's talk more than anything.

"I can smell it, too," he said. "But it's over here."

He was standing by a doorway. A set of steps led down into the darkness. Sean went over there right away. As ridiculous as it sounds, he went down on his hands and knees sniffing like a bluetick hound. "Yup. Trog piss. One of 'em must have marked this spot. Bet you ten to one we got us a Trog down there in the basement. Who's for taking a look?" He stood up. "How about you, little man?"

"Me?" Specs said.

Sean laughed. "You ain't got the balls. I'll go down."

Specs stepped in front of him. "I'll do it."

Sean smiled. "Listen for 'em. They breathe real loud."

I didn't like it. Specs was one of those guys that must have been a toilet in another life because he always took shit. But he didn't like to be challenged. He felt the need to prove himself.

"I'll go with," I said.

Specs gave me a look. "I don't need you."

He turned on his helmet light, took out his .357, and down he went. I told him to be careful. I didn't like any of this. I had a cigarette and I was nervous as hell. I always looked after Specs. I didn't like Sean pulling this macho shit on him, goading him like that.

"He'll be all right," Sean told me.

"He fucking better be," I said.

Sean gave me a hard look and I gave it right back. If anything happened to Specs, I was going to kill him and I think he knew it. We watched each other.

The minutes ticked by.

8

It wasn't long before Specs let out a scream and came jogging up the steps, his eyes wide behind his glasses, his brow beaded with sweat. There were cobwebs on his coat.

"OH GOD! OH MY FUCKING GOD!" he cried out, absolutely hysterical. "IT'S DOWN THERE! I SAW IT! IT LOOKED RIGHT FUCKING AT ME! DON'T GO DOWN THERE! JESUS, DON'T GO DOWN THERE!"

He was ready to jump out of his skin. He was shaking and gasping for breath and I held onto him until he calmed down. Sean was smiling; he thought it was funny as hell.

"They ain't too active in the day, little man," he said.

"Bullshit," Specs said. "This one looked pretty fucking active."

"I'll take a look."

"You better not go down there," Specs warned him.

Sean went anyway. He clicked on his helmet lamp, racked his shotgun, and started down. He made it maybe three steps and came right back up, backing all the way. "I'll be goddamned," he said.

"What?" I said.

"We got one coming up into the light."

I felt a clammy chill run up my spine and there was good reason for it: that piss smell suddenly got stronger. Ammoniated urine and enough to ream the hairs right out of your nose.

"Let's get the hell out of here!" Specs suggested.

"Not on your life, brother," Sean told him. "I been waiting for this."

Specs and I pulled back along the far wall, right near to the door so we could run the hell out of there if we had to. I could hear the slapping sound of bare feet coming up the steps and my mouth was so dry I could not swallow. I could hear the Trog breathing with a hollow hissing sort of sound. That urine stench grew stronger, a low and mean smell that made my eyes water.

"Get ready," Sean whispered.

I saw a shadow emerge from the gloom...it was distorted, semi-human. It was making a low growling sound in its throat. It came up into the light, a grotesque caricature of a human being. It was woman, I thought. Broken, bent at the waist, one shoulder pulled up higher than that other. The left arm reached down near the knee and the other only to the waist. She was naked, her flesh a greasy yellow like leprosy, horribly corrugated, the fissures and clefts in her skin so deep you could have lost a penny in them. Her breasts looked like deflated, fleshy balloons.

"Jesus," Specs said.

Her head was misshapen, long cobweb gray hair hanging from the raw scalp. She looked around with glossy pink eyes that were set with a fine tracery of purple veins like unfertilized eggs. Each set with a tiny black dot that must have been a pupil. Her puckered mouth pulled back from teeth that were black and overlapping, triangular in shape. They looked serrated. A watery brown juice ran from the corners of her lips.

She held a hand up before her face to block the light and I saw that the palm was set with ring-shaped protrusions that looked like the sucker scars of squids you see on whales.

"I'm over here, you bitch," Sean said.

The Trog looked at him and I wondered at that moment if she did not recognize him. She let out a shrill, piercing scream that grew in volume, an unearthly wailing that went right through me, scraping along the inside of my skull like a fork. I thought my bladder would let go. I almost fell over Specs. The scream echoed through that deserted building and came right back at us: it was an agonized sound like an animal being put to death.

Then she spoke...or made sounds like speech. I'm not sure. But this is what I heard: "*Yyyyyyooooooouuuuu,*" she hissed with a timber that made everything inside me pull up tight. "*Yyyyyyoooooouuuuuu...*"

If Sean hadn't had that shotgun, she would have torn out his throat and washed herself in his blood. She stumbled towards him, blinded, hissing, and very pissed off.

Sean let her get within four feet and then he gave her a round right in the belly. 12-gauge shot at close quarters, it nearly torn her in half. She went down screaming and thrashing. He gave her another right in the chest and she flopped, screeched, and then went still. The stink of her blood was just as bad as her urine.

"That's how it's done," Sean said.

My legs went out from under me and I sat down hard next to Specs who'd already folded up. We sat there, speechless. We thought killing that thing would be enough. But it wasn't. Not for Sean. He set aside his shotgun, kneeled down by the Trog. He wrapped her hair in his fist and pulled it tight. Then out came his hatchet. With a couple quick strokes, he decapitated her.

He stood up, holding that vile grimacing head by the hair. Blood dripped from the severed neck. "Either you boys want this for your trophy cases?" We just looked dumbly at him. "Didn't think so." He opened his potato sack and dropped the head in, tied the sack off at his belt.

I finally found my voice. "What the hell do you want that for?"

"I got my reasons, brother," he said. "See, Trogs are superstitious, I think. Maybe they believe in ghosts or something. I don't know. But they don't care for their own dead or parts of 'em, for that matter. I was in a pinch one time with three of the fuckers bearing down on me. I only had one round in my gun. What to do? I threw a trophy Trog head at the others and they ran off like the Devil was coming down to fucking Georgia. You should have seen it!"

I was very happy that I hadn't.

9

There was no way in hell I wanted any part of Trog-hunting. You couldn't have paid me to go after those monsters. They lived down in the sewers mostly, Sean told me, and I was content to let them stay there. But something happened that changed my mind.

We left the building, got out into the sunshine—Sean had promised us he had an unopened bottle of Jack Daniels back at his apartment and I was all for that—and right away we saw carnage. Scabs. About a dozen of them were lying dead in the streets. Their blood was very bright, very red spilled over the rubble. They had been dismembered, hacked and slit, disemboweled. Their entrails were strewn everywhere. One particular set was hung from a STOP sign. They had all been decapitated, the heads set neatly next to one another on the curb.

"Hell's going on?" I said.

Sean went down to a low crouch right away like he was back in the Army, a recon scout sneaking through enemy territory. I didn't know what the hell was going on.

"Who killed 'em?" Specs wanted to know.

"Shut the hell up, both of you," Sean told us and meant it.

He moved towards the bodies, eyes scanning the terrain in all directions. He went over to one and pulled something free of an abdomen. It looked like a broken stick. But when he brought it over, I saw it was a spearhead of all things.

"Hatchet Clans," he said. "Must've swept through while we were inside. Get back in the building."

"I'm not going back in there," Specs said.

"Then you can die out here, little man," Sean said. "Because you *will* die. The Clans leave nothing alive when they sweep an area."

I went back into the building. I decided to err on the side of caution. It was the second time Sean had mentioned these Hatchet Clans. I didn't know what they were, but if they scared Sean they must have been some real bad boys.

We got inside and Sean told us to stay away from the windows. He stayed by them, watching the streets.

"What are these clans?" Specs asked.

Sean let out a long, low sigh. "They're fucking dangerous, that's what," he said. "Scabs are psychotic, but they're disorganized. Half the time when there's no game—people, I mean—they're killing each other. But the Hatchet Clans are organized into large units. They kill anything they see. Those they don't kill, they rape, torture, or enslave. You don't want to fuck with 'em. They're...savage, primeval. That's the best I can do. They don't use guns. They use axes, spears, hammers...whatever. Let's put it this way: you ever seen those shows on TV...when there was TV...about army ants marching through the jungle and fucking devastating everything in their path? That's what the Hatchet Clans do. They're raiders for the most part. They like to scalp people, cut trophies off 'em."

I had a lot of questions, but I didn't ask them. I was scared. Specs was, too. Sean was a badass. I didn't think there was anything he couldn't handle, but the Clans had him spooked and that was enough for me.

After about ten minutes of silence, he motioned us over. "Look," he said.

I saw two or three men come over a heap of rubble. They wore filthy old Army overcoats. One of them had a machete. One was carrying a length of chain in his hand. The other had a fireman's axe balanced atop one shoulder. They were looking around. The most amazing thing was that they had gas masks on like soldiers from the trenches of World War I.

"What are those masks for?" Specs whispered.

Sean shook his head. "Fuck if I know. But they all wear 'em. Must've looted 'em from an Army depot or a National Guard Armory, Army-Navy surplus or something. I've never seen what's under the masks, but I heard their faces are eaten by some kind of fungi."

I'd seen and heard enough.

Sean kept watching them. "You see two or three like this, you can bet there's thirty more. These are scouts. Hate to tell you, brothers, but we're in some real shit here. They swept through before. Now they'll start hunting building to building."

Specs looked at me. His eyes were bulging. "Oh, that's fucking great. Now what?"

"Calm down," Sean said. "We best get down in the cellar."

Specs looked close to a panic attack. "With the Trogs? Are you nuts? I been down there. There's a hole in the wall. That's where that Trog came from."

Sean grinned. "Damn right there's a hole in the wall. It leads into the sewers. And that's where we're going."

10

Under the circumstances, we didn't have a choice.

Our helmet lights on, we entered the jagged hole in the wall. I didn't know if the Trogs tunneled their way out or if it had been hit by a bomb. Regardless, we went into it and emerged in the shadowy labyrinth of the sewers. As far as our lights could see, nothing but a brick tunnel that looked to be crumbling in spots. It was about seven feet in diameter. It was roomy enough, but it was still a sewer. A foot of water washed past us, carrying debris and occasional rat corpses.

"This is nice," Specs said.

Sean stepped down into the water and we did the same. It was warm. Almost unpleasantly so like standing in a stream of urine.

"This is a main rainwater drain," he told us. "It cuts for miles under the city. There's hundreds of lines branching off it.

Some like this and some you gotta crawl through on your hands and knees. Okay, let's go."

I didn't even ask him where we were going.

We splashed along, our lights bouncing with each step, huge sliding shadows moving over the tunnel walls. The smell down there was awful. Just dank and polluted, the stink of moist rot and stagnant water, other things I didn't want to contemplate. Water dripped and bits of masonry fell now and again. We saw huge colonies of corpse-white toadstools that grew from cracks in the tunnel. I swear they were pulsing almost like they were breathing. A fetid mist came off the water.

"How far do we have to go?" Specs asked.

"Quite a bit. At the very least I want to get a good five, six blocks away from here."

"And how are we gonna know when we're that far?"

"I'll know."

"But—"

"Just shut the fuck up for awhile," Sean said.

I suppressed a smile. Specs was like that. He got nervous and he'd talk your head right off. It was his way. Pouting, he walked along at my side, casting sidelong looks at me, maybe waiting for me to rise to his defense. I had no intention; what we needed now was quiet.

We came to places where the tunnel was nearly blocked by fallen rubble. Many times it was because of a collapsed building whose blasted cellar had opened right up into the tunnels below. There was moss growing everywhere, some kind of green mildew that was luminous.

We'd gone about a block when we saw our first living rats. They were immense and filthy, eyes lit like red Christmas bulbs. They let us pass, but they kept a tight eye on us.

I kept hearing things behind us. Subtle sounds like scratching. It might have been our echo because everything echoed down there, even our voices. But the farther we went the more certain I was it was no echo.

Finally, Sean stopped. "You hear something?" he said.

"Yeah."

We all heard it plainly: a scratching and squeaking as of many, many rats. The sound was getting louder. I had dealt with the rats before. They were bad enough when there was only a few, but when they came in numbers you were in trouble.

"Move it," Sean said.

We hurried down the tunnel which sounds easy in the telling, but splashing through a foot of water gets hard going after awhile. Sean knew his way—or I hoped he did—leading us down side tunnels and then into the mainline again, back and forth until I had no idea where we were. We came to a cave-in and stepped around it into a flooded cellar. There was no building above it; it had been blasted away. The sun sure looked inviting. But there was no way to get up to it. Back into the tunnels, this way and that.

We charged into another offshoot and Sean stopped. "Trog," he said, then relaxed. "Shit, it's a dead one."

It was stuck in a little ell, standing up. It was gray and withered looking, near-mummified. Even its hands were folded over its bosom. A fine plaiting of green mildew grew over it like a caul.

We came into another cellar. It was black in there, the water up to our knees by this point. Dead things were floating in the leaves. Broken beams and shattered sections of concrete rose around us like dock pilings. I saw human bones sticking up out of the water. A ribcage here, a yellowing femur there. The air smelled like blood and meat. I didn't like it in the least.

We came around a rubble pile and right into a nest of rats.

II

"Shit," Sean said, his light playing over them.

We all had our lights on them and our guns. Behind us, I could hear the squeaking and scratching of the rat pack that was tailing us. I started thinking the Hatchet Clans didn't sound so bad.

"Kill 'em!" Specs said.

"No," I told him. "Not unless we don't have a choice. No sense riling them if we don't have to. You shoot them, they'll be forced to fight."

"Good thinking, brother," Sean said.

There were eight or ten of them sitting on a section of collapsed wall, huge, fat-bellied rats with glistening red eyes. Several of them were chewing on something white and bloated. It was a human arm. There were maggots on it. One of them looked right at me, wormy growths coming out of its belly making obscene slithering sounds. Its teeth were bared, claws splayed out like it was ready to jump. Its greasy black fur seemed to flutter and bristle as if it was infested with lice. And as I watched in disgust and amazement, a grub-white parasite the size of a jelly bean hopped off the rat's back.

"Good ratties," Sean said, moving around them. "We're just passing on by. No harm in us."

We moved around a pile of wreckage and the cellar opened up into a cavernous hollow. I could see tree roots dangling from the ceiling. All sorts of junk was rising from the water, even several badly rusted metal beams. There were bones everywhere, human bones. All polished white and licked clean. I saw several skulls that were riddled with teeth marks.

"Nash," Specs. "Nash..."

I saw.

There were literally hundreds of mutant rats. Armies of hump-backed things waiting with sharp teeth and shining scarlet eyes. I saw one that was blubbery and shapeless, almost hairless. There were several stubby, blind fetal heads rising from it. The mouths were opening and closing. And the stink...dear God. Where before it had been a high, hot smell of rot and blood and dampness, now it was a seething, noisome envelope of putrid decay.

Nothing nature had birthed could smell like that.

The rats began to inch closer, crowding us. They were behind us now and in front of us, to all sides. Wherever our lights played, we could see rows of shining, hungry eyes.

Sean took a green cylinder from the pouch around his shoulder. It was one of the white phosphorus grenades. He kept it ready.

Some of the rats were the size of beagles and terriers. Big, mutated things, some almost completely hairless, others lost in a storm of writhing, twitching growths. Many did not have the usual compliment of limbs, but three or sometimes two gigantic clawed appendages. They were so large you could hear them breathing. Many were covered with tumorous, jutting humps and open sores. Some had too many eyes, others not enough, a few were blind, squeaking things.

The rats were clustered around us, mutants, abominations of every sort, pushing in closer and closer. Hosts in this black, stinking nightmare world. Closing in, pushing us forward, leading us towards something, it seemed.

We splashed on, ready to fire our guns at any moment...but to what end? The rats would have buried us alive in seconds. There were that many.

Specs came around a section of floor fallen from above and he screamed. I'll never forget the caliber of that scream. It sounded like his mind was venting itself, blowing everything clear so it could look upon this new thing and make room for the immensity of its horror.

He fell into me, clutching at me, pulling at me, trying, it seemed, to wrap himself around me. "Nash, Nash, Nash...it's there, Nash! It's right there I tell you! I saw it...*I fucking saw it looking at me—*"

Then my light found it, too, and something in me sank, submerged forever. I looked right at it and to this day I know I saw it, but I couldn't have. For there are mutants and then there are *mutants.*

It was a rat the size of a pick-up truck.

Maybe not one rat, but two or three that had *grown* into a single flaccid nightmare mass that was horribly puckered, hairless, and fish belly white. That's what I saw. It reposed on a filthy, stinking pile of debris, cannibalized human bodies, and bones in a huge oblong cavity in the wall. It was like some kind of fucking altar. That clownwhite flesh was nearly transparent like some kind of pulsating jelly and you could see the bones beneath it. The skin seemed to move, to writhe, vibrate with a slick, boneless motion as if everything beneath it was in constant, sickly motion. Two bobbing heads sprouted from trunklike necks, jaws of yellow knifeblade teeth gnashing together. But the worst part were the eyes. One head had three oozing, red orbs the size of softballs. The other had but one, filmed and pustulant. There was a third head that was limp, dangling on a stalk of neck

And I swear to you, that growing out of that body were a dozen other smaller fetal heads like on that other rat, each filled with an unnatural, atavistic life that would not die.

Sean was panning his light over it, making gasping sounds in his throat. Its underbelly was set with roping, snakelike growths. I think I saw eyes...yellow, mucus-filled eyes...opening amongst them.

I was floored, sickened, offended...it's hard to put into words. But *terror* belongs there, too, for never have I set my eyes upon anything as revolting, as perfectly loathsome as that gigantic grub-like rat.

The other rats had backed off.

It was all too obvious why: we had been led to this hideous mutation, unharmed, as food. We were living sacrifices laid down at the feet of this deformed, nightmare mother. They had offered her only scraps...until now.

And she wanted more.

Unfurling her glistening claws from the leathery sheaths of her paws, she moved forward. It was almost a hopping, slinking motion, a slithering. Everything seemed to move at once, a biological shuddering profusion.

A ribcage vacuumed free of meat tumbled down from the heap in her pulsing wake. At her feet, wriggling in the human carnage of bone and limb, were her young. Hundreds of hairless, squealing things with transparent hides. Misshapen like deformed fetuses, they wormed through the cadavers and skinless husks like maggots in pork.

This maybe is what put us into action.

The mother hopped down, her clawed, spade-feet slapping the wet timbers. Her lips pulled back from blackened gums, fence-post teeth licked by whipping tongues. A freight train roar of hissing anger vomited from those throats as she came on, her huge, pendulous teats swinging back and forth like sacks of grain.

Sean started shooting.

Something like this...something degenerate and perverse and evil...it had to be killed, it had to be crushed.

The first of Sean's rounds from his shotgun pulverized one of the eyes like a rotten grape, the next blew a snout apart. Specs and I started firing, too. Bullets thudded into throats and clawing limbs. They snapped off teeth and bisected teats in sprays of foul milk.

"Run!" he told us. "Over there! Get into that pipe!"

There was a small junction pipe coming out of the wall. It was big enough to crawl through on our hands and knees. Specs and I splashed our way over there, tripping over things and pulling each other up out of the water. We fired at the other rats. Specs slid into the pipe.

I turned back and saw Sean empty his shotgun at the mother rat and then pull the pin on his phosphorus grenade. He tossed it right at her and dove into the water. There was a blinding explosion of white light and flames engulfed her, they spread over the water and up the jutting beams. Rats scattered.

Sean emerged a few feet away, shouting, "Into the pipe! Go! Go!"

Everywhere there was the awful, nauseating stink of cremated flesh and hair. The squealing, mewling mother and her legions as they were roasted alive.

On hands and knees I went through the pipe as fast as I could. I could hear Sean swearing behind me. Specs was way ahead of us. I could see the bobbing light of his helmet. Behind us there was nothing but the roaring of the mother rat and the shrill, angry squeaking and squealing of her pack. I figured we'd never make it. We'd be devoured alive in that narrow, claustrophobic pipe. But eventually it opened up into another main drainline. It must have been some sort of overflow.

I climbed out and Specs was waiting there, his grime-streaked face pulled tight, his eyes huge. Sean got out after me and led us through the water to a ladder. He went up first and handled the manhole cover. I doubted I would have been strong enough to do it. Then up went Specs. Then me, leaving the subterranean world of echoing scratching and screeching behind.

Sean pushed the cover back on and it clattered into place.

We were all sitting on the pavement in the broad daylight, nothing but rusting cars on an empty street around us.

Sean was breathing hard. With his helmet on, face dirty and sweating, he looked like a coal miner just up out of the shafts. He saw us looking at him and he grinned. Then he laughed under his breath. "Dammit," he said. "I lost my damn Trog head."

12

Sean was crazy.

Make no mistakes about it. After our adventure in the sewer, I was strung out: shaking, sweating, my guts tied in knots. Part of me wanted to scream and another part wanted to laugh uncontrollably. But I wasn't about to let that happen.

"We couldn't have seen that," I said after a time. I was drawing off a stale cigarette, smoking it with both hands because I couldn't keep it steady with one.

"Oh, we saw it, all right, brother," Sean said, slapping my shoulder. "All kinds of crazy shit down below. Things that caught a good dose of radiation and then crawled down there to breed. There's shit down there that'll never see the light of day and we can be thankful for that."

Specs hadn't said anything. He just stared at us, his eyes glassy and fixed. Mostly he stared at Sean. Wouldn't stop staring at him, in fact. Finally, Sean said, "Hell's your problem, bitch?"

Specs was pissed. I could see that. "We could have been killed down there hunting for your fucking Trogs!" he said, letting it all out. "You're a fucking maniac! Worse, you're a fucking inconsiderate, reckless maniac who doesn't give a shit about anybody else! Fuck you and your Trogs! You hear me? Fuck the both of you."

At which point, he stood up and just started walking down the street. We followed him and I calmed him down bit by bit. Of course, Sean kept laughing about it and that only made matters worse.

"Don't worry, little brother," Sean finally told him. "I won't ask you to go down below again. It ain't your thing."

He led us through the streets, keeping an eye out for the Hatchet Clans. About a block from his apartment I saw someone standing in the street. It was a girl. And she looked normal. She stood there, seeing us, and did not move, did not speak. I called out to her, but she didn't answer. I motioned the others to hang back.

"Well don't dirty her up too much, Nash," Sean said.

As I got closer I saw that she was probably around college age, nineteen or twenty, no more than that, girl-next-door pretty with high cheekbones and big blue eyes, a honey-blonde ponytail down the middle of her back. She was dirty and ragged, but you couldn't get around the fact that she was very stunning.

I held my hands out. "I'm normal," I said. "So are they. It's okay. Really."

Her eyes were glacial, emotionless. When I got up close to her she came alive and there was a knife in her hand. I wrestled with her for it while Sean laughed and Specs panicked. Finally, I pinned her and it wasn't easy: she was strong, determined.

"Knock it off," I told her. "Nobody's going to hurt you! Nobody's going to kill you or beat you or rape you!"

"Speak for yourself," Sean said.

"Shut up," I told him.

I could see in the girl's eyes she wanted to believe me, but there was doubt and who could blame her?

"I'm gonna let you up now," I said. "You wanna run away, go ahead. We're not coming after you. You wanna come with us, that's fine. We have shelter and food."

She gave me a hard look. "And what will that cost me?"

"Not a damn thing. You have my word."

I let her up and she ran off, stopped, watched us. We just went on our way and paid no attention to her, but we knew she was following us.

"Well?" I finally said, turning around.

"My name's Janie," she said, offering me a sliver of smile.

13

We hung around for a few more weeks. I'm not sure why. I needed to go west. That's what The Shape wanted. But I was in no hurry then. That didn't come until later. Life in Cleveland wasn't exactly fun and games, but I liked being with Sean. I'd never met a guy who was more resourceful. He knew where everything was. He had stashes of food, survival gear, and weapons all over the city. Later I learned all that stuff had been hidden away by the Cleveland chapter of the Hell's Angels who'd been friends of his. They'd been preparing for war.

The city was full of Scabs. There were some street gangs you had to watch for and the Hatchet Clans, of course. Night was a bad time with the rats and mutants and the Children. The Red Rains came and went. I found a nice piece of equipment at a scientific supply house: a solar-powered Geiger Counter. It was to come in very handy. Whenever the Children showed, the radiation count skyrocketed so it was a pretty decent early warning device. I came to the conclusion that the Red Rains were not just blood, rendered meat, and acid, but were charged with fallout, too. I took readings on a puddle of the stuff and it was hot.

During those weeks I got to know Janie real well.

She didn't seem to trust Sean or Specs. She clung to me. She was always at my side, a sweet and wonderful girl. She was almost twenty years younger than me and for some reason, she took to me and fell in love with me. I figured in the old world, she wouldn't have looked twice at me even if I'd been her own age, but it was a new world with a whole new set of expectations and priorities and Janie had changed with it. She'd been in her freshman year of college—pre-med at Ohio State—when the world ended. Back in high school, I learned, she had been an honor roll student and class president, civic-minded and caring...gone to church, volunteered at the local children's hospital, collected coats for the needy in the winter and canned food for the elderly in the summer.

When the bombs fell, she'd made her way back home with some other students to Painesville, Ohio, and pretty much watched her friends and family die. She left for Cleveland a month ago and the Hatchet Clans had gotten her friends, leaving her stranded in the city.

She'd been through it like everyone else. Regardless, she was a real peach in every way who wore her heart on her sleeve.

We all liked her. We all felt protective of her...even Sean, despite himself. We all, I think, envied the fact that she had survived the end of the world with morals and ethics intact. But for all that we could not be like her. The world was a jungle now and only the strong and the vicious survived. Janie just didn't get that. That's why we had to keep an eye on her. That heart of hers was too big for its own good and there were too many things out there that would take a bite out of it.

Towards the end of our stay in Cleveland, The Shape started whispering in my head again. This time it wasn't about us going west. It wanted something else, but as usual it was vague about what it wanted. All I knew is that it wanted an *offering*. In the back of my mind I knew exactly what that meant, but it was too horrible to consider.

So I told the others about The Shape.

Janie didn't seem surprised at all. She accepted what I told her. But Sean thought I was fucking nuts, hearing voices in my head and all. Specs liked the idea of an offering, of course.

"It wants a sacrifice, Nash," he said. "And we better give it one."

"A sacrifice?" Sean said. "Like what? You mean like a *human* sacrifice?"

"Exactly."

"You are one crazy bastard, little brother. But what the hell? Let's go get some old ragbag and offer him up."

Janie said nothing. Nothing at all. She didn't have to; I could see the disappointment in her eyes. It was barbaric and wrong. She knew it and I knew it, but we went ahead anyway.

Specs was excited at the idea. Like I told you, he was into all that new age shit, crystals and astrology and you name it. He had read lots of books about witchcraft and Satanism and all that high, happy horseshit, so it all came natural to him. We grabbed some old man, some ragbag, tied and gagged him, then dragged him into a vacant lot one night and tied him to a tree. We piled wood all around him in a big heap and then we lit him up. Specs said it was expiation, that we had to make a burnt offering and that would keep The Shape happy and on our side.

It was horrible.

The old man died screaming, lit up like a candle. I saw his eyes actually boil out of his head and his skin superheat like wax and run off the skeleton and into the flames. When he was smoldering I told The Shape to come and get him. That was the first time it ever appeared to us, took on physical form. It took our offering...absorbed it...but somehow I knew it wasn't what it wanted.

It wanted something living, not something burnt.

It was angry at what had been offered.

It wanted another.

Two days later, Specs got sick.

14

We'd just come back from scouting out some vehicles to get us out of the city and Specs had been acting funny all day. He wasn't saying much. After we'd settled in, he came over to me.

"I got something, Nash," he said. "I got something real bad."

"You're just tired," I told him.

"I been coughing for three days."

And he had been. I think we were all aware that something was going on, but maybe we justified it in our own minds by saying it was just a cold or something...even though we all damn well knew that even cold bugs were serious business these days.

"I can't even breathe out of my nose, Nash," he told me. "My muscles and joints ache all the time. Sometimes I have trouble breathing."

"Don't say anything to the others, not yet."

He shook his head. "Afraid I can't do that, Nash. I can't take the chance of infecting them with what I have."

Good old Specs. Guy went through life pretty much afraid of everything. One of those people that God or Nature or what have you had given barely enough strength and fortitude to get through day by day. But when the chips were down, he was as strong as they came. As selfless as you could imagine.

We told Janie and Sean and they would have been totally justified to want to get away from him, but they didn't. He was one of us and we were going to make it together.

"Don't you worry, little brother," Sean told him. "We'll get you on your feet. Before you know it, me and you'll be hunting Trogs again."

Specs tried to smile at that and a tear slid from his eye.

The next few days were bad. Specs' skin began to take on a bluish, cyanotic tinge that concerned us all. He couldn't breathe. He was gasping all the time. He was hot to the touch and a sour-smelling sweat rolled down his face. He'd have choking fits that would go on for ten minutes. In a last ditch attempt, Sean went and found us some military-grade antibiotics and we shot Specs full of them. It did no good. It was simply too late.

Mostly he was incoherent, thrashing in his sleep and even convulsing. There was little we could do. Janie mothered him the best she could. Now and again, he'd wake up, look at me, and start talking about throwing corpses in the back of the garbage truck in Youngstown or sleeping in cars or any of the other stupid things we'd done.

It was then I realized he was going to die. The idea of that cut me open, made me bleed. We'd been through a lot. Specs was like some stupid little brother that annoys you, hangs around, but won't go away and you're secretly glad for it. I didn't want to be without him.

Then one day, he said to me, "Nash...don't let me die like this...it hurts...everything fucking hurts...I can't even breathe. Put me out of my fucking misery."

I just shook my head; it was unthinkable.

But Specs was insistent. "Please, Nash, don't make me suffer. Give me...give me to The Shape."

It was insane and I told him so, but he kept pushing and he made Sean and Janie hear him out, too. See, Specs was of the mind that The Shape was pissed off at him because it had been his idea to do the burnt offering of that old man. That's not what

The Shape had wanted at all, Specs said. So it had let him get infected with some germ as a punishment. Maybe it was true, maybe it was bullshit. Who knew?

"See, that's why this is perfect," he told us. "I'll be a sacrifice. I'll give myself to that monster and it'll save me from dying slow and it'll keep The Shape happy. He'll take care of you guys, keep you safe."

I was absolutely against it. True, The Shape *did* want something more. I knew that. I felt that. I'd heard it in my mind. My big mistake was telling Specs that. But it was too late.

"Please, Nash. Please," he kept saying.

We were all against it...but that pathetic, pleading look in his eyes wore us down. Sean broke first and said it was the only goddamn decent thing we *could* do for him. And then Janie...

"He's our friend," she told me. "I'm against wasting life of any sort...but we can't make him suffer. If this is what he wants...I guess you should allow him it."

There was argument, but he got his way.

We were going to sacrifice Specs.

We were going to give him to The Shape.

15

Sean scavenged us a stretcher and we carried Specs to a warehouse on around sunset. We weren't going to burn him or any of that fucked up pagan madness. We were going to do it the right way and just let The Shape have him. We set the stretcher atop some crates. We lit candles because Janie said we should. Specs loved all that occult pageantry.

Then it was time.

I'll never get that night out of my mind. The candles flickering. The cavernous silence. That creeping chill that came in off the river. The warehouse felt like a tomb.

I held his hand and we talked. "Remember that day when we sat on that bench, Nash? We ate Dinty Moore stew and drank Dew. That's the day I knew you were my best friend in the world."

I couldn't take it. I started balling my eyes out. I told them all that I just couldn't go through with it. I lashed out at

Sean and Janie and they just watched me with defeated, sad eyes. Then I looked at Specs fighting for every breath, then I knew I had to do it.

So I summoned The Shape.

I closed my eyes and concentrated on that sphere of darkness in my mind that I always associated with it. Right away, I could feel it coming and I was flooded with a primal terror that was ice-cold, freezing. The atmosphere of the warehouse immediately went from being simply neutral to *activated.* That's the only way I can describe it. Around us there was no longer just dead air, but an ether that was charged and deadly and thrumming with energy. The hairs on my arms and at the back of my neck stood up like I had come into contact with a charge of static electricity.

I went down on my knees, absolutely senseless.

Janie and Sean pulled me back to safety.

I smelled a sharp stink of ozone and something like burning flesh, hot blood boiled to steam. Then an awful, acrid stench like melting wires and blown fuses. The warehouse seemed to tremble. The concrete floor vibrated. There was a searing hot flash of something like chain lightening that blinded me momentarily and then the Shape was coming: a boiling black mass like thunderheads getting ready to shoot lightening at the earth. It was a spinning, roaring, unstable irradiated elemental force that came with the heat of coke ovens and the toxic glow of nuclear reactors. Looking at it was like looking into the primeval fires of cosmic creation.

Janie screamed.

Sean fell on his ass trying to get away from it.

The Shape was pulsing, revolving on an axis of pure atomic force that was frightening to behold, a storm of fallout and dust and particulated matter with a heart of superhot plasma. It made a buzzing sound like a million angry hornets.

I stood there, feeling its heat burning the fine hairs on the back of my hands. It was matter and force and pulsating energy, but it was not mindless. It was sentient and directed. Absolute nuclear chaos that was living and evil and hungry. At the very center of the whirlwind itself, there was a zone of blackness darker than anything I had ever seen before, the blackness that must exist beyond time and space. And flickering luminously within that shrieking void of antimatter were two red eyes that looked hot enough to melt steel.

Without further ado, it took Specs.

Dear God, it took him.

The mass of The Shape was constantly changing and reinventing itself, but I suppose if you had to give it spatial dimensions I would have said it was probably something like twelve feet in height, maybe six in width. It hovered over Specs for a moment or two and that's when he realized exactly what he had given himself to.

He screamed.

Probably with his last reservoir of air he screamed like I've never heard a man scream before with a wild, cutting, hysterical sound that echoed through the warehouse. Sean made to go to his aid and I held him back. Specs was beyond our help. If Sean had gotten close to that radioactive furnace, he would have been vaporized.

Because that's what happened to Specs.

He was sucked into it and I saw him spinning in that godless void, I saw him bulge up and then literally explode into particles that were vacuumed into the central mass, made part of it, every atom leeched of its energy in the whirling subatomic storm. And then he came back out again. He hit the floor and he was a blackened, smoldering heap of refuse that sparked and popped.

The buzzing sound faded, seemed to come from a great distance. There was a resounding hollow explosion that sounded much like a sonic boom when the air collapses back into the void left by a supersonic fighter.

That was it.

It was gone and so was Specs. What was left was a smoking heap of debris that had been supercharged, disassembled at the molecular level and then, reassembled, and vomited back into this time/space.

Janie and Sean practically had to carry me out of there. They did not speak for some time and I didn't blame them. For I had shown them something no sane, reasoning mind should ever look upon.

The face of the Devil.

16

For weeks afterwards, I had nightmares about that night. I kept seeing The Shape take Specs and what had become of him. I kept seeing the blackened, burning heap of refuse he had been reduced to. He had been my friend. A very loyal, very kind-hearted guy. And I had given him to that fucking nightmare and how in God's name could I ever get it out of my mind or learn to live with myself?

It was that night as Sean went off by himself to brood and drink, that Janie and I made love for the first time. She was so much younger than me that I felt like some kind of deviant, but I did it anyway. I lost myself in her and her hot body against mine was the finest thing I'd ever known. At least, that's what I told myself.

What a wonderful world it indeed was. Empty cities and spawning mutants, bioplagues and Red Rains and fallout and...*The Shape.* I didn't know what it was and I refused to speculate. Though when I had looked on it I was certain that it was the very stuff the universe was made of. The meat, as it were, of primary cosmic generation.

Sean did not come back that night.

We were worried. Around noon he showed up with an SUV and a full tank of gas. He had two men with him. One was tall and lanky, the other shorter and heavily muscled. Pretty as Janie was, they did not even give her a second glance. They stared at me and I was certain I saw something like fear and awe in their eyes. I wondered what Sean had told them and decided it really didn't matter.

"This is Carl and Texas Slim," Sean told me. "They want to go west, too."

"Welcome," I told them, wondering if one of them would have to burn some day to keep the rest of us safe. "Welcome."

There were five of us then.

ELKHART INDIANA

1

I was in league with The Shape.

If I'd doubted it before, there was no mistaking it after Cleveland.

I made sacrifices to it, I did the selecting and I did it not only to save my sorry ass but the asses of my little posse. We took care of The Shape and The Shape took care of us. We were healthy. We weren't riddled with sores and radiation burns like the others. There was no disease in our bodies and our genes weren't going crazy from fallout. The Shape led me on, always pointing me in the right direction and I always found a few treats for him and, in return, we were alive and we were strong, we always had full bellies, safe places to lay our heads at night. No, I don't know how it worked. Not really. Only that being in league with that thing gave us all a sort of protective magic.

2

We stood around by the river watching the woman burn for maybe a half hour or so, the stink of cremated flesh hot in our faces. Long after it was done and she was nothing but a smoldering skeleton, we stared at the flames licking from her ribcage and the hollows of her skull. It was morbid, but we were fascinated, unable to look away as a child cannot look away from a roaring campfire. Something about the mystical call of the flames, I suppose, as transfixing and hypnotic now as they'd been to our ancestors huddled in an Ice Age cave.

The smell was sickening.

You would think after all the incinerated bodies we'd come across—and, yes, *produced*—the smell would be something we wouldn't even notice anymore like a guard at Belzec feeding corpses into the ovens. But we did notice. All of us. The burnt scarecrow tied to the blackened tree was something we'd see in our minds for days. And smell. Because the smell of burnt hair, roasted flesh, and oxidized bones would stay with us, haunting us, coming into our dreams until we'd wake, sweating and terrified, certain that a charred and grinning skull would be on the pillow next to our own.

"I think she's done," Carl finally said, lighting a twig off the burning corpse and firing his cigarette with it.

Texas Slim chuckled. "A little honey sauce, some taters and beans, we got ourselves a barbecue."

I laughed; so did Sean. It was funny. Even funnier the way the human mind works. In the worst of situations there is some kind of psychological trigger or safety valve in the brain that overrides all else, releasing stress by making us joke about the most horrible things. I suppose it's the same thing that made soldiers in the trenches of World War I adopt human skulls as pets, giving them silly names like "Mr. Jingles" and "Lippy" and the same thing that made people burst out laughing at funerals.

"That's enough," Janie said, standing far and away and downwind from the burning woman. "I won't listen to it."

"Sure, Janie," I said. "We were just kidding."

Janie didn't like that kind of shit. She saw nothing funny in the dead even though they were scattered everywhere now. The cities were graveyards and the streets were littered with remains. To her, a body was still a body. To the rest of us a body was of no more importance than a bag of leaves or a cardboard box. But that was Janie. The last of the bleeding hearts. An endangered species.

It had been nearly two months since we rolled out of Cleveland with Carl and Texas Slim in tow. And a hard two months they had been, fighting with the Hatchet Clans, hiding from radioactive dust storms, searching for vehicles and finding food. The days went by in a blur.

And now, there I was, staring at the remains of another offering for The Shape.

Janie stomped off.

Texas Slim and Sean kind of eyed me warily as friends will do when your girlfriend is in a mood. I bummed a cigarette from Carl and stood there, uncomfortably, smoking and watching the St. Joseph River roll on by.

"Hey, Nash," Sean said. "I ever tell you about the time I sold my wife for a dollar?"

Texas Slim giggled. "This is a good one."

Sean smiled in the moonlight, his teeth crooked and missing. "We were in Sturgis, man, you know, the biker rally? Well, sure as shit, me and the old lady were at each other's throats. All day long. It was always like that with us. That's why I got this scar on my forehead, you see. We was at this hop-and-grind joint and she passed out. So things being what they were, I started making out with her sister who was sitting next to me. She'd fuck anything with a third leg. Well, Trixie wakes up and I'm tongue-fucking her sister and she yells something and hits me in the face with a beer bottle. One mean bitch, that Trixie." He laughed. "Anyway, there we was in Sturgis. We'd been drinking and smoking Cee all day long. We're sitting at this bar putting back shots of Wild Turkey, just tearing into each other as was our way. This big dude, think he might have been with the Outlaws or the Pagans, he says, Hey, how much for your wife? I say, you want to buy that shit? He says, Sure I do. How much? A dollar, I tell him. He hands me a dollar and takes hold of Trixie and she screams something at me and that's the last I saw of her."

"Well, what happened?" Texas Slim wanted to know. "He kill her?"

Sean pulled off his cigarette. "No, nothing like that. She shows up back at the hotel about three in the morning, all dirty, clothes torn, and I say, Hey babe, how was it? She near beat the shit out of me. Next day, that big biker comes up to me, says, I want that dollar back. I say, That bad, eh? He don't think it's funny, says, You ought to have a license to sell poisonous snakes, you asshole." Sean sighed. "Yeah, that Trixie. She was something. She was doing a nickel at Utah State Penn for possession last I heard of her."

We all laughed again. But not Janie. She did not like stories like that. Things had changed so much now. You had to stick tight to survive these days, not like the old days where you and the boys went out to the man-cave to swap the salt and talk tit. You had a woman these days, you had to keep her by your side and she had to keep *you* by her side.

Carl said, "We best be on our way, Nash. I don't like being out here in the dark."

"All right," I said. "Let's get gone."

We crossed Island Park, guns in our hands and packs on our backs, keeping an eye on the shadows and the things that might be hiding there. We saw nothing. We got on Jackson Boulevard, went over the bridge and Waterfall Drive, cutting down South Main. We needed a place to sleep for the night. We were all dead tired. Usually, well before sunset, we had a place. But today had been busy.

"Start checking some doors," I told Texas Slim as we walked. "We gotta lay up somewhere."

He did so, but door after door after door was locked. We could have blasted our way in, but I didn't want to make all that racket and draw attention to ourselves. Besides, what good is a door that's been blown off its hinges? I wanted a place with some security against what was outside, hiding in the dark.

"Too bad none of us can fly a plane," Sean said. "Lots of planes at the airport. Maybe I should give it a try, Nash."

"Oh, shut up," Janie told him.

The full moon above was very bright. Main looked like a glowing ribbon of ether as it stretched away into the distance. Everything was silent and surreal. All those empty buildings and shops crowding each side of the street, the abandoned cars at the curbs. If it hadn't been for the skeletons in the gutters and that unearthly quiet, you could have fooled yourself that there was still life here. Still people sleeping in beds and little kids dreaming little kid dreams, all charging up for another day in the life.

But it wasn't that way anymore.

Those buildings were monuments to a way of life that had vanished now. Main Street, Elkhart, was like something kept under glass in a museum: carefully preserved but long dead and gone. As we walked, Carl out front with his rifle looking for trouble, I felt at ease with things. What we had done this night wasn't something I was proud of, but we were alive, we were breathing. We would live to fight another day and another day after that.

I was wondering where we were going to hole up for the night and where in the hell we were going to get a vehicle come tomorrow. Most were either smashed-up or their batteries were dead, engine parts salvaged. But we needed a ride. We needed one bad. We had to get moving west.

"Open door," Texas finally called out, standing in front of a tattoo parlor called INKED AND DANGEROUS.

It was good as any.

"C'mon, Carl," I said, waiting for him as he scanned the streets with the barrel of his AK-47, looking for trouble, always looking for trouble.

We filed inside and I locked the door, pulled down the shade on the window. It was a tight little place, but it had a backdoor leading out into the alley in case we needed to make a quick escape. We rolled out our sleeping bags and the boys had a smoke while I tried to get Janie to act civil.

But after what had happened in the park she wasn't speaking to me. She had retreated into herself, offended at every conceivable level by what we had done to the woman and *what* we had offered her up to. But I didn't much care. All I knew was that it was done. It was over with. We'd made sacrifice and we were safe now. At least until the next cycle of the full moon.

Because that's when The Shape would come knocking at the door again with an empty belly.

2

It seemed like my head had barely hit the pillow when Carl was shaking me awake. "Nash," he said. "C'mon, Nash, wake the fuck up. We got activity here."

"What?" I said.

"I think someone's out there. In fact, I'm sure of it."

I pulled myself out of my bag, looked out the window and saw absolutely nothing. Just the empty street, the rusting hulks of vehicles. Some at the curbs, others pulled right up onto the sidewalk. A few had been driven right through the plate glass windows of shops across the street.

"Looks pretty quiet," I said.

"I think we were followed."

I was still looking and not seeing anything.

"There was someone or something behind us, dogging us. I know it," he said. "They're out there right now."

Carl's intuition wasn't always on target, but usually in situations of danger he was pretty damn perceptive. I watched the streets and though I did not see anything, I had the oddest feeling that as I watched, I was *being* watched. It made the flesh at the back of my neck creep.

Sean crawled out of his bag, stretched, said, "How the hell am I supposed to sleep with you two jabbering like this?"

"We're being watched," Carl said.

"You always think we're being watched," Sean told him. "Go lay the fuck down. Put a tampon in and get a few Z's, for chrissake, you pussy."

Carl almost hit him with the butt of his AK and it would not have been the first time. I stepped in-between them as I always stepped in-between them. Carl was always fighting with Sean or Texas. He had a short fuse and they knew it. He just couldn't take a joke. One of those guys that walks around with a target on their backs.

I peered out the window again. I thought for just a second I saw someone dart behind a car. It could have been my imagination. My eyes were still crusty from sleep. The moon above the buildings had moved clear across the sky. I must have been out for hours.

I had just pulled my face from the window when the first shot rang out.

A bullet punched through the glass and I felt it pass by my cheek. Heavy caliber, too, because not only did it punch a neat hole in the window but it shattered it. Another round came through the glass face of the door. Carl brought up his AK and fired a few liberal three-shot bursts into the streets. And that brought the reports of at least three more rifles. The glass was blown out of the door and black bullet holes were punched into the walls behind us. Carl fired another burst and by then, on my hands and knees, I had everyone together. We rolled up our bags, gathered up our packs and made for the rear entrance.

Carl gave another three-round burst to keep our adversaries from making a rush at the building.

"Get going," Sean told us. "I'll hold off the Indians and catch up with you."

I'll never forget him standing there with his Ruger Mini-14 carbine, bopping and weaving as rounds peppered the tattoo parlor, telling us to get going as he worked the bolt and laid down suppressive fire. And I'll also never forget that crooked, toothy smile he flashed me right before a bullet caught him in the head and blew his skull into mucilage that splashed against the walls.

Somebody screamed. In fact, two people screamed: Janie in horror and Carl in manic rage. I was too shocked to do anything but stare at Sean folded up on the floor, his legs kicking then going still, the top of his head just...gone. I crawled over there, pried the 14 from his hands and whispered something to him, something heartbroken and gushy, and followed the others out the back way. Sean. They'd killed Sean. *Jesus Christ, fucking Sean.*

The alley. Carl was already running and Janie was trying to wait for me, but Texas Slim wasn't having any of that. He had hooked her by the arm and was propelling her along pretty much against her will. The alley zig-zagged, then opened up out into the street. I caught up to them and tossed Carl Sean's Ruger which had much better range than his AK. One of our attackers came leaping out from behind a car and fired a round from what I thought was a .30-30. He got off that shot, but that was it. Carl fired with the 14 and dropped him screaming in the street with a perfect gut-shot.

We ran.

And as we ran, we were pursued. I told the others to scout ahead while I gave our attackers a little trouble and bought us some time. The others ran ahead and hid out. I waited. The silence was unbearable. I heard a breeze rattle the branches of an aspen across the way. A dog howled in the distance. That was it. Then, after maybe five minutes, running feet. They were just down the block. I counted three of them.

They dodged behind a car.

I caught the glint of a rifle barrel in the waning moonlight, raised my .30.06 Savage and fired. I didn't hit anyone, but my round punched through the windshield of a Cadillac and gave them something to think about. A few more rounds came my way. I fired one more time and then took off down the sidewalk in a low run, hunched-over. More rounds punched into plate glass windows and I dodged behind a pick-up truck.

I had no idea where the others were by that point.

I waited for the bad boys to close in, but they were in no hurry. They'd fire a shot in my direction from time to time, but I didn't return the fire. I was trying to draw them out and the longer I was quiet the more they'd want to find out why. If I'd have been smart, I would have cried out or something so they'd think I was hit. But I wasn't that smart. And I didn't want Janie and the others to come running to my rescue and get greased.

Footsteps were coming.

Light, agile. But they were coming from behind me which either meant that the bad boys had circled around me or that—

"Nash," Carl said. "There's a train station about two blocks down. Ground's wide open around it, perfect killzone, we can waste anything that comes knocking. Texas and Janie are waiting down there. Let's go."

It was about that time that I heard vehicles start up. Two of them, racing their engines. We were on foot and the bad boys had wheels. Things were starting to look pretty bad. I ran off after Carl and about the time it seemed my lungs would burst, we caught up with Janie and Texas Slim. They were waiting behind an overturned Datsun. I followed them across Tyler Street, through the gates, and into the parking lot of the train station, which had been an Amtrak hub before the world ended. I saw signs for Michigan Southern and Conrail.

Carl was right: it *was* wide open in every direction, defensible, perfect killzone. Nothing could approach our position without us knowing it. The New York Central Museum was across the way and the Conrail Yards and the Conrail mainline just beyond. The yards were huge and went on forever. Nothing out there but trains lying dead and rusting on tracks. And in that moonlight, you could see for miles it seemed. The only problem was that it was a big, sprawling building and there was no way in hell the four of us could cover all sides.

I saw the headlights coming in our direction and knew we really didn't have a choice. The horizon was getting blue and I knew the sun would be up in less than an hour. That was to our advantage. The station was open and we locked and barricaded the front door once we were inside. Carl checked the other doors, secured them, then we went upstairs into the offices. From the windows up there it would be like a duck hunt.

A pick-up truck and a Ford Bronco pulled into the lot. Two men stepped from the pick-up and three more from the Bronco. They looked normal. I didn't know what they wanted with us and I knew I'd probably never know. Maybe just the ragtag remains of a militia out hunting. Maybe they wanted our weapons. Maybe they wanted Janie.

By the time they got out of their vehicles, the sun was making itself known in the east. They were chatting amongst themselves, pretty much at ease. They did not know we were there. Maybe they suspected it, but they didn't know. I was hoping, really hoping, they'd just go away. I wanted to hurt them bad for killing Sean, but for the safety of the others I was willing to let it go. Carl had already killed one of them.

They started fanning out in the lot.

"Shit," I said under my breath.

We already had the windows open. I raised my Savage, sighted in on a guy with a cowboy hat, squeezed the trigger and dropped him. Carl fired a split second after me and dropped another with a headshot. I caught another guy in the leg. The two dead ones lay flopping in the lot in their own blood. The one I'd shot was screaming. The others pulled back behind the pick-up truck, putting a few rounds in our direction.

"We've got 'em boxed in, Nash," Carl said. "When that sun comes up we'll have 'em."

I nodded. "No shooting until it's light. Unless they move. And they're going to have to pretty soon."

The sun was rising. The world had gone from black to indigo to light blue. It would be fully light in about fifteen minutes. What I didn't like was the idea of playing cat-and-mouse all day long with those assholes. I went over to Carl, whispered something in his ear. He liked my idea. Janie waited behind me. Texas Slim was out in the hallway keeping an eye on the stairwell.

Twice in the next few minutes, the bad boys below tried to make it to their parked vehicles and twice Carl had put a round within inches of them. We had them boxed good. They were hiding behind the rear of the pick-up truck. The Bronco was over a bit and they didn't dare make a mad dash for it. And that was good, because I'd already eyed that baby up. I wanted it. I didn't care if I had to kill everyone of them to get it.

Carl lit a cigarette, blew out some smoke. "Nash?" he said.

"Go ahead."

Janie looked at me, but I wasn't saying. Carl, cigarette clenched in his teeth, sighted in on the pick-up truck. He started squeezing off rounds, working the bolt of the Ruger and squeezing the trigger in rapid succession. He put one through the windshield. Another through the front driver's side tire. He kept them pinned down. Two more shots into the cab. And then the killshot. Leaning out the window, he scoped out the gas tank and pulled the trigger. Dead on target, too. Right away, gasoline started flooding out from under the truck.

The bad boys started shouting.

Carl fired into the tank again and it went up with a resounding explosion, the puddle of gas going up in flames. The three survivors—one of them beating his burning clothes with his hands—appeared from behind the truck. They were firing at the building, trying to make the safety of the Bronco about twenty feet away. I aimed and fired on the guy I'd already pegged in the leg, catching him in the side and pitching him to the pavement. He screamed like he was being roasted alive.

The smoke from the burning truck was thick in the air and it screened the others from us as it screened us from them. The two survivors were going to get the Bronco. I put two or three rounds where I thought they were, but I knew one of them would make it. And they would have.

But something else happened first.

3

Carl stopped shooting and backed away from the window. "Listen," he said. "You hear it? They're coming..."

"That smell," Janie said.

I didn't know what the hell either of them were talking about. I was smelling burning gasoline and scorched metal, melted rubber and plastic, the stink of burnt cordite in the room. My ears were ringing from the shooting. So I truly didn't hear or smell anything for a moment. But then I did: a rising steady drone that seemed to be coming from every direction and a smell: sweet, almost gagging, like sugar liquefied in a pan. The droning got louder until it became a high, whining buzz and that stink...nauseating, like thrusting your head into the innards of a hive dripping with honey. Absolutely overwhelming.

"Close those fucking windows!" I cried out.

But Carl and Janie were already doing so and I joined in. None of us seemed to give a shit about the fact that we had exposed ourselves to gunfire from below. We knew what was coming and we knew very well what would happen if we didn't get those damn windows closed up fast.

"They're down in the lobby!" Texas Slim called out, rushing into the room and slamming the door behind him.

We got the windows closed and just in time—for something landed on the glass outside. An insect. It was about six-inches long, segmented, a pale cream in color like a larval termite with tiny spines rising up from the thorax. Looking like some weird mutant hybrid of a wasp, a fly, and a mosquito, it fluttered wide, transparent purple-hued wings, two sets of them that were intricately veined with a dark tracery. It had bulbous red-orange eyes the size of marbles and I swear it was looking at us, hungering for us. Carl thumped the window and three more landed followed by a fifth, sixth, and seventh. They knew we were in there and they wanted us. They crawled over the glass, buzzing their wings, each extending a fleshy proboscis to the window, investigating it. The most obscene thing about them was that proboscis. It was rubbery, pulsing, the tip flaring out like a set of moist pink lips, suckering on the glass, inflating and deflating like it was kissing.

The dread of insects, especially large ones, is instinctual and that instinct becomes manic when the insects arrive in numbers, swarm like these things did. I don't know what they were. Nobody really did. Just horrors that rose from the ashes of nuclear saturation, the radiation mutating their genes, adapting them perfectly to the hunting grounds of the new lopsided world. We called them *bloodsuckers* and that was as good of a name as any because they *were* bloodsuckers. They flew in dense, buzzing clouds, descending on anything with red blood in them and draining them dry.

I'd seen it happen and it was a horrible thing.

Carl thumped the glass again and something shrank inside me as I feared it might break, but it didn't break. The insects flew off. Out in the parking lot below there were hundreds of them gathered in a huge buzzing swarm like mayflies, rising and falling, darting in and out of the mass, dancing about each other.

But even with that shrill buzzing in my ears I could hear the bad boys below screaming.

It's not a sound I think I'll ever forget. They were covered in bloodsuckers, literally enveloped in them. They were on the ground, writhing, squishing bug bodies beneath them and more poured in to feed all the time. Those blubbery lips—I don't know what else to call them—on the end of the proboscises were attached to the men, suctioning the blood from them and I could hear that, too. It sounded like a kid sucking pudding through a straw.

Janie backed away from the window, shaking violently, hugging herself, then covering her ears. She was crying, her mouth was open like it wanted to scream but all that came out was an airless whine.

Texas was shaking, too. They shared an absolute terror of insects and these things only multiplied that tenfold. He wrapped his arms around her and she held on tight and maybe I would have tried to pacify them with a calm reassuring word if my skin hadn't been crawling.

Even Carl wasn't doing too well and nothing scared him. Beads of sweat were rolling down his face and I bet they were ice-cold. Just like the sweat beading my forehead.

Down in the parking lot, the feeding continued. The swarm found the bodies of the two dead men and were feeding on them. The gasoline had long since burned off and the truck sat there smoldering, but not putting out enough smoke to drive the bugs away.

As I said, the bloodsuckers were a dull, pale cream in color, but as they fed, juicing their veins and capillaries with stolen blood, they bloated up and their flesh went a bright, vibrant red like the ass end of female mosquito after she has just drank her fill on your forearm. Some of them were so distended with blood they could barely get off the ground, they looked almost absurd with their bulging, brilliant red thoraxes. Like glistening scarlet softballs with wings. Several were scrambling along sluggishly on the ground, too fat to fly, dragging their wings behind them. Their fellows chipped in by landing on them and suctioning off the excess with their proboscises.

More bugs landed on the window and when Carl went to thump them, I stopped him. If that glass broke we were dead. It was safety glass and safety glass does not break easily like in the movies, but all we needed was for one of those windows to have an imperfection. If it broke, we'd be drained dry before we even made the door.

And at that point, running from the room was no longer an option: I could hear them on the door, thumping and scratching about, their suckers attached to the wood.

I looked out the window. The bloodsuckers had abandoned the bad boys. They were bled white, every drop of blood vacuumed from them. They were curled up on the pavement like dead, dehydrated spiders. They were contorted, limbs drawn up, faces corded and withered, looking like mummies that had dried out for 2,000 years in a tomb beneath the sands.

"Why don't they leave?" Janie said. "What the hell do they want?"

"They want us," Carl said under his breath.

It wasn't the right thing to say, of course. It was like telling somebody who was terrified of snakes that the snake in the backyard won't leave until it crawls up your pantleg and bites you. But Carl was never known for his sensitivity.

The noise outside the door was growing. The buzzing was getting very loud, the thumping, scraping and sucking sounds going right up my spine.

I looked outside.

The bugs were still out there, flying around, covering the pick-up and the Bronco, so thick on the ground you couldn't see the pavement. More of them were settling onto the windows all the time. Drunken and distended with blood, the fat ones flew around in crazy circles, crashing into the others and hitting the ground. And then one, just intoxicated, flew right at the window at full speed. I jumped just as it hit the glass with enough force to make the glass rattle in its frame. The bug was so swollen with blood it literally exploded on impact like a water balloon. Blood and bits of tissue, a few assorted limbs, ran down the window in a vivid crimson smear.

Janie screamed.

I think I did, too.

The spilled blood drove the swarm wild and they pressed into the glass to lick it up, dozens and dozens of them. The buzzing outside the windows was then louder than that outside the door. More of them flew in, covering the glass and each other, more all the time, until the light was shut out and the room went dark.

Carl fumbled in his pack and lit a couple candles. Texas Slim pulled out his Coleman lantern and lit it. We didn't need to be waiting in the darkness, listening to those things buzzing and sucking, wondering if one might land on our necks. That would have been too much. It would have been living on the edge of panic and we were already there.

"Just wait it out people," Carl said, sounding somewhat calm. "When they realize the pickings are all picked, they'll move on. They always do."

That was sensible. And as the little leader of our little group, I probably should have said it but my mouth was so dry I think anything I might have said would have come out in a broken squeak.

Carl walked over to the door and studied it with the beam of his flashlight. He lit a cigarette. "Too bad we couldn't pump some smoke out there, Nash, it would drive them off."

"Just...get away from the door," Janie told him.

"Had to make sure it was secure," Carl said.

Texas Slim chuckled. "And is it secure?"

"Seems to be."

"That's good news, Carl," Texas said. "You make me feel all warm and cozy like I was in my mother's arms."

"Kiss my ass, peckerwood."

"All right," I said. "Let's shitcan the fighting, okay?"

Texas was still holding Janie to him—and liking it, I'm sure—over on the couch against the wall. "Well, you know it ain't me, Nash. It's Carl. He just likes to pick and the more picking you do the better chance you have of making the blood run."

"Shut up about blood," Janie said.

"Yes, darling," he said. "Whatever you want, my dove. I'm here to comfort you."

"And watch your hands. My tits don't need comforting and neither does my ass."

We all shared a brief laugh at that.

But it didn't last. This time, I heard it: a scratching sound. In that room of shadows, it was hard to say where it was coming from, only that it was there and it was growing more insistent by the moment. I looked around. The couch. The desk. A few leather chairs. The radiator. A potted plant long since wilted. File cabinets. A walk-in closet, door closed. A few stray chairs pushed up to the desk.

"I'm not liking that," Texas Slim said.

Carl and I started looking around with our flashlights. At first we thought it was coming from the walls. But that wasn't it. I walked around the desk, shining my light around. My beam fell on the clean air vent in the floor. It gleamed off two bulging red eyes.

I shrieked and stumbled back.

A bloodsucker came up out of the vent and circled the room lazily like a moth around a streetlight. It was in no hurry. Texas and Janie ducked, crying out. Carl made ready to put a round in it with his carbine. I grabbed up the wastebasket and tried to swat it. The glow of the candles and flickering lantern light cast a mammoth, leggy shadow of the thing against the wall. It flew like a wasp you see in slow mo on one of those nature documentaries on the Discovery Channel: back hunched, legs dangling beneath, just drifting around.

Carl jumped at it, swung his carbine like a bat and struck it. It bounced off the wall, slid across the desk and landed on the floor about three inches from my boot. I instinctively stomped on it and then almost wished I hadn't: the sound of its exoskeleton crunching beneath my boot made me shiver. It made a pained trilling sound right before my weight smashed it to paste.

"Oh God," Janie said.

That cloying stench of hot, seething honey was getting stronger in the room and it wasn't from what I was wiping off my boot onto the area rug under the desk. Because that scratching came again, only there was more of it. They were coming from the clean air vent.

I saw two of them flying around, bumping into the ceiling. Another settled onto a lampshade and Carl swore, brought up his carbine, and fired. He split it into two sections that skittered about on the floor for a moment or two before going still.

"No guns!" I said, looking over at the black, breathing mass covering the windows. "You break that window, we're fucked."

Texas and Janie were clinging tighter than ever. Texas had a throw pillow in one hand and was wildly swatting with it. It was probably the most ridiculous, effeminate defense I'd ever seen.

Carl was chasing the other bugs around. They flew in directionless spirals, bumping the walls, one of them knocking a vase off the desk that shattered on the floor. He knocked one down and smashed it with his boot and I cold-cocked the other with the wastebasket and it nose-dived to the floor. Its wing was damaged only it was too stupid to realize it and kept propelling itself in a buzzing circle on the floor. I killed it with the wastebasket.

But by then there were others.

One of them dove right at Janie and she punched it, knocking it aside and I stomped it. Texas beat another down with his pillow and crushed it under his boot. The sound of it smashing made him wince, say, "Oh Lord."

One of them dove at my head and I swatted it away with the can. Two others went at Carl, one of them attached itself to his fist as he made to punch it and another latched onto the back of his arm. He smashed the one on his fist by punching the wall, but the other got a good grip and its proboscis suckered to his skin. He let out a wild cry and I took hold of him. I reached out and grabbed the bug in my fist. It was hot and greasy under my fingers, its body pulsating rapidly like the beat of a newborn's heart. I squeezed it with everything I had. Its wings crackled like dry cellophane and its bony skeleton crunched like an egg shell, brown goo squirting between my fingers. With a swell of nausea in my belly, I yanked it free, the proboscis refusing to let go. As I pulled the mangled body free, the proboscis stretched like a rubber band, then the lips came free with popping, smacking sound and a ribbon of Carl's blood sprayed against my cheek.

I tossed it to the floor.

Texas and Janie were on their feet, swatting the insects down.

"Cover that fucking vent!" Texas shouted.

Which was exactly what I was going to do, but Carl was way ahead of me. No gun? He had a better idea. He grabbed a can of silicone spray from the shelf on the wall, the kind used to lubricate machine parts and make leather upholstery gleam. He got down on his knees before the clean air vent, pressed the button on the can and held his Bic lighter to the spray. A foot long mushrooming tongue of flame shot out. He held it to the vent. He fried one of the bloodsuckers coming through and it curled up, making a shrill *e-e-e-e-e-e* sort of sound as it died. Others tried to come up but he cooked them and drove still more down the vent. When the lattices of the vent were glowing hot, he yanked one of the filing cabinets over it, sealing it shut.

As he did that, the rest of us killed bugs.

There were about a dozen of them. We smashed and stomped and hit them. One got tangled in Janie's hair and Texas almost cold-cocked her when he hit it, knocking it free. One got on the back of my neck and I screamed. I tried to pull it off but I couldn't get a grip on it. I felt those rubbery pulsing lips attach to my flesh. They were warm. There was a sudden piercing like an ice-cold pin.

Then Carl knocked me to the floor and tore the beasty free.

I saw it laying there, smashed, a long needle-like protrusion hanging from the lips. It was wire-thin and probably used to puncture veins and arteries.

The war we fought was horrendous and by the end we had bug guts smeared on our hands and bug blood on our faces and down our arms. But we won. And when we had, we stood there breathing hard, dozens of mangled insects and parts thereof at our feet.

Carl lit a cigarette. "Fuck of a way to fight a war," he said.

Janie burst out laughing, only this laughter was high-pitched and near hysterical. I understood it: I had the mad desire to do the same. I clutched her to me, that honeyed bug stench so ripe on her my stomach rolled over. Texas kicked bugs into the corner and the rest of us just let the tension run from us.

About the time Carl finished his cigarette, we heard a creaking.

Then a snapping.

And that's when the window exploded inward.

4

The eruption of glass had not even made it more than a few inches, I bet, before we were in motion. I suppose we were all pumped hard with adrenaline and just ready to jump. Later, I was impressed at how we reacted, how we moved as a single unit: fast, cohesively, and without question.

The window blew in and we moved.

Texas threw open the door to the closet and we piled in...along with four or five bugs which, considering that *hundreds* had just blown into the room, was not so bad. I was the last one in, shoving Janie before me, and as I slammed the door shut I saw the room fill with insects.

And I do mean *fill.*

They came in through the shattered window in a droning storm like autumn leaves blown by the wind, an absolute tempest of bloodsuckers that erupted in a single boiling mass of wings and thoraxes and bulbous red eyes, fanning out and inundating the room in their numbers. That's what I saw in the second or two before I slammed the door shut, smashing three or four between the door and jamb that were trying to follow us in.

It was pretty hairy for a moment after we got in there and the room filled with that ominous cacophony of buzzing. First off, I wasn't exactly accurate in calling the closet a *walk-in* closet. It was your basic coat closet with a rod to hang jackets and what not from. About three feet deep, maybe four wide. And all of us in there with rifles. It was like the proverbial sardine can. When you took into account that we were trapped in a confined space with four or five mutant bloodsucking insects, it was not a good thing.

It was pitch black in there, of course.

The only light coming in was from the lantern and candles outside and this filtered through a space at the bottom of the door that was maybe half an inch wide. There was a lot of screaming and shouting as we smashed the intruders. One of them latched itself to Janie's throat and she went absolutely wild. Carl was the one that finally got it off her. When all was settled and done, dead insects at our feet, we were pretty banged up and bruised. My face was scratched from Janie's nails. I think I had punched Texas...or maybe Carl. Janie had elbowed me in the belly and stomped on my toes. Carl had backhanded me or, more precisely, back-*elbowed* me. Texas was complaining that somebody had kneed him in the balls and Carl said his left shin had been laid raw.

I suppose if somebody had watched us in there with a hidden camera or something, they would have found it hilarious.

Basically, four adults in a box beating the hell out of each other as they tried to kill the bugs. It reminded me of that Three Stooges episode where the boys get stuck in a phone booth together.

Anyway, it was your classic closet. No standing room, of course, with the coat rod there. It was hell being packed in like that and having to stoop over. Especially when we realized that it might be hours before the swarm got bored and moved on. They were buzzing loudly outside the door and being in the closet was like being tucked away in the cell of a bee honeycomb.

"Whose hand is on my ass?" Janie said. "Kindly remove it."

"Where am I suppose to remove it *to?*" Texas Slim wanted to know. "I'm simply trying to make use of every available space for the comfort of the group, darling."

"Leave that space alone."

"This is bullshit," Carl said. "We're going to be fucking pretzels by the time we get out."

Texas laughed. "Well, I'm betting you'll make a really awful tasting pretzel, Carl."

"Yeah? Well, fuck you."

Carl shoved into me, knocking me and Janie against the wall. Texas shoved him and soon they were grappling and we were getting the worst of it. Go figure. I shoved back and Janie elbowed me and I made to push Texas and I cracked Janie alongside the head and she kicked me and Carl said we were all a bunch of fucking morons and brought his head back and nearly broke my nose.

"All right!" I finally shouted. "Knock this shit off!"

Everybody calmed a bit and we had three or four seconds of unbroken, cramped peace. Then Carl made a growling sound in his throat. "Texas? You're jabbing me in the ass with your gun."

"That ain't my gun," he said.

"You sonofabitch."

More scuffling. I finally told them to knock it off and told Texas Slim to quit jabbing Carl with whatever he'd been jabbing him with—I didn't want to know what—and we settled in and started waiting. The bloodsuckers were buzzing, bumping into the walls, crawling over the outside of the door and scratching at it, making those appalling sucking sounds that were terrible to hear. Carl switched on his flashlight and, sure enough, about a dozen of those proboscises had slipped through the aperture at the bottom of the door, the flared lips at the ends looking for something to attach to. We stomped them and the bloodsuckers made sharp trilling sounds, but after awhile they learned not to stick their beaks into the crack. That sweet scent they carried was so thick in the closet I thought we would asphyxiate.

We spent nearly three hours like that.

Three hours is a long time when you're cramped and contorted. I defused a lot of fights between Carl and Texas Slim and prayed the insects would leave, but mostly I did a lot of thinking. And what I thought about most was not our predicament or the death that was held at bay by two inches of wood, but about Sean. Sean was dead. I had seen him get his brains blown out but I still couldn't believe it. Sean who had pulled my ass out of the fryer again and again in places like Cleveland, Toledo, and Bowling Green. He was a good guy. Tough, loyal, smart, and very wise in his own way. A guy who had run guns, pushed meth and heroin, been a blood member and enforcer for the Warlocks motorcycle gang back east, and did time for armed robbery and aggravated assault...but when it was just he and I alone, I had gotten to know a side of the man no one would ever have suspected existed. A very wise and compassionate side.

"Nash," he said one night as we sat on the shores of Lake Eerie in this little town called Vermilion. "Nash...what we gotta start doing here in this big crazy fucked up world of ours is forgetting about what we were and concentrating on what we are. The cavalry's not coming over the hill and the U.S. Marines are just another piss-stain. The only luck we got is the luck we make and the only hope we got is the hope we carry. You dig this shit?"

"Yeah."

"It's gonna be up to guys like me and you. Especially *you.*"

"Me?"

Sean nodded. "That's right. You're special. We all know it. We can all feel it when we're with you. You're leading us somewhere and into something. Something important." Before I could disagree, he said, "And it ain't because The Shape let's you pick out sacrifices for it. It could have chosen anyone to do that. It picked you because you're on the road to something big. Might not be a good thing, might be real fucking ugly when you get there, but that's where you're going. That's why The Shape is pushing you along. Because it's out there. Your destiny. And I just got this freaky feeling that whatever it is, it's important to the race, to all of us."

He would always say things like that that made very little sense to me at the time. But, later, when I thought it out, I would understand. In his own way, the man was a prophet. He knew what I could not know and felt things he had no right feeling. But he was right. With what came later, he was absolutely right: I *was* on the road to something big. We all were. And it was more terrible than anything we could imagine.

Wedged into that closet, I just couldn't believe he was gone. I didn't know what I'd do without him. Without his insight and wisdom and his unshakable confidence in me. He was always the first guy into a fight to save us and the last one out. And he was always the guy who made everyone retreat to safety while he held off the "Indians" as he called them. And in the end, trying to protect us had cost him his life and he wouldn't have wanted it any other way.

Thinking about him, I felt tears roll down my cheeks.

It was like losing a brother.

But like he had said so many times, I had to concentrate on the here and now and not the before. Sean was now part of the before and as much as it hurt, I had to let him go.

After the buzzing was gone for a good thirty minutes, we cracked the door. There were dozens of dead bloodsuckers on the floor. Cause of death: unknown. There were two or three living ones clinging to the walls, but they must have been old or sick or something because when we swatted them they fell to the floor, moving very sluggishly. The candles were both tipped over and out. Six bugs had died suctioned to the lantern like they were trying to fuck it. We peeled carapaces off our packs, made sure nothing had crawled inside, and gathered up our belongings.

"Looks like we're clear," Texas Slim said, appraising the parking lot through the shattered window. "Swarm's gone."

"Let's get that Bronco," I said.

We hurried downstairs, found a few more dead bugs, a couple sluggish ones that Carl took great joy in stomping, but other than that it was safe. When we got outside, the parking lot was a carpet of dead and dying insects. I didn't know what had sickened them, but I was grateful for it. There were hundreds of them underfoot, a veritable mat of exoskeletons that made the most revolting crunching sounds as we walked over them. It was like the parking lot was carpeted with peanut shells. They were all over the Bronco, but thankfully the windows and doors had been closed. We brushed off what we could, loaded our stuff, and jumped in.

Judging by the sun in the hazy sky above, it must have been nearly noon by the time we pulled from the parking lot. There were so many dead bugs on the windshield that Carl turned on the wipers and made a grisly brown smear of them that took the wipers and squirting washer fluid some time to clear.

"Let's get the hell out of here," I said.

5

My plan was to head it out of the city and keep rolling until we hit South Bend, because that's where we had to go. Whether that was intuition on my part or The Shape planting ideas in my head, I didn't know and didn't really want to. We had a mission, I knew that much. We had to go west. And I had a feeling that we needed to get moving, that somewhere, somehow, time was running out.

Leave Mother Nature to ball up the works.

We were maybe a block down South Main when a sandstorm brewed-up and within five minutes, visibility was down to maybe twenty feet. Carl didn't waste anytime. A good sandstorm can gum up an engine in no time flat. And to get caught out in one on foot is unthinkable. He took the first opening he found which happened to be the parking lot of the

Concord Mall. We didn't stop and run inside. Nothing so refined: Carl drove the Bronco right through the plate glass front of JC Penney, smashing through displays and tossing silver-skinned mannequins in every which direction.

But we were inside.

Sand was blowing into the store, but we manhandled displays out of the way and drove the Bronco right out into the atrium itself where it was sheltered from the blow. Sandstorms were a bitch, of course. Sand would blow hot and dry for three days or three hours, just burying everything in the streets and then it would just die down and another wind would scour it all clean. You just had to wait it out.

There were worse things than sandstorms.

Dust storms, for example. When they blew—and if you'd survived long enough in the nuclear wasteland you learned to tell the difference—they brought intense radioactivity with them. You got caught out in them, you were dead. But ever since the bombs came down, pissing fallout across the country in seeking toxic clouds, the weather just hadn't been the same. Dust, debris, fine particulate matter had been blown up into the atmosphere and for some time the weather had been cold because the sun just wasn't getting through. But, thankfully, that hadn't lasted. All that dust and sand and what not settled back down. But now and again, a good gust picked it up and blew it around and sometimes it was just sand and sometimes it was dust so saturated with fallout it would burn everything in its path.

There were weird electrical storms, too, that would turn the sky black and boiling, slit through with jagged red and purple seams. Winds would start blowing again, cloud-to-ground lightning splitting open trees and shattering roofs and starting firestorms that would burn for days.

Maybe some day the planet would heal itself, but it would be a long time in coming.

So we were trapped in the mall, waiting it out.

With nothing really better to do, we went shopping. For the most part, the mall was relatively untouched. Maybe when people were dying in numbers from plague and radiation sickness, suddenly Elder Beerman, Footlocker, and the Great

American Cookie Company didn't seem so important anymore. There was some wreckage, of course, but not as much as you would expect. We stocked up on tools and automotive supplies at Goodyear, got new boots and socks over at Champs Sports, jackets at Leather & More, and while Texas and Carl fooled around in Spencer's gifts, Janie raided Bath & Body Works. By that time I was shopped out and I stood around in the food court staring with lust at the things I missed most in life: Papa John's Pizza and Taco Bell.

The mall was depressing. Personally, I find malls depressing on a good day. But empty, forlorn, and dusty, the Concord was far worse. It was creepy, disturbing. The world had gone toes up and dragged things like civilization, art, intellect, and poetry into the grave with it. Libraries and schools had probably been burned or bombed, but synthetic places like this were still standing. Plastic museums of greed and money and fuck-you-I-got-mine mass consumerism. The dark side of the American dream, the cancer that had rotted us from within, the hungering worm that was never full. But buying and spending had been our drug, hadn't it? All those things you couldn't really afford. All those things you bought anyway. And the corporations got rich and the credit card companies got fat and the little guy sold off his soul and dignity for a phony lifestyle that was never his in the first place.

Standing there, looking at the stores and displays, I couldn't help but feel nauseous at it all. And I couldn't help but think that maybe, just maybe, if we'd all been less concerned with our wallets and more concerned with our brother man that the world might have still been green and sunny and filled with the laughter of children and not a radioactive wasteland haunted by mutants, crazies, and pandemic germs. I had to wonder, really, if maybe we had deserved this. That with the road we were on, becoming shallower by the day, if something like Doomsday hadn't been inevitable.

But ultimately, in a way, we weren't to blame. Nature had engineered us into what we were. Our ancestors were greedy by necessity. They had to be to survive. The more your tribe had the better chance you'd make it through the winter. And that greed, of course, became materialism. The human animal always wanted more and there were those that profited obscenely by exploiting this common, inbred need. And somewhere down the line, we destroyed ourselves.

I suppose if visitors from another star ever showed up, they'd look around, shake their heads, and go somewhere else.

After awhile, I got off my soapbox and found Janie looking around in Underground Attitude. "Do you ever wonder," she said, "how long we can keep playing the odds like we do and survive?"

"Long as we have to."

"Do you really believe that, Nash?" she said, her face very long. "Do you really believe we can keep fighting against the inevitable?"

"And what's the inevitable, Janie? Death? Should we just lie down and not bother? Is that what you think?"

"I don't know, Nash. Is it what I think?"

"Don't talk in riddles. I'm too tired for that shit."

Janie just stared at me. There were vast crystalline depths in the blue of her eyes. "What I'm saying is that we keep running and running, moving west. What are we running *from?* And better yet, what are we running *to?* What do you think is out there, Nash? Do you expect we'll find paradise, some kind of oasis from all this or do you know better?"

"I don't know shit, Janie."

"You know more than you're saying."

I hated when she did things like this. It was all hard enough without over-analyzing why things were and why they weren't. "Janie, all I know is that we're being driven west—"

"Like cattle."

"—it's what The Shape wants and you know what? It's what *I* want, too, because I'm just optimistic enough to believe there's something better than this. There has to be."

"But the germs..."

"I'm fully aware of the germs. I have nightmares about them."

She sighed. "What I mean is that we can't keep playing the odds. Sooner or later, we're going to pick up one of these germs. One of us is going to get infected. And if one does, we all do."

"Maybe we're immune."

"Specs wasn't."

"No, but the rest of us didn't get what he had, now did we? Maybe there's a reason for that."

"The Shape? Do you really believe that, Nash?"

I honestly wasn't sure what I believed anymore. "Listen to me, Janie. All I know is that since The Shape picked me I have skirted one danger after the other. That's all I know. That's my convoluted logic. We do what it wants and it keeps us alive. Maybe it even makes us immune...I just don't know. We've got an edge that no one else does, we'd be goddamned stupid not to use it."

"Even if it means taking a life every month?"

"Yes."

"You really believe that?"

"I do. And deep down, you do, too." I went over to her and put my hands on her shoulders. "I *have* to make selections, Janie. You know it. I know it. If we don't...if we *don't,* The Shape will do its own selecting. Me, you, Carl, Texas, maybe all of us."

Her arms loaded with clothes, she turned and walked away from me. Just like that. She was good at heart, she was true gold. But her morals were having trouble with how we lived. I wished to God there was another way. But there wasn't. There just wasn't. The germs floating around out there were unbelievably infectious and deadly. I didn't want to go down with black plague or cholera, typhoid or the flu. And especially not with Ebola. If that meant sacrificing an innocent each full moon to protect me and my friends, I was going to do it.

At least, that's what I told myself as I watched her walk away.

I felt very grand, very high and mighty, maybe even noble at that moment like I was some kind of fucking hero, some errant knight sacrificing all for God, country, and queen. But later, my delusions failed as they often do. I found a place where I could be alone, the very back aisle of Waldenbooks where I sat on the carpeted floor, surrounded by racks of kidlit—Junie B. Jones, Dr.

Suess, Horrible Harry, the Boxcar Children, Henry Higgins, assorted Roald Dahl's and Beatrix Potter's—and I cried. Face in my hands, I cried my eyes out, remembering when I'd had a wife, a life, and, yes, some dignity.

Not like now.

When I opened my eyes again, I stared at the neat rows of books. At cardboard standees of Harry Potter and Max from *Where the Wild Things Are.* Surrounded by books that made me remember my secret childhood worlds, I had never felt so broken, so frayed, so fragmented. A post-apocalyptic Humpty Dumpty.

The sandstorm blew on and off for five days.

We were nearly ready to tear out each other's throats by then. Any diversion would have done, even a pack of crazies and a firefight. When it ended we piled into the Bronco, barely speaking. Carl drove us out of the mall and into the world. Entire streets were blocked with sand dunes. The city looked completely different blown with sand and whitened with dust.

"Where to, Nash?" Carl finally said when we were rolling down South Main again like five days before.

"West," I told him. "Get us to the highway, to U.S. Twenty. We have an appointment, I think, in South Bend."

SOUTHBEND INDIANA

I

We didn't make it there for a week.

We had one problem after another. Suffice to say that when we did arrive, as luck would have it, the Bronco blew a tire soon as we rolled in and left us stranded there on the dirty backside of Indiana. And at night yet. Nothing worse than being on foot at night. Too many things out there. Too many predators haunting the ruined carcasses of the cities. Wild dog packs, mutant rats, swarms of bloodsucking insects, things much worse that it was hard to put a name to.

The radiation had done funny things.

We found a little ranch house in a devastated neighborhood at the edge of town and laid low. Nothing out there but wild dogs picking in the gutters, rats, lots of wrecked cars, sand blowing in the streets.

I thought we'd be safe for the night. I was wrong.

The house was empty. It was solid. And it appeared to be defensible. Of course, it wasn't real easy to ascertain the latter, it being dark and all. And I didn't want to be using any flashlights. Batteries were hard to come by and I didn't exactly want to telegraph our position to whatever was waiting out there...because something was, you see. I could feel it right up my spine and I knew better than to dismiss such a feeling.

Ten minutes after we got there, we all heard it: a high, almost electronic piping that sounded oddly like a locust being imitated by a machine. And there was only one thing that made a sound like that.

We got ready.

Breathing in and breathing out, I waited with the .30.06 Savage cradled in my arms. Because it was coming. It had been scenting us for the past hour and now it was closing in.

The others were back in the kitchen—Carl and Janie and Texas Slim—huddled up in the shadows, trying to keep quiet and failing at it. Whatever came through that door, I wanted first crack at it. Believe me, I was no hero, but the idea of whatever was out there flooding into the room in numbers and us being boxed in together...no, it was a recipe for disaster.

That feeling at my spine went electric.

"Get ready," I called out.

The others were anxious to run, to fight, to bust caps or retreat, as long as it was *something*. The waiting was hard. Very hard.

"Anything?" Carl whispered from the kitchen.

"Nothing. Be quiet. We wait."

"How long?"

"Always in a hurry, our friend Carl," Texas said. "Notice how he's always in a hurry?"

"Yeah...and who dropped a quarter in you, dipshit?"

"Knock it off!" Janie warned them.

I just shook my head. Those two were like a couple kids sometimes.

It was times like these, in the dark and the quiet, that I remembered the way things were before the war. How I'd been married. Had a life. Ancient History 101, I guess. Now I was just a scavenger trying to stay alive, killing and taking and running, always running, just hanging on by my fingertips, suspended uneasily over some yawning black pit filled with human bones. Thirty-seven years old, a chromed-up Beretta 9mm jammed in the waistband of my jeans and a knife with a seven-inch blade in my boot. That's who I was now.

I lit a cigarette, sweat trickling down my spine.

I blew out smoke and walked over towards the window, staying in the shadows along the wall, keeping clear of the cool moonlight that flooded in. The windowpane was grimy, speckled with dust and soot. I wiped a clean spot and studied the streets out there. In the semi-darkness of a moonlit night, it could have been ten years ago. Cars at the curbs. Trees lining the boulevards. Houses lined up in neat little rows. It was only when the moonlight washed it all down that you could see the cars were all rusted and wrecked, the trees gnarled-looking, leaves and dead limbs scattered about, the houses weathered gray from the blowing sand, yards overgrown, windows broken.

Nothing else.

"Carl?" I whispered. "What's the Geiger saying?"

"Pretty cool, Nash. Getting twenty to twenty-five."

I thought it over, wondering if maybe the wind had made a lonesome howling sound and my imagination had channeled it into something else. But if it had, then we had *all* imagined it. And I didn't believe in mass hallucination.

Outside, it was silent.

Nothing moved.

I leaned against the wall, finishing my cigarette. If nothing happened in another twenty minutes, I figured, then we'd relax, wait out the night, go scavenging in the morning. Had to be a decent ride in this town somewhere.

And it was as I was thinking this that I heard the Geiger Counter in the other room start to click.

"Carl?" I said, my breath barely coming.

"Yeah...going up. We got...forty, fifty, sixty...she's climbing, man."

The Geiger was clicking madly now, ticking like a bomb. My heart was pounding, trying to keep up with it.

"We spiked a hundred...it's getting hot."

The Geiger was clicking so fast now it sounded like one steady clicking roll.

"One-fifty and climbing, man...shit."

Sweat running down my face, I looked out the window and there they were. The kids. The fucking *Children.* Just standing out there on the sidewalk like they were waiting for Susie or Jimmy to come out and play with them.

"They're here. Get ready to bust."

Out on the walk, the Children waited, just standing there. There were six of them. If you squinted your eyes real tight, you might mistake them for real kids, but they weren't. Just wraithlike things that looked like they'd been blown from a tomb, clothes hanging in rags, faces gray and corrugated, eyes burning a hot noxious yellow like seething reactor cores.

We had to move now, take them out. There could be no hesitation. They were walking atomic waste, kicking out deadly roentgens in a hot rain of fallout.

Using the butt of the Savage, I broke the window, shattering it from its frame.

I took aim.

And as I did so, the six of them out there raised their fists, extending their first fingers, and pointed at me. Their oval puckered mouths opened and they emitted that high droning whine that rose in volume until it was nearly hypersonic, making my ears ring and then hurt, my brain filled with waves of agony.

I jerked the trigger, took out a girl in the middle.

The round caught her dead in the chest and the effect was instantaneous: she was tossed back, the entry wound spilling some black steaming fluid and right away she began to writhe and twitch like she'd just taken hold of a high power line. Black smoke boiled from her, something like blue fire erupting and consuming. She blazed up like one of those snakes you burn on the Fourth of July, just smoking and popping and going to black ash.

That's how she died.

And before I could sight in on another, they all let loose with that discordant droning noise that was howling and lonesome. Like insects. Enraged insects droning in a desolate summer field. They converged on the house, not running or even walking, but *gliding* forward with some insane locomotion I couldn't even guess at.

The rest of my posse were in the room by then, all with guns in their hands. Even Janie who hated guns. The Geiger was clicking away, registering the massive radioactivity coming from the Children.

They were at the door.

A flickering cold light licked around its edges. The door cracked and buckled, great jagged rents running down its face. It blackened, smoke rising from it. Then it blew in and the Children were filling the doorway, eyes lit with a terrible xanthic glow that reflected off their scabrid faces. Lamprey mouths were open to reveal rows and rows of tiny hooked teeth, radioactive steam blowing out in hissing clouds that crackled like static electricity.

A girl stepped in the room first.

Her bare feet sizzled on the dirty carpet, burning footprints right into the fibers she was cooking so hot with radionuclides.

Everyone fired before they cooked with her.

Carl had a Mossberg 500 12-gauge, Texas Slim had a .50 cal Desert Eagle, and Janie had a .30 Smith. We laid down a considerable volume of fire, cutting down the Children as they tried to ghost through the door with a glowing shroud of radioactive mist.

We kept shooting until there was nothing left to shoot.

The Children had fallen in a whining/screeching heap just inside the room, pissing that toxic black blood and going kinetic with their own nuclear saturation, burning and twisting, clouds of black oily smoke filling the room. Their flesh went to hot running tallow, then ash. Their superheated skeletons were phosphorescent and arcing with juice, rising up one last time like they were trying to escape the smoldering wreckage of their flesh...then they crashed back down into it, crumbling into fragments.

I saw a blackened skull roll free, smoke rising from it, jaws sprung open as if to scream. It made me think about how close those little fuckers had gotten and how hot they were with radioactivity. *One of these days we're gonna absorb too much and we'll all be popping with tumors. Gotta happen.*

Then Carl grabbed my arm. "Man, we better get the fuck out." He was holding the Geiger up and it was clicking fiercely. "It's pretty damn hot in here."

I followed him out the back way, out into the shadows and consuming darkness of the night.

And whatever waited there.

2

The Children.

Who were they and, more importantly, *what* were they.

Nobody I had ever talked to had any real good answers. But the same radiation saturation that killed adults by the hundreds of thousands and *millions* did something else to the kids. And not just certain ones, but *all* kids, anyone under ten years of age for whatever reason...but none older than that. Maybe the onset of puberty made them biochemically infertile for the change. But under ten, well, it mutated something in them.

Your own kids or the kids next door, the charming little girls playing dress-up in the backyard or the rambunctious little boys playing sandlot baseball...they were not human anymore.

They were monsters.

The radiation had gotten hold of them, turned them into deranged night stalkers with yellow luminous eyes and fingers that would actually burn you to a cinder if they got a hold of you. They hunted by night in packs like wolves or *vampires*, killing anything they could catch. Somehow, some way, maybe because they were young and still growing, their cells had absorbed the fallout, made it part of their natural rhythms. Nobody really knew and most were too scared to find out.

There were survivors out there that thought the Children were ghosts or ghouls, supernatural things that crept out by night to feed. That wasn't true, of course, but you could hardly blame anyone for thinking it. For it was really hard to imagine anything as scary as the Children. Radioactive fallout was part of life here in the new spooky world. You had to live with it and learn how to detect it, what places were hot and how to avoid them.

But the Children made that difficult.

Because they were, essentially, fallout and fallout that was cunning and evil. Fallout that hunted its victims.

I figured they did it for a reason. Maybe they absorbed something from people, something they needed. It was hard to say, but it had to be *something.* I knew they were not supernatural even though sometimes they acted that way and they *did* only come out at night. They were not flesh and blood as we understood flesh and blood, but a *different* sort of flesh and blood. Something completely alien right down to their blazing hot subatomics.

But they could be killed.

If you put a bullet in them, they'd literally burn up like atomic piles right in front of you. I suppose if you stuck a spear in them the same thing would happen, but if you got that close you'd fry.

So bullets worked best.

The smart thing was to avoid them, to hide out by night and stay off the streets. That was your best bet. I had no idea where they laired themselves for the daylight hours and I honestly didn't want to know. In the back of my mind, I always envisioned them stretched out like the undead in reactor cores. Nobody really knew.

These days, everyone was afraid of kids because all kids became *Children.* It was rumored that they were coming right out of the womb like that and pregnant women were being killed on sight by gangs to avoid any more Children being born.

It didn't bode well for humanity's future given that the next generation were hideous mutations.

Extinction was only a matter of time.

3

We took time to reload when we were an easy block away, darting beneath an old oak and planting ourselves in its shadows. We caught our breath. Had a drink of water from our bottles. The Geiger was reading forty micro-roentgens which was strictly background radiation. That was pretty normal. Before the war, background rad was something like ten to fifteen micro-roents in your average American city. Now twenty was the low end and fifty to sixty being the high end...of course, that didn't take into account places like LA that had taken direct hits and were still cooking hot.

"We gotta find us a place to hide out for the night," Carl said.

Texas Slim chuckled. "It amazes me, Carl, how you get to the root of the problem every time."

"I got a root for you, asshole."

"If that's your root, sonny, then it must've been a real bad growing season."

"Fuck off."

I sighed. "Zip it, both of you."

"Another house?" Janie suggested.

But I didn't like that. The Children were out there, they would find us again. I had hoped that they wouldn't be in this town, but they were here like everywhere else. No, another house wasn't an option. It had to be something different.

"Hear that?" Texas Slim said. "That's not coyotes."

I heard it all right: the telltale baying of dogs echoing out through the shadow-carved town. Children. Dog packs. Jesus. South Bend was no different than every other town. I supposed they were all like that now, maybe some even worse.

We needed to get downtown. But that meant getting farther away from the Bronco with its flat tire.

"Let's go," I said.

"What way?" Texas Slim wanted to know. "All ways being the same, I suppose."

"Towards the center of town. We'll scout back for the Bronco come first light. Right now, let's get off the streets."

.30.06 in hand, I led them away.

The night was warm, but not unpleasantly so. Just the sort of night you might have spent out on the front porch with a cold beer in your hand in the old days. I led them down alleys and streets, through a maze of avenues, and across an empty field.

Downtown.

Main Street. It was a graveyard like every other main street in the world now. Windows broken, buildings half-burned out, the corpses of cars and trucks clogging up the streets. Drifts of sand pushed into doorways. Desolation and nothing but.

The sidewalks were choked with leaves from the past autumn. Nobody was there to sweep them up now. There were things beneath the leaves, probably skeletons, but nobody bothered to look. The windows were all dirty from sandstorms.

We moved past storefronts draped in shadow.

A video store. An insurance office. A café. Several stores with soaped out windows and badly faded going-out-of-business signs. We passed a department store with dusty, cobwebbed Halloween costumes behind the dirty windows, saw yellowed and curled Halloween decorations in the windows of several others. A theater with the lofty title of The Grande Ballroom still had an all-night horror show up on its marquee. Many of the letters were missing, but it looked like it was really going to be some kind of All Hallows hoot with four movies and a couple stage acts.

"See that, Texas?" Carl said. "Halloween horror show. Be like a fucking family reunion for a peckerwood like you."

"Quiet," Janie said.

As I saw the marquee, the decorations, the memories weighed down on me. Good God, Halloween. I'd forgotten about that being that every day was fucking Halloween now. The bombs had come down a week or so before Halloween and that was almost a year ago now.

Shit.

We kept going, waiting for something to show its ugly face, but so far nothing had. Janie was right behind me, Texas Slim behind her, and Carl taking up the backdoor with his shotgun.

So many shadows...spilling, pooling, spreading over the streets in tar-like lagoons of night. A light breeze was blowing, leaves skittering about, sand trickling against windows. I led them around a car stalled on the sidewalk, a Chevy. It looked like it had popped the curb and been abandoned there, two of the doors still thrown open. Moonlight flooded it. There was sand and leaves inside. The browned skeleton of a child was curled up on the back seat nearly buried in sand. It still had blonde curls. A girl. Looked like she had gone to sleep, gone peacefully, probably waiting for her mother to come back.

Radiation. Plague. Who could say?

We skirted more wrecks, refusing to look inside them, but always wary of anything moving in them. Nothing did. We came around a dead minivan and there was movement. People.

"Stay back," I told them, keeping my rifle on them. "Just stay back and we won't have any trouble."

But these people were not going to try anything.

We all saw what they were. Four or five of them...a man and a woman and a few kids, a family maybe. They were crouched there, holding onto one another. The stench coming off them was nauseating, like hospital dressings rank with gangrene and drainage. And there was a good reason for that: their faces were lumpy with rising sores, splitting and bleeding. It looked like one of the kids had some kind of growth coming out of his eye. They all breathed with rasping, phlegmy sounds. The man reached out a hand, broke into a fit of coughing, and vomited a dark slick of blood onto the walk.

The stink was unbelievable.

"Fever," Janie said. "They have the Fever."

Everyone backed away.

The family crawled towards us with squishing sounds, but nobody fired. Last thing we wanted was to be blasting blood and fluids into the air. Lot of the germs that had mutated with the fallout were airborne pathogens. These days, it was all collectively known as the *Fever*: a lethal zoo of what military biohazard specialists call "hot agents." And unfortunately, at this zoo, the cages were wide open and all the creeping beasties were in the air, the water, you name it.

I jogged away and the others followed. Next to the Children, there was nothing scarier than bodies hot with plague.

I ran across the street kicking my way through drifted sand, around a rusting furniture truck, and my luck almost ran out right there. A dog was waiting for me, a big one, in a pool of moonlight. Looked like it might have been a shepherd once, but it was hard to say. Its hide was patchy, threadbare, grotesque pink tumors and open sores rising like bread dough. A dark sap dripped from them.

I went down on my ass to avoid colliding with it.

I crawled away and then the others were with me. The beast was making a low mewling in its throat. Its fur, what there was of it, was sticky and spiky with discharges from its open wounds. It had only one eye, the other consumed in a pulsing pink growth that had burst out of its skull. The entire body was flabby and loose.

It opened its jaws and growled, slime dripping.

"Well, come on then," I told it.

And it did.

It tensed itself to leap and as it vaulted up I fired twice, dropping it to the pavement. One round punched through its chest and the other smashed its head open, cleaving it apart almost perfectly. It lay there, mewling and jerking around, its head waving from side to side on a snaking trunk of a neck that almost looked boneless. Blood spattered the walks.

We got out of there.

I could hear more dogs howling in the distance. I had no idea what I was looking for, but I knew I'd recognize it when I saw it. And then there it was: an Army/Navy store. The door was open, a down of leaves and sand having blown in.

We went inside, clicking on flashlights.

Displays were tipped over, a case of war medals smashed...but other than that, the store was relatively unscathed and that was a real rarity these days. All of which made me think that South Bend must have been hit pretty hard by disease.

"Carl? Get that door shut. Lock it and prop something against it to keep it closed," I said. "Help him out, Texas."

"I suppose somebody's has to."

I turned away from them. "Janie, let's find a place for us to spend the night. Dawn won't be for six hours yet."

Everyone did what they were told and the long night began.

4

Good thing was, save for the barking of dogs and the occasional sound of rats running in the streets, nothing at all happened. We found a storeroom in the back and crashed there for the night, sleeping in shifts.

And so the night passed.

When daylight finally came, sweeping the night terrors back into their holes, it turned out that the Army/Navy store was a real windfall. We found another locked storeroom in the basement and it was just full of goodies...once we popped the door with a crowbar. Cartons of military MREs and freeze-dried hiking food, cases of bottled water and packets of water purification tablets. Sleeping bags and flashlights, waterproof raingear and parkas and blankets and first aid equipment. Upstairs there was camo clothing in every size, some of it American and some of it British DPM.

While Janie and I took inventory, Texas Slim and Carl went out hunting a new vehicle. They bickered their way out the door, trying to decide whose mother had entertained more bikers in a single night. I was glad to get rid of them. That shit went on almost constantly, the nipping and arguing and insulting. It was what they did and they enjoyed it, but it got old after awhile.

"There's a ton of stuff here, Nash," Janie said, standing amongst heaps of blankets and clothing and green metal boxes.

"We'll just take what we need."

That was an unwritten rule these days. No sense being a glutton, no sense being a hog, just take what you needed and leave the rest for some other unfortunate soul. I believed in this completely. I knew others did, too. There were always plenty who didn't, of course, but I truly believed that karma would sort their asses out in the end.

"What do you think the chances are they'll get us a decent ride?"

Janie laughed. "Pretty good if they don't kill each other first."

"Ah, they're pretty tight, I think. They just express their feelings for one another in a strange way."

"Let's go to the storeroom, Nash. I want to show you something."

I followed her downstairs and when we were in there, she locked the door.

"What do you want to show me?"

"What do you think?" she said, something blazing just behind her eyes. "You've been thinking the same thing I have so quit playing innocent."

The heat that burned inside her spread out and consumed me. She was beautiful...but still the image of my wife came to me unbidden and dominating as it often did. Shelly. Dear God, *Shelly*. I remembered the mole on her thigh and the way she laughed and the little notes she would stick inside my lunch pail and the way her hand felt in mine and how she had looked the day we were married and how lucky, how blessed, I had felt knowing that she was *mine*. And then I saw her, as I would always see her, dying in my arms that night from cholera, nothing but bones wrapped in yellow skin, her chest trembling with each shallow gasp of air, and my own voice saying again and again, *this is Shelly, this is my wife, this is how I bleed.*

But that was gone.

It was faded with age.

Janie looked at me and something crossed her eyes like a shadow and then was gone and I was with her, losing myself in her.

She came right up to me and grabbed my hands and put them up her shirt and on her breasts. They were hot to the touch. I could feel her heart pounding with a steady delicious rhythm. I kissed her with my lips and then with my tongue and that's how it started. Later, thinking about it with a warm satisfaction, I thought I actually *melted* into her. It sounds like something from a cheap paperback romance, but that's how it was. It was no gentle seduction, there was nothing subtle or soft about any of it...just a union born of absolute need, trembling fingers working buttons and zippers and then I was on top of her and inside her, pumping, and she was breathing hot and heavy in my ear. Moaning. Begging me never to stop. I think I told her I loved her. When we came, we both cried out. It didn't last long, but what there was of it was completely molten.

Later, still wrapped together in a twine of hot flesh and cooling sweat, she balanced herself on one elbow and said, "You think about your wife a lot, don't you?"

"I guess."

"But you never speak of her."

"No."

"Why not, Nash? Don't you think it would be better if you did?"

I pulled away, pain breaking loose inside me. "I can't. I just can't."

Janie didn't push it, it wasn't in her to do so. She lay next to me, her skin golden and her limbs long. "Do you trust me, Nash?"

"I think you're the only one I *do* trust." I meant it.

"I want you to tell me about your wife. Not now. But some day. When you do that, when you share it with me and trust me with it, I know I'll trust you, too."

The idea that maybe she didn't trust me, not completely, hurt. I knew the others were with me because they thought I could keep them safe. It was not devotion, really, it was need and maybe it was even *fear*. Fear of what I could do and what I would call up on the next night of the full moon. That made me somehow omnipotent in their eyes. They respected the power, feared how I wielded it.

They did not fear me.

They feared what I called: *The Shape.*

But Janie?

No, Janie did not fear me. The connection between us was different, deeper, hard to know or understand. But it was there. It was always there. Sometimes I feared that she would leave and I would be alone. Completely alone and when I woke in the night, shivering and sweating from nightmares, she would not be there to hold onto. Then it would be just me, the memories of Shelly coming in the dead of night and sucking the blood from my soul.

I reached out and touched Janie, loving the smoothness of her skin. And as I did so, that old voice said, *Jesus Christ, she's just a kid...she's nineteen and you'll be forty in three years. You could be her father for chrissake. Don't you see that? And yet you cling to her and you sleep with her, and how do you feel about that? Do you feel dirty? Unclean?* But I didn't. Maybe once I would have but that once was so far gone, dropped into the deepest well imaginable, and I could no longer know what was right and what was wrong. I only knew that it felt right and that was enough.

It was all I had.

I thought I loved her.

And loving her, wished she were dead.

She was just too good to be thrown into the ashcan with the rest. She had morals and ethics. And those things just didn't have a place now.

"I want you to trust me," I said. "I need you to."

"Do you trust me?"

"Yes."

"I hope so."

"I love you," I said.

She laid her head on my chest. "Then I suppose I love you, too."

"That's pretty noncommittal."

"It's a noncommittal world now, Nash."

I laid there, feeling her, feeling part of something and more alone than I'd ever felt in my life. There was pain inside for what I had done and what I had lost and what I would never find again. I could feel it in each heartbeat and in the steady flow of my blood. I opened my mouth to tell Janie about it, but I closed it again as I saw my wife's face looking down at me from some window in my mind.

Yes, pain. Nothing but pain and it did not need to be given a name.

5

I think it was our first night in South Bend that I began having the nightmares. I, like you, have had my share of night frights, but this was like nothing I've ever had before. To call them *dreams* is like calling a 500-megaton thermonuclear weapon just a *bomb*. And the real scary part here, you see, is that I'm not really sure they *were* dreams. The experience was too...corporeal, too organic, if that makes any sense.

All I can tell you is we were in the storeroom. Janie was sleeping at my side and Texas Slim and Carl were across the room. In the dream, I opened my eyes and what I saw was the shadowy storeroom. I sat there, blinking, looking around, filled with a terror that was positively nameless. I wanted to get out, to do anything...but I could not move. Or maybe I was *afraid* to. There was no window in the room, but the entire far wall suddenly lit up like it was washed by pale moonlight. More than moonlight. Luminous, flickering, energized. That's when I saw that the light wasn't just light but some whirling vortex of phosphorescent matter that was alive, expanding, engulfing the entire wall until there was no wall. It made a hissing, boiling sort of noise that put my nerves right on edge.

I was filled with revulsion and horror. I wanted to scream and maybe I did.

It kept expanding, swirling, a great worming mass like thousands and thousands of corpse-white snakes squirming and roping and tangling, being born from their own serpentine lengths, pushing out from a central mass that looked almost like a face...it had a contorted, leering slash for a mouth and something like eyes, evil, upturned eyes pulsating with the formless blackness of the void. The rest of it kept changing form, compressing, elongating, mutating. The face of Medusa. That's what I thought in the dream: I was staring at the face of Medusa. Except this Medusa was absolutely alien, absolutely obscene, a corpuscular entity with a grotesque blur for a face made of thousands of those reaching white tendrils. Like the face itself, they were not a solid mass, but composed of millions of squirming threads and filaments who themselves were made of millions of roping fibers braided together down unto infinity. As I watched, the entire thing began to unwind until it looked the entire far side of the room was a nest of billions of writhing, smooth white cobras made of plaited, conjoined worms.

But the face wasn't gone...not entirely.

It was eroding, flaking apart, unwinding into viscid living threads, but still those malefic eyes stared out at me. They watched me. As I cowered with bunched fists, a pounding heart, and a sour sweat running from my pores, it took a wicked delight in my terror. *You can run, but you can't hide, Nash. I'm coming just as you've always suspected, born in the microscopic ether and into the real. East to west, that's my path. I leave nothing but graveyards and gleaming white bones in my wake. As you go westward, so do I. And you better hurry because I'm right behind you. Youngstown is a cemetery now. Those streets you played in as a child...filled with bloating white corpses and strewn with well-picked bones, nothing but flies and rats and buzzards, nothing more. Just the rising hot stench of decay and the silent blackness of tombs. I'm entering Cleveland now. Soon I'll be coming for all that you have left. Will you scream when I take Janie, your sweet little cherry away from you? Or will you barter for your own miserable life as her flesh blackens with the pox, as she drowns in a yellow sea of her own infected waste and diseased blood bursts from her pores and she vomits out the black slime of her own liquefied intestines? What will you do, Nash? What will you offer to me?*

It was bad, that thing getting inside my head and tormenting me, but what was worse was that it *touched* me. All those coiling, unraveling threads came at me, covering me, sliding into me like slivers of ice, impaling me and filling my body with their pestilence and contamination. The agony of infestation was unbelievable. My body shook and gyrated with waves of agony as I was absorbed, assimilated, remade in the form of that monstrous Medusan parasite, my blood gone to cold clotted venom, my internals dissolving to a marrowy sauce, my brain rendered to a gray slopping jelly. My cells were polluted one by one, distended with waste, each finally exploding in a drainage of diseased cytoplasm. I was literally a living corpse, drowning in my own filth, poisoned bile, and putrescent blood.

My mind was gone, pulled into some sucking black hole of insanity...but still I could hear a voice, my voice, wild and screeching: *Nash, Nash, Nash! Can't you see what it is and what it will do? Look behind you, look to the east, it's nothing but a great bird-picked bone pile now! No more sunshine, no more light, no more anything! That thing destroys everything in its path and leaves a spreading ink-black swath of darkness in its wake! And it's coming, getting closer day by day, for the love of God or Janie or yourself, you better run, you better run as fast as you fucking can—*

I came out of the dream at that point, if dream it was. Drenched with hot-cold sweat, I stumbled to the door and got out of the storeroom. My guts were flipping over themselves, rolling with a greasy peristaltic motion. My legs were so weak I could barely stand. I stumbled into walls and tripped over my own feet. My muscles were sore and throbbing. My back kinked. My hands trembling. White bolts of pain were trying to split my skull in two. Tears rolled down my face and my teeth chattered. I was filled with a sense of loathing as if I had been embraced by a wormy corpse.

But what had embraced me was far worse.

Not the corpse, but *The Maker of Corpses.*

Outside the Army/Navy store, I fell to my knees in the cool night air. I didn't care about dog packs or the Children or rats or any of it. That shit was pedestrian in comparison with what I'd just been through. I did not know if it was sheer nightmare or reality or some feverish, fucked up brew of both, all I knew was that I could smell the hot green odor of rotting corpses in the cities to the east and taste something in my mouth like hot-sweet bile. I threw up and kept throwing up until it was all purged from me. And even then the raw, fetid stench of it on the sidewalk—far unlike any vomit I'd ever known—made me shake with dry heaves.

Somewhere during the process, Janie came out. "Are you all right, Nash?"

I looked up at her, my face warm and waxy, my eyes bloodshot and tearing. I swallowed. Swallowed again. I could not speak. We went inside and I drank some water, smoked a cigarette, and all the while she was staring at me, wanting answers. "Nash? Nash? God, Nash, speak to me..." Oh, but I couldn't. Because if I opened my mouth and powered up the old voice box what was going to come out in a gushing flood of pure unbridled terror was the scream to end all screams. I was afraid I would start and never, ever stop.

So I said nothing. Absolutely nothing.

I could see it in her eyes, the concern, yes, but also the fear as she wondered if I was shot through with the Fevers. But what I couldn't say, what I dared not frame into worms, was that I was not sickened with Fevers but had been embraced by *the Mother of Fevers.*

And it was coming.

Getting closer day by awful day.

An unnamable horror that had come to exterminate what remained of the human race.

6

Texas Slim and Carl found a vehicle for us and it was really something. They came back with it about an hour before the sandstorm hit, noticing with some discomfort the uneasy silence that lay between Janie and I. They did not ask about it. They took us out to show us what they had found.

I started laughing when I saw it.

So did Janie.

Of all the dinosaurs in the automotive jungle they had somehow come across a VW microbus that had been new when the Vietnam War had still been raging. The bus was worn and dented, painted up with ancient flowers, peace signs, and other psychedelic hieroglyphics that had faded with age. It was an ugly vehicle for an ugly world.

"Where in the hell did you find this?"

"Some guy's garage," Carl said, scratching his thick black beard. "We were checking out this neighborhood, just looking in garages for anything we could get. We found this. Looks like shit, sure, but it moves and it can get us out of here. Maybe Michigan City or Gary, wherever."

"It's been serviced some, Nash," Texas Slim added. "We found the fellow what owned it. He was on the floor, still had an oily rag in his hand."

"Fever?" I asked, almost breathlessly, remembering my dream.

Texas Slim shook his head. "No...looked like radiation. His hair had fallen out and that sort of thing."

"Yeah, but we almost didn't get it because of the dog in the yard," Carl said.

"Oh, you're going to go into that, are you?" Texas Slim said.

"Dog?"

"Sure," Carl said. "Big black mutha. Probably chained out there for days, crazy and foaming at the mouth. Texas here, he tries to make friends with it. Tries to pet it."

"I didn't try to pet it."

"Sure you did."

"No, I didn't."

"Yes, you did, you idiot. You were talking all sweet and sassy to it like you wanted to bone that fucker. Not that I'd be surprised."

Texas just laughed. "Now see, Nash, that's sheer invention on the part of my friend here with the small penis. Carl gets confused sometimes. His head isn't right. But, you know, what with his mother mixing it up out in the barnyard with anything willing, it's no wonder he turned out this way."

Carl took a step towards him. "What I tell you about my mother?"

"Nothing I hadn't already read on the bathroom wall."

"Keep it up, you peckerwood sonofabitch. One of these days you're going to dip that wee little pee pee into something and it's going to get bit off."

"So I'll keep it out of your mouth."

I had to break them apart at this point because the last thing I needed were these assholes swinging on each other and busting out each other's teeth. Like we didn't have enough to worry about. And it was about that time that the sandstorm started kicking up. I told Carl to find a garage somewhere to store the bus and by the time he got back the sand was already blowing.

So we hid out in the Army/Navy store and just waited.

There was nothing else to do.

We spent another four days in South Bend because we could not leave.

Visibility was down to a few feet. We listened to the sand blow and blow. It was driven by high winds that howled through the town, burying the streets in drifts and swirling eddies, churning sand-devils whipping and lashing against the building. For days it was like that, the moaning wind and the sound of sand grating against the windows and walls in a fine granulated grit. It found hairline cracks and seams and blew into the store, dusting the floor and covering the displays and shelves in a powdery down.

We waited downstairs in the storeroom, listening to it rage.

Even down there we could feel the sand on our skin, clogging our pores, getting in our hair and dusting our faces. It went on and on.

We huddled together and paged through old magazines and nobody said much. We all wanted to be on the road. We wanted to ditch this desolate burg.

But Mother Nature had other ideas.

As we waited, Carl and Texas Slim tried to stare each other down almost constantly and Janie was pretty much ignoring them and giving me the cold shoulder. It was a long goddamn wait. I spent my time consulting the dog-eared map in my pocket, wondering what we might run into out on the interstate, the whole time my belly filled with needles because we were trapped there. *Waiting*. I couldn't shake the dream. Maybe I was paranoid—*definitely*—but I was feeling that hideous something coming from the east as maybe I'd been feeling it for a long time. I did not doubt its reality. The bottom line was we had to keep moving west. That's the way it had to be and nobody asked why.

They knew.

They knew, all right.

Just like they knew that the next full moon was less than a week away and it would soon be time for me to make a selection.

The time of The Shape was nearing...

GARY INDIANA

I

We came into the city on a day that was still, ominous, and hazy. Our VW hippie microbus was on its last legs. Like the wild free-loving days of Haight-Ashbury, the bus was past its prime. She seized up twice out on I-80 coming into Gary and Carl said her bearings were shot and her carb was gummed up. As it was, we pretty much coasted into the city, the love machine wheezing like an asthmatic old man. We needed new wheels because hoofing it across country just wasn't an option.

We skirted Tolleston and cut through Ambridge until we reached downtown. Coughing out clouds of blue smoke, our VW microbus rolled to a stop before a row of tenements and died with a backfire.

Inside, Carl swore. And then swore again.

I stepped out, fanning my sweaty face with a Cleveland Indians baseball cap. I lit a stale cigarette with a cupped match and then looked around at the devastation...the overturned cars, the rubble, the garbage blowing in the gutters. Drifts of sand were pushed up against the buildings. A crow sat atop the traffic light ahead, cawing. The day was hot and hazy, picked dry as desert bones,

Other than that, there was nothing.

Just the deathly silence that was uniform to most cities since the bombs had come down. A pick-up truck was pulled up to the curb, a crusty yellow skeleton behind the wheel. Birds had built nests in the slats of the ribcage.

I was trying to get a feel for things. Where we should go and what we should do when we got there.

From inside the bus, Texas Slim called: "Nothing here, Nash. Let's pack it in."

I ignored him, stepping away from the bus and studying the ruined buildings around me. I saw no life, no movement, but

I knew it was out there somewhere. Hidden eyes were watching me, gauging me. The days had long since vanished when you welcomed strangers with open arms.

That's not how it worked now.

There were people here, I knew, and not all of them were thick with radiation and Fevers. I had to find one of them. Somehow. Some way. The full moon was coming fast now.

If I couldn't find someone, it meant selecting one of my own and I didn't like that idea.

There were five of us now—Janie and I, Carl and Texas Slim, and the new guy, Gremlin. We called him *Gremlin* because we'd picked him up in Michigan City, found him trapped in the trunk of an old AMC Gremlin. Scabs were out the night before, he said, looking for recruits and he jammed himself in the trunk and then couldn't get out. He was so wedged in there it took all of us to yank his sorry ass free.

I hadn't made my mind up about him yet. There were things I didn't like about him—his perpetual bitching—and things I *did* like: he did what he was told without question. Janie was neutral on him. Carl and Texas Slim liked to pick on him a lot, which was their way of feeling him out and finding out what he was made of.

I scanned the streets, looking for a decent vehicle but all of them were wrecks. I turned my back on the VW and then I heard something. At first, I wasn't sure what it was, only that it seemed to be coming from the alley across the way. I called out for the others to stay in the bus in case it was a trap and walked over there. Plugging my cigarette into the corner of my mouth, I pulled the Beretta out of my waistband. I worked the slide and jacked a round into the breech, got ready for what might come.

In the alley, shrouded in shadow from the buildings on either side, there was a man.

Barely a man, in fact. Just some emaciated stick figure pulling itself along like a worm. He had three riders on him—rats. They were huge, the size of cats, their bodies swollen and tumorous beneath pelts of greasy gray fur. They looked up with shining rabid eyes and then got back to work eating the man. This is what I had been hearing...the chewing sounds of rats feeding, moist and slobbering like dogs working juicy bones.

There wasn't much meat on the man, but the rats were taking what they could get. One of them had its snout buried in his throat and was tugging at something in there. The other two were digging in his belly, yanking out his entrails and gnawing on them.

Bold bastards...and in the daytime yet.

The rat that was digging in the man's throat pulled its gore-smeared snout free and made a low hissing sound. It was ready to defend against all and any poachers. It rose up on its haunches, ready to fight. Droplets of blood glistened on its whiskers. There were wriggling worm-like growths suspended from its belly that looked like teats...except that they moved, pulsed. I aimed, fired, knocking the rat free of the man and pulverizing its head into splashing meat. It rolled over once, legs kicking, and died.

The other two abandoned the man's belly, leering at me with flat red eyes. They both opened their mouths, blood-stained teeth bared. Strips of tissue hung from their jaws. I shot first one and then the other. The first took a head-shot and died quick enough, the other, a hole punched through its belly, tried to crawl away, squealing and bleeding, dragging its viscera behind it over the dirty pavement. I shot it again and it did not move.

The dying man looked up, his face contorted in utter agony. He had crawled out from behind a dumpster, the rats eating him the entire time, no doubt. He left a smear of blood in his wake. I watched him, wishing there was something I could do. Times were hard, savage, yes, but I still felt compassion at times like these and I wanted nothing more than to help the poor guy.

But it was too late and I was no surgeon.

The rats had done irreparable damage, the trauma gruesome and unpleasant. The guy's belly was open, his throat was open, his bowels had been pulled out and bitten. Bad enough, but he was obviously dying long before they attacked. Radiation poisoning. I had seen it plenty of times by then and I knew it when I saw it. Most of the guy's hair had fallen out, his scalp and skin split open in jagged ruts. There were sores everywhere. Most of his teeth were gone and those that remained were rotting brown in the gums. He was bleeding from his ears, his nose, his mouth, even his eyes.

He held a hand up to me, a sickly blotched claw really, as if needing to make contact with a human being one last time. Then his arm fell and he lay there, bleeding, vomiting out bile and blood, gasping in pain.

"Sorry, old man," I said. "Wish there was something I could do."

Tensing myself, I put a bullet in the old timer's head to alleviate his suffering. It was the only thing I *could* do, but doing so made me feel cold and empty inside. Had I known any good prayers, I might have used one then.

"Don't mean nothing," I said under my breath, amazed, as always, that after all the shit I'd been through there could still be something as intangible as guilt in my soul.

Deeper in the shadows of the alley...a rustling, a skittering.

More rats.

Probably a colony near.

I walked quickly back to the van. It was mid-afternoon and usually the rats didn't get too active until night, but you never knew. They could be unbelievably vicious if you threatened their nests. If they came after me in numbers I could empty my gun into them and it still would do no good. They'd bury me alive in teeth and claws and lice-infested bodies. My bones would be licked clean in minutes.

When I got back in the van, I told Carl to get us the hell out of there.

The van started to roll again, jerking and wheezing, but gradually picking up speed.

2

The thing I hated about Janie most of all was that she was brutally honest, absolutely not a shred of bullshit in her soul. Way things were, deceiving yourself and those around you was a way of life. It kept you sane, kept your feet on the ground. But not Janie.

Whenever we were alone, Janie would look at me with those eyes so clear and so blue, and she'd ask me that same question again and again and again: "Where, Nash? Where are we going? Where are you pointing us to?"

"West," I'd say. "We're going west."

"Why west? What's out there but more of the same?"

"Because that's where we have to go. That's all."

Janie would keep her mouth shut for a few moments. Then she'd say: "Is that what it wants? Is that what The Shape tells you to do?"

And I would suddenly feel absolutely numb with fear, a gnawing anxiety rising up from within that threatened to swallow me alive. I would not be able to speak. I would lay there, dumbly, Janie in my arms, feeling the cool sweat on her body, smelling her musk and sweetness. The Shape, The Shape, The Shape. Oh dear God. What it wanted, what it demanded.

What I had to give it once a month during the cycle of the full moon.

Jesus.

See, that was Janie: no bullshit. The others would never dare ask me something like that. They knew about The Shape. They knew what it wanted...but it didn't make for pleasant conversation so it was not brought up.

But Janie wasn't like that. She'd hit me with questions and I would have to answer them. I'd find my voice, some old and scratchy thing that sounded distant and tinny like an old 78, and tell her, "Yes, that's what it wants. It wants us to go west. There's something out there."

"What?"

"I don't know. Something out there and maybe something we have to get away from back here. I don't know."

I wouldn't say anymore than that. She did not need to know what I suspected was behind us, chewing its way across country, city by city, leaving charnel waste in its path.

Janie would breathe in and out and I'd run a hand over her naked back, that deliciously smooth tanned skin, thinking how she was so much like Shelly. Except that Shelly was dead and Janie was alive.

"How long, Nash? When will it be satisfied? When will The Shape have enough?"

But I would never answer that one because it sickened me to contemplate it. What I would have to do and who I might have to do it to. For I knew with an awful certainty, sure as there was blood rushing through my veins, that there would never be an end to it. I didn't know what The Shape was exactly, but I sensed that it was part of this new world, a natural force now like wind and water and sunshine.

It would ask things.

I would do them.

And if it ever asked for Janie? If it ever did that...if it ever goddamn well did that...I didn't know what I'd do. Because there was no fucking way it would touch her.

I would not allow it.

I didn't care how hungry it was...

3

Although we found no vehicle that day, we caught a woman for The Shape. Carl got her while out scouting on foot. She was hiding in a building. As he passed by, she threw a rock at him. So he went after her, beat her into submission, bound and gagged her and brought her back.

Janie wasn't real cool with that.

The woman was barely human, that's all I can say. She wasn't infected like a Scab, not yet, but from the look in her eyes that wasn't too far off. She looked like she wanted to tear out somebody's throat.

Janie pulled the whole sympathetic thing and told us how that woman was a human being with rights like everyone else. "I want to talk to her, Nash."

"She's fucking whacko," I said.

"Please."

"Well," Carl said. "She wasn't acting real human or ladylike when I found her, Janie. But you can give it a try if you want."

Carl pulled the duct tape from her mouth.

She watched us with beady, metallic eyes.

Janie put a hand on her shoulder. "Honey..." she said.

The woman flinched, screamed full in Janie's face, then lunged forward trying to bite her. Carl knocked her to the floor, crouched on her back, and taped her mouth shut again.

"So much for that," I said.

"She's nuts," Janie said. "Absolutely fucking nuts."

Carl and I laughed our asses off.

4

Night.

We holed up in a little machine shop after a day wasted looking for better wheels than the VW. I chose the machine shop because it was defensible and set back from the street. There were even bars on the windows. If anything or anyone tried to get at us, we'd see them just fine in the moonlight and the street outside would make an excellent killzone.

I pulled up a chair before the window, cradling my Savage bolt-action .30.06 in my lap. I was figuring there wasn't much Gary could throw at me that I couldn't cut down with that.

I was sitting watch. Carl was snoring in the back room with Texas. Janie was sleeping, too.

There was nothing to do but watch that empty, waiting street. Now and then I'd lean forward up against the glass and see the moon up there above the town. It was not quite full, but damn close. Just round and fat and leering like a yellow eye, its gaze painting the buildings a phosphorescent yellow.

It reminded me of when I was a kid.

There was an older girl named Mary LaPeer who had this flowing dark hair and brilliant blue eyes. I was just absolutely in love with her. Mary had a telescope and on warm summer nights she'd take it out in the backyard and look at the moon and stars, sometimes until one or two in the morning. I'd watch out my window, my heart beating with a slow and expectant roll, waiting for Mary to come out. When she did, I'd slip out my window and join her. Mary showed me the moon and Mars and the Crab Nebula one time, but no heavenly body she showed me burned brighter than the stars in my eyes when I looked at her and listened to her talk about the rings of Saturn or the misty yellow orb of Venus.

Mary was five years older than me. I was infatuated with her until the day she graduated high school and moved away, off to college. On that day, I cried and cried because I knew I'd never see her again and I didn't. Even now the memory of that pained me, cut something open inside my belly and made me bleed. But I never forgot those summer nights or the crickets chirping, the soft whisper of Mary's voice and the Milky Way spread out over the sky and Mary telling me that one day, her and I would travel out there. Together.

Sitting there at the window, peering off into graveyard of the world, that moon poised above, I remembered Mary and missed her and wanted to sob. Maybe I lost myself in my memories too much, because I think I drifted off.

And when I woke, the Geiger Counter was ticking madly at my feet.

There was someone out in the street.

I started in my chair and nearly fell right out of it. I blinked my eyes a few times to see if I was imagining things, but I wasn't.

There was a girl standing out in the street looking right at me.

She was like some wraith that had burst the gates of a tomb, just thin and ragged and flyblown. And that's when I knew she wasn't a girl at all. That's when something jumped in my stomach and I could smell the acrid stink of fear sweating out my pores.

She was one of *the Children.*

I think I tried to call out to the others, but my mouth went all rubbery like I'd just gotten a shot of Novocaine in the gums. I made a sound, but not enough of one for anybody but myself to hear. More than anything, I just sat there stiffly like something whittled from a log. Maybe I thought if I played dead, pretended I wasn't alive, then that awful little girl out there would just go on her way. But no dice.

She saw me.

She knew I was there. Maybe she saw me move or maybe she smelled me, tasted the fear rising from me and decided she wanted more. In the dappled moonlight, I could see her just fine—the colorless hair falling to her shoulders, the gray skin and horribly seamed face that looked more like an African fetish mask than human features, something worked with a knife and chisel. Her eyes were yellow and luminous, sunk deep into exaggerated bony orbits like candles burning from the depths of mine shafts.

Breathing hard, the spit dried up in my mouth, I brought up the .30.06 with what I thought was a careful, confident motion. But the truth was that my hands were shaking so badly I could barely hold onto the damn thing.

The girl out there had not come any closer.

She stood her ground and I stood mine.

I had to shoot her. I had to put her down. I had to spray the irradiated filth in her skull all over the pavement and I had to do it soon. Because whether it was out and out telepathy or something biochemical, when one of them knew where you were, they *all* knew.

But I hesitated.

I knew Carl wouldn't have and not Texas Slim either. But even after all I'd seen and done, the various encounters I'd had with these little ghouls, I still was human enough where the idea of killing a child...or something that had once been a child...just turned something sour inside me, filled me with rot and venom, made me want to vomit out my stomach.

A voice in my head that did not belong to The Shape, but was probably simple old instinct told me, *Look at that fucking thing, Rick, it's not human, it's not a child. It's gray and shriveled and embalmed-looking, dusty and filthy like something that crawled from a grave. It's walking meat, nothing more.*

Great advice. I brought the gun up and I was going to kill that thing because I knew I had to. But as frightening as that child was, she was also somehow pathetic, more victim than victimizer even if she was lethal as the glowing rods pulled from a reactor core. At that moment, perhaps sensing my indecision, she brought up her hands, held them out palms up like some miserable waif begging for alms, for a couple dirty nickels to feed her starving siblings with.

Just do it, you idiot.

I sighted her in with the rifle, seeing her for what she really was: a monster. A seething, creeping horror from a pit of radioactive waste. Even at that distance, I could see those eyes perhaps too well and they seized something up inside me. Maybe they weren't luminous exactly, but a shiny translucent silver-yellow staring from those depressions like shimmering opals planted in the sockets of a skull. There was nothing in those eyes. That were flat and dead, voids filled with a blankness, a blackness that existed, perhaps, beyond the rim of the universe.

I hesitated too long.

Her hands fell away and then one came right back up, pointing at me and her oval mouth opened like the maw of lamprey, moonlight winking off all those tiny hooked teeth. And she screamed. Made a shrill droning sound like a locust in a summer field, but loud enough to make my ears bleed.

And the others started coming.

I heard a commotion in the back room that I knew was Carl and Texas coming to do some killing.

I took aim again and put a round right into that little girl. It shattered the plate glass window and caught her right in the chest, throwing her back and down, spraying blood and meat twenty feet or more. It happened immediately to her as it always does with the Children: she began to burn up. It was like whatever was stored up inside her went at once, potential energy going kinetic. By the time she hit the pavement, about as dead as dead gets, she was already smoking like a bag of burning shit. Some crazy blue fire erupted inside her and her flesh liquefied like hot tallow, steaming and sputtering, her face sliding off the bone and her blackened skeleton trembling in the street for a moment, than crumbling away.

It happened that fast.

But by then there were other Children.

I never saw where they came from, maybe from under the rusting wrecks of cars or out of sewers and cellar windows, spilling from chimneys and skittering down the brick facades of buildings like spiders. No matter, they were in the street. A dozen of them and more on the way.

They ringed the front of the machine shop, chattering and squealing with delight, eyes shining and mouths opening and closing like eels sucking air, skeletal fingers all pointing at me while each and everyone of them made that high, keening noise that I knew meant, *there, there he is, one of the different ones, the alien in our midst, kill him, kill him, kill him...*

They started to close in, a ragged and emaciated band, heads tangled with matted hair and faces contorted and vicious.

"Motherfucker," I heard Carl say, "it's the goddamn brats again."

He kicked out what remained of the window and by then Texas was at my side, a Browning .45 in one hand and a Desert Eagle in the other like some death-crazy guerrilla that wanted to die hard with smoking pistols in both fists.

The Children, maybe twenty or thirty of them, swarmed at us like insects, hopping and jumping, screeching and droning. I dropped three of them and Texas four others. Carl cut two of them nearly in half. And it was sheer pandemonium, the dying ones sending up great clouds of ash and greasy smoke and the living ones pouring forth right over the tops of them.

But none of them made it through the volley of fire.

A few got within three or four feet of us and we blew them away, opening skulls and perforating chests. I put my last two rounds in the belly of a little boy and he actually stumbled and fell almost on top of me, impaling himself on a shelf of jagged glass, burning up right in front of me. Carl kicked his carcass back outside before we asphyxiated on the fumes.

And about the time the others started to pull away, the street out there blazing bright like the mouth of a crematorium, somebody hit us from behind. I heard Janie cry out and then somebody knocked me and Carl aside and the next thing I knew, the crazy lady we'd captured was diving through the missing window, rolling across the sidewalk and coming up on her feet, hands still tied behind her back. Carl reloaded and was about to put her down, but he didn't get the chance.

A half dozen of the Children fell on her, taking her down effortlessly, putting their hands all over her and suctioning themselves to her with those lamprey mouths. The woman screamed and shook, but she couldn't throw her riders. They clung on, incinerating her, reducing her to a smoldering, insane thing that vomited out loops of cremated entrails.

We shot through her to get the Children.

And then they were all blazing and smoking and writhing, curling up and sputtering like bacon on a hot skillet. One of them broke free in its death agonies and shambled maybe five or six feet in our direction, then collapsed to the sidewalk, shuddering and flaking away, finally puking out some black and bubbling mass before going still.

And that was it.

We'd survived another attack by the Children. We just stood there, gasping and shaking, twenty or more Children lying in the street, fused into some blackened, steaming mass of bones and bodies.

"Those are some mean little shits," Carl said.

"We better get out of here," Janie said, refusing to view the carnage. "Those bodies are burning hot."

So we went down into the cellar and waited for dawn.

There wasn't much else we could do.

5

It was on those glaring, overcast days where the world was sank in a saffron haze that you could never see danger until it was right upon you. Sometimes when the dust storms came we were caught out in the open. It always started the same way with a silence that was heavy and sullen, a stillness that would make your flesh crawl. Then the wind would come howling like banshees, screaming through the streets, engulfing the world in a whipping tempest of radioactive dust. If you couldn't get to cover and fast, the wind would scrape your skin right off and the radiation would roast you from the inside out.

I had once seen a pack of ragbags out picking through the gutters get caught in a storm like that.

They didn't make it ten feet before the wind nailed their coffins shut. When it lifted and the dust had dispersed, the roentgens dropping away to near-normal, there was nothing out there but six bodies laying in the street. They were blistered and baked, brown as old shoe leather, tendrils of smoke rising from them with a nauseating stench of burning flesh.

Regardless, Gary was desolate.

About what you'd expect a year after Doomsday. The Geiger was reading fifty micro-roentgens per hour, background radiation, which was warm but certainly not hot. Livable. Other than that, it was more of the same: deserted streets blown with rubbish, smashed vehicles, burned-out houses. Lots of rubble from the last days when Martial Law was declared and the Army tried to put down all the private militias.

Gary was no worse than any other city, of course, but I wasn't for hanging around and either were the others. We needed a dependable set of wheels. We needed to be free and mobile. We needed something else, too, but we weren't talking about it.

Carl, being military-minded, wanted a Hummer with a mounted fifty-cal. Texas Slim wanted a hearse. Janie didn't care either way and I just wanted something dependable. Gremlin, of course, had no opinion. He'd bitch whatever we got.

With a third of the human population wiped out in thirty-six hours and millions more dying from fallout in the weeks and months following, you'd think autos would be easy to come by.

Not so.

"C'mon, you piece of shit," Carl said, turning into a crowded avenue that was strewn with the hulks of rusting cars and trucks. All the tires had been stripped away for fires. Most of the windshields were shattered. He had to snake his way through them and it was no easy bit with that wheezing old bus jerking and stopping and flooding out all the time. "Cocksucker...fucking cocksucker."

Texas Slim giggled. "I like that. I like how he does that. Swearing like a sailor."

"Kiss my ass," Carl told him.

"See? He keeps doing that. It's hilarious."

Texas Slim was a little odd. He wasn't from Texas at all. Somewhere in Louisiana, he claimed, but Carl called always called him *Texas* and so did we. He was good with a gun, good with scavenging, good with doing what he was told without question. He was just a little off sometimes and it was often hard to tell whether he was serious or just laughing his ass off at everyone and everything.

"Hey, you suppose they have any willing ladies around here?" he wanted to know. "Or even a few that aren't so willing?"

"You just keep fucking your hand and shut up," Carl told him.

Janie sighed and I leaned back in the rear seat, thinking about what we would have to do once we got some wheels and who we might have to do it to.

"Hey," Gremlin said. "Check it. We got some local action here."

There were a couple old ragbags in their tattered salvation army coats picking up dead rats and dumping them into potato sacks. Once upon a time before the world went mad, they had been bums, homeless people, but in this brave new scary world there were no more bus stations to sleep in and no soft tourists to panhandle. Now they were scavengers and they'd eat just about anything.

Carl eyed them warily. "I got me a real funny feeling here."

"So get your hand out of your pants," Texas Slim told him.

I waited, not putting much on Carl's feeling, but then Janie began to tense up next to me and I knew something was going on.

"Shit," Carl said.

The ragbags had no sense of intuition. They just kept picking up their goods and dreaming of browned rat-stew and humbleberry rat-pie, happily ignorant in the fog of their own stench. Carl hit the brakes and everyone almost fell out of their seats. But nobody bitched, because by then we all saw what Carl was seeing.

Scabs.

Three of them were standing on top of an old rusted station wagon. They had metal pipes in their hands. They were paying no attention to anything but the ragbags. They jumped off the wagon, hit the dirty street running and, just like that, they fell on the ragbags and started piping them. The ragbags just went down, curling themselves into protective balls, and the Scabs just beat them until their pipes were red and crusted with hair and tissue and the ragbags were no longer moving.

Then they looked over at the us.

Just the three of them. They were naked, their faces a scabrous dead-white, burst open with sores.

"Get us out of here!" Gremlin said. "Why are we just fucking sitting here?"

Carl got the van moving. The flesh at the back of my neck was prickling, every muscle in my body standing taut and trembling. That's when the other Scabs showed.

Not just two or three, but dozens. Most of them were naked.

They were coming from every direction. Leaping off cars and running from ruined buildings, crawling out of alleys and dropping from broken windows. They had knives and axes, pipes and broomsticks, hammers and meat cleavers. This was their turf and they were going to protect it. Up until then, I had never seen Scabs organized like that. It was not a good thing.

There was no going back and everyone knew it.

Time to go hunting.

More of them were pouring into the streets now, streaming out of their coverts and hides, all carrying axes and pikes and hammers. But no guns. I looked real closely and saw no guns. And at that point, it was all we had going for us. I didn't need to tell anyone what had to come down. Their hands were already filled with guns. We were going to cowboy our way out, Wild West it.

Janie looked at me with raw panic in her eyes, but there was no time for reassuring words. Carl had his Mossberg 500 across his lap. The beauty of the Mossberg was that it was no longer than your arm but it had real killing power. Texas Slim had his big bluesteel Desert Eagle .50 cal ready to bust and Gremlin was holding a chromed-up Smith .357. I jacked a fresh magazine into my Beretta.

Janie wouldn't take a weapon.

"Put your head down and keep it there," I told her. "Okay, Carl. Roll."

Carl eased the bus into motion, got it rolling to ten and then twenty miles an hour. Windows were rolled up, doors locked.

The Scabs converged.

"Come on, you ugly pricks," Texas Slim said. "Come get you some lovely fifty-cal."

They went after our hippie bus like it was a living thing that needed to be brought down, a primal beast in need of slaying. Like stone-age hunters attacking a mammoth, they charged right in. Hatchets and axes flew, pipes rose and fell, hammers banged and knives gouged. The rearview mirrors were knocked free, the windshield feathering out with cracks as rocks and bricks glanced off it. The front passenger side window collapsed inward in a spider-webbed tangle as Texas Slim fired three rounds from his Eagle point-blank at the screaming Scabs. A cluster of them fell away. Nothing speaks quite as loud as .50 cal. Carl didn't wait for them to get his window. When they crowded in, jabbing and pounding and scratching with their long white fingers, he brought the Mossberg up and fired. The window disappeared and a couple Scabs had buckshot sprayed in their faces.

There were too many.

Gremlin looked at me and I nodded.

We brought our weapons up and fired simultaneously right through the windows. The .357 shattered the glass and it dropped away, but it took two or three rounds from my 9mm to do the same. Everyone was shooting then, knocking the Scabs down and watching more swarm in, bodies dropping and faces splashed off skulls, the bus lurching as it smashed into one after the other, jerking as it rolled over their writhing bodies.

A Scab with the craziest, glassiest eyes I had ever seen knocked two or three of his brothers away, holding a long-handled axe up for the swinging. I put a round in his left eye socket and he fell back, twisting around in a circle, screeching, hands pressed over his face, blood gushing from between his fingers.

"KILL 'EM!" Carl shouted with a sort of manic glee as he steered and fired his Mossberg. "GREASE THESE MOTHERFUCKERS! PUT 'EM DOWN!"

The bus was taking a beating and there was only so much ammo. Already the inside was filled with smoke and glass and blood from the Scabs, everyone's ears ringing from the close-quarter firing.

We made it through the first gauntlet of Scabs and most fell away as the bus rounded the next block, but others still chased on foot and there was just not enough room to get up any speed out of the old VW. I drilled three more before my Beretta was empty and then I started smashing faces with it. But the Scabs, juiced to the gills on hate and rage, didn't give in easily. They kept coming, leaping right over the bodies of their comrades. I caught a fist in the jaw, another in the temple, nails scraped across my face. Then hands had me, yanking me right out of my seat. Janie was pulling on me, shouting, screaming, but she was losing the tug-of-war.

I fought the best I could, clawing and punching, but there was only so much I could do. In my brain, defeat already echoed: *I'm done, I'm fucking done in! Them sonsofbitches have me!*

Then Carl swiveled around in his seat, driving with his knees, bringing out a .38 Airweight and putting a round right into the face of the guy who was trying to drag me out. The bullet passed so close to my left ear I could feel the heat. But it was right on target. The Scab took it right in the nose and he fell away like he was kicked. Carl fired two more times and cored two more Scabs just like that.

Texas Slim knocked one more away then he was out of ammo, too.

So was Gremlin.

There were more guns and ammo in the back, but there was no time to get at them. Carl stomped on the accelerator and the bus jerked, coughed, sounded like it was going to stall out, then it found some speed and flattened two Scabs that ran at it. Another was hanging on the driver's side and Carl shot him with the Airweight, but he wouldn't let go. So he shot him again and again. Another tried to dive through Texas Slim's window and Texas Slim drove a lockblade right into his throat and still he hung on, blood bubbling from the wound.

"You need to die, friend! Let me show you!" Texas Slim cried out and started stabbing him in the face, the neck, the head, and finally he dropped away.

Janie was holding me so tight I thought she was going to break my arm, but we made it through.

"Well, that was a fucking trip," Carl said.

And we all started laughing. Just laughing like crazy, everyone cut and bleeding and dirty.

But in the confusion and haze, Carl never saw the little overturned Ford Focus until it was too late. He jammed the brakes and spun the wheel and the bus glanced off it, jumped the curb and smashed through the plate glass window of an old video store.

And there it died.

6

"Everybody out!" I said.

We were unharmed for the most part, just bruised and cut. We grabbed the guns from the back, the Geiger and medical kit, a few nylon bags of odds and ends. Carl had his AK-47 and I had my .30.06. Texas Slim reloaded his Eagle and Gremlin had done the same now with his .357. I made Janie take the .45 Browning, but she wasn't too happy about it. She held onto it like I'd given her a moist brown turd to call her own.

Outside, I saw no more Scabs.

We were lucky, real lucky.

Radiation had made the Scabs. Who they were before did not matter. The radiation stewed their chromosomes, made their hair fall out, made their faces go white and, yes, *scabby*. Most of them had black glistening eyes, but some had pink eyes like albinos. Dosed with radioactivity or not, they were mean and violent as hell. And insane. Just crazy mad. They'd come at you with weapons, with their bare hands, with their teeth. All anyone knew was that they were dangerous like rabid dogs and you had to put them down the same way.

Anyway, things were real quiet in the streets.

A dirty, glaring haze hung in the sky, glancing off the buildings and the cracked windshields of cars. You had to squint to see anything. And that's probably why we didn't see the three Scabs waiting for us.

One of them was drooling, his body twitching with spasms like he was amped up on Meth. The one next to him was doing the same, his eyes rolling in their sockets, his entire body jerking around like he was a marionette hooked up to strings. There was some kind of bubbling gray slime coming out of his left nostril. Both of them were grunting like rooting hogs. They all had knives and they wanted to use them.

Knives against guns...didn't make much sense, but nothing about these guys made sense.

The third one was semi-coherent. "The cunt," he said. "We want your cunt. Give us that cunt. We want her."

"Only cunt here is you," Carl said.

Texas Slim giggled. "I don't think the lady cares for the term."

"Shut up," I told him.

"We want that cunt," the Scab said again.

I kept Janie behind me. "Come and get her. She's yours."

Their brains were so melted, they just didn't get it.

They stepped forward and I dropped two of them with the .30.06, both gut-shot, and Carl put two rounds in the other guy. He fell over dead. The other two were squirming around, bleeding and moaning, making weird squealing noises. They were in pain and death would be a long time in coming.

"Let's go," I said.

"Nash," Janie said. "You can't let them suffer."

"Fuck I can't."

"Rick."

"C'mon, Janie. Enough already. Save the Pollyanna shit for another time."

"Rick, you can't."

"Sure he can, Janie," Texas Slim said, pulling out his knife. "In fact, if one were to employ a bit of creativity, they could die that much slower."

He bent over to have a little carefree fun mutilating the dying Scabs and I told him to knock it off. Goddamn Texas Slim. He'd spawned in the shallow end of the gene pool. Maybe he had tortured puppies as a boy and had moved on to bigger things since. You had to keep your eye on him. He claimed to have studied mortuary science in Baton Rouge and had an unhealthy interest in corpses and those about to become so. I had seen him do some things with the dead that were not only unpleasant, but obscene.

"You're going to let them die like that?" Janie said.

"They're not even human," I told her.

I pulled her away and she wrenched free and I knew we were about to have a fight and make the others uncomfortable, but suddenly then and there, out in the middle of that hazy dead street, we all just stopped. The only sound was the dying Scabs rolling in their own blood. Just silence. A silence that was so heavy it seemed to have physical weight.

Nothing moved.

No breeze stirred.

The air suddenly grew very dry, charged with static electricity. And hot. Sweat popped on Janie's face. It rolled down my brow and dripped off my nose.

"Oh shit," Texas Slim said. "Here comes the blow."

Dust storm.

The ground started to shake and there was a distant rumbling. I looked around, wondering where we were going to make shelter. My throat was dry. The world began to thrum as the storm grew nearer.

Gremlin looked desperate. "Nash! C'mon, fucking Nash! Are we just going to stand here and wait for it or what?"

I wanted to backhand that bastard, put him to the ground and leave him there until that storm cycled in and fried his shit. The need to do that was very strong.

"Look," Carl said.

There it was. It was coming out of the east in a raging tempest, gathering up dust and dirt and refuse and anything that wasn't tied down. It was huge and hungry and roaring like a primeval monster. Everything was shaking now: the streets, the buildings. As the storm came—and it came really fast—it cast a murky shadow before it. That shadow engulfed block after block and—

"Run!" I said. "Over there!"

There was a building across the way that looked pretty sturdy and pretty solid. We made for it, but the door was locked. Carl blew it open and everyone jumped in, clambering around in the darkness. Texas Slim found an old desk and used it to secure the door shut.

"Okay," I told them. "Let's find those stairs."

Through a grime-streaked window, I watched the street out there darken as the storm moved in. And by then, the whole building was shaking.

7

Ever since Doomsday, germs terrify me.

No, I'm not talking OCD here or anything so trifling, I'm talking about the horror that I feel when I think of all the really nasty germs floating around out there and what they can do. The radiation, as I said, did something to those germs, made bigger, badder, more virulent bugs out of them, creating deadly strains and mutated life forms of the sort I didn't even want to think about. I suppose some are the same old bugs, but many I know for a fact are much deadlier than they once were. Case in point, it was rumored that some exotic form of hemorrhagic fever similar to Ebola was burning its way through Akron and had already devastated what was left of Philadelphia and Pittsburgh.

Except, as it turned out, it was no rumor.

The form of hemorrhagic fever we're talking about here is, like I said, very much like Ebola. You remember good old

Ebola, don't you? It laid waste to quite a few villages in Zaire, the Sudan, and the Ivory Coast back when the wheels of the world were still turning and not completely flat. It was big news. Scary news. A deadly, communicable "hot" virus that was filling graveyards with no end in sight. But it did end. It came and then left, ostensibly of its own choosing.

Now this lethal strain of hemorrhagic fever—let's call it Ebola-X, that sounds suitably frightening—is like Ebola squared, Ebola to the tenth power, Ebola with a seriously pissy disposition, Ebola jacked-up on Meth and feeling extremely virile and kill-happy. I know these things because, at the very end, after Doomsday and right before our government collapsed, this new virulent Ebola-X was already laying siege to places like Washington D.C., Baltimore, and Boston.

And it's still out there, mutating, generating, taking what godawful form I can only guess at.

Let's say for the hell of it that you have contacted Ebola-X. From what I understand, communicability is roughly 98% and fatality 100%. This is death row, people, with no governor's last minute reprieve. It begins with muscle aches, the sweats, and a spiking fever. Next comes agonizing abdominal pains, pinpoint hemorrhages in your brain. Your eyes go a bright, glistening blood-red. Your skin goes yellow and cracks open with sores. By this point your brain is pretty much jelly and blood gushes from any and all orifices while you vomit out black goo, infected blood, and macerated sections of your stomach and intestines. Death is within sixteen hours of first contact and those sixteen hours are the longest sixteen hours imaginable. I personally am not religious. I don't believe there's a little invisible deity in the sky who watches over us. It's a nice, comforting thought, but I don't believe in spiritual fairy tales and I'm pretty sure neither do the millions who've died in concentration camps, from mass murder, witch hunts, race crimes, and disease outbreaks. So while I don't believe in God—though I would like to—I do believe in the Devil and the Devil is Ebola-X.

So, you get the picture, Ebola-X to human beings is pretty much like direct sunlight to a vampire...except that crumbling to dust would probably be far less painful (and messy).

Now let me tell you about Texas Slim. I haven't said much about him; I've let you form your own opinions from my, hopefully, objective impressions and memories. Now Texas has an unusual past. He's a bit quirky, offbeat, possibly borderline sociopathic. He laughs at things that make others cringe, tells very unpleasant stories that like piss in the punch don't go down well in mixed company. Enough said. But I think beyond all that, he's okay. He's tough, he's disciplined, he's loyal, and unusually compassionate. Maybe that's how they breed 'em down there in Dixieland Louisiana. Regardless, I like him. He stands by me and I stand by him.

Now it would be easy enough to dismiss him as a weirdo, but don't make that mistake. Let me tell you what happened to him before he joined up with my posse, which we could call the Loyal Order of The Shape or the Fraternal Order of the Esoteric Shape. Neither of which is very funny.

Anyway, Texas was living in Morgantown, West Virginia when the bombs fell. Being that he had a second cousin in Pittsburgh, he went there. His cousin—a large, pear-shaped woman named Jemmy Kilpatrick, who sported more tattoos than teeth—was holed-up in her apartment building with a posse of twenty others. Texas joined the posse. He was warmly welcomed...even if he did not find the romantic attentions of Jemmy so welcoming, that is. Things at the "commune," as he called it, went well. Everyone pitched in. Everyone scavenged for food, weapons, fresh water. They did a high, fine job of it.

Then Jemmy came down with a fever.

Her symptoms pretty much followed those I mentioned above. Within six hours, her eyes were bright red—"Dracula eyes" as Texas Slim himself put it—and blood was literally gushing from her nose, her vagina, ass, bubbling out of her pores and dripping from her ears. She was like a ticking bomb for several hours, then she exploded. Burning with fevers, smelling of dank rot and drainage, she could no longer sit up and just stared off into space as the blood welled out and her skin went the waxy yellow of a transparent apple. Her flesh cracked open and bled. She became a seething mass of fevers and running blood and then...she "crashed and bled out" as the biohazard specialists say. She began shuddering with spasms. She vomited out great gouts of black-red arterial blood, spraying it liberally around and spattering those, Texas included, who were trying to care for her. She heaved out a great quantity of some greasy black substance as well. Texas said the room smelled like "a bag of hot vomit." I don't doubt it. But the most horrible thing of all, he told me, was the ripping sound of her anus as it opened to vent blood and tissue, which was probably what was left of her bowels. She died very quickly after that, submerging in a pool of her own blood and waste.

Now most people would have run off long before and most of the commune had.

But not Texas Slim. He stayed right to the end, drenched in Jemmy's blood and drainage. He said the idea that he was infected by a lethal organism did not occur to him. I think he's bullshitting. He knew, but he was not the sort to abandon those in need even at the risk of his own life.

Of the twelve people who stayed behind, all of them—save Texas himself—were infected within twenty-four hours.

For the next two days Texas was busy taking care of them as they crashed and bled out. It was as close to hell as he'd ever want to go, he told me. All those infected people stuck in that tight room stinking of rancid blood and sour vomit, convulsing and shitting out their insides, their bright red watery eyes staring at him as they fell into terminal shock and vomited out everything that was inside.

He buried all of them in a vacant lot next door.

When he told this story, it was just him and me with a bottle of Jack Daniels. He would not share it with anyone else. And as I listened, it was like the poison was being squeezed from his soul. It scared me. Scared me because I wondered if he still carried the virus and scared me because I finally had a first person account of exactly the sort of shit that was making the rounds out there. What he had been through made my own experiences with my wife wasting away of cholera sound like pink party cake and balloons.

But he survived. Both the bug and the experience.

But you can see now why I'm terrified of those germs. What they were and what they are even now becoming. Because they're constantly changing, mutating. It's their nature. But the very worst thing is that germs make me think of that dream I had in the Army/Navy storeroom in South Bend. For what were they now mutating into? What sort of twisted, hideous evolution had spawned that thing I saw or dreamed of? What sort of pathogenic viral horror had the moldering plague graveyards finally given birth to?

I didn't know.

But I could feel it out there, getting closer and closer, spreading a tenebrous shroud over the ruined cities of men as it came creeping ever westward.

8

In the building, after a meal of Spam and crackers, I sat by the window listening to the radioactive dust blow through the streets below. We were up on the fourth floor in a locked room. It was good to get up as high as you could because the truly lethal supercharged dust was near ground-level. It was saturated with fissile waste materials such as Strontium-90, Cesium-137, and Plutonium. The higher dust was really just plain old dust and debris caught in the cyclone. So the higher you were, the safer you were.

But down on the streets it was deadly.

I sat there, body aching, eyes crusty from lack of sleep. The storm had died down somewhat and the building was no longer shaking, plaster falling from the walls, but it was still blowing. Every now and then a good gust would grab the building and shake it like a fist and we'd cling to each other and cover our heads, blessing the people who had built that pile of bricks to last.

Janie was leaning up against me with her head on my shoulder. Her eyes were closed, but she wasn't really sleeping. Just shutting out the world, the moan of the wind, the stink of the apartment that smelled like cat piss and woodrot. The boys—Texas Slim, Carl, and Gremlin—were trading tales as they did, each trying to outdo the other like old men discussing who had the most miserable childhood or teenage boys boasting of sexual excesses.

"We're going to have to spend the night, aren't we, Nash?" Janie whispered.

"Yeah. It's too hot out there right now."

The wind had died down some, but not enough for my liking. Once the wind blew itself out and the dust dispersed, the roentgens would die out. But not until.

So we were staying.

"What's the Geiger saying?"

Carl took a reading. "Were getting sixty up here. It's dropping."

Two hours before it was pegging nearly a hundred micro-roentgens and that was getting a little warm. Still not too bad, not like down below where the dust was probably putting out at least 400 or in places like Chicago, which had taken a direct hit from a 500-megaton device and had a lingering radioactivity so high it could only be measured in *rem*. There were a million micro-roents in one rem and, before civilization passed, rumor had it that Chicago was cooking at something like 5,000 rem. If anything was still alive there, I didn't want to know what it was.

Gremlin's voice was droning on and on about some black chick named Homegirl he had known in Fort Wayne. Hatchet Clans got her one day, just outside the city, he claimed. They gang-raped her in the street, scalped her with a butcher knife. Then, while she was still breathing and the last Clan-boy was still pumping on her, the others started cutting off her fingers and pulling her teeth and slicing off her ears for souvenirs as the Clans were wont to do.

"What did you do?" Carl said. "Just fucking watch?"

"What was I supposed to do? There was ten of them and one of me."

Texas Slim thought that was funny. "Thought you said you loved her?"

"I did. Every chance I got."

That sent Texas Slim into gales of laughter. "Ain't that something? Ain't that just something?" he said. "I loved a girl like that once. She was colored, too...no, maybe she was Indian. I use to bone her in the ass every chance I got. She only had one tit, though. But that was okay."

"One tit," Gremlin said. "You ain't real picky are you?"

Carl laughed. "Oh, he's picky, all right. He only fucks his left hand. Got himself a thing for it."

"I fuck them both. You know that," Texas Slim admitted. "And when I do, I only think of your mother."

"There you go again."

"That's sick," Gremlin said. "Real sick shit talking about somebody's mother like that. When I jack off, I think only of hot, young stuff."

He cast an eye on Janie when he said that and nobody missed it. I saw it. I think he wanted me to see it.

Texas Slim said, "Hey, Gremlin? Are you aware they have a romantic day for couples, Valentine's Day?"

"Yeah. I heard that."

"Well, they have a romantic day for single fellows like you, too. It's called Palm Sunday."

"No shit?"

Janie was trying not to laugh, but she couldn't help herself. Either could I. This was my bunch, my posse. Like kids in a locker room. Christ.

Gremlin laughed for a bit, too, then got right down to doing what he did best: complaining.

"I'm so sick of this waiting I could puke," he said. "We gonna have to stay in this shithole all damn day, Nash?"

"Yeah, and probably the night, too."

"Shit. I ain't got nothing to drink and nothing to fuck. I can't stand this waiting around." He stood up and paced back and forth while Texas Slim and Carl talked about radioactive women they'd known. "I mean, shit, Nash, what we need is some wheels. Get our ass out of this city."

"Sure. And if you want to go out and look for one in that dust, you go right ahead. Me? I'm staying. Too hot out there for my ass. My dick is already glowing in the dark."

Janie punched me and Texas Slim laughed.

"Yeah, quit your fucking whining, man," Carl said.

"Yeah," Gremlin said. "But it stinks in here."

"So do you, man, but you don't hear me complaining."

Gremlin didn't even laugh at that. "I'm sick of this shit. We left our food in the van, nothing to eat. This fucking bites it."

"You had Spam like the rest of us," Janie said.

"I don't want Spam, woman. I want a steak and a baked potato with sour cream. I want some bread and butter. I want a piece of pie and some ice cream and—"

"That all?" Carl said.

"No, that ain't all. I want some decent grub. I want some booze. I want some cigarettes that aren't stale and I want a blowjob."

Carl just shook his head. "Texas, suck his dick, will ya?"

Texas Slim smiled, shook his head "No sir, doctor told me to go easy on the sausage and gravy. I follow his orders."

"This is fucked up," Gremlin said. "You guys just joke and laugh and where the hell's any of it getting us?"

He was starting to get on everyone's nerves. We were getting sick of listening to him. At first, it had been kind of humorous the way he'd complain about anything, from sleeping bags to canned beans to the lint in his belly button. Always bitching about something and complaining about something else. But it was not humorous anymore, it was just plain bullshit. Way things were these days, you just had to take what you could get. Wasn't anybody's fault that the Scabs attacked and the storm came. Shit happened. You lived through it, that's all. Armageddon taught a body patience if nothing else.

Carl said, "Hey, Nash, wanna get high? Wanna get *reeeeaaal* high?"

I declined as a joint was lit.

We were always finding dope. There was no shortage of it. There was just a shortage of people to smoke it, was all.

I couldn't stop thinking about the world and what it had been and what it was now and what it might be in ten years or a hundred. How do you live through something like Doomsday and not become as shattered as the cities around you? And how do you find the plaster to patch up all those jagged cracks and crevices that have split open your mind and your soul and made you maybe something less than human? How do you hold yourself together and find any sort of optimism again? God knew, I wanted to be like Janie. Wanted to be kind and caring and tolerant like I once was. Part of me wanted that very badly. But it was fantasy. And another part of me knew that only too well and that part was the dogged, grim realism that cemented me to this new fucked-up world.

The world was shit.

To survive you had to be an animal.

The end had brought things into being that had no right to exist and it had changed others to absolute nightmares. That was the world these days. Like something Roger Corman had envisioned back in the fifties...mutants and roving gangs, religious crazies and nature run wild. Like in one of those old movies that I used to watch on the late show when I worked three to eleven at the shoe factory in Youngstown, *The Day the World Ended* or *Panic in the Year Zero* or *World Without End.* Just laying there on the couch, chewing takeout pizza and drinking beer, never once thinking I would be living through some kind of fucked-up horror movie.

But I was.

We all were.

Things had changed. The fallout had killed hundreds and hundreds of millions. There were resulting mutations and degeneration and savagery on the part of those that *did* survive. I had seen my share, but I knew there were worse things out there. Things I could not or would not want to imagine and one of them had come to me in a dream. Regardless, I knew very little about radiation or nuclear physics or genetics or any of it. Yes, I had a solar-powered Geiger Counter. But I didn't really know how it worked or how radiation affected things like atoms or biology.

Back in Youngstown, after it happened and everyone was just kind of wandering around in shock, the germs started sweeping the cities. There was a guy in my building named Mike Pallenberg. He taught physical sciences at East Palestine High. A real smart guy. He was an assistant football coach for the Bulldogs and when I was in high school I was a running back for the Lisbon Blue Devils. So we had a little rivalry going. A friendly one. When he was dying from radiation sickness, on his deathbed, he said, *You just wait, my friend, you just fucking wait. There's things gonna happen now I'm glad I won't be around to see. All that nuclear energy released at once...it'll affect the weather, living things, everything. You wait. See, it's the molecules. They've changed just as cells have mutated and physics as we understand it has been bent on its ear. This world is mutating, organically and physically, microscopically, matter and energy and subatomics going haywire. Nothing will ever be the same. Not for a hundred-thousand years.*

If ever.

Mike was absolutely right.

I had seen mutations. They were real. The radiation wrought evolutionary changes that would never have to come to be in a sane, sunlit world beneath the eye of a loving god. And it wasn't always the changes you could see. Much of it was, as Mike hinted, microscopic. Diseases that men had beaten off years ago mutated and spread like wildfire after the bombings. And that's what worried me now. The germs. What they were becoming. Because I had seen cities where plagues, super-plagues, the *Fevers,* had turned them into leper colonies.

And those germs were still out there.

Mutating, waiting to burn through what was left of the human race.

Like David Bowie said, this ain't rock and roll, this is genocide.

9

If you're reading this, then no doubt you know how the world ended. Feel free to skip this part. I'm putting this down just to clarify things in my mind and maybe leave some kind of record.

Okay.

It started with an exchange of nuclear weapons in the Middle East. Iran launched one against the Israelis and the Israelis responded in part. Maybe it could have stopped there, but the fuse had been burning a long time and by then it was just too late. Nukes were used in Africa, Asia and Europe. About thirty such weapons were used worldwide. Mutual assured destruction, just like they'd always said. Four of them were detonated in the continental United States—one in New York, one in Chicago, another in Atlanta, and the last in LA. The initial strikes killed fifty million people, the news said...when the stations were still broadcasting, that is. Resultant contamination killed another three million and fallout tripled that within six months. All of the weapons used against the U.S. came from North Korea. The U.S. responded by turning North—and much of South—Korea into a radioactive dead zone. We hit it with some eight nukes. The Russians hit it three times, the Chinese twice.

Just goes to show, we should have taken out that crazy little dictator when we had the chance.

Nukes were being fired by just about everybody in the wake of mass nuclear destruction. Africa and the Middle East were particularly hard hit by a variety of tactical nukes that killed millions as armies attempted to destroy armies and succeeded mainly in thinning the already teetering civilian populations. By the time it all came to an end, there was no more civilization as such. Just billions of people dying from fallout and rampant infectious disease. Firestorms raged and cities cooked hot with fallout and nuclear winter descended.

And that is how the world ended.

The Doomsday scenario.

Not with a bang, but with big motherfucking *BOOM!*

10

I dozed for an hour or so and when I woke, Gremlin and Texas Slim were giggling. I had been dreaming of my wife. What a waste to open my eyes to this fucking nightmare. I drank some water and smoked a cigarette, watched Janie's long legs cross over one another and wished we were alone so I could screw the hell out of her. Typical male thoughts. Even Doomsday couldn't change the male animal.

Carl was cleaning weapons. Texas Slim was humming some old John Cougar song and laughing as he did so. Gremlin was staring at me. He had a funny look in his eyes.

"What is it?" I asked him, already suspecting it would be trouble.

Gremlin smiled. "Just wondering when it's gonna be and *who* it's gonna be. That's all."

"Hell are you talking about?"

"You know."

"No, maybe you ought to elaborate."

He kept smiling and I wanted to slap that grin off his face. "When you gonna do it, Nash? When you gonna call The Shape? When you gonna call it up?"

That snapped my eyes open.

Yes, it *was* time to make a selection, to offer someone up, but I didn't need this sonofabitch to remind me of the fact, to rub my nose in it. Now and then I liked to forget. Pretend my soul wasn't dirty. The wind out there was still blowing, dust and grit scraping against the building. I listened to it, felt a different sort of wind blowing through my heart. A wind that was hot and ugly and searing.

Janie saw it coming, said something, but I wasn't hearing her.

Gremlin saw then that he'd crossed the line. "Listen, I just mean—"

I don't know what came over me. I balled my hand into a fist and punched him in the mouth. Gremlin's head jerked back and his lips mashed against his teeth and then the blood was flowing. I hadn't really even thought about it; it was a reflexive kind of thing.

"You stupid motherfucker!" I shouted at Gremlin's cringing, bleeding face. "We don't talk about that! We never fucking talk about that!"

Gremlin babbled out some silly excuse, his lips and teeth all stained red, and he was so pathetic, so ridiculous that the anger rose in me like lava up the cone of a volcano. It burned bright and hot. I lost all reason and just started swinging. Gremlin warded off a few with his upraised arms, but most of them landed and I had the satisfaction of hearing him beg and bleed and hurt. Gremlin's left eye was blackened, his nose bloodied, lip split. There were some nice eggs on his head. I would have kept going, lost in the idiotic violent splendor of the thing, but then Carl pulled me off and Janie shouted at me with such utter disappointment and hopeless resignation that I just curdled inside.

Carl finally let go and by then there was no fight left. "It's cool, Nash," he said and you could tell by the sound of his voice that he didn't think it was cool at all. "You got him good. Taught him a lesson and all. Got it out of your system. Chill now. Step away."

"Well, you certainly whomped his cookies, Nash," Texas Slim said. "You worked him like three miles of dirty road."

They were all staring at me and I didn't like it one bit.

But I guess I would have stared, too. Irrational, violent outbursts have a way of attracting attention just like they have a way of shaking your trust in people. I felt foolish, guilty, angry with myself. I'd always prided myself on my cool head. Patient, understanding. This *wasn't* me. I didn't hit people. Not unless they were a threat. And what threat had Gremlin been? He was just an annoying little windbag that never knew when to shut up.

"Nice job," Janie said. "Jesus Christ, *Rick*."

The others just kind of turned away. All of them except for Gremlin. He kept eyeballing me with an accusatory stare. There was blood all over his face, purple welts. His lower lip was swollen like a sausage and his right eye was nearly closed. It hurt just looking at him.

"Feel better now, Nash?" Gremlin, said spitting blood onto the floor. He chuckled. "I've been beat worse. A lot worse. That's okay. I got out of hand and you showed me my place. I know better now. I know how I rank."

I reached out to him, to put a hand on his shoulder, and Gremlin slapped it away, almost putting me on my ass in the process. "Don't you fucking touch me, you goddamn asshole."

Nobody disagreed with what he said.

I went and sat by myself, smoked, brooded, listened to the storm. Pouted. I was angry and at the same time I was beside myself with guilt. I kept thinking: *You could kick them all to the curb right now. Get rid of 'em and in a week you'd have a new posse.*

Who are they to fucking judge you? Who the hell do they think they are?

Crazy thinking, I know. I couldn't kick Janie to the curb without kicking a big part of myself there, too.

Shit.

Ultimately, I had just shaken their confidence in me and I knew it. I didn't really know why it happened, only it had been coming for a long time. It just happened as such things will. Partly it was the damn depression that ate me open most days, made it feel like there was a black hole south of my belly that wanted to suck me into the darkness alive and kicking. And another part was probably general frustration, unhappiness, and the very real fact that Gremlin was really, really getting on my nerves. Add to that that the waiting was killing me. We had to move. We had to get west before...well before something caught up with us.

Nobody spoke and I kept my mouth shut.

Gremlin hadn't bothered washing the blood off his face. He wore it like warpaint. He sat on the floor, legs drawn up, arms wrapped around them, head cradled between his knees. His eyes were crazy and wild and full of pain and they were on me. Only on me.

Staring.

Hating.

I had the most ugly feeling that as soon as my eyes were closed Gremlin would slit my throat. So I watched him. Watched him close. And as I did so, feeling that my little posse was fragmenting, I felt more alone and vulnerable than ever. I started thinking about Shelly. I started thinking about Youngstown.

I remembered standing on the roof of our building the night the bombs came down. Lots of people were up there. New York City had taken a direct hit. Though it was a long way from Youngstown, if you looked to the east you could see where it was...or had been...because the horizon was glowing blue.

II

Beneath the bleached eye of the moon, the rats came out.

They came out of gutters and cellars, ruined buildings and ditches, places of dark and dampness where corpses rotted to foul ooze. They became a great black squealing river that flooded the streets and sank them in greasy, skittering bodies. Nothing with blood in its veins stood a chance. The rats were swarming, infesting, pressing forward like driver ants in some steaming jungle, driven to frenzy by a relentless hunger, living only to feed and breed and sink the world in their numbers.

The crazies in the streets never stood a chance.

Five minutes before, the dust storm finally having blown itself out, they were still shouting out psalms and raising their hands skyward to the Lord God above, shouting about salvation and deliverance...and now they were inundated.

Buried alive.

The rats hit them from every direction and you could hear flesh tearing and bones crunching and distant screams extinguished by plump, ravenous bodies. It became a feeding frenzy as the rats devoured the crazies, devoured each other, and even themselves in their mania. And it was quick. Just three minutes from the time the first wave hit to when the black river evaporated into the shadows, leaving nothing behind but stripped rat carcasses and five sets of well-picked bones that gleamed white as ivory in the moonlight.

There was not a drop of blood to be found on those bones.

Janie refused to watch, of course. She wasn't squeamish by that point, but with her there was always a line of common decency that she refused to cross. The rest of us watched the action from the windows. Carl and Texas Slim had a bet going and that made it all a little more exciting for them. Carl said it would take the rats at least five minutes to strip the crazies; Texas Slim said three minutes, tops.

And he was right.

"You're one cool hand, Carl," he said. "That's six joints you owe me. Feel free to pony up right now, dear friend."

"Shit," Carl said, pulling off his cigarette. "Feel like I been suckered."

"You have," Janie told him.

Texas Slim shook his head. "No, Janie, that's not so. See, I know rats and I understand rats. I've made a study of them. It's quite scientific. See, rats are different now. They've changed. They're fiercer than they once were. There are some real big mutants out there now the size of cats and dogs. Now, these new rats...it'll take a pack of thirty of them about thirty minutes to strip five bodies, right? So it stands to reason that *three-hundred* of them can strip five bodies in three minutes. What you do is you take the number of people and divide it by the number of rats and thereby arrive at your sum, which in this case you round off to three minutes, give or take."

It was insane how his mind worked. "You've got the most fucked up head I've ever seen," I told him.

Texas Slim smiled. "Thanks. I appreciate that."

"Don't encourage him, Nash," Carl said. "He's got enough problems."

I figured that was probably true.

Carl butted his cigarette, looked around. "Hell is Gremlin? He's been gone a long time."

"He's out pouting since Nash cocked his block," Texas said. "He said he was going to scavenge around in the building here, but I know better."

He had that one pegged pretty damn good. That's exactly what Gremlin was doing...licking his wounds, feeling sorry for himself, and pouting. I didn't doubt it a bit. Since I lost control on him, cocked his block, he had not stopped staring at me with that vicious gleam in his eye. It did no good to apologize. He just wasn't having it. Even Janie had tried to talk sense to him. The bottom line was that I had lost it and pounded on him for no good reason other than the fact that I was probably externalizing some inner turmoil. That's how Janie explained it. Maybe that was bullshit, but it sure sounded good.

"He's been gone awhile," Janie said. "Do you think you should go look for him?"

I shook my head. "He'll come back when he's ready."

"I will then."

She started to rise from the sofa but I yanked her back down again. "Janie, no. He's just being a pain in the ass. Give him some time, he'll come back. Besides, I don't need anyone else risking their necks out there. It's dark out."

She didn't need any more convincing after that. Truly, though, I didn't want to go look for him because I was almost afraid to, afraid of stumbling around in the dark with him out there...*waiting*. He had an axe to grind and I didn't want him grinding it against my head. And I sure as hell didn't want Janie doing it, either. I had seen how Gremlin looked at her...like she was a piece of meat and he was hungry. There was five miles of hell in that look.

"What if he goes outside?"

"I hope to hell he doesn't. Not in the dark. The rats'll be bad. Who knows what else?"

"The Children," Carl said.

It was possible. And if Gremlin was crazy enough to go up against them, then he was asking to die a hard, ugly death.

So we sat around as night came on, just bored silly. Carl got a few candles out of his pack and lit them. It made everything nice and Medieval, stuck up in that stinking apartment by candlelight while rats and worse things prowled the streets below. It was like living during the 14th century.

Texas Slim started chatting away about the good old days in college studying mortuary science. How you'd shoot Permaglo into cadavers through the carotid artery after you'd drained them to firm up muscles and organs.

"I used to like to wash them," he told us. "You have to soap and lather them up and then knead them like bread dough to work the Permaglo through. Gives the skin a nice, natural tint. You can see it happen right before your eyes. You shoot it in the mouth to keep it toned. That way, Uncle Joe or Aunt Tillie doesn't get all gray, mouth sagging, lips shriveled back from the teeth. People don't care for that. Don't like that death-grin. They like them fresh-looking so they can say, looks like he's just sleeping, ain't he sweet?"

"That's it," Carl said. "You sick goddamn fuck. I'm not going to sit here and listen to you talk about that shit. You're creeping me out."

Texas Slim chuckled. "Just telling you how these things work. Might come in handy someday, you knowing this."

"How the hell could it be handy?"

"Well, hell, son...it's a mean world out there...am I right? Sure. All manner of nasty things out there. Germs and Fevers and plague and nasty microbes. Could be someday we'll be dead and you'll be alone. Say that happens. There you are, so lonely you could fuck a fence. Then you happen upon some attractive lady, only she's dead—"

"Knock it off, you fucking ghoul."

"—so you take this knowledge of mine and you whisk her off to your friendly neighborhood mortuary and fix her up. Paint her, polish her, firm up her attributes, spray her female parts down good with disinfectant—"

"I'm warning you."

"—get her all prettied up, crack yourself a bottle of wine, and see what happens. Let nature take its course. But don't forget the eye caps, my friend. Slip 'em under the lids...otherwise they get that sunken look. And that's a turn off, trust me."

"I'm going to kill him, Nash. I swear to God I am," Carl said.

And it looked like Janie might just join him in that particular endeavor.

I just sighed. I truly dreaded these down times because it always went this way. Texas Slim went out of his way to annoy Carl and he rarely failed at it.

"Change the subject, will ya?" I said.

Texas Slim shrugged, didn't have a problem with that. And for maybe five minutes we had blessed silence. But it didn't last. Of course it didn't last.

"In Morgantown, before the germs got out of hand," Texas Slim said, launching into another tale, "we had some big rats. I saw them. I was bopping and hopping with this Chinese guy they called Ray Dong. We got along good, Ray and I. He had once been in the time-honored business of embalming like yours truly, so we had all kinds of things in common—"

"This isn't about fucking corpses, is it?" Carl said.

Texas Slim laughed, but laughed in a secretive, conspiratorial sort of way as if maybe he *did* have a few amusing anecdotes about corpse-fucking but he wasn't about to share them in mixed company. "No, this is about rats. Big rats and a fellow I knew named Ray Dong. He was Chinese. This happened in Morgantown, which is in West Virginia."

"We gathered that," Janie said.

Texas Slim went on: "Ray was one of these guys who could eat anything. Dogs, cats, green crawly things. A rare stomach had he. He just liked to be eating all the time. So one day he says to me, he says, Hey, let's go rat hunting. I say, Rat hunting? What for? To eat 'em, he says. Some of 'em are pretty big now. We get one, cook it over a fire, be like roast pork. Only I get the heart. I like the hearts best. I say, I don't want to eat rats. But he talks me into it. It's dangerous stuff, rat hunting, but Ray...well I simply couldn't say no to him. Eating something that's been dosed isn't a good idea as you all know and those big black rats, oh boy, they've all been dosed for certain. You know what happens when you start eating mutants."

Radiation changed a lot of things. There was a rumor going around that if you ate mutated things, you absorbed what was in them and it became *you*. Something to do with the DNA. Essentially, you are what you eat. You start eating a lot of rats with their chromosomes all wigged out from radiation saturation...it fucks up your genes and pretty soon, well, you start becoming something else, something rat-like.

But it was a rumor. That's all.

"So we go rat hunting," Texas Slim said. "We go out at night and I don't like it. We have to hide from night things. Lots of night things in Morgantown, you know. As luck would have it, we find rats. Hard not to. But they're in packs, so we lay low. Finally we see one big ugly thing about the size of a pig. It's chewing on a corpse, gnawing on an arm like a chicken leg. Never seen anything like it before. Big, like I say. All kind of gray and wrinkly, no hair just a lot of black bristles like a hog. It saw us right away, made a squealing sound like a mama boar. Ray put the flashlight beam right in its face and...ho, Jesus and his holy mother, it sure was ugly. Hairless and flabby, big slobbering mouth dripping juice and black eyes, real black shiny eyes. Had a nub growing out of the side of its neck like a second head that never took.

"Ray...oh hell, he was crazy, *crazy*. He ran right out there, hooting and hollering while I was filling my pants. He had a .45 and he pumped three rounds into that ugly mother-raper. The rat made a squealing sort of noise and came right at Ray, took him down right in front of my eyes. Poor Ray. It took him right by the face and started chewing and slurping. That's when I saw that there were a dozen rat pups clinging to its back, all kind of bald and wormy-looking, all of them screeching with those little pink sucker mouths. I ran. Last thing I heard of old Ray Dong, the best Chinese man I ever knew, was the crunching sound when mama rat bit through his skull."

There was silence for a moment after that one. Then I said, "And what was the point of that story?"

"Just passing time."

Goddamn Texas. He never quit. We had enough troubles without him giving us worse nightmares than we already had. I knew about the rats. So did the others...we just didn't like to spend a lot of time thinking about them was all. I could have told him about the rat that Sean, Specs, and I saw in the Cleveland sewers, but I didn't like to think about it.

Janie wasn't much on horror stories and especially since these days most of them were true. She just sat there staring at Texas Slim and I was feeling the heat coming off her, knowing she was about to read him out.

But she never did.

For down below, out there in the world of crawling shadows, there came a sound which sealed her lips.

12

It was a great resounding roaring/howling sound.

It rose up and up until it took on the shrill baying of an air raid siren and I could feel it thrumming through my bones and scraping right up my spine. The windows practically rattled. It was hollow and primeval in tone. We had all heard things at night before, but never anything like this. It stirred some instinctual terror in us. At least it did in me.

Janie was gripping my arm so hard her nails actually broke the skin.

When it had echoed away finally into the night, Carl swallowed and said, "What in the hell was that?"

But there were no answers. I was picturing some mammoth horror rising from the ooze of a Mesozoic swamp and howling at the misty moon high above.

Nobody said anything for a moment or two.

We were all waiting for someone else to break the silence, but no one did. And the reason for that was very simple: we were *waiting*. Just waiting. Waiting for something else to happen, for that howling to rip open the night again. Only this time it would be a little bit closer.

I opened my mouth to say something ridiculous and reassuring, but I never got that far. For there was a thud. A sudden, immense thud that shook the whole building. It came again. And then again. Plaster fell from the walls, dust trickled from the ceiling. Downstairs somewhere, something crashed, something else made a high-pitched splintering sound. There was lots of noise suddenly down there: things falling and banging and then only silence.

Everyone waited quietly after that.

But whatever it was, it never came back.

But, then, neither did Gremlin.

"Should we go look for him?" Janie said after a long time. "I mean, *all* of us?"

I shook my head. "No. It's too dangerous out there. We'll have a look in the morning."

"He'll probably be dead by then."

"He's probably already dead, darling," Texas Slim said.

There was no more to be said on the subject. I set up watches for the night and that was it. The others got what sleep they could, trying not to think about what had been rooting around downstairs.

My dreams were far from pleasant. They started out with nightmares about being stalked through a wrecked city by some kind of horrible beast I could not see and ended with a real doozy about Youngstown. I dreamed the city split wide open like a rotting pumpkin and millions of hungry graveyard rats began pouring out.

13

Morning.

Just after first light, I got them moving. We ate something quick out of our packs and went downstairs. Soon as we made the lobby, we stopped dead.

"Will you look at this," Carl said.

The lobby had been ransacked.

All that racket from the night before, the banging and crashing, well here was its source. Plaster was gouged right down to the lathes, holes punched in the walls, doors torn off hinges. Everything was broken and shattered. And for about six or seven feet up the stairs, the railing balusters had been smashed like somebody had taken an axe after them. A goddamn big axe.

"What happened here?" Janie dearly wanted to know.

But I had no idea. Something had come into the building last night, that same thing that had been howling, and it went on a real bender down here. But what that might be I could not even guess.

"Look," Carl said.

The front door was missing. Texas Slim found it outside, cast into the street. Its surface was cut with triple ruts like it had been worked with a scythe. A sturdy, century-old hardwood door...it must have taken something damn nasty with big claws to do work like that.

"Fucking monster," Carl said.

"Guess I'd be inclined to agree with you," Texas Slim said, though it was obvious he didn't care for the idea.

We stood around in silence and I knew I had to get them going, get them doing something constructive before the significance of this made them want to hide under the beds. And I was just about to do that when somebody walked up.

"About time you people got up."

Gremlin was standing there.

His olive drab fatigue coat was dusty, a ribbon of cobwebs hanging from one sleeve, but other than that he looked no worse for wear...that is, if you discounted his bruised face, split lip, and blackened eye.

Nobody said a word for a moment.

I went over to him. "Where the hell have you been?"

Gremlin offered me a grin that was downright creepy. "That's some nice welcome," he said. "I was hiding out. Some kind of thing down here last night. I hid out in an old coal bin in the basement."

For some crazy reason, I just did not believe him. His eyes were glazed, shell-shocked almost. And that grin...it was dopey and strange, seemed to be saying, *I know something you don't, oh yes.*

"We figured you were dead," Carl said. "Too bad."

I said, "Did you see what did this?"

"No, I heard it, but I wasn't getting close enough for a look. Fucking thing was sniffing around...I think it was looking for me."

Janie, who was usually the most sympathetic person in the world, did not say a word.

I was getting a bad feeling, but I couldn't be sure what it meant.

If the others had misgivings about Gremlin's story, they tried to hide it, but not Texas Slim.

He stood there looking at the destruction, the .50 cal. Eagle in his hand. I was watching him. Watching him real close because I knew two things about Texas: he was fucking weird *and* he had a very good head on his shoulders. So I watched him run it all through his brain, see what he came up with. Texas stood there, holding his gun and wrinkling his brow as he did when he was vexed. Then slowly, he turned his gaze on Gremlin. Kept it there.

It was a hard stare and Gremlin quickly started to squirm.

"What the hell is it?" he demanded. "Fuck are you looking at me like that?"

Texas Slim shrugged. "Just wondering certain diverse things, I suppose."

"Yeah...like what?"

"Like how it was you were down here last night and you didn't see what did this. Strikes me as funny, that's all."

Gremlin looked to me for support and got nothing but a cool blank stare. "I *heard* it, same as you did. But I hid out. You think I was going to come out and face that fucking thing with the way it was howling and tearing this place apart?"

"You were armed, weren't you? You had a three-fifty-seven. Why didn't you try and pop our visitor?"

I stood there, waiting, as did the others.

Texas Slim was interrogating the guy, but someone had to. Something just didn't wash about Gremlin's story and it didn't wash so much that it just plain stank rotten.

"What is this? What are you insinuating?"

"Yeah," Carl finally put in. "Fuck are you insinuating, asshole?"

But Texas, being Texas, just shrugged and smiled thinly, let it all go. He'd made his point and he knew it. He'd cast doubt on Gremlin and a doubt that was tangible enough so that even thick heads like Carl picked up on it.

After all that, I got them organized, got everyone loaded up with their duffels and sacks and on the road. There was only so much daylight and I didn't want to waste a second of it.

14

By late afternoon the next day, we still had no wheels.

We wandered for hours, searched as far west as the Tri-City Plaza on 5th, but the Geiger started beeping because we were getting too close to Chicago. So we cut back to Midtown, then down as far as Glen Park, searching Gleason Park and the University lots and still came up with nothing. Then back downtown to Union Station to check parking garages. Just about everything had been stripped of tires or was smashed-up or had a dead battery. It seemed pretty hopeless.

We were marooned in Gary.

Trapped in that cemetery.

We had to get out. That was the bottom line. The background radiation was a little high, not too bad, but we were practically on Chicago's doorstep and if a good gust came blowing east from the Windy City we would be in trouble.

As we walked, I thought about all the things I missed. Fresh food, TV, and motorcycles came to mind right away. There were bikes around, but most of them were either wrecked or in pretty bad shape. All the dealerships had been looted after society and law and order had collapsed. People being people had helped themselves to all those little extras they'd never been able to afford. It was tough finding good vehicles, too. Most cars and trucks were either smashed up out on the roads, abandoned and rusting, or had been stripped of useable parts. You'd see a lot of that. Really nice pick-ups, SUVs, sports cars sitting around on flat tires with shattered windshields, engines stripped or destroyed. Oh, there were plenty of drivable rides out there, but the people who had them also had guns. Lot of times you'd just find cars with skeletons in them.

Nobody was in a real good mood. We were tense, expectant, waiting for something truly horrible and truly dangerous to come around every corner. Because it was there. We all felt that. It was watching us, waiting for us, we just didn't know what form it would take. And after those sounds we'd heard last night, we expected only the worse.

But that was night.

This was day: a misty, damp sort of day that carried an unpleasant chill to it. I didn't like us being this vulnerable. In a vehicle we had the luxury of protection, of shooting and driving off...but not on foot. Any pack of crazies could chase us, corner us, and we only had so much ammo.

As we walked down yet another street, scoping out the rusted hulks of vehicles, the rubble and refuse, the bones heaped in the gutters, I was thinking about Gremlin.

Gremlin in general annoyed me in ways I could not exactly put a finger on...but after that weird howling last night, he had popped back up this morning and something had been very off about him. I was not sure what. There was something there and my gut-sense told me it was trouble, but of what variety I could not imagine. The howling. Gremlin coming back. That fucked-up, creepy grin on his face. Maybe I was just tired and wigged, but I was also certain I was not wrong in my assessment of him.

We kept going. Another street, plodding along. More wrecks, more staring empty buildings. Drifts of sand in the street. A light breeze that smelled dirty and low. I watched Texas Slim watch Gremlin and wondered what was going through his mind.

"Years ago," Texas was saying, "I worked at a quaint little establishment called the Horas Brothers Family Mortuary in Lafayette. That's in Louisiana, Carl, case you were wondering."

"Yeah, I know where the hell it is."

"I had...well, gotten myself into some difficulties with a young lady in New Iberia and it necessitated that I seek gainful employment to pay my child support, you understand," he said, chuckling to himself. "Well, one day we received the body of a criminal named Tommy Carbone. He was known in underworld circles as Tommy the Tripod and the reason for that should be quite obvious. Anyhow, this poor soul died in prison. Apparently...and you'll excuse me, Janie...all this poor man did was masturbate three, four, five times a day, I learned. And then it became worse and it was every hour on the hour. In his cell, the prison workshop, the dining hall. Finally, the prison authorities took him to the infirmary and strapped him down. Poor Tommy. He laid there hour after hour with that quite mammoth penis of his standing straight up.

"Finally, he went into convulsions and died and then he came to us. The problem was, you see, that his large and particularly ungainly member was still quite hard. Death will do that, you see. Even after we suctioned the blood from him, it would not lay down like a good dog. Well...we had a sheet thrown over him and it looked like a tent. As it was, his manhood being so long, we simply couldn't close the lid on the casket so, necessity being the mother of invention—"

"Do we have to hear this?" Janie said, slapping at a fly.

"—we used a rotary saw to cut it off. I'll never forget that day as long as I lived when I felled that high timber. I felt just like a lumberjack. *Timber!* I cried when it came crashing to earth.

Of course, the director, Archie Horas, being a man of the most morbid imagination, had that gargantuan member stuffed, shellacked, and made into a fine walking stick."

"Oh, shut up," Carl told him. "A walking stick. Jesus Christ."

"I smell smoke," Janie said.

I did, too. It could've been a good thing and it could've been a bad thing.

"Let's follow it," Gremlin said. "Might be somebody cooking grub."

"And could be somebody cooking somebody else," Carl pointed out.

"All right," I said, a headache beginning to thread its way through my skull. "Let's shitcan the talking for awhile. Everybody keep their eyes open. We gotta find something here."

And we did as we reached the western edge of the city, skirting what had once been Tolleston and moving north towards Westbrook across West 6th and Taft. The stink of smoke grew very heavy.

"Just ahead," Carl said.

Plumes of smoke were rising over the roofs of buildings.

And there was something on the warm, dusty wind: the stink of death.

15

I took point, ready for just about anything.

In the overcast sky above, I saw birds circling: crows, buzzards.

I led my posse down an alley and around the collapsed remains of a building which had fallen into its own gaping cellar. There was water down there, black and clogged with leaves.

Scanning what lay ahead with my rifle, I said, "C'mon. Move slow. Move quiet."

There was rubble in the streets, of course, the fire-scarred facades of buildings, buses and cars and trucks scattered about, some smashed, other overturned, many just rusted to hulks of iron in which birds and rats nested. But it wasn't just this or the bullet-pocked storefronts, the broken glass, and rivers of sand blown over everything.

There were bodies. Fresh ones.

At least a dozen bodies in the street in every imaginable state of mutilation. Some were missing arms or legs, one woman looked like she had been partially skinned. Another had apparently been trying to crawl beneath an overturned truck and somebody had pinned her to the ground with a homemade spear shaft.

I led the way in with my .30.06 and the others fell in behind, Carl and Texas Slim flanking them, ready to start busting.

"You know what happened here, don't you?" Texas Slim said.

And I did, all right. But I had other things on my mind and I wasn't spending any effort thinking about it, doing anything that might divert my attention from what might be waiting out there in the wreckage and the shadowy ruins of buildings. The stench of recent death was in the air. Flies were buzzing in clouds, carrion crows circling high overhead. Three of four cars were burning and I was guessing that they had been running before this happened.

We came upon a young couple spread-eagle in the street. There was blood all over their naked, pale bodies. They had been decapitated, the heads nowhere in sight. Flies swarmed over the stumps of their necks. With a sickening lurch in my stomach, I figured that some of that blood was from what had happened to them *before* their heads were chopped off.

I was not only sick to my stomach now, I was pissed off. And getting more pissed off by the minute. We moved around a pickup truck that was still blazing with a sharp stink of burning rubber, plastic, and oil. Smoke twisted in the air, ground mist blowing around in damp sheets.

"Oh, God," Janie said.

There was a heap of bodies on the sidewalk. All of them were naked. They had been slashed and hacked and disemboweled, dumped here in a bloody heap of limbs and staring, sightless faces. Their eyes had been carved out, noses slit free, and the bleeding ovals of their mouths bore witness to the fact that their teeth had been yanked. And every one of them had been crudely scalped.

"Fucking Clans," Carl said.

Yeah, it was true. The Hatchet Clans always scalped their victims. People said they wore belts and sashes of scalps. Nobody but them came through an area and butchered like this. The Scabs and the other gangs of crazies were violent and bloodthirsty, but they were not this methodical, this viciously creative. The Hatchet Clans were—as Sean had pointed out—like army ants on the march, killing and destroying everything in their path. I knew little about them other than that they were brutal and deranged beyond belief. And that they came in numbers, in huge mobs like swarms of locusts come to devour a field. I didn't know what held them together, whether it was some social or religious grouping or just a shared bond of insanity.

One thing was for sure: they were tribal and they had gone native. I had heard they were all infected by some kind of morbid fungus. Maybe that was it. Beyond that, they were sinister and smart. They liked to set up ambushes, draw you in by sacrificing a few of their own. Make you think you had the upper hand and then storm in by the hundreds and overrun you.

Everyone was very tense. Other than the Children or the risk of Fevers, nothing could inspire terror like these guys.

We found seven heads, mostly women's, that had been arranged in some kind of spiraling circle on the hood of a sedan. Symbols were painted in blood on their foreheads. Two men were laying in front of an apartment building. They had been dismembered completely...then with a wicked sense of humor, their torsos and attendant limbs had been arranged in proper anatomical order...just no longer connected.

From a street sign a woman had been hanged by the feet, her fingertips just brushing the pavement. She had been eviscerated, her body cavity hollowed right out. Her breasts had been cut off, her scalp and deathmask peeled free. On her back were more bloody symbols of the sort we were beginning to see everywhere...on dusty windows, car hoods, sidewalks not covered in sand. They looked almost runic and there was something especially frightening about that.

"Goddamn Gary," Carl said. "This place has always been nothing but a shithole. I told you that when we came in. Fucking sewer. It wasn't much before the bombs and it ain't much now."

"Over here," Texas Slim said.

There was a Greyhound bus parked at the curb. I saw curtains in the windows. I moved around towards the bifold door. It was open. The safety bars you pulled yourself up the steps with were dark with sticky blood. There was a bloody handprint on one of the windows.

Even outside, I could smell the death cooking in there.

"Carl," I said. "You and me."

I went in, Carl at my back. The bus had been converted into a dormitory of sorts with the seats removed and cots lined up in orderly rows...at least they had been. Now they were flipped over, tossed aside, everything painted a shocking red. Blood was sprayed in wild loops and whorls. The floor was sticky with it. Bits of flesh and clumps of hair were stuck in it.

And bodies, of course.

I figured at least a dozen or more, all cut and slit and hacked. And scalped. Limbs and entrails were scattered around, dangling from the shelves on the walls and tangled in old army blankets. It was hot in there, hot and closed-up and revolting with the smell of blood and meat and bowels. Several spear shafts were still sunk in torsos. They had been painted up with symbols that were unreadable because of the dirty handprints and bloodstains.

I got outside before I threw up. And then, to my surprise, I did anyway.

"Don't go in there," I told the white, drawn faces of my friends. "Don't go in there."

When I felt better, I drank some water from my bottle, had a cigarette with Carl. I felt hopeless and helpless, outnumbered and just beside myself. The carnage. Dear God, the carnage. There must have been a somewhat thriving community of people here before last night. Before the Clans marched in and slaughtered them. I thought they had been normal, too. In the bus, I had seen baskets of clothes, books, tools. These people had not been crazies, they had not been animals.

Texas Slim had been sweeping the area, finding nothing but more bodies. But he had found something else, too. "Got one," he said. "Over here."

We followed him. He stopped and there, lying in a twisted heap just inside the display window of a store, was one of them.

A dead Clansman.

He was perforated with bullet holes and must have taken quite a volume of fire before he went down. He wore a filthy green army overcoat and heavy scuffed boots. His hands were curled up like dying spiders. They were yellow, bony, mottled with open sores. His head was shaved bald, but he wore a greasy scalplock like an old time Pawnee warrior. And he had a gas mask on. They all wore them like some kind of fetish mask. Strictly war surplus, as Sean had said, it was made of leather with an oval breathing filter and two glaring buglike eyepieces. It was strapped on.

Finding a dead Clansman was rare because they always carted off their dead with them.

"Let's see what this fuck looks like," Carl said. He shouldered his AK and pulled out a K-Bar fighting knife. Being careful not to touch the corpse, he slit the straps and peeled the mask back with the tip of his knife. And then recoiled in horror.

"Shit," he said.

The face was an atrocity. The flesh was yellow and spongy, grotesquely distorted like the skull beneath was swollen. There was only one eye which was glazed white and staring. The other was gone, a bubbly white mass of fungus growing from the socket and engulfing the entire left hemisphere of the face and head. It seemed to be dissolving the tissue. Tiny rootlets had grown from it in a wiry mass, feeding right into the flesh and up the nostrils. The growth had contorted the muscles, pulling up one side of the face in a hideous toothy grin. The blind eye that had once been powered by a diseased brain watched impassively.

"Let's get the fuck out of here," I said.

We turned away, turning a blind eye to the slaughterhouse around us. Even Janie, who was helplessly sympathetic, just turned away because there was simply too much of it to take inside and hold there. She was drained. We were all drained. The first normal people we'd seen in months and they had been butchered.

I pushed on farther down the street, getting us away from the carnage and the smell, wondering if we should have searched the buildings for survivors and knowing that it was pointless. I rounded the corner ahead and that's when the first shot rang out.

16

I hit the ground with the others, crawling towards the safety of an overturned car. Bullets zipped around me, thudding into storefronts and street signs. Whoever was doing the shooting was not real precise. Another shot rang out and punched through a plate glass window, knocking a dusty cobwebbed mannequin over.

"Hole in one," Texas Slim said.

"Coming from that building over there, Nash," Carl said, pointing to a brick walk-up across the street. "See the glint of the barrel? Second story window?"

I did. The window was gone and pink curtains were blowing out.

"Sounds like a medium caliber. Maybe a thirty-thirty or a thirty-ought."

"You, sir, are a violent man," Texas said. "Such a knowledge of firearms. Shame on you."

We were effectively pinned down. Other than a few wrecked cars the street was wide open. A perfect kill zone. The only thing we had going for us, way I saw it, was that the sniper out there wasn't much of a shot. The bullets came intermittently and always pretty wide of our position as if the shooter was just trying to scare us off or keep us contained.

"Well, what do you think?" Carl asked, sighting on the building with his AK.

"I'm not sure," I said.

"Maybe they'll just go away," Janie said.

"And maybe Carl's mother should have kept her legs closed, child," Texas Slim said.

"You better shut your fucking hole," Carl warned him.

I put a hand on him. "Easy."

"I'm all for waiting until they run out of bullets," Gremlin said.

Carl laughed. "You would be." He turned to me. "Let me see your Savage."

I wasn't sure if it was a good idea or not. Carl had a way of stirring up the hornet's nest and particularly when he had a gun. And then another shot rang out and punched into the hood of the car and I handed Carl the rifle.

Carl jumped up, sighting as he did so. He fired, ejected a shell, and repeated the process twice in quick succession. I couldn't have done it in a matter of seconds like that and even if I did, I wouldn't have had any accuracy. But Carl did. His first two rounds punched into the face of the building mere feet from the window and the third went right through it.

And then a figure—a woman, I thought—leaped in front of the window and fired twice, the slugs hitting the street in front of the car. She kept trying to fire, but she was out of rounds and that was obvious by the temper tantrum she threw at that moment before crying out and jumping away from the window.

Carl handed the .30.06 back to me and took up his AK. "I'm going to get the bitch."

"Leave it," I told him.

"Leave it? Full moon's not far off, man. We need something before then if you know what I mean."

I just nodded and Carl raced off. I felt the guilt cut into me as it always did and I could feel Janie next to me, disapproving. She just didn't get it.

Texas Slim said, "Well, I'd better go accompany him. Boys do get into trouble when unsupervised."

I sighed and leaned up against the car. Sometimes I felt like I was leading and sometimes I knew I was being led. Janie was looking at me. Her face was unreadable.

"If nothing else, they get her she might know where a car is."

"Oh, is that what you want her for?"

I lit a cigarette to keep my nerves in check and probably so I didn't slap her right across the face. "Listen to me, Janie. Do me a favor and pack away your fucking morals and ethics, okay? In case you haven't noticed we're at war here. We're fighting for our lives. Do you think I care about some crazy bitch who's trying to kill us? Well, I don't. I care about Texas and Carl. You, me. Gremlin. If she dies so that we live, fuck it. That's how it has to be. You think she cares about us?"

Janie was ready to answer that, of course, but in the building across the way there was the distinctive staccato of Carl's AK-47 doing some talking over there. He wasn't cowboying it...just two rapid three-shot bursts and that was it.

"Well, he either got her or she got him," Gremlin said.

Then we waited. The silence was heavy, almost crushing as we watched the building, listened to the wind make things creak and groan in the deserted street. Dust devils whipped around. Birds cawed in the sky.

I crushed my butt. "Hell are they?"

And then they appeared, pushing a woman before them. Carl shoved her out the doorway and Texas took her by the arm and guided her down the stairs and out into the street. I figured she was probably in her twenties, tall and long-limbed, very attractive. She was tanned and fit, swearing and bitching and fighting the whole way. Texas Slim and Carl, being quite resourceful, had torn up some bedsheets and tied her arms behind her back.

And she didn't care for it much.

They brought her over and Carl shoved her to the ground. She twisted and squirmed, struggling up to her knees. "You fucking asshole! I said I'd go with you! Quit fucking pushing me, you prick!"

"Quite a mouth on her," Texas Slim said.

"We caught her in the corridor. She was making a run for it. I convinced her otherwise."

She was wearing a pair of cut-off jeans and a yellow shirt with a picture of Sesame Street's Cookie Monster on it extending his middle finger. EAT SHIT, was printed above this. And that pretty much summed up her feelings concerning her captors.

Carl put a hand on her shoulder and she jerked away and spit on him. He laughed.

"Settle down," I told her. "We're not fucking crazies. We're not going to hurt you."

"Oh no, I can see that."

"You shot at us first, honey. Not the other way around," Texas reminded her.

She sat there looking at us with big dark eyes, lips pulled away from white teeth that wanted to snarl. Slowly, by degrees, she mellowed. She was still breathing hard, but she wasn't as predatory.

Her T-shirt was ripped and I could see a fine expanse of flat belly and a pierced navel. I cleared my throat, dug a water bottle from my pack and gave her a drink. "They didn't...ah...hurt you, did they?"

She shook her head.

"I'm Nash," I said and made a quick round of introductions.

She licked her lips, still looking ready to claw out eyeballs. "Mickey. Mickey Cox."

Texas Slim giggled. "Cox, did you say? I like women named Cox."

Carl started laughing.

Gremlin was just staring, his mouth hanging open. He wasn't drooling at our captive, but he wasn't too far from it.

Janie went to her, pulled a jackknife from her pocket and cut the knotted sheets from her wrists. "Are you all right?"

"Yes."

Janie smiled at her and Mickey relaxed almost instantly. No one could refuse Janie's eyes, I knew, when she put them on you. There was such honesty and sincerity in them she could have melted a rock. "Are you sure these idiots didn't hurt you?"

"They were rough. But I've been handled rougher."

"I'm certain you have, child," Texas said. "And often."

I thumped him on the arm to shut him up.

Janie looked her up and down. "You sure they didn't...touch you or anything?"

Mickey shook her head. "They're still walking aren't they?"

"C'mon," Carl said. "Nash, you know I wouldn't do something like that. I might kill her ass, but I wouldn't fuck it."

"True, very true, that's our Carl," Texas Slim said. "He's a noble sort. And you all know I wouldn't hear of such a thing. I would never assail a woman's virtue unless she asked me to."

"Comedians," I said by way of explanation.

Mickey drank her water, kept an eye on us. Particularly me. The others she didn't much care about, but she kept her eyes on me. I was very aware of it, but pretended I didn't notice. She was eye candy. Or maybe, and more bluntly, *hand* candy. Unlike Janie who was petite and fair and porcelain doll-pretty, Mickey was tall and dark and long-limbed. She was pretty, too, but in a blatantly sexual sort of way. She had the curves and the legs, the high tits, the big dark eyes and full lips. The sort of girl who could talk about eating a salad and make it sound positively sensuous and carnal, make you want to dash out and fuck your hand. Here was a girl who'd gotten along on her looks her whole life. She knew what men liked and she knew she had it, knew how to use it.

I figured she might be trouble if she started trying to manipulate my people.

I told her what we were doing and how we needed some wheels.

"Where you going?" she asked.

"West. Just west. Out beyond the Mississippi, I think."

"That's kind of funny," she said. "You see...I was moving west, too. I was in Philadelphia when New York was hit. Everything went to shit there." She dismissed that with a wave of her hand. "A bunch of us got out, started heading west. I'm the only one left now. You know how it goes. There were six of us. Rats. Hatchet Clans. Fallout. My boyfriend...Mike...we lost him in Canton one night. Something attacked our car. They yanked him and another guy out, left us for some reason."

"Something?" I said.

"Yeah...it was dark I couldn't see. But they had claws. Big claws. Smelled like piss...like rotten meat."

"Trogs," I said.

"Were you with those people...back there?" Janie asked her.

Mickey nodded. "Yeah. For the last two or three weeks. They were nice, you know? Real nice. Real normal. They had a little community set up. All of it was run by a guy named Fisher. He'd been some kind of minister once. He was cool. They had some doctors and nurses, carpenters, teachers, all kinds of things. They were all working together. Lots of families were living with him. A few kids even, ones that hadn't changed over yet...you know how that is."

She told us Fisher was planning on getting out of the city. He had a bunch of buses stashed away on the south side over in Hammond. Trailers of supplies, military surplus, medical, everything. He had his sights on a fortified monastery down in Hebron County. They could have lived there in safety.

"What happened?" Carl asked her.

"Clans came, man. They must have been watching us awhile because they just came out of nowhere...we never had a chance." But that was something she didn't want to talk about and everyone saw it in her eyes. "So you guys are going west? Yeah...I can't explain it, but ever since this started I've had the strongest urge to go west, too. Funny, huh?"

"It's a funny world, dear," Texas said.

I thought of my dream of The Medusa exterminating the human race city by city. Moving westward. I wondered if maybe Mickey was just one of many that would be trying to escape west, part of some exodus.

"Can I come?" she asked. "Can I come with you?"

"Sure."

Carl was looking at me and I could feel those eyes. More so, I knew what he was thinking which was very much along the lines of, *course you can come, sweet thing. Wouldn't be a party without you. Next night of the full moon, we gonna get down, we gonna bust a move you'll never forget.* I guess I was thinking it, too, more or less. But maybe not as bluntly as Carl.

Mickey kept watching me. "I know where there's a nice Jeep Cherokee just north of here across the river. It's in a garage. Fisher had vehicles stashed everywhere. It might work out."

I smiled. "Welcome aboard," I said.

And then there were six.

At least until the full moon began to rise.

17

I decided Mickey was going to come in handy because she was a resourceful girl. I just had the feeling that she was going to work out. We stood around talking more for a bit, ducking into a building nearby for a bite of MREs—freeze-dried spaghetti and meatballs, yum—and started swapping war stories while Gremlin drooled over Mickey and Texas Slim watched Gremlin and Carl watched everyone and Janie...Janie just kept her eye on the new girl.

There was something between them that was unspoken. At least on Janie's side of things. What had been sympathy and understanding was blossoming into something along the lines of jealousy and you could plainly see it in her eyes. Women sometimes got territorial, I knew, without meaning to. And I was sensing that in Janie.

She had competition now. And she didn't look like she cared for the idea.

Mickey was an interesting girl. There was no doubt about that. Not just easy on the eyes, but smart. Maybe she'd never be invited into Mensa or win the Nobel Prize for physics, but what she lacked in book smarts she more than made up for in practical schooling. And intuition. She had an almost sixth sense where danger was concerned. Something we all soon learned about.

After our impromptu luncheon, it was out into the streets again. It would be dark in a few hours and I wanted the Jeep before that happened. Mickey led the way, knowing exactly where we had to go. She barely made it to the end of the block before she stopped dead and started shaking her head back and forth.

"What is it?" I asked her.

"I don't know...something's wrong. I can feel it," she said. "Something's wrong."

Texas Slim and Carl just looked at each other.

"She's giving me the willies," Carl said.

"That ain't what she gives me," Gremlin said.

Mickey shrugged. "Sometimes...sometimes I just sense things before they happen."

Texas laughed nervously. "Had a grandmother on my mother's side, a Taney from Terrabonne County. Swamp country. She had the gift, too. Oh...she was old, old, old, was old Mother Taney. Had but two or three working teeth and a narrow face, big old nose looked like a coat hook. One eye was bad...lost it when she was a child in an unpleasant spearfishing accident...but the other was just big and round, kind of yellow and staring. Made her look like that witch in the old comic book...you know the one I mean? Gave me the creepy-crawlies, it did, that staring yellow eye. One day she says, Whet yee looking fowa, booy? Cause that's how she talked. I says, I lost my socks, Mother Tee...that's what I called her. *Mother Tee.* She says, Thems socks bee out yondah the sweetgoom, hear? And they was. Right where I left them by the sweetgum. Couple weevils made a home in them, but that was all. She had the sight and she could find anything, anytime—"

"Quiet," I told him. I knew Texas was just nervous and whenever he was nervous he started telling wild tales, but now was not the time. "What is it, Mickey?"

Everyone was waiting and Janie was getting perturbed, liking the new girl a little bit less all the time. The poison between them was thickening away on the back burner.

Mickey turned and looked at me. She was pale beneath her tan, her eyes huge and wet. "Clans. The Clans are coming."

To which Carl immediately disagreed...but then he heard it. We all heard it.

Heard them coming.

Six or seven rose up from behind the hulks of smashed vehicles, screeching and wailing. It was an ambush. I was certain of that. A carefully staged ambush of the sort that the Clans were so very good at. But for some reason...they just couldn't wait.

Maybe it was that Mickey had somehow sensed them out there and stopped everyone in the street. Maybe they'd known the gig was up.

But now they were waiting no more. They charged from their hides, screaming and hissing. They ran in zig-zagging patterns through the street, just insane and bloodthirsty.

"Son...of...a...bitch," Carl said.

I brought my Savage up and dropped two of them. When a third got in range, Carl opened up with his AK and stitched him...or her...or *it,* crotch to throat. They were merciless, these things. Remorseless, relentless. For even when they squirmed dying in the streets, riddled with bullets, they still fought and shrieked. Only a couple of them carried crude weapons...clubs and spears. Carl and I dropped all but two, but it wasn't going to be enough. For these few had only been the spearhead. The others were coming now.

A beat-up pick-up truck came rambling down the street, glancing off dead vehicles and bouncing over drifts of sand. There were two Clansmen in the cab and a dozen more in the back. I saw them, swallowed, figured I knew what the Romans must have felt like when the Picts came at them.

Berserkers.

That's what they were. Every one of them just psychotic and vicious.

They hopped from the truck while it was still moving and fanned out into the street. They looked much like the dead one we had found. They were all bald with warrior scalplocks, distorted faces hidden behind gas masks. They wore flapping overcoats and leather trenchcoats, jackets that were stitched patchworks of other coats, even what looked like ponchos made from tarps. They swarmed forward, brandishing homemade spears, spiked clubs, axes and pikes and, yes, hatchets.

We laid down a volley of fire and then got the hell out.

We ran for our dear lives like spooked rabbits. It was all confusing and there was no cohesion whatsoever. Should we make our stand in a building? On a rooftop? Behind a wrecked car? In the end we found ourselves back in the vicinity of Fisher's little commune, which was now a commune of corpses. We spread out, armed, and got ready.

The truck came storming forward and I sighted on it, put a couple rounds right through the windshield. It blew into the cab in a spiderwebbed mass of candy glass. The passenger slumped over and the driver jammed on the gas.

I sighted again. I knew the only weapon that would work from this range was my .30.06. This was my baby. Maybe I could have passed the rifle to Carl but Carl was behind a station wagon on the other side of the street. There just wasn't the time.

"Nash," somebody said.

I breathed in and out. Sighted. Squeezed the trigger with a half-assed prayer brushing past my lips. I caught the driver in the throat, I thought. He snapped back in his seat, hands flying from the wheel trying to stem the flow of blood from his neck. The truck went out of control, bouncing off a minivan, and spinning up onto the sidewalk and ramming the remains of a police patrol car. And there she died.

The driver struggled out and Texas ran up on him and blew him away with the .50 cal Desert Eagle. But the others were coming.

As they got in closer, I saw it was true what they said about these animals. They *did* wear the scalps of their victims. They wore them in scarves and belts. And not just those things, but necklaces of blackened ears and teeth strung on wires, a wide and gruesome collection of mummified body parts.

Carl dropped two with his AK and it was just sheer pandemonium as we all cried out, firing, pouring everything we had at our attackers whose numbers were swelling as more of them came running down the street. Already, eight or ten of them were down and writhing and they'd been replaced by twice that many. Even Janie was shooting with the Browning .45. Mickey had Carl's .22 Airweight.

One of them got with twenty feet of our position by crawling underneath some cars and I popped him right in the face. The slug went right in through one of the plexiglass eye ports and the Clansman was thrown up against a truck. But he did not go down. He took three or four shambling, zombie-like steps forward, bright red blood spouting from the entry wound and then went down, face-first.

Others closed in.

One jumped on top of a truck and threw his spear. It barely missed Janie. Carl blew him away. I ran out of rounds and had to switch to my Beretta 9mm. I shot one and then another and then something clubbed me in the back and I went down. I hit the ground and twisted away just as an axe bit into the pavement where I'd been. I jumped up and emptied the Beretta into my attacker and then another jumped me, tossed me against the car. He lashed out with a knife and I just avoided it, kicking him in the belly and hammering his scabby bald head with the butt of the Beretta until something gave in there with a wet snapping.

Carl emptied his AK and starting blasting away with his Mossberg. Texas Slim was hit with a spear in the side and went down. Gremlin was beaten down with a club. Mickey fired her Airweight, jumping around with great athletic grace and popping them one after the other and then she was out of ammo and two of them grabbed her. She fought and kicked and they slammed her face-down on the hood of a car. They were going to rape her then and there because that's how the Clans operated...not with military precision or organization, but with sheer mania.

Carl blew one of them away with the Mossberg, scattering his guts for twenty feet and, dropping and turning, wasted another. Then three of them knocked him down and it was all over as they raised their hatchets.

But Janie grabbed an axe from one of the dying ones and buried it in the back of a Clansman. He spun around, axe sunk in his back and smashed her with his fist. She went down and he leaped on top of her, tearing away her shirt, her white breasts exposed. He grabbed them with his filthy, pocked hands.

"JANIE!" I cried out.

And then I was in the mix. I ran and punted the Clansman in the head like I was kicking the winning field goal and the Clansman rolled away, limp as a rag. Then I leaped, diving, and took out two more like bowling pins, jumping to my feet and kicking one of them until they were no longer moving.

Then I took up Carl's dropped Mossberg and cracked another in the face hard enough to rip the gasmask right off him. He stood there, his face like a fleshy, grinning skull covered in clots of oozing white jelly. Mickey hit him from behind with a club and his skull cracked with an audible snapping. I gave him the butt of the Mossberg full in the face and down he went. Four Clansman were left and they came on screaming and swinging chains and throwing hatchets.

And that's when the birds came.

18

There was a sudden wild squawking and chirping and trilling and we all looked skyward. Even the Clansmen. Except there was no sky. Above the surrounding buildings it was black and the air was thrumming with the flapping of hundreds of thundering wings. Janie was on her feet, zipping her coat shut and covering herself when they came. I threw myself at her, knocking her down as two- or three-hundred birds came swooping down in a single shrilling mass. There was nothing to do but cover my face and roll into a ball, covering Janie's body with my own.

The birds came down.

The world was a cacophonous storm of cawing and pounding wings. I felt them beating around me, feathers filling the air. Beaks pecked me, clawed feet tore my skin. There were so many I could not breathe. I was going to suffocate in feathers and bird shit. As I lay there with Janie, I thought I heard her scream and I was certain I did. I was gasping for breath. Crying out as beaks drilled into me again and again. With one hand I swatted at them and they pecked away at my palm, my fingers until they stung and bled. The air was thick with them, with that awful humming and fluttering and squawking.

And about the time my mind began to unreel from the crowding of birds, the feel of oily feathers and nipping beaks and the gagging stench of dander and rot...they lifted. They pulled away and were gone.

Then I looked finally. They weren't gone at all.

They were attacking the Clansmen.

It was incredible but it was happening. Something about them had drawn the birds. I saw ravens and crows, buzzards and even a few huge vultures, as well as mutated forms with greasy green wings and scaly, knobbed heads, leering red eyes and hooked beaks that almost looked like sickles. They went right after the Clansmen and clawed them with their feet and pecked away at their gas masks, their mottled heads and yellowed hands. They hit them from every direction.

One of them tried to run with twenty or thirty birds on him, some circling and dipping in for attack, but most clinging tight and pecking away mercilessly. He looked like some kind of contorted, grotesque scarecrow that was finally getting his due from the birds he had frightened away for so long. He finally went down and the birds settled over him, pecking him until he was writhing red meat. I was astounded and I was pretty sure the others were, too.

Another Clansman who'd been making a pretty good show of himself by batting away birds with a swinging chain, their broken bodies littered at his feet, suddenly let out a piercing, guttural cry and...*disappeared.* He vanished as a flock of birds simply enveloped him. The crows and buzzards and the rest just kept cawing and squawking as their beaks rose and fell, coming away stained red, yanking out strings of tissue. It was an appalling sight. When he was down, crushing a few of his attackers beneath him, the birds kept at it, crowding in, fighting for space like piglets at their mother's teats. The sound of the Clansman being stripped was simply awful...moist tearing sounds and crunching noises and pulpy hammering as beaks dug deeper for hot goodies.

It went on for about twenty minutes. We did not move. We didn't dare.

After a time, many of the birds flew off, but most stayed and discovered the corpses and remains of Fisher's people and began to feast. And that's when I figured it out. *Of course.* What did vultures and buzzards, crows and ravens have in common? They were carrion-eaters. That's probably why they had come in such numbers in the first place...to feed on all the corpses in the streets. But when they came—separate species flocking together for reasons I could not hope to guess at—they discovered the Hatchet Clans. They decided they looked tasty.

But why was that?

The Clansmen were hideously infected and disfigured by some creeping fungus, but they were certainly not dead, not soft and greening. But there was something that attracted the flock.

Something.

The birds were still everywhere, happily feeding, fighting amongst themselves for the tastiest bits, but they were paying no attention to my posse.

"All right," I called out in a calm, cool, non-threatening tone of voice. "We're going to leave now. Just everyone stand up and follow me out of here. I'll get up first."

Tensing, I slowly got to my feet, breathing nice and slow, trying not to gag on the stink of the carrion birds or what they were eating. A raven flew over my head, unconcerned. A huge buzzard pulled a stringy red flap of meat from a corpse's neck, chewed it down, and made a sharp hissing sound at me. Its jaws yawned wide and it hissed again, then it got back down to its meal. I started breathing again.

The Clansman were nearly reduced to skeletons by this point. The one that had tried to run wasn't much more than that. A raven was pecking through a gash in the gas mask, tearing out pink scraps while a pair of crows sat atop the bloody exposed ribcage, spreading their wings now and then, cawing, and digging out some juicy morsel overlooked.

Around me, the others began to get up. Very, very slowly. They were seeing that they were dead center of the feeding grounds now. The birds were everywhere. Lined up atop wrecked cars and trucks like soldiers in ranks. Flying though the air, circling high above and not very high above at all. Buzzards walked around with chunks of red, ragged meat hanging in their jaws. Vultures were pecking their entire heads into the body cavities of sprawled corpses, shaking their entire bodies as they ripped at something within. When they pulled their heads free, savagely gulping down morsels, they were red and dripping.

I led my people forward, thinking the whole time, *this is either gonna work or we're all about to die in the worst way imaginable.*

But I did not hesitate. Years back, in Youngstown, I'd known a guy named Roger Sweed who worked at the zoo with the big cats. He claimed that when you had to deal with them you never showed fear. When you were in their areas you had to act like you belonged there. So that's what I was doing now: just threading my way amongst the corpses and birds, being perfectly casual and disinterested in what they were doing. Which was not real easy when a raven plucked an eye out and stood there watching me, the eyeball dangling from its beak by the optic nerve.

I walked on, my empty Savage in one hand and Janie's hand in the other.

There was bird shit and feathers everywhere, scattered bits of human, dead birds lying in tangled heaps and others dragging injured wings that scampered away as I approached.

Birds squawked at me, but I ignored them. I moved through breaks in their ranks, paying no attention to the ones that flew just over my head. Flies lit off corpses and scattered limbs and viscera, huge buzzing clouds of them. They droned at my ears and crawled over my neck but I did not swat at them. The entire time I thought the birds would attack at any moment.

But they never did.

19

"It'll be dark in an hour," I said, as we paused to reload our weapons, hiding out in a trashed pharmacy.

Carl looked around the devastated city. "So we better find somewhere to lay low for the night."

"Shit, shit, shit," Gremlin said. "I thought we were going to be out of here. Somewhere else. Fuck."

Using the U.S. Army medical pack I'd gotten from Sean, I attended to Texas Slim's spear wound. It was a nasty looking gash across his ribs, but hardly fatal. I disinfected it, closed it with a couple butterfly bandages, taped a sterile battlefield dressing over it, and gave him a shot of antibiotics just to be safe. He'd be sore for a few days but nothing more.

Janie was off looting through the store. She was gone quite awhile. When she got back there was a funny look in her eyes.

"Where you been?" I said.

"Just looking around," she told me. She was lying and I knew it. But I wouldn't realize how big of a lie it was until much, much later.

"Why don't we keep going...we have guns," Mickey said. "Within an hour, I think, we can be at the garage with the Jeep. Why wait until tomorrow?"

Texas Slim grinned. "Because when it gets dark, child, out come the oogies and the boogies and the things that go bump in the night."

"Let's risk it," she said. "We get that Jeep we can be out of Gary in twenty minutes."

"Why don't you just do us all a favor and shut up?" Janie said.

"Take it easy, Janie," I told her.

Her eyes were not just blue at that moment but glacial. "Jesus Christ, Nash. She's been with us a few hours and she's calling the shots? Who the hell asked for her advice anyway?"

Mickey shrugged. "I was just saying."

"Oh, shut up."

They stood there, staring at each other while I was getting annoyed and Texas Slim and Carl were silently amused and Gremlin was practically in heat. "Hey," he said. "Just like Roller Derby. We're gonna have us a cat fight. Out come the claws! Fur is gonna fly!"

"Why don't you go fuck yourself?" Mickey told him.

"No, I wasn't thinking about fucking myself. I was thinking about fucking somebody else."

I got in there then. God knows I'd had enough of that fucking idiot by then. I shoved Gremlin and put him on his ass. "Knock it the hell off. What did I tell you about that shit?" I had a sudden desire to throw him another beating. The only time that asshole took a break from whining and complaining was to start panting over one of the girls. "Keep it in your fucking pants. Christ."

I turned and saw that Mickey was smiling at me like I'd come to her rescue and I also saw that Janie was steaming. The green-eyed monster was out of its cage.

"Let's all just settle down here, okay?" I said to them. "We're not going to accomplish anything like this."

Gremlin got up, brushing dust off himself. His face was still bruised from the last time we'd tangled. He touched his fingertips to a purple welt under his eye that was slowly fading. "Sure, Nash. I got ya. We got to keep our new girl nice and fresh, eh?" He winked. "Our friend don't want damaged goods, do he?"

"Here we go again," Carl said.

"What the hell is he talking about?" Mickey wanted to know.

Texas Slim hooked her by the arm and led her away. "Nothing to worry about, my dear. You see, many years ago, Gremlin's mother took a large healthy shit and fell quite in love with one of the turds she saw in the bowl. So she nursed it and fed it and brought it up and the result of that you see standing over there."

Carl burst out laughing.

We all did...except for Janie and Gremlin himself.

Sighing, I led them outside.

It was about that time that I noticed we had an audience. At first, I went for my gun...but then lowered it. There was a man standing not fifteen feet away on the sidewalk. He was naked except for an outrageous cranberry bathrobe that was hanging open, his business on full display. His fingernails and toenails were both painted purple.

"Boy howdy," Texas said to him. "Join the party?"

The guy just stared at us. He had a brilliant, fluffy head of trailing blonde locks. He also had a beard that was more white than gray.

Texas Slim had no fear of crazy people. He went over to the guy and tied his bathrobe shut for him. "The ladies, you understand," he said, pressing a hand to his wound.

The guy had a phonebook under his arm. He pointed down the street and said, "They came in silver buses. I saw 'em. They had orange suits on. They took Reverend Bob and threw him in the bus. I saw it happen. I saw lots of things happen. I wrote all down in my book here." He showed us the phonebook, shrugged. "I ate my dog because I was hungry."

Carl laughed in his throat and turned away. "Who's the fucking Gomer?"

"Pay no attention to Carl," Texas Slim said. "He hasn't had a serious romantic encounter since his dear mother passed."

"Kiss my ass," Carl said.

Bathrobe wandered away down the street. Texas called to him, but he kept going.

"Want me to grab him?" Carl whispered.

"Why?"

"You know why. It's almost time."

"Let him go. I'm tired of this shit."

I started walking again, Mickey at my side.

"Where are we going?" Janie said.

"To find that Jeep."

"Tonight?"

"Why not?"

She just shook her head and Mickey grinned. We walked in silence, Texas Slim and Carl out front with their guns keeping an eye on things. I was thinking about everything and trying hard not to. We trudged on, getting closer to the river. In the distance I could see the mills and refineries Gary was famous for. A few birds circled in the sky and sand blew over the roads in a fine spray. We went over a grassy hill, crossed railroad tracks, cut through some wilted thickets and then before us, stretching in all directions, a great blackened pit.

It was full of bodies.

20

Well, *bodies* was not exactly accurate, for the pit was actually filled with skeletons that had once *been* bodies. There was nothing fresh down there. Just what looked like thousands of skeletons heaped and broken, disjointed and blackened. There was ash everywhere. The pit stretched easily for three city blocks in either direction, as far as I could tell.

"Must've burned 'em here," Mickey said. "I saw a pit like this outside Allentown."

Texas Slim nodded. "The germs and fallout must have been very bad here. Too close to Chicago. They must have dumped them here and torched them. Judging by the ashes everywhere, I'd say it went on for some time."

I saw that it wasn't just bones down there, but the wrecked hulks of cars and trucks. Lots of things had been dumped down there. It was a junkyard.

"You didn't know this was here?" Janie asked Mickey.

"No...how would I?"

"Well, you led us right to it."

"So what?"

"So, you're leading us to that Jeep. You know where it is. You didn't know this was here?"

"No, I didn't. I came out here once. But not on foot. We were on the road north of here, on the other side of the river. I-ninety."

Janie did not look satisfied and I knew I had to get the show rolling again here or another fight would break out. My little group was getting frustrated, tired. They needed something to set their sights on. That's why I was going after the Jeep now rather than wait until tomorrow. At least, that was one of the reasons. The need to keep moving west was getting very strong, you see.

The sun was hovering just over the horizon now. I saw that there was a trail cut through the pit and up the other side. If we tried to go around, it would probably be dark by the time we hit the river.

"Let's go," I said.

"Down *there?*" Gremlin said. "I'm not going down into that cemetery."

"Then you can stay behind."

I started down, moving easy so I didn't go sliding on the sand. Pebbles and loose rocks went rolling into the bone pit. The others fell in behind me without a word. Gremlin, too. It must have been a quarry or sandpit at one time that had been abandoned and then opened back up, enlarged, when thousands were dying by the day and infectious disease was burning hot through the city.

The hillsides were littered with stray skeletons wrapped in threadbare rags. They were rising from the sand, their bones so white they looked luminous. As we neared the bottom, I noticed there were great jagged slabs of slag everywhere along with sections of broken concrete that looked to have been part of sidewalks at one time. Ancient lengths of cement drainage conduits rose from the refuse along with rusted staffs of rebar and old porcelain sewer piping that must have been down there for decades and decades. Sure, first it had been a quarry, then a junk pit, then a body dump.

The shadows grew long and I felt Janie slide her hand in mine and I was glad for the feel of it. I gripped it tightly. Things rustled in pockets of spreading dark. Birds winged from one wrecked vehicle to the next. A rat stood atop a rusting engine block, watching us pass. The trail wound through the wreckage and bones, zig-zagging this way and that. Somebody had beat the trail through so it was definitely in use.

But I bet they don't go down here after dark.

I kept going as night settled in. There were things jutting from the shadows everywhere. I tripped over a curled piece of rebar and almost went down. I dug a flashlight from my back. Working batteries were getting scarce now, but I didn't like the idea of gutting myself on jagged metal.

"Nice place," Texas Slim said.

"Yeah, nice place to die," Gremlin added.

I fanned my flashlight around, picking out old refrigerators and heaps of tires, the rusted and pitted remains of an old swingset rising from the sand. And bones, of course. They were everywhere. The light glanced off ribcages and femurs and spinal columns. And skulls. Dozens and dozens of jawless skulls that had been picked clean. Bones rose up in great ramparts through which rats scurried.

When we hit dead center of the pit there was really nothing but skeletons. Some still dressed in rags and articulated, but most blackened and broken and tossed around. I started seeing a lot of small bones and skulls which must have belonged to kids. As we cut around some termite-pitted dock pilings, there was a little baby buggy with weeds growing up through it. I put the light on it out of some ghoulish curiosity and saw that the carriage was all rusted and black, the bonnet burned to flaps. Inside there was a tiny skeleton with jaws wide in a scream.

"Oh God," Mickey said.

More derelict cars and piping, bones and shattered hills of concrete. I was moving everyone along faster now, needing to get out of there. Maybe it was nerves and maybe it was something else but I was getting very apprehensive. It felt like there were needles in my belly. I was sweating. I could feel the beat of my heart at my temples. Rats squeaked and bats winged overhead.

"We should find the trail up and out in a couple minutes," I said, either to reassure the others or myself.

"I hope so," Mickey said. "I don't think we should be down here."

"Oh, shut up," Janie told her. "Don't be so damn dramatic—"

But her words were cut right off...for somewhere out in the shivering darkness that filled the pit like the blackest oil, there rose up a roaring which sounded positively primeval.

"I'm guessing we're fucked here," Texas Slim said.

21

The roaring came again and this time it was closer.

And there was a smell on the night breeze: sharp and vile like rotting hides piled in heaps.

It became a matter then of making a run for it or standing and fighting. The beast was out there and I figured it was the same one we'd heard last night. I had the most unpleasant feeling that it had been following us, scenting us across the city. Maybe that was just my imagination working overtime, but I had the strangest feeling that it was right.

"What do you think, boss?" Carl said.

"Let's go," Janie said. "Please, Nash."

There were a few other mutterings on the subject, but the one person who seemed to have no opinion was Gremlin. The first to complain, the first to bitch, the first to interject his opinion on any subject...but now he had nothing to say. Sure, maybe he was scared but I was not so sure.

"Let's draw it in and fucking waste it," Mickey said.

And that's what I was leaning towards. I just didn't like the idea of making a run for it with that thing...whatever it was...at our backs. It was stalking us. And only now had it announced its presence because it had us here in this pit and it knew we were not going to escape.

"C'mon, Nash, this is crazy," Janie said, just riven with fear. "Let's just—"

"Sshhh," I told her.

Nobody spoke; they just listened now.

The beast was coming. We could all hear it picking its way towards us in the darkness. The crackling of leaves and sticks, the crunch of bones, the thudding footsteps of something very large like an ogre in a fairy story coming out of a dark wood to eat children.

Another sound now...a grunting, sniffing sound like a rooting hog.

I didn't bother using the flashlight. Not yet. It knew where we were and it was coming. I'd wait until it got in close, close enough to shoot. I motioned the others forward to some concrete pilings. They got behind them and spread out, guns held in sweating, shaking fingers. And there we waited as that monstrosity out there edged in closer, stealthy like a jungle cat hunting its prey. There was so much junk and refuse in the pit that there were dark shapes rising all around us. Everyone watched, waiting for one that moved. I thought more than once that I saw some hunched-over shaggy form of immense proportions.

Maybe it was my imagination.

We waited for five minutes, then ten, sweating bullets. Everyone was tense. There was nothing but the sound of our breathing, the distant sound of wild dogs barking, tiny creatures rustling amongst the wreckage.

I kept my .30.06 up and ready. Janie was trembling next to me only I didn't feel it so much because I was trembling myself.

"Anybody in the mood for a nice quiet ghost story?" Texas Slim said.

"Shut up." I sighed. "I think someone should go have a look. How about you, Gremlin?"

"Fuck that. I ain't going out there."

"You afraid?" Texas Slim said. "You didn't seem afraid of that thing last night."

And it would have been interesting to hear Gremlin's rebuttal to that, but a wild screeching noise came scraping out of the darkness and it sounded almost like laughter...shrill, hysterical laughter. The laughter of something that grew fat on fear and sharpened its teeth on human bones. The stink was overbearing...high and hot. I thought I saw two huge eyes shaped like crescent moons reflected out there.

"It's coming and we're going to kill it," I said.

I tried to swallow but my throat was so dry that my tongue stuck to the roof of my mouth. Something moved out there. Something made a hoarse guttural noise that became a slobbering sound like the beast was drooling.

"Get ready," I whispered.

I couldn't have imagined a more tense, threatening situation. That ugly bastard out there, whatever in the Christ it was, had our number. It had been following our trail and now it had us right where it wanted us. Yet...it was hesitating out there. It could have jumped out at us at any time and started killing, but it didn't. It was cautious. Careful. Predators were like that. They wanted the upper hand. Even a tiger in the jungle or a great white shark in the surf aren't as gutsy as most people think. They want to take their prey, *yes*, but they want to do as easy as possible without harming themselves. And like them, this creature wanted a sure thing, a clean kill, the upper hand. I could almost sense its hesitation out there.

"Come on, you fucker," Carl said under his breath.

The waiting was hell. We couldn't go on like that. We had what I thought was a perfect killzone: sheltered by the concrete pilings, there was a sandy clearing right in front of us and wreckage piled up in a rampart behind. If that thing wanted us, it'd have to charge through the clearing. And I wanted it to do that. What I didn't want was to play cat and mouse with that fucking horror. I didn't want it sneaking in on our flank or getting ahead of us and lying in wait when we tried to make our escape. No, we had to draw it in.

"We have to bait it in," I said. "Gremlin, take a walk out into that clearing."

"Fuck you," he said.

"Why not, Gremlin?" Texas Slim said. "He won't hurt you, will he? You're his friend."

At the moment what Texas was getting at did not occur to me, but later I understood perfectly: we had been set up. Gremlin had set us up.

"Give me the AK," I told Carl. I handed him the Savage. "I'm going out there."

Janie's hand on my arm was like an electrical wire juicing with current. I had to pry it loose.

"No, Nash," she said. "*Rick...*"

"I don't think that's a good idea," Mickey said.

Nobody did except, of course, Gremlin. But it had to be done. "Carl? I'm going to draw it in. Aim for its head, its eyes. Killshot."

Carl got ready with the Savage.

Texas said, "Still say we send Gremlin here."

"No, not him," I said. "We're going to need him tomorrow night when the moon comes up."

He made a whimpering sound in his throat because he thought I had just selected him. Maybe I had, but if so then I'd selected him many days before. I said it mainly to shake him and it worked just fine.

I stepped out into the clearing with the AK. My knees were shaking. Beads of sweat rolled down my face. Yet, despite the fact that I was ready to have kittens, I walked out there very casually. I did not even hold the AK up; I kept it at my side as if I didn't have a care in the world. I reached into my breast pocket, took out a cigarette and lit it. I was shaking, but I was doing everything I could to give the impression that I was perfectly at ease. Then I waited. The holes in my plan were many. If that thing had sniffed us across the city, then like any other predator it might be able to smell the fear on me. If it was intelligent—and I suspected as much—then it might suspect the trap I had laid. All I had going for me, I thought, was the fact that it wanted us bad. And such animal desires often cancel out common sense.

I had almost finished my cigarette when I sensed, rather than heard, motion out there. A chill went up my spine and there was a sudden hot, reeking stench of putrescence that nearly put me to my knees. Then it charged, leaping out of the shadows. I had a momentary glimpse of something massive, muscular, and distorted. I threw myself backward and a split second after my ass hit the ground I opened up with the AK on full auto, just spraying rounds into the shadows.

I saw it clearly as it came at me in the moonlight.

I saw my rounds pepper its chest, saw it flinch and draw back. It was much larger than a man and I don't think I'm exaggerating when I say it stood eight feet in height. A hulking thing with skin like oily leather, threadbare with twisted tufts of gray hair or bristles. Its misshapen hide was split open in a dozen places with knobs and rungs of bone protruding out. A mutant. One arm was longer than the other, the right shoulder high and ridged, the left almost flat, the chest a rack of bones. It lacked any sort of body symmetry.

And it had claws, huge curving claws.

It moved with incredible speed. Carl fired and missed and in that split second, it jumped at me, standing over me. I could feel the acrid, pungent heat rolling off it in waves. Smell the rank decay of its hide. Tiny crawling things fell off it and skittered over my face and bare arms.

I heard Janie scream, Mickey cry out, Texas shout.

It looked down at me and why I didn't fire the AK again I did not know. I guess I froze. Its face was an obscenity: gray and seamed, almost like some demonic version of a wild boar with a flattened snout and huge maw filled with gnarled yellow teeth and what might have been tusks. One eye was huge and staring and the other drawn into a slit, everything out of sync.

The way it stared at me with those glistening red eyes, I got the sense that, yes, it was going to kill me, but it would not be a quick, merciful affair. My death would be sport. Amusement. Like a cat torturing a mouse. No more, no less.

I remember wondering why Carl didn't shoot again, thinking that this had been going on for minutes. But later they told me that it was probably less than five seconds from the time I went on my ass to when it stood over me.

Then Carl did fire.

He caught the beast right in the head, his round right on target despite the shadows. It punched through that slit eye and exited with a spray of meat and blood. It was a killshot. A perfect fucking killshot. That thing should have fallen over dead as a stump. But it didn't. The impact of the bullet tossed it backwards and it stumbled for a few feet, but instead of dying it raised its taloned hands to the sky, threw back its head and let out a shrieking cry that nearly deafened me. It wasn't a roar or a baying, nothing like that. Not the sort of thing you'd expect from a monster like that. No, it was a high, piercing wail that sounded very much like a woman in utter anguish. Inhuman, yet definitely female.

Then it darted into the shadows.

By that time I was crawling madly towards the concrete pillars and hands found me and yanked me to my feet. I was nearly delirious with terror. It took me a moment to screw my head on straight.

"Let's get the hell out of here," I finally said.

Mickey instantly took charge. With a flashlight borrowed from Carl she found the trail and led us out of there. Texas Slim was at her side with his Desert Eagle. They got us through that maze of bones and junk and found the trail leading up the hillside. Carl and I took up the back door, Janie and Gremlin sandwiched in-between.

Out in the enshrouding darkness of the pit we could hear the thing.

It was wailing with that shrill unearthly sound, its voice echoing out all around us. It seemed to come from behind us, then off to the left, then the right. We stopped dead twice in our climb because it sounded like it was right in front of us. It must have been the echo. Once, when we paused, I swore that I heard it sobbing out there pitifully. Then, seconds later, there came a maniacal screeching that went right up my spine and that, too, dissolved into a cold, dry, hysterical laughter like the braying of a hyena.

We kept moving up the sheer face of the hill, Mickey's light picking out skulls and ribcages, a few fully articulated skeletons in rags rising from the sand. Half way up we heard more of that grisly, fragmented laughter and it was directly behind us. There was no doubt of it. We froze again, weapons drawn.

It was there, but we couldn't see it.

The moonlight in the pit was uneven with all that heaped refuse down there casting jagged shadows in every direction. Every time we heard a noise, our flashlights revealed nothing.

But it was coming. Getting closer, tightening the noose around us.

We came to a halt, bunching together in a circle, weapons pointing in all directions. But on whose flank it would attack, we did not know. My mouth was dry as sawdust. I couldn't even summon the spit to swallow. It felt like every muscle and tendon in my body had drawn tight like wires.

We heard it, seemingly in several different directions.

It was casting around out there, cat and mouse. I heard things crunching like it had stepped on skulls and crushed them flat. Something huge fell over and the ground shook. I felt the stomping of its feet. A section of cement pipe came flying out of the darkness, whooshing right over our heads and impaling itself in the hillside.

"This is fucking bullshit," Carl said, his voice weak with a sort of manic desperation I'd never heard in it before.

"Quiet," Texas told him

The pit was silent as a crypt suddenly. I could hear the others breathing but nothing else. Sweat rolled down my neck. I could feel the heat rising from the others. It was close, the beast was close. I knew that much. It had been playing games with us, trying to drive us into a state of absolute fear and it had succeeded quite well. Now the end game was at hand. Mickey scanned her light around with a trembling hand and picked out nothing but bones, broken slabs of pavement, the rusting hulk of an old stove. Suddenly, the air was thick with a sickening stench like spoiled meat.

The beast came leaping out of the shadows, roaring with primeval appetite.

We shot at it, but it was like trying to kill a ghost. It was there. And then it was not. Panic set in and we just scrambled madly up the hillside. Mickey led the way, Texas right behind her. Gremlin knocked me aside and then grabbed Janie and tossed her back. She lost her balance and rolled ten or fifteen feet down the hillside.

"Take her!" Gremlin cried. *"Take her and leave us alone! She's the one you want!"*

I went after Janie and Carl went after Gremlin. I heard them tussling. Heard screams and cries. I pulled Janie up and fired into the darkness where I heard the beast. As I led Janie back up, I saw that Carl had Gremlin on the ground. Gremlin was screaming and crying and Carl was drilling him in the face. By the time I reached him, he had yanked Gremlin to his feet. Then, grabbing him by the hair and the back of his jacket, he lifted him right up and threw him. Gremlin went airborne about five feet, hit the ground rolling. He rolled right down to the bottom and when he finally stopped he let out a demented scream that was about as close to raw insanity as I've ever heard.

We saw him in the moonlight.

Just as we saw the grotesque figure standing over him. The beast picked him up with very little effort, hoisting him over its head and shaking him like an offering to the cold moon above. He was squirming, crying, screaming. If I hadn't have hated that bastard so much at that point, I might have felt sorry for him. The beast brought him down on a sawtoothed plate of exposed metal. His scream ended instantly with a wet, shearing sound.

We ran up the hillside and out of the pit in record time.

Behind us, we could hear the sounds of Gremlin being battered to a pulp.

Thirty minutes later we saw the bridge. It stretched about half a mile over the Calumet River and the railroad tracks below. It was a steel bridge with two high arches near the center, sagging and twisted like it had withstood an airstrike. Maybe it had. I estimated that it was probably a good hundred foot drop to the river below. The closer we got to it the more we all saw the wreckage: mangled girders, blackened uprights, overhead beams sheared and hanging, the whole thing crowded with debris, smashed cars and trucks. Everything from big semis to minivans. It almost looked like they had been driven up on the bridge to form some kind of barricade. Many of them were charred.

As we neared it, Janie said, "Are you sure this thing is stable?'

Mickey nodded. "It doesn't look like much, but it's safe."

I don't think any of us were very reassured. It looked like some kind of war had been fought up there and not that long ago. In my mind, the bridge was the monstrous exoskeleton of some gigantic insect, shattered and broken and rawboned, just waiting to fall into the polluted depths of the river below.

I checked Texas Slim's wound by flashlight, just to see if all the commotion had torn it open but it was okay. So on we went.

Mickey led the way, seeming to know it quite well as she slipped around the burnt hulks of cars, trucks, and nameless machinery. We saw quite a few skeletons, some cremated behind the wheels of vehicles and others scattered underfoot, birdpicked and disjointed. It was like a graveyard. My flashlight picked out more than one skeleton that was punctured with bullet holes and that made me certain that a war *was* fought up here, or at the very least dozens of small skirmishes. Several trucks had burst through the railing and hung precariously on the edge, their noses pointed out into the misting blackness. A sluggish, gray-green fog with the consistency of ectoplasm drifted over the river below. Now and then there was an opening in it and I could see the wrecks of vehicles rising from the murky, stinking water.

Mickey continued to lead us on, threading us through the wreckage. Five minutes into it, both Carl and I lit cigarettes to calm our nerves. "You know she could be leading us into a trap, don't you?" he whispered to me as he cupped a match to light my smoke.

It had occurred to me, of course.

A sleek, attractive woman like her. How easy it would have been for her to draw in men and then use their own raging hormones and that very male need to protect women—especially sexy ones—against them. But I didn't really doubt her. I had a good feeling about her. Maybe her motives weren't entirely altruistic, but then again whose were? I did not get the sort of bad feeling from her I'd gotten from Gremlin after he hooked back up with us. And that had probably not been any sixth sense on my part, but maybe an intuition planted in my head by The Shape.

We walked on.

The bridge canted slowly upward and leveled out beneath the arches where it ran flat for about two city blocks before canting back down to the other bank. The closer we got to the arches, the more wrecked vehicles I saw. The entire thing was nothing but a vast junkyard. It made me nervous. With all that scrap metal lying around, we could have walked right into an ambush at any moment. It would have been tricky in full daylight, but at night...just death waiting to happen.

So when Janie stopped walking and said, "I think there's something out there," I was not really surprised. Maybe I'd been feeling it for awhile, too, telling myself that it was nothing but shellshock, post-traumatic stress from our encounter with the beast. But as I stopped, yes, I was feeling it, too.

Carl and Texas looked around, then looked at each other. They were not convinced.

"I don't see anything," I said. "Maybe you got the jitters."

"Sure," Texas Slim said.

"No, it's not that," Janie assured us.

Mickey was hugging herself, looking troubled. "She's right, Nash. I feel it, too. Like a hundred eyes are staring at me."

Well, by that point I had learned to trust Mickey's intuition. Janie's was pretty well developed, too, but Mickey's was practically a sixth sense. I decided we'd wait a moment. We got up by the arches, sidled around a fuel tanker, and then kept an eye on what was beneath us, that strip of bridge running back towards the bank we'd just left. The moon had abandoned us. It was rafting through clouds high above. The tension inside me was like hot metal. I was waiting for the moon to come back out. Without it, all those cars stretching out below were just shadows heaped upon shadows.

"Let's move," Carl said.

"Wait," I told him. "Just a few more minutes."

A few more minutes became five and then ten before the moon broke free of the clouds up there and illuminated the bridge. I saw the wrecked vehicles, but I also saw other shapes down there in-between. I thought one of them moved.

I handed Carl my Savage. "You see that minivan with the crushed-in side? Right there by the Land Rover? There's a shadow on its right side that don't belong. Put a round in it if you can."

Carl was more than happy to. He stepped away from us, balanced the rifle on the roof of a Mazda, sighted, and squeezed off a shot. The report was booming, echoing out across the silent river. But a split-second after I heard it, I heard somebody down there scream.

"Shit," Texas said.

There were lots of moving shadows down there, all mulling about like worms on tasty roadkill. And there was no doubt who and what they were: Hatchet Clans. And they were coming.

We all spread out and got ready to start shooting. The Clansmen were moving up through the wreckage and I had to wonder how long they'd been dogging us. In the moonlight, I could see the masks they wore, the shine of the eye pieces. They were no longer practicing stealth. They were shouting and screeching, letting out that wailing war cry I knew so well. Down at the foot of the bridge I saw what looked like hundreds of them. Maybe it wasn't that many, but it was more than enough to overrun us even with the guns.

I told the others to hold their fire until they had something closer to fire at.

Carl was firing at them indiscriminately, trying to kill a few, but mostly trying to drive them back. My plan was to have

Carl hold them off while I got the others away. Maybe it would have worked...but we never got the chance to find out.

"They're here!" Mickey screamed. "They're here!"

And they were. About a dozen of them had slipped up on us, probably crawling amongst the smashed cars on their bellies. They waited until they were in range and then leaped up, brandishing spears and axes and clubs with spikes driven into the ends. Strictly Stone Age shit, but lethal at close range.

They charged.

We started shooting with wild abandon, putting rounds in them, over their heads, to all sides. We put up a manic defense and our firepower was enough that they didn't make it within ten feet of us. A wounded one dragged itself off. And another with no less than six smoking bullet holes in it dragged itself at our position and Texas killed it with a headshot.

"We won't stop the next wave," Carl said.

And I knew he was right: I could see them advancing on us, ducking low and slipping amongst the cars and trucks, staying low so we couldn't draw a good bead on them. I was guessing there were thirty or forty of them. And behind them, at least three times that many.

"We have to run for it," I told the others.

But Texas Slim had other ideas. "What we need here is something that will tip the odds in our favor. Something like a down-home barbecue, if you catch my meaning." He was staring up at the tanker truck just behind us. He was smiling. "That is...if you catch my meaning."

"Carl?" I said. He had driven trucks for a living once upon a time.

The tanker had stalled out or been stopped just as it had reached the first bridge arch, which meant that its hind end was not perfectly level, but sort of hanging down on the canting road way. The cant was slight, maybe 12º at most, just a gently sloping incline you had to drive up until you reached the arches and the perfectly vertical plane of the bridge itself. I had some crazy idea of popping the emergency brake on the tanker...but it would only have rolled twenty feet before crashing into more wreckage.

We needed something better and Carl had it.

23

"There's a discharge valve at the rear of the tank," he said. "It's where you hook up the hose for unloading. Manual. Strictly gravity feed."

As the girls and I watched the Clansmen picking their way toward us, our hands sweaty on our guns, Carl and Texas went at it. I didn't watch what they did. I heard the doors to the truck cab open and shut a few times. I heard them argue. I heard the clanking of a dropped wrench. I couldn't seem to take my eyes off what I was seeing below: the Hatchet Clans. I wondered how many there were in Gary. What I was seeing was not only horrendous but amazing. They were literally everywhere—creeping amongst the vehicles, crawling over the tops, massing like a swarm of hornets. There were so many that it was absolutely ridiculous to pick a target. It reminded me of when I was a kid and I stomped an ant hill and the ants, black and angry, literally boiled out.

There were that many.

Mickey was next to me and she was trembling. "C'mon, Nash...Jesus Christ, we have to get out of here!"

Janie didn't say a word. Oh, she was scared, too, but she wasn't saying a thing. She was just waiting as death moved towards us, either with absolute faith in what the boys were doing or maybe accepting her end. You could never be sure with her.

I smelled gas.

"Okay," Texas said, tapping me on the shoulder. "Time for a very hasty retreat..."

We pulled back and I had him take the girls and get moving while I stood off to the side. Carl looked at me. Gas was dripping from the discharge valve. It smelled very sharp, very pungent. I gave him the thumbs up and he opened the valve. The gas didn't just run from the outlet, it sprayed. It came out in a gushing, high-pressure stream that shot forward a good five feet before striking the bridge. It hit with such force that it washed away the corpses of the dead Clansmen, catching them in a rolling stream and pushing them beneath cars. The smell of raw gasoline was so overwhelming, I started to get dizzy from the fumes.

"Let's go," Carl said.

We retreated with the others. I told them to keep going until they were off the other end of the bridge. They didn't like it, but it had to be. I didn't know what was going to happen when Carl put a bullet in the spilled river of gas. His plan was fairly simple: he'd shoot into the gas. The bridge was metal. The slug from my Savage would kick up some sparks when it hit and that's all it would take. The gas should ignite, but the truck would, too, and when that happened it might be like ground zero on the bridge.

Carl and I climbed up atop the cab of a flatbed truck loaded with lumber. We had a good view of the tanker and the gas flooding down through the vehicles. The Clansmen stopped when it hit them, several were washed right off their feet, more falling as the gas rushed past them. Some retreated. Others came forward. Most were just confused, mulling around, wondering maybe what it all meant.

The gas had been running for over five minutes at that point.

It had flooded right down the bridge and I could see the swirling lake of it on the road where you drove up. Carl raised the Savage. His face was glistening with sweat. He sighted in and fired. Nothing. Swearing, he did it again, aiming down farther in-between two cars right into the gas. He squeezed the trigger. The shot rang out and this time I saw the sparks fly as the round chewed into the steel plating. I saw the spark and then a wall of flames was rushing towards the truck and right through the legions of the Hatchet Clans. They screamed and threw themselves around as the fire enveloped them. There was no escape from it.

We jumped off the cab, landed on the hood, found the bridge and started running. We made it maybe twenty feet when the world exploded into daylight and the aftershock threw us to the bridge. Behind us, it was an absolute inferno. The explosion had tossed the tanker into the air about forty feet and then it came back down, a flaming mass that erupted on impact in an ocean of fire that engulfed the bridge, ran right up the farthest arch, and flooded everything in a blinding blaze. Twin fire balls about the size of two-story houses went rolling up into the sky. A wave of heat hit Carl and I, singing our eyebrows. The Hatchet Clans were incinerated, I was guessing, because nothing could have lived through that cremating firestorm. From the first arch right down to the road below was nothing but a rampart of fire that rose twenty feet into the air. I saw burning Clansman leaping off the bridge or blown right off it. I heard their death cries as they roasted in hell.

We were quite a distance from it, yet the consuming heat was like standing before an open oven door. We got to our feet and ran, gasping for breath. The air was foul with smoke and fumes and it was hard to breathe as if the explosion itself had sucked all the oxygen from the air.

When we reached the others, we were dizzy, out of breath. We fell to our knees and they pulled us to our feet, got us off the bridge.

Lying on the grassy riverbank, I watched the bridge burn. It was so bright you could have seen it for miles, just blazing away as Dresden must have after it was fire-bombed. As we sat there, watching the pyrotechnics, all those cars and trucks started going up as their gas tanks caught fire. I saw a propane truck shoot straight up like a burning missile before coming down into the river below, a huge puddle of flames spreading over the surface of the water. It expanded right to the far bank and started the grass and trees on fire.

It was quite a show.

24

I came awake to the sound of a horn blaring. It tore me out of some crazy, almost hallucinogenic dream about The Medusa. I jumped up and nearly elbowed Texas in the face. I didn't know where the hell I was or what was going on.

"It's okay," Janie told me.

"Must've been quite a dream," Texas Slim said.

I wiped the sleep from my eyes. Slowly, it all came back to me and I slid back down in the seat of the Jeep, relaxing a bit.

We had found the Jeep in the garage just like Mickey said. It was a good vehicle. Well-maintained. Battery charged. Full tank of gas. We'd driven out of Gary last night, crossing the Indiana state line into Illinois and, cutting well south of Chicago, got onto to Route 80 which was our ticket west. The highway was a mess with stalled cars and trucks, overturned buses and you name it. We'd been on it all day, creeping along, and now it was night again.

Mickey was driving. Carl was snoring in the passenger seat.

"Hell we at?" I asked.

"Signs say we're outside some little dive called Utica," Mickey told me. "Road's been clear the last twenty miles or so. How long you want to keep going?"

That was a good question. All I knew is we had to hit Des Moines on our way west. That's what The Shape had said inside my head. Then again, maybe I'd imagined it, but I didn't think so because the need to reach Des Moines as fast as we could was overpowering. It's hard to explain. But when that voice whispered in my head—and I can't honestly be sure it really was a voice as such—and pointed me in the right direction, it became an obsession to get there. It was almost a physical need. Like getting to a toilet when your bladder is full to bursting, if you can dig that.

"Why'd you hit the horn?" I asked.

"Your girlfriend thought a giant bird was attacking us," Janie said.

"I didn't say it was a *bird,*" Mickey told her, practicing great patience, I thought. "Something swooped us. It was big and it was dark. It came out of the air, hence, I'm assuming it had wings."

"I'd say that's a good assumption," Texas said. "And blaring horns are known to frighten off giant birds."

I looked out my window, watching the moonlit countryside passing by. There was mist or smoke hanging in the sky as if something nearby was burning. I could see streaks of color that were pink and almost luminous. I don't know what they were or what could have caused them. Then I saw the moon. It was full. Everything inside me dried up at the sight of it. Full moon and no offering for big bad Brother Shape. A selection would have to be made some way and somehow. It filled my belly with poison just thinking about it. I saw a flock of winged creatures pass over the face of the moon. They looked kind of like giant bats, but maybe they were witches out on a lark. Nothing would have surprised me. Mickey definitely wasn't seeing things.

"We need to stop sooner or later," Janie said at my side. "These people need to rest, Nash."

Sure, rest. Like food, one of those things the human body just had to have sometimes. Janie was not stupid. She knew it was the night of the moon, she knew what that entailed. I got the feeling from her that she was nursing a secret joy inside her that I had nothing to offer up. That my feelings for the others would prevent me from choosing from their ranks. This is what she wanted. To tell Big Brother Shape to fuck himself or herself or *itself*. No more free lunches. No more offerings. We're better than that, we will no longer sink to the dehumanizing, uncivilized depths of offering one of our own to some malignant horror from the pit.

But, once again, sweet and kind as she was, she was also naïve.

The Shape would come.

I would have to make a selection.

We drove on for another hour. We saw a few wrecked vehicles but no more giant birds or much of anything else, unless you wanted to count the pack of wolves or coyotes or whatever the hell they were that cut across the road in front of us. We had to slow down so we didn't hit them. They watched us as they passed. Their eyes glowed green in the darkness.

Finally, Mickey said, "There's a turnoff for Utica. Something about a campground, Nash."

"So what?" Janie said.

"You think that's the place to crash for awhile?"

I nodded. "Yeah, I think so."

"Then pull us in there."

Janie was boiling next to me in the dark but I didn't really have time to assuage her ego. She was feeling very threatened by Mickey. I understood that. I sympathized with it. Unfortunately, Mickey's intuition was so well-developed that it was nearly prophetic. I would have been a fool not to use a tool like that to safeguard us.

The place was dead. No fires burning. No vehicles. The campground had gone wild, most of the sites grown over. There were lots of rock formations and a big river. I figured it was a pretty nice place back in the day, the perfect getaway from Chicago. Mickey scouted us out a spot on a hill that overlooked most of the park and we stopped there. We found some wood at a ranger station down the way and started a blaze in the firepit. It was nice. All we needed were some marshmallows and hot dogs.

No such luck.

We ate Chef Boyardee ravioli and canned mandarin oranges. But outside like that by the fire, it tasted pretty damn good. Nobody was saying much of anything. They were all tired. Nobody had slept much in the past few days. Carl was just staring into the flames. Texas Slim did not regale us with crude stories. Janie kept her eye on Mickey who kept her eye on me. Meanwhile, I watched the moon and it watched me.

I could feel The Shape out there like some malefic dark star orbiting around us, each pass bringing it a little closer. I sat there and chain-smoked. I had no idea what I was going to do. It was the night of the full moon. There was a possibility The Shape might wait until tomorrow night before making an appearance, but there was no guarantee of that.

"What're you going to do, Rick?" Janie said to me, reading my mind.

"About what?"

"You know what."

All eyes were on me then. Mickey was watching me especially close. I knew then that Texas or Carl had told her, tipped her off about the whole business. That was okay. She knew now. We all knew. We all understood. We were thick as thieves, coveting our dirty little secret.

"Nash," Carl said.

I looked over at him.

He had his AK up. "Somebody out there. Out in those trees."

"He's right," Mickey said.

"If they were bad boys, they would have attacked," I said. "Let's assume they're friendly. Let's assume they're in need of company."

We waited. A few insects buzzed and a coyote howled low and mournful in the distance. I could hear our friend moving around out there. Carl slipped away from the fire and took up a shooting position by the Jeep. The rest of us stayed put.

I heard a stick crack, saw a dark shadow slip behind a tree.

"You out there," I called. "Come on in. We're friendly. We got food and coffee. You're welcome to it."

Silence.

Then the shadow came around the tree and walked almost sheepishly towards the fire. It was a woman, fortyish, but so ragged and dirty that she looked like a ragbag. I wondered who she was before the bombs fell.

"Your welcome to what we have," I said.

She came in closer.

Mickey knew exactly what I was doing. She smiled at me in the firelight.

25

The woman enjoyed our coffee, our meager food. She ate with her fingers like an animal while she watched us warily like we might steal her dinner away from her. About the time I was pretty sure she was a deaf mute or something, she said, "Ronny got the pox, had the Fevers something terrible. Blood came out of his eyes. It squirted out. I think he threw up part of his intestines. Looked like intestines." She shook her head, very matter-of-fact about it as if the true horror of the situation had lost its power to shock. "Ronny didn't want to get burned. He was always saying, Marilynn, don't you let them burn me. But I didn't have a choice. Army said so. We put him in the pyre. They made us put him in the pyre with the rest. They burned him. Thousands of 'em burning in the pit. You could smell it all the way to Beloit. It stank."

"Where are you from, Marilynn?" Janie asked her.

"Janesville, Wisconsin. Lived there my whole life. Army started clearing us out block by block. Put us in a camp. Like one of them German camps you hear about it the war, kind with the Jews in 'em. Little huts we lived in. Barbwire all around. We couldn't leave. They wouldn't let us," she told us, the firelight reflected in her eyes. "Lot of us fought. Didn't want to go. Shiela Reed fought, too. She was hiding her husband's body. Shiela was manager at the Rite-Aid, started as a checker but she blew her boss in the storeroom every day, they said, so she got manager. She was crazy. Hiding that body. Army came in and she shot at them. They gunned her down. Threw her in the street and left her there." She looked around at us as if realizing for the first time that we were there. "Where you going in that Jeep?"

"West," Carl told her.

Marilynn's eyes got wide, filled with light. "West, you say? Hear lots of people are going west. Funny. Where west you going?"

"Des Moines."

"That's an awful place. I was there two months ago. I ain't going back."

"What's going on there, darling?" Texas Slim asked her.

"Ain't you heard? Half the town is burned down, rest of its wreckage. It was bombed by the Air Force to clean out the militias. Nothing there now but rats and corpses and big craters from the bombs, lots of fallen down buildings. I been there. I know. Yes sir, I know. Bones everywhere. Lots of cars with skeletons in 'em. Not much else."

"No people?" Mickey said.

Marilynn was sucking tomato sauce from her fingers. "Oh, sure. There's people. Wild people. They run around in animal skins or go naked. They're all crazy. They drool. You don't wanna go there in broad daylight, let alone the dark. Don't get there after sundown. That's when the bad ones come out."

But that's where we were going. I don't know why, but the need was very strong and I wasn't about to ignore it. I kept watching our guest. I didn't speak to her. If I spoke to her, I would feel connected to her and I didn't want that kind of connection. I had to look at her like a farmer looks at a pig he's going to slaughter. That's what it had come to.

I felt like shit. This woman...Marilynn...was dirty and smelly and probably crazy, but she was harmless. Very pathetic, really. I felt sorry for her and I knew that I couldn't and the guilt of what was coming was eating a hole straight through me. Carl and Mickey kept watching me, amused by what was coming. Texas Slim did not look at me. I dared not look at Janie because I knew what was in her eyes and I didn't want to see it.

"Where are you going now?" Janie asked her.

Marilynn considered it as she licked at a sore on her thumb. "Got a sister in Streator. She was alive last I heard. I'll go look her up. Maybe I'll live with her. Maybe together we can make it. All I want is just to make it."

I looked away from her.

Janie said, "Well, I hope you make it to Streator. I really hope nothing gets in your way."

Which was directed at me, of course.

"Yup," Texas said. "Sure would suck the old willy wonka if something prevented you from reaching your sister."

Carl giggled.

Janie glared at him. I glared at Janie. What had to happen now was for the good of all of us, but try and make her get off her soapbox and realize it. Mickey, on the other hand, was a totally different sort of woman. She saw the way things were and knew how they would never be again. I'm not saying that she was a better person—because she sure as hell was not—but she was more like the rest of us: desensitized, desperate, willing to do whatever it took to see another day.

"Well, maybe you should be on your way," Janie said, starting to get nervous. She knew she couldn't guilt me out of this one.

"Was hoping I could sleep the night by your fire," the woman said.

"Well, of course, darling," Texas Slim told her. "Our fire is your fire."

Carl giggled again.

"Nash," Janie said and her voice was pleading. *"Rick..."*

"Why don't you go take a walk?" I told her, beginning to lose my patience with the Pollyanna shit. "Texas'll go with you."

"Stay the fuck away from me," Janie said. "All of you."

She stomped away into the darkness. I didn't like it because there were too many things out there.

In the distance you could see a faint greenish glow at the horizon that I thought was Chicago. There were weird pale blue auroras licking over the city, just pulsating like electrical fields. I saw occasional flashes of something like cloud-to-ground lightening that were a brilliant orange. I couldn't even imagine what that hellzone was like at ground zero.

"Okay, Carl," I finally said. "Let's get this done."

Marilynn put her bovine eyes on me. I'll never forget the way she looked at me as if she knew, as if she sensed the horror that was coming. One human being trying to make a connection with another, looking for mercy, for compassion, for understanding. What she got instead was the butt of Carl's rifle to the back of her head. Her eyes shut and she fell over.

Ten minutes later, we had her tied to a fence with some bailing wire from our heaps of firewood.

Then Carl and Texas Slim backed well away. They knew what was coming.

I just stood there, sweat rolling down my face. The self-loathing and hatred filled me, hatred of who I was and what I had let myself become. And guilt. Oh God, the guilt of it all, knowing that once I had been an ordinary guy with an ordinary life and I wouldn't have hurt a fly.

Mickey stood next to me. Her eyes were huge, dark, liquid. She was breathing hard, her long limbs tensed with excitement. She was getting off on it. Really getting off. I could feel the heat coming off her, the musk that made my cock unfurl itself and go hard. As crazy and twisted as it sounds, I wanted nothing better than to throw her to the ground and fuck the hell out of her.

That's testament to the bizarre workings of the human mind.

"Do it, Nash," she breathed in my ear. "Call The Shape."

So I did.

26

It was coming.

The Shape was coming.

It was cycling itself into being, burning through the ether.

Gutting the fabric of this world.

I had called it and now it was coming. Right away I felt something in the air around me change...break open...twist in upon itself as if the very atoms were being realigned or shattered, turned inside out. The air was heavy. Heavy and thrumming and I could not move. Some yawning, pulsing electromagnetic field had seized me and squashed me flat, pushing me down to my knees at the altar of my god.

Expiation.

Sacrifice.

Burnt offerings.

I tried to forget that the woman tied to the fence had a name. I turned my face away, the air crawling with static electricity. The woman moaned, thrashed, cried out. But I did not hear her. I refused to hear her. All around, a humming and a crackling. A raw, cutting stench of ozone. And then the heat, the burning cremating heat of the living thermonuclear oven as it took on physical form.

Hungry.

Starving.

The heat...the blazing energy...the sound of a million, billion hornets buzzing...sawblades ripping into steel...a screeching...a whirring...the world shrieking out as it was disemboweled at the subatomic level. Then the woman—Marilynn, God yes, *Marilynn*—screamed. A single economical scream that lasted only seconds.

The Shape took her, consumed her.

I did not look.

But Mickey did. You could not have pried her eyes from it. She stared in rapt, almost erotic fascination at what was happening.

Marilynn...

I heard her melt with a crackling sound like burning cellophane. And then it was over and the world was just the world again. I opened my eyes. I made myself look as I made myself look every month on the night of the full moon.

Marilynn was a blackened scarecrow, still smoldering.

A pall of greasy black smoke hung in the air.

Burnt offerings.

She had been melted, reduced to a fused clot of bone and meat and marrow. A bubbling black slime that liquefied, smoking and popping, oozing down the fence into a pool of superhot irradiated refuse. The dry grass blazed where it made contact.

The stench of her burning flesh was still in the air.

I vomited.

And later, still feeling The Shape and knowing that it owned me, I looked up at the night sky, the pale moon brooding high above like a skull.

I opened my mouth.

And screamed.

DES MOINES IOWA

1

Did I like it?

Did I get off making offerings to that monstrosity?

No, I did not. The guilt was thick on me like an infection, it was rotting me from the inside out. My dreams were sweaty, disturbing, goddamned ugly if you want to know the truth...people lined up, people I knew and didn't know, people I'd admired and, yes, even loved, all waiting for me to decide who lived and who died. I'd wake up seeing their eyes, accusing and hating. I felt like a guard in Birkenau or Treblinka, deciding who went to the gas chamber and who didn't. You think that was easy to live with? That it didn't eat my guts out? You can't do what I did without losing part of yourself and after I'd been doing it for a year, I couldn't honestly remember the sort of person I'd been before.

But I didn't do it alone.

My posse did it with me. A communal guilt. We were like soldiers doing a really terrible job...we just didn't talk much about it. It made things go down easier that way. I had a lot of graves out there on my conscience, a lot of ghosts trying to claw their way out, and, Jesus, I had to keep them down. Some how, I had to.

2

The city was a cesspool of standing water, rubble, and unburied bodies. It looked like the mother of all battles had been fought here and maybe it had been. The buildings were shattered, blackened like charcoal, trees standing up like solitary masts, entirely devoid of limbs. Skyscrapers had been reduced to heaps of slag. No birds sang. Nothing grew. Nothing moved. There was only the stench of old death on the faint breeze, pungent and pervasive and secret. The way a tomb might smell.

"This place is dead," Carl said. "Absolutely dead. Can't you smell it?"

I could, but I didn't mention the fact. Nobody else did either. They could feel it, all right, and they did not like it. The silence in the Jeep was heavy, almost crushing. They were waiting for me to tell them what this was all about or at least point them in the right direction. But I was clueless, absolutely clueless. Like every other city, every rawboned urban graveyard, we rolled in with no clear reason of why we had to go there other than the fact that I said so. I doubted if it was enough for my people because it sure as hell was not enough for me.

As we drove in up 94, I was thinking about Marilynn. She was the last thing I wanted to be thinking about, but I couldn't forget what she had said.

Nothing there now but rats and corpses and big craters from the bombs, lots of fallen down buildings.

How right she was. But there was something else here, something important and I could feel it in my guts.

The city lay around us like some crumbled, exhumed corpse. Entire neighborhoods had been bombed to rubble while others were relatively unscathed. It made no sense really, but even those still standing were desolate and eerie, silent and forlorn like monoliths erected over the grave of mankind. Some buildings had walls blasted free and you could see the tiny cubicles within...offices, apartments, like cross-sections of a doll's house. Many were nothing but twisted and mangled skeletal frames of girders waiting to fall and still others were marked by but a single standing chimney or façade. Roads were often cut by jagged crevices like fault lines, sewer piping thrust up through the pavement like the bones of compound fractures.

It was no easy bit navigating our way through.

Entire thoroughfares were blocked by rubble and mountainous debris or had fallen into the sewers below. I saw the huge bomb craters that Marilynn had talked about. They pocked the landscape like the craters on the dark side of the moon. They were filled with pools of foul-smelling water, caked with leaves and garbage and the occasional rotting hulk of a half-submerged SUV. Other streets were blocked by buses and trucks and overturned cars, the burnt husks of military vehicles.

There were bones everywhere, scattered in the streets, rotting in the slimy gutters. Some were still dressed in rags, pushed up beneath the overhangs of standing buildings or huddled in cars that were perforated with bullet holes.

Carl was playing with the Geiger Counter. "Rad's a little high...about fifty. Not too bad. Net yet."

We passed a cathedral that was nothing but heaped stones spread out for nearly a city block. All that was left standing was the steeple and it was leaning hard. Neighborhoods of homes were reduced to kindling or blackened from raging fires long since burned out.

"Well," Texas said, pulling off a cigarette, "this is lovely country. Looks like Berlin in '45. But despite its scenic charm, I'm all for heading out. Getting a funny tickle at the base of my balls and I'm pretty sure it ain't Carl's middle finger."

"Kiss my ass," Carl said.

I giggled...a high, nervous, frantic sort of giggle. I couldn't help myself. Something was very wrong here. Des Moines felt like a cemetery and the comparison was applicable...yet, I knew there was life out there in those blasted ruins. I could feel it watching us.

"He's right," Mickey said. "There's something out there. I can feel it."

"What are we after here, Nash? You got any idea what it is we're looking for?" Carl wanted to know.

But I could only shake my head. "I'll know it when I see it. Keep driving."

Janie was sitting next to me, but she hadn't said a word to me since I gave Marilynn to The Shape. I loved Janie. I would never pretend otherwise. But I was starting to get tired of her moody bullshit. I think we all were. It was getting to the point that her high blown ethics and morals were getting the best of her. Time was when we did what we had to do, she disapproved, but she moved on, let it go. Now she kept sinking into these deep blue funks and would refuse to even speak to anyone. It was immature and whiny. Like dealing with a bratty five-year old. I didn't have the patience for it and I was pretty sure the others didn't either.

"We need to start getting some gas here, Nash," Mickey said. "We got about a quarter tank...but it won't last long."

Fuel was never a problem in the brave new world. If you had a running vehicle it was very easy to siphon all the gas you wanted from the armies of dead vehicles. Carl always carried his little siphon pump with him.

"All right, we better get that done. Let's look for a parking lot or something, a car dealer."

Mickey drove on, steering the Jeep through those devastated, war-torn streets. She was a good driver, steering us around heaped rubble and squeezing in-between wrecked cars. I watched the desolation around us, looking for anything that moved and saw nothing. Not even a stray dog drinking from a puddle. Street signs were missing, stoplights laying in the streets. Telephone poles had fallen right over and those that still stood were leaning badly, their lines strung like limp spaghetti.

"Here we go," Mickey said.

She pulled into the parking lot of a huge white building that went on for about a city block. In huge blue plastic letters it said: CHEVROLET, HUMMER. There were lot after lot of cars, many of which were damaged or rusting, tires stripped away and windshields shattered. But many were untouched.

We piled out.

2

Inside, the dealership was dusty and messy, offices ransacked, computers shattered, file cabinets tipped over, their contents strewn about. We walked over a floor covered in papers, dealer's brochures. The plate glass windows were either broken, entirely gone, or so dusty you couldn't see out of them. It was dim in there, shadows everywhere. It would have been the perfect place to spring an ambush and I think we all knew it.

We went down into the garages and collected up a dozen plastic five-gallon gas cans. Carl had his siphon and we were ready to go. Mickey was there by my side. As was Carl and

Texas. But I didn't see Janie. Shit, I thought, there were only five of us for chrissake! It wasn't like I had to be accountable for a hundred fucking survivors. Yet, Janie had slipped through my fingers.

And it probably wasn't by accident.

The mechanic's bays were huge. You could have parked twenty cars in there and had enough room for a couple trucks. Add to that the metal cages of automotive parts, the dusty red tool cribs, the cars parked on dead hydraulic jacks, and she could have been anywhere.

Immature, Nash, just like you thought. She's got a size-D bug up her ass and she's been feeding and mothering that fucker so that it's now the size of a B-movie monster insect. Ain't that sweet? Little Miss fucking Princess-Prom Queen-cheerleading-blue-eyed-blonde-haired-Nordic-uberbitch is pissed off at your lack of sympathy for all the shitballs and dirtbags in the world, so she just fucking wandered off and endangered you all.

Maybe she's just pouting back in the showroom.

But maybe she walked away from it all.

In which case, somebody's gotta go get her and that somebody might die a hard fucking death out in the ruins.

I was pissed. I was guilty. I was speechless. My mind was going a million miles a minute, exploding with star-shot, and I hated myself for making her feel so poorly and I hated her for standing up on her soapbox and espousing her old world, dead-and-fucking-gone bleeding heart values.

Jesus H. Christ, this was survival.

"Where's Janie?" I said.

"Who cares?" Mickey said, giving me a molten look that said all that needed saying about how I no longer needed Janie, that she was expendable, that my dick was in finer hands now and would soon die and go to pussy heaven. Christ.

"I care," I said.

Texas Slim came over with a calendar. He shoved it in my face. There was a naked redhead with her fine, pointy tits on display. They looked almost as good as Mickey's.

"Look at this fine display," he said to me, clucking his tongue. "Now therein lies the deepest pits of black sin and the voluptuous joys of carnal godhood."

"Fuck are you talking about, dumbass?" Carl said to him.

"I'm saying, my small-minded friend, that this here sweet lick of cherry-red devil's food is the sort of meal a man don't need no spoon nor fork for. No sir, this is a feast best fit for bare hands and slavering mouths."

"Janie's gone," I said, walking across the bay. "Find here. Right now, goddammit. Find her."

I could almost feel Mickey rolling her eyes behind my back.

I didn't give a shit. I had to find Janie. Beretta in hand, I went off looking for her and Mickey tagged along. Carl started searching the bays and Texas went out into the offices. We were all calling for her and I wasn't too happy about that. I didn't particularly relish the idea of making a lot of goddamn noise and drawing unfriendlies in. Because, believe me, they were out there, circling like vultures looking for some tasty red meat to pick at.

The dealership was huge. Unbelievably huge. Mickey and I started going through the showrooms, searching around the Corvettes and Aveos, Silverados and Hummer H3s.

"Janie!" I called. "Janie!"

My voice echoed out and died, affirming the dead and empty voluminous spaces around me. I could hear Texas in the distance doing the same. We were all split apart now. Armed, but split and that was just plain dangerous. I was starting to sweat. My stomach was filled with sharp nettles. Part of me was seriously pissed at Janie for putting us in this position and another part was just plain scared. For what if she hadn't disappeared of her own free will?

What if she had been snatched?

Hell, while we circled around like chickens looking for feed, something might be peeling the flesh from her bones in some dark, webby place. I moved faster, looking, searching, calling out. Mickey did the same, but with a noticeable lack of enthusiasm. I started imagining us, hours from then, still looking and not finding a damn thing and me having to admit that Janie was gone, gone, *gone*. It made me feel empty inside. And every time I didn't hear Texas or Carl shouting out her name for a few moments, I was sure that whatever had gotten her had gotten them. Something vicious and stealthy, something so terrible it could take them silently without so much as a cry or a busted cap.

I felt like I was in one of those old haunted house movies where people disappear one by one. A couple times I looked back at Mickey just to make sure she was there. And I knew at that moment if I hadn't before what my true Achilles heel was: I was absolutely petrified of being alone. That was my ultimate nightmare, that was the form my private hell would take.

Just me alone in a dead world. It reminded me of a story I read in high school, the opening lines of which had stayed in the back of my mind all these years, boiling away like a vat of poison:

The last man on earth sat alone in a room. There was a knock at the door.

I came around a Chevy Avalanche, keeping watch on those dusty windows, thinking more than once I had seen a shape slide past them...but not upright and human, but low and twisted like a troll from a dark enchanted forest.

"Nash," Mickey finally said, hooking me by the elbow. "Nash. I know you've got a thing for Janie. That's cool. And I know she's one of us and we don't want to lose her. But I got a bad feeling, man. I got a bad feeling right up my spine and I don't think this is the right time for us to be separated like this."

I wanted to tell her to go to hell...but I knew she was right. My stomach was filled with fluttering wings; I was sensing something, too. And more than once I had wondered if some bad boys or nameless things had orchestrated the entire thing, snatching Janie so we'd separate and they could take us down that much quicker.

I put a hand on Mickey's shoulder. "Listen to me. Go out into the offices. Find Texas and stay with him, link up with Carl. I'm going to find her."

"Nash—"

"Fuck that. Get going."

She did, giving me one last look of longing or pity and taking off, her long black hair swishing from side to side. I didn't want to be alone as you full well know, but on the other hand I always favor fighting alone so I don't have to worry about anyone else. I waited there, everything inside of me wired full of electricity. But I waited, fumbling a cigarette into my mouth and lighting it. The smoke was acrid, unpleasantly so. Its smell was almost gagging. The heat of the filter against my lips was burning. I didn't get it at first—thought for sure I was going to have a panic attack or something—but then I did.

I was in battle mode.

Every muscle was taut, my nerves jangling, my brain pushing its sensory network to the limits so that all five senses were amplified. Nothing would get by me. Nothing would throw down on me or take me by surprise. When I heard Mickey calling out for Janie with Texas, I tossed the cigarette and ran charging through the showrooms, my heart pounding like a kettle drum. I found a double doorway that led down into the body shop. Other doorways led to other departments but this is the one I wanted.

I rushed into the body shop which was quite large and echoing.

A few dust-laden cars still waited for new fenders, doors, or sidewalls. I could smell the ancient odor of primer and putty. I looked around the tool cribs, darted into the electrostatic paint booth, snooped in a parts cage. Then I went into an office and rubbed some of the grime off the window.

I saw someone across the street.

3

It was Janie.

I circled around in frenetic rage until I found a door, unlocked it, and ran across the street. Janie turned and saw me, kept right on going. I held my gun high, watching every heap of refuse, every shadowy alley, every overturned dumpster and cracked window. *Eyes.* God, I could feel the eyes watching me, cutting into me like drill bits.

I caught up with her, grabbed her shoulder and swung her around. "What in the fuck do you think you're doing, you little idiot?" I cried in her face.

And that face...oh boy. Pinched with grief, eyes swollen from tears. She was absolutely stunning even like that. I wanted to sweep her into my arms and hug her because I could see what she looked like as a little girl, so beautiful she would make your heart sliver, your breath catch in your throat, so vulnerable you only wanted to protect her and make the bad things go away.

"Janie...please," I said.

The stubborn pissiness was gone from her. She was a shell that was cracking apart from the inside out. I could feel the waves of pain coming from her. "Rick...just let me go. I can't do this anymore," she told me and there was no drama in her voice, just a hollowness. "I can't go on murdering people. It's not what I am or what I'm about. I turned a blind eye to it long as I could...but it won't work anymore. I'm sorry."

"Janie...c'mon, don't do this."

She reached out and touched her fingers to my face, smiled very thinly. "I don't want to hurt you. I don't want to be a burden to these others. But I can't go on like this. Just go back to the others. They need you. I'm going to walk away and I don't want you to follow me."

I was speechless. Totally speechless.

"I'm sorry, Rick. I know you think I'm weak and you're right: I am. But I can't justify what we're doing. I'm going to walk away and let fate take its course. I don't have the strength to kill myself, so this is the only alternative. Goodbye, Rick."

She turned away just like that and walked on.

But I caught up with her. "You can't do this. I won't let you. I won't let you die like a dog in the streets."

"You can't stop me and you don't own me."

"It'll get better," I said, knowing it was utter bullshit.

"There's no future, Rick. Accept it."

She started walking again and all the fight had dried up in me. I didn't know what to say or what to do. I was helpless. She was right and I knew it. Janie had lost focus and saw no reason to prolong the inevitable. The rest of us were deluding ourselves. I didn't know why I was bothering. I knew there wasn't any pot of gold at the end of the fucking rainbow; just misery. I wasn't racing towards the light at the end of the tunnel, I was fleeing the darkness that was getting closer day by day, moving west as we were moving west.

I'm not really sure what I would have done if something hadn't happened that gave me a good square kick in the ass. A naked man stepped out of a doorway. He was pale as a bleached corpse, hairless, and there were great holes eaten into his skin like something had taken bites out of him. His face beneath his eyes was just...gone. It had been eaten away right to the pink muscle beneath. He grinned at us like a half-dissected anatomy specimen. His eyes were like depthless black catacombs.

A Scab.

One chewed up by some flesh-eating virus or fungus. He saw me, saw Janie. He walked right over to her and she did not shriek, did not draw back, but stood there with eyes filled with hurt and just waited for it. I brought up the Beretta and fired a round at him point-blank. He jerked with the impact, folding up and pressing his hands to the red jelly frothing from the bullet hole. He made an anguished growling sound.

And it was *answered.*

I swung around and there was another Scab. Naked and bald, a teenage boy. He was down on his knees like a dog, growling at us, yellow foam coming out of his mouth. I shot him in the head and he flipped around, trembling, a perfect stream of dark blood gushing from the wound.

I grabbed Janie by the arm, pulling her away with me, and as I turned I saw that retreat to the dealership was impossible: we were in as nest of them. Scabs came pouring out of every hole and hide and shadowy crevice, they came out like slugs boiling from salted earth. All naked, all full of sores and morbid disfigurements, and all eaten up with those yawning ulcers.

They had all worked themselves up into some kill-happy rapture, some deranged and bloodthirsty mania. It was just unbelievable. They were crawling on their hands and knees, running around in circles, jumping up and down on the hoods of cars in one of the lots. Some were hopping in frantic circles like monkeys. Others fornicating. Some dry humping each others legs. But they all had one thing in common: they were watching us.

And they were gradually moving in our direction.

Janie and I ran down the sidewalk and I heard the thunder of dozens of bare feet following in pursuit. I came to one locked door after another, rounded a corner and a Scab jumped out at me. He knocked Janie to the pavement and I brought the butt of the Beretta down on the crown of his skull. He went to his knees and I kicked him in the head, gathered up Janie, and off we went.

We lucked out and found an old department store. It was open, the plate glass door shattered. We ducked in there. It had been broken up into countless trendy little shops selling everything from gourmet dog foods to golf clubs to designer fashions. We hopped behind the counter of a leather goods shop and held onto each other, not daring to so much as breathe.

Right away, one of them sought us out.

I didn't have to hear or see them: the fetid stink was enough.

As we crouched under the counter, I saw the reflection of a large fleshy man in a diamond-cut mirror. He was breathing heavily with a clotted, gurgling sound like his lungs were filled with some semi-viscous fluid. Under his breath he kept talking, muttering mostly unintelligible things, but I heard this: "Oh, oh, oh, oh. Here? Not here. Over here? Not over here. Somewhere. Oh, oh, oh." He passed on by, stumbling into some mannequins and stomping on them. A plastic arm went sailing over the counter.

More of them now.

From the footfalls, I was guessing a dozen or more. Now was the time for Carl to come bursting in with his AK on full auto, but I knew that wouldn't happen. We were on our own. We either thought our way out of this, fought our way out, or we died. That's all there was to it. I had thirteen rounds left in the clip for my Beretta. I was mentally counting them as I always did. And in the back of my mind, I knew I was saving a bullet for Janie. I would not admit it even to myself, but I knew, I knew. I wouldn't let them get their diseased paws on her.

More of them were in the building now, grunting and puffing and making those gurgling noises. I heard the slapping of skin against skin, heard some obscene female moaning and I knew a few of them were fucking. Because that's all they liked to do: kill and fuck.

We could only stay hidden so long.

Then I saw the reflection of a man in the mirror again. He was paused right in front of the counter, cocking his head to the side like he was listening. There was some kind of phlegmy snot all over his mouth. He slapped his hands on the counter and brought his head over to look behind it.

He saw us, grinned.

I splashed his face right off the bone with two rounds. Janie and I broke from cover and I shot two more. Ten rounds left. We rushed through the store, dashing around displays and hopping over tables. The Scabs were converging from every direction. I kicked one out of the way and shot another and then another. Eight bullets. A set of stairs led upwards but more Scabs were coming down. They were in no hurry. Like afternoon shoppers sluggish with the day, they came down the steps in twos and threes, holding hands, ulcerated faces grinning. It was insane.

Another door. A fire door. Reinforced steel with a tiny square of glass you couldn't have squeezed a greased puppy through. It was open and we went in. It opened outwards and I saw a set of steps leading below. The idea of going into a cellar was not too appealing, but we had no choice. I slammed the door shut, but there was no lock on the other side. But there was a hydraulic door closer up near the top, the sort that store the pressure of the opening door and then release it to seal the door shut. All fire doors have them. Handing Janie my gun, I jumped up, grabbed hold of the arm with both fists and yanked down with all my weight and strength. I succeeded in bending it and then bending it again until its crook nearly touched the door. It was mangled good.

Then the scabs hit the other side of the door.

They got it open maybe an inch, but the bent opener would move no more. It would keep them at bay for awhile. I took my gun back and took Janie by the hand. Her hand was limp. She could have cared less whether we lived or died. But I didn't have time for that. I led us below and it was pitch black. We came to another door and on the other side...light. There was a modular sky light above. It was nearly buried in filth, debris, and fallen leaves but there was plenty of daylight to see by. We must have been along the back of the building, some sort of atrium that had been designed to enhance the natural lighting.

"We're going to make it," I told Janie.

She barely lifted an eyebrow.

We went through another door and into some kind of long, narrow storeroom with stacked skids of boxes piled along one wall and crates of bulging file folders along the other. There was light because we had a few panels of the skylight. I breathed a sigh of relief because there was a lock on the door. I had almost exhaled that breath when I realized we weren't alone.

4

There was a boy standing there.

He couldn't have been much more than ten or eleven, but the last year had been real hell on him. His skin was bleached white, pocked with sores and mats of fungal growth, his eyes a shining translucent yellow. Ulcers had eaten great infected holes in him that oozed a green bile that almost looked fluorescent against his greasy, pallid flesh. I saw him. I saw the death he brought. But he was fast. He charged out and went after my eyes with hooked fingers. I backed away, terrified of coming into contact with any of the infectious, evil germs that had colonized him.

I fell over a box and promptly went on my ass. The gun fell from my fingers and he could have had me right there. But he didn't want me. He wanted Janie. So when I pitched on my ass he quickly lost interest. He targeted Janie and went right after her. She ran towards the door and he tackled her, brought her down like a lion with a tasty gazelle.

As I scrambled to my feet and grabbed my gun, he had Janie face down. She fought and squirmed, but he was on her, dry humping her ass, sliding his erect penis between her legs.

I ran over there and kicked him in the head twice before he fell off her.

Then Janie was up and behind me and the Scab boy got to his feet. The side of his head was damaged—it looked fucking *dented,* to tell you the truth, like it was an aluminum can—and smashed-in from my steel-toed boot. Green puss and a pink tracery of blood ran from the wound.

He made a growling, snapping sound and went right after me.

I put two bullets into him. I tried to get him in the head, but my hand was shaking so badly they both went right into his throat, tearing it open in a jetting splash of arterial blood. It was like slitting a high pressure hose. He danced around in wild, drunken circles, gnashing his teeth, making choked gargling sounds, blood pissing from his neck. It probably only went on for a couple seconds, but that grisly dance macabre was forever imprinted in my mind.

He went down and that's when the most horrible thing happened.

"Rick!" Janie said.

I heard a scream...a series of screams...but none of them were from Janie and they sure as hell weren't screams of terror, but screams of *delight.* Of ecstasy. Three women came rushing out from behind the stacked boxes where they'd been hiding. They brought a high, sharp smell of rotting fruit with them. Scabs. They came bounding out, bald, corpse-faced, graying, flesh hanging in discolored folds. They didn't come after us; they went after the dying boy.

They rushed in with a frenzied hunger, fighting for the blood that pumped from his neck. They drank it, licked it from their hands, bathed in it. While Janie and I watched in amazement and horror, they crowded the boy, slurping and sucking, pressing in like piglets at their mother's teats. It was appalling. The sight of it. The sound of it. I should have shot them all dead because it would have effortless.

But I didn't.

I stood there, disgusted, shocked, paralyzed like a fat juicy bug wrapped up tight in a spider's web. They had to die and I knew it, yet I think some perverse part of me just had to see how it played out.

Finally, one of them made a belching sound and pulled her lips from the boy's neck. She looked right at me. Her face was like yellow tallow, melted, hanging in runnels and loops, her mouth smeared with blood. A low, revolting odor of spoiled meat came from her. Her naked body was covered in scabs, eaten through with ulcers. One of her breasts was flattened, the other hung low and pendulant, ghastly white, the vein lividity beneath a purple that was almost shocking in contrast.

"You are a beeeee-utiful man," she said with a voice that scraped dryly like a shovel across a tomb lid. "So pretty, so lovely." She licked her flaking, blackened lips with a tongue that was bloated and gray. "How about a kiss, a hot little kiss on the mouth?"

It was like déjà vu. She reminded me of that other crazy Scab bitch back in Youngstown that I'd met up with at that deli. She was no less offensive, no less horrible, and certainly no less horny. What she did then I almost hate to put into words. She advanced on me, grinning with gray-black teeth, her tongue hanging out and rapidly licking the air. She put one scabrid hand between her legs and slid a few fingers into herself. The sound was juicy, repellent like somebody jabbing their thumb into a swollen, rotting peach. She worked herself, breathing faster and faster, some kind of drainage running from between her legs and striking the floor like piss. The stink of it was indescribable.

She got closer and I think I screamed or cried out. I remember jerking from the sound of my own voice. Then I remembered the gun in my hand. I brought it up and jacked a round right in her face. Tissue and blood splashed out the back of her head and she went down hard with a violent splatting sound. Her body shook with convulsions and then there was a hissing, bubbling sound and slime pooled out from between her legs with a stink of rotting fish.

It was enough to make us gag.

I didn't want to look, but I did. And that's when I noticed something was *moving* in that discharge. No, many things were moving. What I saw were literally dozens of red beetles, each about the size of your thumb. They were crawling in the slime, more of them coming out all the time and moving up over the dead Scab with a horrid, flesh-crawling clicking sound. They engulfed her, hundreds of them. Her flesh was mucid, pulpy, and they burrowed right into her.

And then the other two women came over, looking for food and for love, I assume. Their faces were gray, pocked with sores, wrinkled and sagging. Their eyes were radiant yellow like candleglow. They grinned and their teeth were very long, very sharp. I shot one of them in the head and fired at the other and missed. And I missed because the moment I squeezed the trigger on her sister, she went airborne. She hit me and knocked me flat. She didn't seem as interested in fucking me as in feeding on me.

I heard Janie scream.

The Scab woman straddled me, greasy and undulant. It was like trying to wrestle a jellyfish. She breathed hot tomb-breath in my face. She spit on me, yellow foam breaking against my cheek. She tried to get her teeth at my throat and I punched her in the face again and again, her flesh soft and spongy. Then I got my hands around her throat. I would squeeze until her fucking head popped off, I decided. The flesh of her throat was like living pulp, seeming to crawl and ooze and flow beneath my fingers. She fought against me, scratching at my face, panting, making hideous slithering sounds.

She was strong, godawful strong.

But I had her, thought I had her. As disgusted as I was, I would not let go and I could feel my fingers and thumbs sinking deeper into her gray mushy flesh. Then there was a loud resounding bang, a flash, and she fell away, dead putrescent weight.

Janie stood there with my Beretta nine in her hands.

"You okay, Rick?" she said, truly concerned.

I brushed some of the woman's remains off me. "I'll live," I breathed. Then I looked over at the corpse, smelled what flowed from between the legs, saw what crawled in it, and promptly vomited. It was an economical vomiting and lasted only a few seconds and then the waves of hot nausea passed.

I heard the sounds of fists pounding on the door.

Jesus, would the lock hold?

And then a voice, a very calm voice said, "You better come with me."

5

The voice belonged to a graying, rather distinguished-looking man in a brown leather jacket. He was standing at the other end of the room. "I would suggest some expediency."

I didn't know who he was or what his game might be. But he seemed sane or close to it and there were no sores on him. We followed him to the end of the room as the door shook in its frame. Down at the end of the stacked rows of boxes there was a little ell with another fire door set in it. He opened it for us and we went in. He closed it and threw a couple locks.

"They won't get through that," he said, "trust me. My name is Price. And you?"

We told him our names.

"Very good," he said. "You made short work of them out there. Nice shooting."

"Thanks," I said, not knowing what else to say.

We were in a storeroom, boxes and crates everywhere. There were candles flickering and a Coleman gas lantern burning away. And that's when I saw that it wasn't just Price in there. Over near the wall, there was a guy stretched out on a sleeping bag and he looked to be in rough shape. His breathing was ragged and hoarse. It sounded like his lungs were filled with fluid. But I didn't look any closer, not then, because there was another guy in the corner. Some dude with a bushy afro that looked like a badly pruned bush. He had a Nikon 35mm camera. He was snapping shots of me with it.

"What's his thing?" I asked Price.

"This is Morse," he said. "He was a photographer once. He's harmless."

He snapped a few shots of Janie.

"He has no film, but it doesn't seem to concern him," Price told me.

Janie scowled at him. "Tell him to stop it. It's weird."

Morse did.

"Nice to meet you," I told him.

He snapped a shot of me.

"He doesn't speak," Price said. "We'll never know what happened to him. He does whistle sometimes, though. Now and again he'll write something for me to read. That's how I learned his name and his profession. Other than that...who can say?"

I looked over at the man on the sleeping bag. I could almost feel the heat coming from him. "He's got the Fevers," I said.

"Yes, he does," Price said.

Price went on to explain that his name was Bedecker and he'd been a first class accountant at one time, had gotten sick only yesterday and had finally fallen down as they looted through the wares upstairs. Then the Scabs had come and they'd brought him down here. He couldn't be moved. So they were waiting. Waiting for him to die.

Looking at the poor man, I wasn't sure which was worse. Being out there with the Scabs or being in here with this man and his germs. His mouth was smeared with blood, his eyes bright red and glossy as he stared into space. This is what Texas Slim called *Dracula eyes*. His face was slack, mottled, set with expanding red sores. He looked bruised, swollen with purple contusions. Every now and then he would tremble and make low hissing sounds or he'd vomit out tarry black blood. It was all over his shirt, the sleeping bag, the floor. It smelled horrible.

"Ebola-X," I said, very near panic.

"Yes, exactly," Price told me, studying the man without emotion, almost analytically. "It's dangerous to be in here with him. He's burning with virus. Quite literally biological toxic waste. The best we can do is keep our distance and avoid his body fluids, particularly that vomit. It's loaded with billions of particles of virus, highly infectious, all of which are lethal hot agents."

"You seem to know a lot about this stuff," I said.

"Hmmm. Yes. Once upon a time I was a microbiologist, a military biohazard specialist," he told me, shrugging. "Now I'm just a survivor. Like you. Like us all."

Price just stood there, staring at Bedecker, watching it happen with the sort of cold detachment that I suppose only a scientist could have. He was mumbling stuff under his breath. I went over to Janie. Morse was standing there with her. He snapped another shot of me.

I motioned Janie over to me, away from our intrepid photojournalist. "That guy's boiling with fucking Ebola-X over there. We're all in danger being in this room."

Janie didn't seem concerned. "Too bad it's not the full moon."

"Yeah, okay, Janie. Point is, we're all in danger here."

"There's nothing we can do about it. Not unless you want to be a hero and throw him to the Scabs."

"Why don't you just stop it?"

She looked at me long and hard. There was no warmth in her eyes. "I know what you're thinking," she said to me. "You're thinking you have two new sacrifices for your friend. Which one goes first? Price or Morse?"

"I wasn't thinking about them, Janie. I was thinking about *you*."

"Prick."

She walked away from me. So that was the state of our relationship. I was beginning to realize that Janie was no longer in my corner and probably could not be trusted. The Shape was the farthest thing from my mind. For the next two weeks I would not allow myself to even think of a selection. It wasn't until the third week that it began to creep into my mind. By the fourth week it became an obsession, one born not just out of fear of what The Shape might do if we didn't offer it something, but of what we would do if The Shape abandoned us.

But right now there were bigger fears.

I went back over to Price and smoked a cigarette with badly shaking fingers. "What's going on?" I said.

"Hmm. We are watching a man die from an infectious organism. And as we do so we are at ground zero of an explosive chain of lethal transmission." He was very clinical about the entire thing. "You see, Nash, when a hot virus infects its host, what it's trying to do, essentially, is to convert that host into virus. The process, of course, is not successful and what happens is what we're seeing here: a man literally turned into a morbid mass of liquefied flesh."

Price told me he had worked for the U.S. Army's Medical Research Institute of Infectious Diseases at Fort Detrick, Maryland. After the bombs came down, they were still in operation for several months, tracking outbreaks of infectious diseases in conjunction with the CDC. After nuclear winter lifted, one plague after another swept the country. It wasn't until late January that the first reports of a highly infective hemorrhagic fever appeared. It started in Baltimore, then swept like a firestorm through the northeast, devastating Pennsylvania, Maryland, Virginia, and New York before setting its teeth into Ohio. The symptoms were similar to those of Ebola and the Marburg Virus—both of the *filoviridae* family—only much more virulent. There just wasn't enough time to completely study this enhanced bug and it was never determined exactly whether the vector was airborne, through interpersonal contact, body fluids, or whether it was all of these things. Price saw enough of it, though, he said, to be certain that it could contaminate in all these ways.

"What happened?" I asked him. "What the hell are you doing in Des Moines?"

"I was born here. When Ebola-X nearly wiped us out in Maryland, a lot of us ran. I came back here. To my family." He uttered a sarcastic laugh. "I watched them all die, one by one. Not from this organism, Nash, but from radiation sickness, typhoid, cholera. I believe my brother died from Septicemic Plague. My sister's family was disease free. But the Hatchet Clans took care of that."

"How the hell did it get here?" I asked. "That virus? I mean, I heard of outbreaks in Africa and that one in the States in Washington DC, but that was just in monkeys."

He sighed, shook his head. "We needed more time, but we didn't have it. It was probably brought here by someone from Africa. There was a rumor floating around that the U.S. Army Medical Command had weaponized a strain of Ebola. I suppose it could have been loosed during the turmoil of the final days.

Russian virologists apparently weaponized a strain of Marburg at the Vector Institute in Koltsovo. It's possible this strain could have found its way into the hands of bioterrorists. It's anybody's guess."

I decided to ask a stupid question. "Could...I mean, is it possible that a virus could actually convert an *entire* body?"

"You mean turn a man into a walking viral body?" He shook his head but I saw uncertainty flash through his eyes. "We'd be giving the virus far too much credit, I'm afraid. It would have to perfectly assimilate the host cells, many of which like neurons are extremely complex."

I kept thinking about my dream of The Medusa, the Maker of Corpses, an immense disease entity, trailing us, always just behind, turning the devastated country into a graveyard city by city. I had no doubt whatsoever that Ebola and similar pathogenic germs had mutated in the radiation and were continuing to mutate. I imagined them evolving through countless generations every week, becoming something much more complex each time, finally transforming themselves into something diabolically intelligent and unbelievably deadly.

I didn't mention any of that to Price, though.

He said that viruses are the bridge between the living and non-living, the undead, as it were, of the microscopic world. They only act alive when in contact with living cells. They are parasites, entirely dependent on their hosts for biological processes. They are more or less protein capsules filled with genetic material encoded to replicate the virus itself. That's it. A virus lays around like its dead until it comes into contact with a compatible cell, then it adheres to it and uses the cell's machinery to make copies of itself. This goes on until the host cell literally explodes and out come countless baby viruses, each out to do the same thing to infinity unless the host dies or something like antibodies attack them.

"The virus has no lofty, ambitious plans, son," he told me. "They live only to replicate themselves which ultimately, in the case of Ebola-X, destroys the host. They are cellular predators, but not organized, not thinking. I can't imagine a line of organic evolution which would allow them to do more than this. They are probably one of the world's oldest life forms and as such, achieved perfection many, many eons ago."

I listened and learned, but I was not convinced. And I sure as hell was not about to argue with an expert and particularly when my only evidence was a series of fucking nightmares.

"Ah, now we see the unpleasant results of extreme amplification of the viral body," Price said, watching Bedecker's torment. "See how he is now rigid as of a corpse? He is filling with bloodclots. They are forming everywhere. Brain, vitals, organs, skin, bones. Hmm."

I looked at Price like he was crazy. I didn't know Bedecker, but he had been a human being once. Possibly a friend of Price's and here the old man was carrying on with this insane running commentary like this was a sport's event.

Morse was on the scene, of course, snapping shots of the dying man from every imaginable angle. He even took a telephoto lens from his bag and got some good close-ups. It was insane.

"See, Nash?" Price said. "Bedecker's not really suffering now. His brain is liquefying. His vitality and humanity have been erased. This is called *depersonalization.* What you are watching now is no longer a dying man but a biological machine choking on its own poisoned by-products," he told me. "The vomiting will continue, as will the bleeding..."

He was right. Bedecker was vomiting almost continually now, that same red-black stinking mush. Blood came from his eyes. His ears. His nostrils. He made an obscene farting sound and more drainage ran out from under his ass. Price said that liquefying sections of his stomach and intestines were being passed now, orally and anally. Blood flowed, gushed, poured as the hot agent ran from him, hungry to find a new host.

I was sick to my stomach. I tried to turn away but Price stopped me. "He is about to crash and bleed out."

Morse made sure this was documented.

I lit another cigarette to get the stink out of my face. I told Price that I had friends over at the dealership, that we should link up with them soon as possible.

"A wise idea," he said. "It'll be dark soon. The Scabs aren't active after sunset. We'll slip away then, though I fear there are worse things out there, much worse things by night. But we can't stay here."

Bedecker was thrashing around, literally sloughing apart as poisoned blood and bubbling fluids came out of every opening.

"It won't be long now," Price said.

6

I took the lead. Janie was right behind me with Morse. Price was in the back. I had three rounds left in my Beretta and that was about the only safety net we had. Scared? No, I was absolutely fucking terrified.

I was thinking hard about Carl and the others. I wondered what they were doing and I prayed they were still alive. But I knew Carl. It would have taken quite an assault by the Scabs to take him out. He was a survivor as they all were. I was surprised that he hadn't tried to come after us, but maybe he had. I just wanted to link back up with them.

Des Moines by night was dark and forbidding.

The moon was still pretty bright above, but shadows were everywhere, circling, shifting, tangling in the streets. As we rounded the corner from the department store, I could see the vague hulk of the dealership in the distance. On a sunny day it was a short, pleasant hop in the old days. Now, by darkness, it was a slow, hellish crawl through no man's land. The air was damp, acrid-smelling. Off to the west I could see a flickering red glow. I assumed parts of the city were still burning or had been ignited anew. I could smell a slight odor of smoke, other things I didn't like to think about. We moved on very carefully. I scoped out the car lots across the way, looking for anything moving out there. I heard a brief, shrill squealing in the distance. Like the sound of an insect...only it was a *big,* scary sound.

Just relax, I told myself again and again. *It's really not that far.*

In the phosphorescence of the moonlight, everything was forbidding and ghostly. Buildings rose like defiled tombs and haunted monoliths. Parked trucks looked like ghost ships rising from the gloom. The skin at the back of my neck was crawling, moving in subtle prickling waves. Something was out there, something was moving around us in the shadows and I new it.

"What was that?" Janie said, suddenly stopping.

The sound of her voice in the stillness made me seize up. "What? I didn't hear anything." I wanted it to be true, but I knew it wasn't. There had been a sound. Something.

Price said, "I would advise a bit of haste on our part, people. Survival by night in the streets of Des Moines is rather minimal at best."

There he went being clinical again, couching everything in his uppity verse. What he meant to say was, *we don't haul ass, motherfuckers, ain't gonna be nothing but a stain out here come morning*. I ignored him. I stood there with Janie, tensing, my hand greasy on the butt of the Beretta. I decided to start moving when I heard it very clearly this time: a squeaking sound. This was followed a strong odor of decay, of dampness and subterranean dank. The way a sewer might smell, I suppose.

I had smelled it before. I knew what we were up against.

"This is disturbing," Price said.

"It's okay. Nash won't let anything happen to us," Janie told him like he was some kid in need of reassuring.

Morse circled around us, snapping off shots.

"Knock it the fuck off," I told him.

What we were facing, if I was right, was something that not even good old Nash could do anything about. I moved forward slowly and I made it maybe six feet before I saw the first of our visitors.

A rat.

It was about the size of a tomcat, its entire body swollen and misshapen with bulging pink cancerous growths that rose from the sparse gray-black fur like fleshy bubbles. In the moonlight I saw them moving.

Every time I saw one I remembered that monster in the storm drains of Cleveland.

"Stay put, don't panic," I told the others. "This is probably a scout out scavenging ahead of the main pack."

Click-click, went Morse.

The rat's snakelike, scaly tail twitched on the concrete like it knew what I was saying. Its eyes were fixed, blood-red, shining like wet marbles. Its jaws were open, loops of saliva hanging from them. I knew from experience how fast these bastards were. I brought up my Beretta very slowly, very calmly, and drew a bead on old Mr. Rat.

He made a sudden high-pitched squealing sound.

I shot him in the head and he pitched forward, blood running from him in a scarlet pool. I could see the fat, grub-like parasites jumping in his hide.

I pulled Janie away and our chain was on the march again. I knew we were in terrible danger; I just didn't know what to do about it other than continue on. Maybe, possibly, somehow, we'd make it through. We started to cross the street in the direction of the dealership which looked huge and tomblike in the moonlight, just crawling with shadows. We hadn't gone far before the rats came out of their hides. They'd been waiting amongst the cars, the main pack, and now here they came. I heard Janie make a disgusted sound in her throat. The rats were everywhere with more arriving all the time. They were huge, absolutely huge. Some of them were the size of full-grown German Shepherds. And all of them dirty and stinking, eyes shining in the darkness, drool running from their jaws, noses twitching.

I knew then that the squealing noise the other rat made was either a cry for help or a warning to the others.

Well, they had the advantage now.

They crept out of the shadows, mutant horrors with growths and white twitching things coming out of their flesh. I did not look too closely. They had closed in on us and there was no way in hell we were going to make the dealership. Going back was out of the question, too, because more rats were filling the streets behind us. Our only avenue of escape was into the buildings behind us. But Janie and I had checked the doors pretty carefully in our run from the Scabs.

There was only one possibility and it was slim.

A narrow dead-ended alley cut between a couple buildings. I saw a fire escape hanging down. The ladder was pulled up, but if it wasn't rusted too badly, I might be able to pull it down.

"Okay," I said. "Price, slowly lead us into that alley. That's where we're going."

He didn't argue. I think by that point even his arrogance had somewhat paled. He led us to the fire escape and the rats moved in, taking their time, closing off any avenue of escape like soldiers in battle formation. They had us and they knew it.

The fire escape. I leaped up, grabbed it and pulled down with all my strength and weight. It slid down an inch, two, then seized. I threw everything into it, flopping and twisting, wishing I still had my beer belly. Janie jumped up and grabbed me around the waist and we swung together like a couple acrobats and I could feel my pants pulling down and I had sudden ludicrous vision of how ridiculous I'd look with my pants around my ankles when the rats feasted on me. Particularly with our crazy photographer taking pictures of my torment.

The ladder let go and let go fast. Next thing I knew we were on our asses in the alley. I got Janie onto the ladder. "Go, go, go!" I told her, the rats moving now, sensing something was terribly amiss with their midnight snack.

Morse went up it like a monkey and Price moved pretty quick and then I was climbing. A rat leaped and seized the toe of my boot. I shook him free and kicked another away and I made the platform above. Two rats were climbing. I stomped one on the snout and he fell, the other was too big so I shot him in the head and down he went. And by then, the alley was a sea of mulling rats. We slid the ladder up and there wasn't a damn they could do about it.

They were squealing and squeaking, feeding on the one I'd shot, but mostly just pissed off. A few of them tried climbing the alley wall, but only made a few feet before they fell back. I waited there until they grew bored and left the alley.

We made it.

7

We broke a window and slipped into an apartment. It was dirty and dusty and dark in there, but there was nothing waiting for us. We made a quick check of the place and the only thing we found was the mummy of a woman in bed holding onto the mummy of an infant. Both were festooned with cobwebs. Their meat was long gone, but their skin had dried to a fine, flaking parchment that clung to the bones beneath. Both had black hair.

We decided we weren't comfortable in there and went to another apartment. No bones, no nothing. We sat in the darkness and waited. The minutes ticked by. I had two bullets left and I was painfully aware of the fact.

"I would think the cautious thing to do would be to wait until sunup," Price said.

And as he said it, I heard a sound from the floor above us. Something large and weighty had shifted up there, sliding its bulk across the floor.

"No," I said. "I don't think that would be a good idea at all. Let's give it an hour or so."

I knew the rats well by that point. They were industrious, cunning, relentless, but not the most patient creatures in the world. If their prey escaped as we had, they would move on to greener pastures. So we waited in the dusty darkness while Morse got a few shots for *Better Homes and Gardens*. We were silent. I could smell the perspiration coming off the others, feel their warmth, hear their slow breathing. They were counting on me to deliver them from this mess. I considered our options. The only logical thing to do was to make another try for the dealership, link up with the others.

After about thirty minutes, I said, "Let's scope out the downstairs."

We moved down the dim hallway, guiding ourselves by the moonlight that spilled through a narrow window at the end. I found the stairs and down we went. The bottom floor was occupied by a health food store which appeared to be untouched for the most part. I guess tofu and shirataki noodles weren't a big draw when the world ended. It was damnably dark in there. Peering out the plate glass windows, I saw that the streets were empty.

Looking around, I saw that the store was not as untouched as I first thought. Something had happened here. There bones scattered over the floor, unarticulated skeletons of human beings and various animals, all just heaped and tossed around in no particular order. It was too dark to see properly, but I was guessing there were the remains of dozens.

"Why would this be here?" Janie asked. "Why here? Why dumped like this?"

Price shrugged. "Who can say? We might have stumbled upon somebody's private ossuary."

But I wasn't buying that either. I kicked a skull out of the way and grabbed up a long bone. A human femur, I thought. I brought it to the next aisle amongst the moldered, crumbling organic pasta. I examined it in a stray patch of moonlight. It was scratched up, gnawed, riddled with minute punctures. Something had been chewing on it and I was guessing the same went for all the bones.

"What is it?" Janie said when I came back and tossed the bone into the heap.

I was about to tell her that the bone had been nibbled on by rats, though I honestly didn't believe it was anything as prosaic as mutant rats. I opened my mouth to do so and I heard a shifting, leathery sound from somewhere overhead and then Price cried out and Janie screamed.

"Look out!" I shouted.

Something had Price. Something twisting and undulant had looped around his throat. I threw myself at him and tried to peel it off his throat. It was scabby and pulsing and felt almost like braided rope. But it was no rope. It was alive. I pulled my gun and fired up at the black bulk above Price. In the muzzle flash I saw a series of tendrils or tentacles, black and oily, squirming and writhing. And mouths. Something with two or three mouths that were vibrantly pink with fine sharp teeth like fish bones.

Morse was trying to take its picture. I knocked him out of the way.

It made a weird squealing sound when I shot it.

But it dropped Price right away.

I could feel a sickening, feverish heat coming from the thing as it rustled and slithered above, a rank stink like decaying hides. It was a dark shape in constant motion. I took aim and fired again and it made that shrill squealing again. In the muzzle flash I saw...I *think* I saw...something like a huge bat retreating into an oval cavity in the ceiling. I saw something like membranous wings unfolding, shiny flesh like greased vinyl set with a tiny hairs, mouths, and more than two beady, bulbous eyes. It moved quickly and was gone, in-between the floors.

I couldn't even guess what it might have been.

I was only glad it wasn't in the mood for a fight.

I got Price to his feet and got him over by the doorway. There was a circular burn around his throat like something that might be left by a hangman's noose. But he was all right. The streets were empty and I opened the door.

"Everyone hold hands," I said. "We're going on a run."

We raced across the street and nothing came loping out of the shadows to stop us. We crossed first to one car lot and then another and came around the side of the dealership. We went in there and made the first showroom and a blinding light hit me in the face.

"It's about fucking time," Carl said, lowering his flashlight.

8

The morning dawned gray and pale like the blood had been sucked from it. The dark pulled away and vanished into holes and cellars for the day. After crashing for a few hours, I was awake with Carl and Texas Slim to greet the new day.

"Tell me something," Texas said as the others stretched and yawned and got their stuff together. "You think this is why came here? For this Price fellow? You think that's it?"

"Yes, I have a feeling it is."

"But why?"

I shook my head. "I don't know. It's just a feeling. Take it or leave it."

He looked like he wanted to leave it and I did not argue the point.

"I say we ditch that Morse guy," Carl said. "He takes another picture of me and I'm drilling him."

"Go easy," I said. "He's just confused."

The Jeep was untouched and we were thankful for that. Texas and Carl carried plastic jerry cans of gas out to it that they had siphoned from other vehicles and set about filling it up. Janie was off packing up our stuff with Morse. I stood there, leaning up against a Chevy Cobalt, pulling off a cigarette. Mickey was there. She was watching me but not speaking.

After a time, I said, "Go ahead. Say it. Say what's on your mind."

I looked over at her, expecting to see the fire in her eyes. She quite often gave me the impression that she was in heat. "I was never much in the old days," she said. "I was the kind of person you probably think I was. I made a living getting my picture taken, if you catch my drift. Sometimes I wore a bikini or something equally as scanty, sometimes I didn't wear a thing. No porno, though. Believe me, I was offered, but it wasn't my thing. You'd be surprised at how many calendars I did."

I smiled. "No, I wouldn't be surprised at all," I told her, wondering what the sudden need for confession was all about.

She gave me a smile, threw her hair back. She knew I liked to look at her. What sexy woman doesn't know men like to look at her?

"Bottom line is, Nash, is that I was never much. I considered myself a model. My mother considered me a whore. But I made good money posing with motorcycles and trucks and ATVs, wearing tool belts and hardhats and nothing much else." She shrugged. "But I never felt like I was part of anything. Not until now."

"Now?"

"You'll probably think it's crazy. Now that I'm with you guys I feel...needed, part of something. It makes no sense, I know. But it's true. You make me feel safe, protected. This world is fucked up and dangerous, but I feel secure with you, Nash. I felt it right away. There's a power coming off you. An energy. We all feel it. It's what draws us to you."

"I'm nothing special, trust me," I told her.

"Oh, yes you are."

She told me the secure feeling came from me, not the others. They had nothing to do with it. She said that when Gremlin was with us he just gave her the creeps because he was like the men she always assumed salivated over her calendars. The sort that would have fucked a toilet seat if they thought her ass had touched it. Gremlin had been like that.

"A small mind with surging hormones," she said. "A walking idiot penis."

I started laughing. Yeah, she had that asshole pegged, all right.

"I study people, Nash," she told me. "I always have. People and their relationships interest me."

"And what do you think of the relationships in my little posse?"

"I think they're tight, solid. You have a good group," she admitted. "Carl's okay. He's like your obedient watchdog. He'd never betray you. Texas Slim? Oh boy, how do you categorize him. He's weird, but loyal. He sure likes to talk about mortuaries and embalming bodies. I have to think his interest in corpses is not purely professional. Then again, he's about ninety percent bullshit. Underneath he's okay."

Mickey admitted that Janie intimidated her a bit. Probably because Janie didn't like her and felt threatened by her presence. But there was no reason for that, Mickey said, because Janie herself was pretty, features finely-sculpted and perfectly Nordic from her blue eyes to her high cheekbones and the blonde hair that was not so much yellow as silver.

"She's really got it going on, Nash. But if you don't mind me saying so, she's a little cool. Not just to me, but to you, to everybody. She's caring and compassionate, though. She gives you that feeling that she cares a lot more than she's willing to admit, but it's sort of a, I care, honey, but from the end of a stick."

Mickey said that she'd felt the bond between me and Janie right away. Like she was plugged into me or I was plugged into her and together we completed some sort of arcane circuit.

"Sure," I said. "But I'm beginning to think that circuit is dead."

"If it is, I'm sure she'll blame me for it," Mickey told me. She stared at me for some time. "You have the power and I knew it right away. Just looking at you made the hairs stand up on the back of my neck. But I wondered what it was at first. Everybody walked light around you, except for Janie with her mood swings. I knew you had something going because whatever it was, the others were terrified of it."

I could feel myself warming to her already. She was honest. Honest like Janie was honest, but more straightforward, no games, no subtlety, no esoteric feminine mystery. With Mickey, everything was on the table in plain sight. There was something very refreshing about that.

"And what do you think now that you know about The Shape?" I asked her. "Do you think I'm some kind of horrible monster? Some psycho who gets his kicks hurting other people? No mercy, just a fucking animal. That's what Janie thinks."

Mickey put the full force of her hungry eyes on me and it was considerable. "No, Nash. That's not what I think at all. You do it for the good of all even though it scares you and you hate it. But I don't hate it," she said, moving in a little closer. "I respect the power you have. In fact, it turns me on."

I could have laughed, but I didn't. It was true. I could see it in her eyes. Power got her off and she wasn't too proud to admit it.

"How's you intuition working?"

"Just fine."

"You feeling anything?" I said. "About what might be coming our way?"

"Yes."

"And?"

She licked her lips and looked away. "We're in terrible danger."

9

We were driving.

It was decided that the simplest route out of the city would be the one we took in. Follow I-80 out and head west. I didn't have the slightest idea where in the west we were going, I only knew that we had to keep heading in that direction. For it was out there somewhere. What I was looking for or what The Shape wanted me to find. In just about every way entering Des Moines seemed like an awful waste of time, yet I knew it had been important. Somehow. Was it Price? Was that it? I couldn't say for sure, but it seemed likely. The idea of it scared me. For the only real use Price seemed to have was that he was an expert on infectious diseases.

Time would tell.

Carl was driving, complaining about all the wreckage. Mickey was sitting up front with him. I sat in the back with Price and Texas. Janie was in the way back seat with Morse. I turned to say something to her, but she held a finger to her lips. Morse was sleeping and that was a good thing. I started plying Price with questions. Maybe I just wanted to hear somebody talk who knew something about what was going on.

So Price talked. "Even in the old days nobody wanted anything to do with Ebola," he told us. "Even your veteran biohazard experts were scared of it. It gave virologists the cold sweats. The way a lot of us were thinking was that Ebola was the doomsday machine of germs, the only life form we had encountered thus far that could truly put a serious dent in the human population. Maybe more than a dent, maybe a big ugly hole. The Ebola organism was the most frightening thing we could imagine. We knew too little about it. It popped up along the Ebola River in Africa, wiped out some villages, continued a pattern of sporadic, though minor, outbreaks in the next few decades, but never really broke out. Maybe if it had, we could have nailed the bastard. But it was all sketchy. We couldn't be sure of the vector. Was it airborne? Waterborne? Both? Neither? Were the corpses of its victims vectors? We tracked it to central Africa and there the trail went cold. We knew it was there somewhere, proliferating, but we never could find the headwater, the reservoir. Yet we knew it existed. And that scared us. We were all envisioning a massive breakthrough into the human race, the virus crashing from one individual to the next. Millions dead within weeks. So it was no wonder that biohazard people wet themselves at the idea of working with this deadly little bug.

One little tear in your protective suit...well, that's it, isn't it? The virus will flood into your system through any tiny cut or abrasion."

Price went on to tell us that Ebola was the perfect microbial firestorm. Once it gets inside you the war is over before the first battle is fought. So it was all bad enough on the old Ebola front, he informed us, then Ebola-X showed.

It was even worse, if such a thing is imaginable.

Basically the same bug, just pumped up and with a very bad attitude. It spread faster, it killed quicker. Ebola-X attacks every part of the human body, sparing nothing: nervous tissue, marrow, organs, lymphatics. It goes after everything, absolutely laying waste to the immune system. It begins with massive blood clotting which restricts blood supply to the various systems of the body. Starved of nutrients and oxygen, tissues go necrotic. Connective tissue become mush, the skin is covered with bright red lesions which seem to expand as you watch. The flesh goes to pulp and internal bleeding begins. Your gums go to putty and your teeth fall out. Your eyes fill with blood and blood runs from every available orifice. Black infected vomit comes out in great quantities, tearing the skin off the tongue and bringing up sloughed, dead tissue from the windpipe and stomach while blood flows from your ass thick with macerated chunks of your intestines. The organs bloat as they fill with clotted blood and begin to decay. The testicles swell up like hard blue balls, nipples bleed, and vaginas eject infected tissue and copious amounts of black-red drainage. If the unlucky victim is a woman and she is pregnant, she spontaneously aborts the child who emerges infected with Ebola-X, blood running from it, eyes brilliantly red. The child, like the mother, is toxic biological waste.

"The end result...well it's horrible, like something thrown together by Hollywood special effects people. The body literally liquefies into fleshy soup hot with virus." Price stared out the window at the ruin of civilization. "Ebola was bad enough, but we knew with Ebola-X we were looking at the perfect killing machine. The hand of a very angry god. A species threatening event."

After that little discourse, nobody said a damn thing. Not for quite while. The gruesome details had done their job on us.

"Well, you certainly are a cheerful fellow," Texas Slim told Price after a time and there was absolutely no humor behind his words.

I was still thinking about The Medusa. I wanted to relay my fears to Price somehow without sounding like some kind of paranoid whacko who couldn't tell the difference between nightmare and reality. Later I knew, if the chance came and I could get him away from the others, I would tell him. I would make him listen. And if he thought I was raving, so be it.

We drove on and I saw Mickey watching me in the rearview. When I caught her eyes, she smiled. I was glad she was with us and at the same time I saw her as a possibly destructive element. I believed for the most part everything she'd told me that morning, but I wasn't naïve. I knew women like her with all the right stuff in all the right places made a career of manipulating men. I knew I had to be careful.

"If I might ask," Price said, "what exactly fuels this desire to travel west? You seem to have no clear idea of where you're going or even why you want to go there. I find that a bit confusing."

Texas looked over at me and I didn't dare meet his eyes. I could feel Janie's eyes on me, too, probably bitter with hate and recrimination. I had to tell him; he was part of this, he deserved to know. But I was hoping for a more intimate chat. I don't know what I would have said and I never had the chance because there was a sudden impact and the Jeep fishtailed in the street, glanced off a parked car and smashed into a pile of rubble.

10

Of course, Morse came out of his peaceful sleep screaming and immediately reaching for his Nikon. Everyone was yelling and shouting and wondering what in the Christ had happened. Me among them. Something had hit us and hit us damn hard. This was no accidental run into a parked car or a slab of building. Something had hit us. Something really damn big. Through the windshield I could see nothing but a swirling cloud of dust.

"Is everyone all right?" I said, once things calmed down.

"We're okay, I think," Carl said. "Have to check the Jeep, though."

"What was it?" Janie wanted to know.

"Perhaps our friend Carl drove us into something," Texas Slim suggested.

"Fuck I did. Something hit us. Something big."

But what? That's what I kept asking myself. We had come around a blind corner created by a shattered building and its attendant rubble and then...I don't know...I saw a flash of silver. Then...*boom.*

"I think it was a bus," Mickey said. "It came out of nowhere...but it looked kind of like a big bus."

"That's what I saw, too," Carl said.

I looked from one to the other. "A school bus? A Greyhound? Hell kind of bus?"

"Nothing like that," Mickey told me. "It was bright silver. Like a train."

We piled out. The front passenger side quarter panel of the Jeep had a good dent in it, a very big dent, but it wasn't pushed in enough to rub against the front tire. Carl checked the engine, the undercarriage. Everything was okay. For once, vehicle-wise, we'd caught a break.

"I'm still wandering what it was," Texas said.

"Look," Mickey said, examining the dent. She scraped something out of it with her fingernail: a strip of silver paint. "See? I told you. It was a big fucking silver bus."

Morse got a shot of the paint.

I was picturing one of those chartered coaches that used to take elderly people down to Bransom, Missouri for foot-stomping country music. One of those out on a wild joy ride. It was ridiculous, but the image in my mind persisted.

"It didn't have windows," Janie said.

We all looked at her.

"That's what I saw. I wasn't really looking. I think I was nodding off," she explained. "But then I opened my eyes and I saw this metal, silvery thing. It was huge. But it had no windows. No windows at all."

I thought maybe some kind of military vehicle. But *silver bus...silver bus...*those words kept running through my mind. Where had I heard something about a big silver bus?

Mickey was tapping a long index finger to her lips. "That guy...do you remember? That weirdo in the bathrobe? He was saying something about a silver bus."

Carl laughed. "That fucking Gomer? Shit, he had painted purple toenails and he was carrying a fucking phonebook. He said he ate his dog."

But I was remembering now, too. The bathrobe guy, crazy, deluded, shellshocked...but not necessarily wrong. What had he said exactly?

They came in silver buses. I saw 'em. They had orange suits on. They took Reverend Bob and threw him in the bus.

"Might I ask what you people are talking about?" Price said.

I told him. I told him about the guy and what he had said which had struck me as being very odd at the time. Now I was wondering if it wasn't so odd after all and I think Price was wondering the same thing.

"Hmm. A silver bus. Men in orange suits, did he say? Interesting."

There was no time for speculation then. We were wide open in the streets. We got back in and Carl got behind the wheel and got us rolling. As we drove out, I tried several times to engage Janie in conversation but she wasn't having it. Every time I spoke to her, she'd ask Texas or Price a question or pose for one of Morse's photos.

She's gone over the line, hasn't she? I kept telling myself. *Bitch is alive because you've taken care of her and now she's turning on you. You gonna put up with that, Rick? Maybe you ought to introduce her to big brother Shape next month...*

An angry, betrayed sort of revenge fantasy, that's all it was. I wouldn't do that to Janie. But on the other hand, if it came down to it, who *would* I select? Looking at the faces crowded into the Jeep, I knew it wouldn't be easy if it came to it.

Every corner we turned, every street we prowled down, I expected trouble. But there was nothing. Nothing at all. My guts in my throat, Carl drove us out of Des Moines. And even then I think I really knew where we were going. Because I'd heard it in my sleep last night.

Nebraska.

II

We left Des Moines and drove for a few hours until we spotted a little roadside park with a historical marker. A river ran through it and there was a waterfall back along the trail. We were dirty and we needed to clean up. So we took turns bathing and it felt wonderful. Janie and Mickey went first. Then Price and Texas and Carl. I made Morse go alone. I figured nobody wanted him clicking shots of them in the raw even if there was no film in the camera.

I went last. The water was chilly, but refreshing and I could have stayed in there all day.

I needed to think.

We were right on the outer edge of something and I knew it. Some great abyss was opening before us and it had everything to do with Nebraska, where The Shape wanted us to go. The endgame was coming soon. Destiny was just over the state line and I knew it. I felt it right down into my marrow.

As I stood under the cascading water, I thought about all that I had lost. I thought about Specs. I thought about Sean. But mostly I thought about my wife. I thought about Shelly and it seemed she'd been dead a hundred years. Her image was still in my mind. But it was no longer clear, no longer fresh, almost like an old photograph that was slowly fading.

And that scared me. It really did.

I remembered Shelly dying and I started to cry. I was happy that she had not died alone and unloved like so many others. I was glad that I held her hand as she passed. She was out of it by then and probably didn't even know I was there, but I don't believe that. I don't believe that at all. I think she was aware. I think she died knowing I loved her.

You would have been such a good mother, I thought. Remember how we talked about kids, Shelly? Remember that? Oh, our children would have been so lucky to have you as a mother. You would have been so perfect. You were an angel in every way and I'm glad I told you so and I only wish that we'd have had kids so I could be telling them now how wonderful of a woman their mother was.

These were the things I was thinking.

I couldn't seem to think much else. I stood there in a daze and somewhere during the process, I realized I was not alone. Mickey was standing there at the edge of the river, up to her ankles in the water.

"Mind if I join you?" she asked.

Well, I wanted to tell her to go away and leave me brood, but I didn't and I honestly didn't want to. "Sure. Come on in."

Mickey stepped out of her shorts and her T-shirt and she was amazingly beautiful. Just long-legged, high breasted, her skin bronzed by the sun, long dark hair sweeping down one shoulder. I don't think I'd ever wanted anyone as badly as I'd wanted her at that moment and she damn well knew it. She'd been orchestrating this since she joined us and I hated her for it. Almost as much as I hated myself for giving into it.

"Come here," I told her and it was not a request.

I swept her into my arms and her flesh was cool from the water, but I could feel the heat blazing between her legs. I took hold of her roughly and she did not fight. Her tongue was hot in my mouth. We fondled and kissed like that for a moment and then I grabbed her by the hair and pulled her down, slid my cock in her mouth. I forced her head up and down on it and made her gag. When I was hard, I grabbed her by the hips, digging my fingers into the cheeks of her ass and she wrapped her legs around me.

There was nothing tender about it.

I brought her over to a waist-high shelf of rock and put her down. I spread her legs apart and slid into her. She was a fantasy fuck, there was no doubt about it. I took her like I hated her. I slammed into her and made her cry out. And when I came, I shoved her away from me. There was no love involved. It was brutal, violent.

And that's exactly what she wanted.

By the time I was done and I stepped out of the water with her trailing behind, I knew one thing for sure: Janie had been watching us.

12

And she had been. I knew it. I could see the recrimination in her eyes, the way she looked at me like some squirming thing that had slid out from under a rock. Maybe it was my imagination. I don't know. She'd been giving me the evil eye for so long it was hard to be sure.

That night I dreamed of The Medusa moving east to west like some immense malefic vacuum cleaner sucking up the last of the human race from decaying cities like dust from a carpet and leaving nothing but polished white bones behind.

It was getting closer and closer and I could not get away from it. I saw its face. And worse, it saw me. It called me by name.

And then hands were shaking me awake.

"Nash," Janie said. "It's just a dream. That's all it is. Just a dream. You have to be quiet. I finally got Morse to sleep." She told me this like he was some little kid she had to tuck in. Maybe he was.

I laid there, looking up at her, sweat running down my temples. "I saw it," I told her. "It's coming for us. It's getting closer."

She just nodded. "It's been coming for a long time."

"You've...you've seen it?"

"In my dreams. We probably all have."

"Janie..."

"Go to sleep, Rick."

"Stay with me," I said. "Don't leave me alone."

She shook her head. "It can't be that way anymore and I think you know why, don't you? Go to sleep. When you wake up you can tell yourself it was only a dream."

I never felt so alone before.

13

As we drove to Nebraska, Price and I spent a lot of time talking. He was a very intelligent man and there seemed to be little he did not know about. One night, sitting by a fire in a sheltered field off the highway, I told him about The Shape. He was part of it and I figured he needed to know.

It was just the two of us.

I was expecting him to laugh at the very idea. He was a scientist. An educated man. But he did not laugh...he looked very grim as I told him about The Shape. Afterwards, he went silent for a long time, lost in thought.

Being Price, he had a few theories on my friend.

He said that The Shape was the ultimate cosmic chaos, something born of nuclear fission and plutonium saturation from the very blast furnace of creation...something that was nothing until the radiation brought it into being, gave it body and mind and attitude, if you can dig that. A wraith essentially, a spook birthed from a thermonuclear womb, a supercharged flux of sentient radiation.

A brand new devil for a brand new world.

"The destruction of our old world, Nash, has given birth to a new one that is very frightening in all respects," he said. "The biological mutations we've all seen are really minor in comparison to things like this Shape of yours and other things that may be coming to pass out there now. There's nothing supernatural about any of it...but at the same time, it's all so beyond our science and our meager simian powers of reasoning, that it seems almost godlike."

"You haven't seen The Shape," I told him. "But when you do...well, let's just say it's enough to put you to your knees."

"I believe it would be."

The Devil of the new world, as it were, Price believed to be a random series of particles that became organized and cohesive and organic, for lack of a better word, as a result of massive fallout. And let's face it, as crazy as that sounds, this particular bogeyman had been waiting to be born a long time. All the raw materials were there in barrels of radioactive waste, the cores of atomic reactors, and stores of unstable isotopes. Just laying there waiting, waiting to be born. Much like the inorganic chemicals of Azoic earth had waited to become life.

I had always wondered why The Shape only showed on nights of the full moon. Sometimes I could talk to him in my head on other nights, but only on the nights of the full moon would he show for his latest meal. I figured it was all impossibly esoteric and mystical, something supernatural that my poor little brain could never hope to understand.

But Price had a theory on that, too.

In fact, wasn't much that guy didn't have a theory on. From female orgasms to the mating cycles of katydids, Price had a very definitive opinion. He was one of those guys that were just too smart for their own good. I tried to argue with him about a few topics, but that was a mistake. He made me feel like a striped ape wallowing in my own shit. He was a professional debater and he took me off right at the knees, leaving me feeling stupid and annoyed and goddamn uneducated. Annoyed mainly, because he never seemed to see me as an equal, but as an object of amusement like a cute little puppy that had learned not to piss on the furniture, but hardly an intellectual equal.

And you would think that I would have been offended by that, but I wasn't. I admired people like him. I really did. Often in blue collar people like me you get a sort of reverse snobbery where anyone with money or higher education becomes an object of ridicule. And, yes, sometimes it was warranted, but very often not. In Price's case, it was not. He was highly intelligent and intuitive and if I were to have dismissed him out of some Neanderthal bias, then the only fool would have been me.

So I did not dismiss him.

I listened; I learned.

Price had a theory on the full moon bit, too, as I said.

And he gave it to me in the form of a lecture as always. He said that if you looked through the body of folklore and tradition concerning the moon—he had, of course—then you would see certain underlying principles that were intriguing. The moon, he said, had a history of inciting the human species. It drove men mad. It regulated the menstrual cycles of women. It was forever an object of religious importance. To many primitive societies, the moon was considered a goddess, the creator of time and space, the repository of human souls...those unborn and those awaiting reincarnation. This Moon-Goddess ruled the cycles of creation and fertility and death and this was why ancient calendars were very often based on lunar phases *and* the menstrual cycles of women which were very often identical in duration. The moon ruled not only the tides, but human and animal life, rebirth and procreation. That's why Scottish girls at one time would only wed on a full moon and why certain crops could only be planted beneath its glowering eye. Witches were said to draw down the moon, to call up demons and familiars only on this blessed night.

But much of that was superstition and yet, he told me, there was a germ of underlying truth to it all. For the geomagnetic pull of the moon had a decided impact on all living things and their individual electromagnetic fields and maybe it was at these times of greatest influence—the full moon phase—that certain doors were open that might be closed on other nights. Maybe witches really did call down demons and nameless monstrosities and maybe those things were much like The Shape in origin and composition. The same geomagnetic force that made crops and women fertile, might also create an ideal environment for something like The Shape to physically manifest itself, exploiting cosmic and lunar energies to give itself substance.

Just a theory again, but I liked it.

Price was a smart guy, like I said.

I think he was dead right about not only the moon's influence, but about the nature of The Shape itself. And I told him as much. Not that being right came as much of a surprise to him; he was usually right.

"It wants us to go west," I told him. "It's been pushing me in that direction ever since Cleveland. I don't know why. But there must be something out there. Something..."

Price put his analytical mind on it and right away said, "Maybe it's not pushing you *towards* something, but *away* from something."

God, the guy was good.

There were other things I wanted to say to him. Things about my dreams, about The Medusa, but I wasn't ready just yet. It was coming, though. I knew that much. Because The Medusa was out there, chewing its way through the ruined cities of men, picking the last meat off the last bones of humanity. And it was coming for us.

Knowing this, feeling death and plague gathering behind us, I said, "You worked in a lab back east, right? Tell me what that was like. Tell me what happened at the end."

14

"As I told you," Price said, "I was a biohazard specialist. My area of expertise was Level 4 hot agents, highly infectious organisms capable of causing pandemics. At research facilities like Fort Detrick, there were four levels of biohazard, you see, Biohazard Level 4 being the most dangerous. This is where we manipulate and study infectious diseases for which there are no vaccines: hantaviruses, dengue fever, hemorrhagic fevers, the Marburg and Ebola viruses, other hot agents that have been weaponized or genetically altered to increase their virulence."

Price said that in order to gain access to a Biohazard Level 4 complex it was like going into outer space. You went through multiple airlocks in a self-contained Hazmat suit that looked very much like a space suit. So much that everyone called them this. You were decontaminated going in and out, subjected to chemical showers and ultraviolet lights, low-level radiation, scanned by mechanisms that could detect the presence of lethal bioorganisms. It was quite a process, apparently. Level 4 containment zones are kept under negative air pressure, he told me, so that if there is a leak, the air will not flow out into the world, but be sucked back into the hot zone itself.

After the bombs came down, there was one pandemic after another and everyone was scrambling to keep up with them. The team Price was part of—the Special Pathogens Branch—were interested in Ebola-X which had broken loose in Baltimore. They needed to study it before it was too late and this was no easy thing with the infrastructure of the country crumbling around them.

"But we had priority and we were under military jurisdiction," he said. "We were ordered to begin a massive biocontainment operation. So this is what we did. To begin with, we needed specimens to work with. So a Biocon SWAT team swept down in full Hazmat and secured us some thirty people from an apartment complex. They were taken to the *Slammer*, which is a biologically secure facility, half hospital and half working laboratory.

"I was there during the op. Several of those we took—and we did *take* them, Nash, make no mistake on that, civil rights be damned—had already slipped into terminal comas. Many were bleeding out. The majority were obviously infected, but really just terrified."

And it was only the beginning of their terror.

They were brought to the Slammer and each was sealed in biocontainment cells. Within hours, even the healthier individuals were beginning to crash. This new enhanced Ebola moved very swiftly, Price and the others soon learned. It was a pathetic sight to see human beings being destroyed in such a way, he said. Their eyes were staring out, glassy and brilliantly red, blood running from their noses, their faces transformed into rubber fright masks from massive destruction of facial connective tissue and the fact that their brains were degrading into a pudding of gray matter.

There was no time to lose.

Although blood and other tissues had been collected, they needed liver tissue collected at the moment of death. This was called an agonal biopsy. A biopsy syringe was inserted into the liver which, like the other organs, had begun to liquefy. And it is here, at the point of death, that the cadaver undergoes spontaneous liquefaction as necrotic organs and tissues literally melt and fluids drain free in copious amounts, the blood black as tar, all of it cooking hot with virus.

Within forty-eight hours, all the subjects were dead.

Price said it was interesting to note that Ebola-X—while mimicking ordinary Ebola or Marburg in that it attacks the skin, soft tissues, organs, etc. like some ferocious viral wolf—also mimics radiation sickness. They ran into a lot of that at Detrick.

Subjects whose faces were splitting open from sores, whose hair and teeth had fallen out. It looked like exposure to toxic levels of radiation. But it was just the virus. He said all of the subjects became delusional as their brains were eaten away and more than a few became psychotic. And all of that—from the sores to the baldness and the rage—made me think of the Scabs. Maybe there was no connection.

Price went on, "We performed a series of autopsies and found exactly what we knew we'd find," he said, his face sculpted by shadows. "The liver was yellow and liquefied, kidneys ruptured, intestines filled with blood and decayed. It was the same with all organs and connective tissue. They had gone necrotic and dissolved. Each cadaver was the same...biological waste as the result of extreme viral amplification.

"The next stage was to cultivate the organism," Price said. "We put organ tissues from the dead into flasks with living cells from the liver we had biopsied. We did a series of these with blood, mucus, various discharges and mashed organs. Then we put them into an incubator which mimics the temperature of the human body. Within two days we had a thriving culture of virus. We got our first look at our monster."

Price was silent for a few moments. I had the feeling that what he was telling me were things that he maybe hoped would die with him. Though he could be clinical to the point of cruelty at times, when he was telling me these things he was filled with pain.

"The virus?" I said finally.

"Yes. We put it in the beam...that is, under the eye of the electron microscope. We were looking at a filovirus very similar to Ebola or Marburg."

Filoviruses, or "thread viruses," are quite unique in the world of virology. While many viruses look like balls or plugs, the filoviruses are quite alien in appearance and resemble braided rope or coiling worms. Many think they look much like spaghetti. Price said that even to a microbiologist there is something invidious and evil about them and no one who has studied them has not felt it.

"What we had was Ebola, no doubt of it, but mutated from its ordinary state. A new strain, unspeakably deadly."

Under the microscope was a sort of elongated viral body with dozens of slender threads looping from it. Like white worms or tentacles, he told me. They watched Ebola-X invade healthy cells with savage abandon, an unstoppable army of killer microbes. They would send out their thread-like tendrils, grab a cell, overwhelm it, on and on. Once they had infested a cell, they pretty much gutted it of nutrients and genetic material, forming *inclusion* bodies—crystalline blocks of pure virus—which were replicated viral broods getting ready to hatch and infest. The cell itself would be grotesquely swollen by this point, literally pregnant with virus. Each inclusion body moved outwards toward the cell wall, touched it, and exploded into hundreds of new viruses. These viruses then penetrated the cell walls, causing the cell itself to distort and bulge and finally burst...releasing newborn viruses to find more host cells where they drain them, multiply, and burst free again. The process begins again. An absolutely alarming geometric progression.

"Such a process is horrible when you think about it," Price said. "Viruses making viruses ad infinitum, blocks forming, blocks exploding with hundreds of hatchlings, the host cell bursting, the viruses turned loose, traveling through the bloodstream and clinging to any available cell in a relentless amplification of the original virus."

It was horrible, all right.

It was downright scary, in fact. I was starting to get ideas that left me cold and it all tied in with what I saw in my dreams and what Price was describing to me:

"I'll never forget my first view of the thing," he told me. "It was an absolute obscenity. I was always fascinated by the deadly beautiful horror of Ebola, but this mutated variety literally terrified me looking at it. You would have to see it, Nash, to appreciate what I say. That elongated body with dozens of serpentine white worms coming from it...like snakes, undulant vipers. I thought...*yes*...that first glimpse of it...I thought I was looking at the face of Medusa." He wiped sweat from his brow. "I had the strangest feeling that nightmare was *aware* that I was watching it. That it was looking at me and knowing it was my master. It was pure evil and I knew it. I...dear God, just looking at it made me want to slit my wrists."

Medusa.

I sat there for some time, just smoking my stale cigarettes, staring into the fire and contemplating the end of my own species. Because it was coming and there was no denying it now. The war had thinned the human population considerably, weakening what was left...and Ebola-X would now kick the race's legs out from under it. It would exterminate us. And not as some mindless germ, but as a mutated, hideously evolved germ that knew exactly what it was doing and took grisly pleasure in the same.

Before I could stop myself, I blabbered it all out to Price. My dreams. The Medusa. What it looked like and what I thought it to be and how it was sweeping east to west and leaving well-picked graveyards in its wake.

"It's unbelievable," was all he could say. "And you think The Shape is leading you away from it...to some unknown destiny?"

"Yes. It wants us to get to Nebraska. It wants that very badly." I shook my head. "Why Nebraska? Why not South Dakota or Wyoming or Montana? I don't know. I just don't know."

"Well, there could be one reason," he said. "The Creek."

"The Creek?"

"Yes, Bitter Creek. At Detrick we called it 'The Creek.' The Creek is a Level 4 Biocontainment facility in Bitter Creek Nebraska," he told me. "It was a research complex and storage facility. I've never been there, but I knew of it. We all whispered about it."

I felt a chill up my spine. "And what...what is stored there?"

"Bioweapons," he said. "Every nasty germ we've been genetically engineering is stored there. That's the rumor. In the worlds of virology and microbiology, it's like Area 51. It carries the same mystique."

Bitter Creek.

I could feel The Shape warming to the idea of it. This was it then. The end was in sight. That's where we were going. I would lead and the others would follow. Straight into the heart of darkness, straight into the valley of the shadow of death.

Straight into Hell.

BITTER CREEK NEBRASKA

I

A storm hit us when we crossed the Nebraska state line. It started with rain and hail and fierce winds that tried to strip the Jeep right off the highway. Pretty soon it wasn't just rain hitting us or chunks of hail the size of golf balls, but all manner of debris. The winds picked up anything and everything, creating a lashing, wet whirlwind of flak that made the Jeep shake and jerk like it was pushing through an artillery barrage.

If that was our welcome to the Cornhusker State, it wasn't a very friendly one. I suppose my old pal Specs would have called it a bad omen.

Carl got us off I-80, cut through some farmland and pulled before a huge barn that seemed to be about as long as a football field. Covering our heads, we ducked inside. We were glad for the shelter.

There were cattle stalls up both sides with lots of hay and a concrete drive down the center. At one time, they must have had quite a few head of cattle in there.

Carl and Mickey and I watched the storm through the doorway.

It was really something. The rain was still coming down along with occasional barrages of hail. The sky was flat black, seamed with brilliant scarlet and indigo bands that seemed to flicker and expand like Northern lights. We could see bolts of lightening sweeping the countryside in the distance, just flashing and arcing like airstrikes. The thunder made the barn shake.

"Fucking storm beat the hell out of the Jeep," Carl said. "She's drivable...at least for now."

"We just have to get to Bitter Creek," I said.

"And where is that?"

"According to Price, it's north, up in Boone County."

Mickey nodded. "Okay. And what's in Bitter Creek?"

"That's what we have to find out," I said.

I wasn't about to tell them what I thought or felt or what Price said about the Level 4 facility there. No sense spooking anyone more than they already were. Because I could see it in their eyes: a combination of excitement and dread and there was no mistaking it. They knew we were nearing our destiny, that something very big was just around the corner.

"Maybe it'll be paradise," Mickey said with all due sarcasm. "Maybe it'll be the light at the end of the tunnel."

Carl pulled off a cigarette. "Sure, honey. And maybe it'll be hell on earth."

"Let's just ride this storm out for now," I said.

I left them there hashing it out. I went over to the others. They were sitting on a low stone trough. Janie had broke out some MREs and Texas Slim was regaling them with a story of a tornado at his aunt's farm in Oklahoma. This was his version of dinner theater. I wasn't hungry, but I listened to Texas tell of cows getting sucked up into the funnel, their badly worn carcasses getting deposited in the parking lot of an all-you-can eat barbeque joint twenty miles away.

"So at least none of that beef went to waste," he said.

I walked away, Morse snapping a few shots of me, and leaned against one of the stalls. The smell of hot food made my stomach flip and flop. I stayed there by myself, chain-smoking and wondering if I was leading those poor people to their deaths.

Lost in thought, I looked up and Janie was standing there.

"What're you thinking about, Nash?" she asked me, though I could see by the set of her face that she had absolutely no interest. "Something important or just musing over Mickey's tits?"

"I was musing over Mickey's tits."

Janie shook her head and turned away.

"It was a fucking joke," I told her. "C'mon."

She stayed though it was obvious that she no longer cared for my company and could you honestly blame her? All men lust in their hearts, don't they? But only the stupid ones let it go any farther than that.

"I was thinking about these people, Janie."

"What about them?"

I pulled off my smoke, wishing to God I could quit and knowing there wasn't much point to it at that stage. "They're following me because they have some kind of faith in me or they fear The Shape or they think it—or *I*—will keep them safe. For the most part, they don't question; they accept. And that bothers me. The faith they have."

"Well, faith of any sort would bother a guy like you," she said and then noticing that I was oblivious to her barbs, said, "They need something to believe in, Nash. Everyone does. Especially now. And you have to admit, for the most part they've been lucky with you."

"Specs and Sean weren't so lucky."

But she had no interest in discussing the dead. "And you're bothered by this faith?"

"Yes, I am." I ground out my cigarette. "We're going to a place called Bitter Creek, Janie. All I know is that somewhere near there Price says there is a storage facility the Army kept its germ warfare agents at. That's all I know. But I know it's where I'm supposed to go. I know, somehow, that it all ends there. I have to go there...but I don't know about the rest of you. I wonder if I shouldn't tell you people to keep heading west and just drop me off. I don't like the idea of the rest of you facing what I know I have to face."

"Hmm. Suddenly you have some overwhelming desire to protect their lives?"

"Yes."

"It's too late, Nash. They'll follow you and you can't get rid of them."

"What about you?"

She studied me with her cold blue eyes. "I have my own reasons for staying with you and, believe me, they have nothing to do with love for who or what you've become."

"Why don't you tell me what I've become?"

"What good would it do?"

She turned away and I grabbed her hand. She yanked it away like she'd just touched a rattlesnake. "Don't touch me,

Nash. You don't have the right anymore. I'll stay with you like the others. But only because I need to, not because I want to."

2

"You smell that?" Carl said about ten minutes later.

I stopped brooding. The wind was coming from the other direction, through the half-open door at the far side, and I could smell death on it: hot, putrefying. It was a smell I knew well, the bouquet of every city in the country and the world for that matter. But in that barn you did not expect it. It was high, nauseating and it was getting stronger.

Carl, Texas, and I grabbed our guns.

We tracked the smell to the far end of the barn and each step I took on the way there made my heart sink a little lower. We didn't need more trouble. We had to get to Bitter Creek. And with what might be waiting there, wasn't that enough?

"Something around that stall," Texas said, his Desert Eagle .50 cal in his hands.

Carl moved forward with his AK. I followed.

Corpses.

There was some kind of trough cut into the floor and its purpose was unknown to me. There were five or six bodies in there. They were greening, going soft with rot. They were all bloated up, that stink so thick it was nearly palpable.

"Shit," Carl said.

One of the bodies moved. Then another. It was incredible, but I saw it and despite all I knew about horror by that point—which was considerable, I might add—I found myself gripped with an unreasoning superstitious terror at the idea of a moving corpse.

But there was nothing supernatural about it.

The bodies were infested. That's all it was. A corpse-worm that was perfectly white and perfectly smooth slid out of the eye socket of one of the bodies. It was slimy and steaming, about three feet of it wavering side-to-side in the air, that bulb-like head opening and closing like it was breathing.

Carl shot it, cut it in half before it could spit some of its digestive enzymes at us. The bullets shattered it into a fleshy sauce of black bile. The rest of it slid back into the eye socket.

"We should burn those bodies or something," Carl said.

"Why?" Texas asked him. "Once those worms are done eating, they'll just starve anyway with no more meat to be had."

"True," I said.

Texas and I turned away and walked towards the others. I called out to them that it was nothing but a worm and they relaxed. Carl was right behind us. He couldn't help himself, he pointed his AK into the pit and gave the remains a couple of three-shot bursts.

And that's when we all heard the screaming.

3

A man came charging out at us. He had a shovel in his hands and he planned on using it. I don't know where he'd been hiding—maybe under the straw—but he charged right at Carl before any of us could intervene and before Carl could get his weapon up. He swung the shovel and Carl ducked out of the way. It barely missed his head. The shovel blade hit the concrete with such force it sparked.

Then Carl cracked the guy with the butt of his AK and down he went.

He was some raggedy old man with a white beard. He was on his knees, breathing hard, blood running down his temple.

Carl got his rifle on him.

"We won't hurt you," I told him and he just looked at me with wild, confused eyes. The eyes of an animal. He muttered something, but it made no sense. The others were circled around us by that time. He saw them, panicked, and crawled away on all fours towards the door.

Carl made to go after him.

"Let him go," I said.

He made it to the big door, slid it open and the rain poured in. It was coming down in sheets. The old guy was soaking wet in seconds. He cried out something and darted out into the storm. All of this happened in under less than a minute.

We saw him out there, the rain and wind hammering into him. He started first this way, then that, and then...then he screamed. We all saw something huge and undulant move in his direction. It hit him and dragged him off into the rain. None of us could be sure what it was. It just happened too fast. In the back of my mind I had an image of a gigantic snake coming out of the murk.

He screamed again and that was it.

Guns in hand, we watched, we waited, but there was nothing. Just the rain spraying into puddles and lashing the sides of the barn.

Nothing else.

4

The storm ended a couple hours later and by that time we knew without a doubt that there were things out there, out in the pastures and cornfields. We had no idea what they were, but we could hear them. For some time we'd been hearing low squealing and sharp screeching sounds. And once a resounding booming noise as if something had placed an extremely large foot down.

The storm had left a pinkish fog in its wake, but the Geiger told us it was harmless. Still, it was heavy and claustrophobic and I didn't like the idea of legging it out to the Jeep with what we were hearing. As it was, the Jeep was only a vague phantom in the mist.

"It might be advisable to wait until the fog lifts," Price said.

I was going to disagree with him because I really had to; we had to get moving. Whatever it was, it was building in me: the need to get to Bitter Creek as soon as possible. The idea of waiting was just not an option. His suggestion was greeted with a stony silence by everyone.

Everyone but Mickey. "I think he's right, Nash."

But nobody wanted to wait; I saw that.

"I'll lead the way out," Carl said. "Nash, you come with me. Texas, you get my signal, lead the others out."

I knew then it wasn't just me. The others felt it, too. They were as filled with anxiety as I was. We had to go. We *needed* to go.

Carl went out and I was right behind him. The fog felt moist, almost sticky against my face. Ten feet from the door, the barn vanished. It was swallowed by the consuming fog which seemed to thicken by the moment, stirring itself into an opaque soup that began to look less pink and more blankly white and suffocating.

We found the Jeep and sighed.

"Okay," I called out to the others, wiping a dew of moisture from my face. "Come on!"

Carl jumped behind the wheel and turned the Jeep over. The ignition sputtered a few times and my heart dropped. Sometimes those weird lightening storms will fuse out the electrical systems of vehicles and you'll never get them running again. The ignition caught finally, the engine holding a fine idle.

I allowed myself to breathe.

I knew we weren't alone out there. I could hear occasional dragging sounds in the distance. I was aware of ghostly shapes moving through the fuming mist.

Something moved near the back of the Jeep and was gone before I could draw a bead on it.

"Hurry!" I called to the others, trying to watch every direction at the same time.

Something else moved past me. I could have shot it. It was close enough...but what I saw, well it was too crazy. Just a hunched over shape running on all fours. It looked almost like a hog, a huge and barrel-bodied hog, bristled and corpse-white. That's what I saw. I thought it had the face of a man.

I heard others hopping about in the mist.

Carl got out of the cab. "Are they fucking coming or what?" he wanted to know.

The words barely got out of his mouth when I heard the hopping sounds again and something made a shrill squealing and dove out of the mist, flattening Carl. I ran over towards him and some pig-faced mutation came at me. I put two rounds in it, fired three more into the mulling, hopping shapes in the fog, and something hit me from behind and put me face down.

I came up fast, fired a shot, and heard Carl cry out.

I scrambled over to him and one of those things...whatever in the Christ they were...had him pinned down. It looked like a hog, all right...except that it was swollen a blubbery white. Carl was fighting against it as it pummeled him with its split hooves and tried to get its snout at his throat. I got over there and kicked the thing two or three times until it fell off. I should have shot it...but I was afraid of hitting Carl. It rolled off him, greasy and shining white, and came right up, its face caught somewhere between a hog and a man. Its pink, glistening eyes were on me. It was snorting and squealing madly, its mouth almost like a blow hole and filled with sharp yellow teeth that were curled back like those of a rattlesnake.

It dove and I put three rounds into it, which dropped it but hardly killed it.

Carl had his AK then and he blew its head apart.

It lay there, legs kicking in the mud, splattered with dirt and leaves and splotches of dark red blood that looked almost black against its luminously white flesh. Its head was drilled open in three or four places, jelly-like blood pulsing out with a horrible sputtering sound.

"Jesus," Carl said turning away.

Texas, I knew, had gotten the others back into the barn for safety. He was calling out to us.

"Yeah, bring 'em over," I said.

I saw no more of those hog things.

The others were coming now. I couldn't even see them, I could only hear them stumbling over the muddy drive, splashing through puddles. That's what I heard, the Beretta 9mm tight in my fist. And then I heard something else and if the engine coughing dropped my heart, this made it plummet into black depths. It was a deafening, almost primeval roaring sound that shook the world.

I had the doors open and I pushed Janie and Mickey inside, then Texas and I almost made it. Yes, we almost did.

Then Price cried out. He'd been coming around the rear of the Jeep to get in on Carl's side...and then something took him.

I heard him scream.

Something coiled around him like the thing that had taken the crazy old farmer. It was black and smooth and serpentine, flattened, the outer edges set with spikes like the traps of a carnivorous plant.

I fired at it. So did Carl for all the good it did.

I saw Price get taken. He didn't get pulled off into the fog, he got pulled *up* into it as if whatever had gotten him was hovering right over us.

Morse started snapping pictures like a combat photographer and I pushed him inside.

Carl jumped into the cab and I made to follow suit, except something like a whip lashed out of the fog and hit me. Not only hitting me, but tossing me ten or fifteen feet away.

Carl called out.

I heard someone in the Jeep scream my name. I wanted to believe it was Janie, but I'm sure it was Mickey.

Getting to my knees, the breath knocked out of me, I looked up.

The thing was right above me. It had to be nearly the size of a mobile home. Huge and swollen and lumpy, covered in greasy mats of fur or wiry spines. It was hanging there like it was buoyant, filled with gas. Maybe it was. First thing I thought—although it makes no sense—is *spider*. But it was no spider. I don't know what the hell it was. I saw clusters of orange globular eyes, appendages of some sort akin to legs or tentacles, but segmented like the tails of scorpions, pink and pulsing, the edges serrated with spikes. In the very center of that grotesque, rolling profusion up there was a great black abyss that might have been a mouth.

Those limbs were draped everywhere.

I felt very much like a fly in a spider's web. I knew whatever way I moved, it would have me. So I did not move...I crouched there, stunned, feeling an aching need to piss. The beast hung above me like some freakish nightmare that had being birthed from the fog itself. Slimy and dripping and bristling. The appendages trembled from time to time with shuddering tremors.

It had something in its mouth.

I think it was Price.

It was working him, rendering him. Sucking and slobbering and chewing. Something fell from that colossal maw and clattered to the ground. It was a human femur, polished and gleaming.

I felt a wet peal of hysterical laughter bubble in my throat.

Slowly, painfully slowly, I began moving forward, towards the Jeep which seemed about two city blocks away.

I was a human slug, inching and wriggling forward, moving at such a lethargic pace it took me ten minutes to make it five feet. And even then, I kept moving. The beast was still chewing and slurping, but its limbs twitched and quivered from time to time. Perhaps sensing prey or merely flexing their alien musculature.

The Jeep.

It was close now.

When I was within six feet of it, I panicked. Panicked and crawled madly through the mud until I reached it. The beast moved and slithered and its many limbs—Christ, dozens of them—contracted and fluttered and a few of them began to search over the ground like questing fingers.

It was insane.

The beast kept eating, dropping bones and other things.

I could see it pretty clearly. Or at least that part of it that was hanging from the fog.

It looked like something from a 1950's B-movie, some blasphemy from a Roger Corman flick...a gigantic, hairy jellyfish with those coiling pink appendages.

That's all I could see and it was enough.

I jumped up and ran to the door of the Jeep. I got it open and jumped into the front seat just as something brushed over the top of my head. When the door was closed, that thing got pissed. It dropped appendages and they slithered over the roof of the van, looking for what had gotten away. For one terrifying minute, those limbs were covering the Jeep windows, squirming and scraping, pink suckers kissing the glass. As crazy as it sounds, it was much like being in one of those car washes with the soft flaps brushing up against the windows. I watched those dozens and dozens of pink suckering mouths. They looked like lips.

When the thing pulled away, Carl gunned us out of there.

Something scratched against the roof and something else pounded the tail gate and made the Jeep shake. Then blood, very red and running, splattered over the windshield and Carl cleared it with the wipers. I saw one of those semi-human hog's heads roll off the hood.

Then we were back on the main road, racing through the mist.

I never asked any of them why they didn't try to come after me when I was trapped out there and I didn't think I needed to. I knew why: they'd been paralyzed with fright.

5

Carl stayed well outside of Omaha, cutting north up to U.S. 30, and the farther we went the quieter it got in the Jeep. Even the small talk petered out after awhile.

We drove on through the fog, moving slowly in case there were stalled cars or trucks on the road.

Carl drove and drove and drove.

The silence grew thicker, almost permanent.

We drove for an hour and then stopped in a little town to gas up. I do not remember the name. It was dead, completely dead. A black silence echoed through the streets. The houses were gray and sagging, paint beginning to peel from their boards. The lawns were overgrown, weeds spouting up through cracks in the streets. The windows were all dusty and blank. Nothing had lived there in a long time. Mickey found a few skeletons in a little park across from the gas station where Carl did some siphoning.

But that was it.

We drove away.

I slept for awhile and when I came awake, Mickey was sleeping with her head on my lap, her knees pulled up to her chin. I looked over at Carl and he smiled at me with a wicked grin. Mickey came awake and looked like she was ready to do what Carl had been insinuating.

The fog was still pretty heavy.

We rolled into another little town and the streets were deserted, burned-out houses to either side. Lots of wrecked cars, weedy lots, and shattered plate-glass windows.

"Look," Mickey said.

I saw them: people. They were lined up on the streets as we passed, faces distorted from sores and growths, raw and rotting. Ulcers had eaten holes right through them. For every one that stood, a dozen more were sprawled on the pavement or rotting in the gutters. They were all hot with plague. They threw things at us that splattered against the Jeep. I want to think they were rotting tomatoes.

We drove for a few more hours and then slowed down. I saw a town ahead.

"Bitter Creek," Carl said.

6

We didn't go in the first night. We camped outside at a little roadside park. It was getting late and I don't think anybody wanted to charge in there in the dark, especially without knowing what it was we were charging *into.* We built a fire and we ate and we sat around. Nobody said much.

It was a nice night.

The fog had lifted and the stars were bright. It could have been a sky ten years ago or anytime before Doomsday. The only telltale giveaway was an occasional flickering purple-blue corona at the horizon. Other than that it was perfect.

I was thinking about Price and all the things he'd told me, how they all fit in with what I knew and what my dreams told me. I was sorry Price was dead. He hadn't wanted to go out in the fog, but we had made the decision for him. Was that a portent of death? Probably not. Just a very wise man recognizing a fool idea when he saw one.

I squeezed my eyes shut and all I could see were the faces of dead friends. Then that faded and I saw the cities to the east—

lifeless, wind-blown, heaps of smoldering bones. Nothing but death to the east of the Mississippi now and nothing but death creeping slowly west. Iowa was dead now. So was Minnesota, Missouri, Oklahoma, Arkansas, and East Texas. Dead. Kansas was going to its grave and so were the Dakotas. Nebraska would fall next and I knew it.

The Medusa was getting closer, moving faster and faster.

I started to sweat and shake because like The Shape, I could feel it out there chewing westward town by town. I had some kind of vague psychic uplink with it and I could feel it getting closer, seeking me out on a hot wind of pestilence.

"You okay, Nash?" Mickey said. "You look funny."

"He always looks funny," Texas said.

"Yeah, I'm okay," I said.

Nobody believed it and neither did I.

I studied my posse each in turn.

Good old Carl, always at my side. Just like Mickey said, my loyal watchdog. Texas Slim, perpetually amused by all around him. Mickey, eyes burning hot and salacious, always ready to please. Janie, her love grown cold, nursing secrets and resentments. And Morse, just crazy as crazy got, fooling with his camera. I think I was attached to them in one way or another and that's why I wanted them gone.

But I knew they wouldn't leave.

Because something was out there and they wanted to see it, too.

7

We walked into town that first day, armed to the teeth. I needed to see Bitter Creek up close and personal. I wanted to know what it looked like and felt like and smelled like.

We found our first corpse within the hour.

Some guy twisted up in the grass, a four-leafed clover tattooed on his right bicep. It hadn't brought him any luck at all. He was slashed open, burnt, crushed...almost looked like he'd fallen out of a burning plane a half a mile up. But that wasn't it. His death had been ugly and brutal, certainly, but it had nothing to do with planes because there were no more planes. Just like there were no more trains or baseball games or TV. Not much of anything, you came right down to it.

Just the six of us.

We were crouched in a cornfield, watching the little town below us in the valley. There was a sign ahead on the side of the road, its Day-Glo surface blasted with bullet holes. BITTER CREEK, it said. And beneath that: CLASS C BASKETBALL CHAMPS 1996.

I wondered if Lucky had played basketball.

I figured he hadn't. He was so mangled and misused it was hard to tell if he was thirty or sixty, but with that tattoo, I figured he was some kind of tough. Guys with tattoos are always trying to tell the world something. But this guy? What was he saying? Not much. He looked like something you scraped off the bottom of your oven. But that tattoo was unscathed. Go figure.

Carl said, "I figure this guy ran out of luck."

"Sure as hell," Texas said.

There were lots of things that could have killed the guy, but we all knew the Children had gotten him. When they got their hands on someone they always left them looking like this.

"All right," I said. "Let's go. Let's find out what all this is about."

Morse took a couple pictures with his Nikon and nobody mentioned the fact.

We cut back to the road and followed it towards town. We hadn't gone too far when we came to yet another gruesome sight: scarecrows. A ring of scarecrows circled the town like a noose. Except, of course, they weren't scarecrows exactly, but mummified human corpses that had been picked by birds, blown by the dry wind and baked in the sun. The crosses they'd been nailed to were very tall, maybe twenty feet, and they rose high above us like the masts of galleons.

"Looks like a warning," Carl said. "Something to scare outsiders off."

Morse got a few shots of them.

"I don't think it's anything quite that simple," Janie said, but would elaborate no more.

She was becoming increasingly mysterious and mystical. But, all that aside, I had to agree with her. This was no warning. Not exactly. I was thinking more along the lines of an *offering*. I wondered if those poor bastards had even been dead when they were nailed to the crosses. I decided I didn't want to know.

I stood there, smoking a cigarette with Carl, staring up at them, senseless and transfixed

"You boys might want to watch those cigarettes," Texas Slim said. He pushed a boot down into the yellow grass. The grasses crunched, broke apart into tiny fragments. "Awful dry here. Awful dry. One dropped match or cigarette..."

I could imagine the place burning and it made me smile. Because even then, hovering at its perimeter, I knew it was nothing but a vile pesthole. It had the same atmosphere as a plague pit.

"Be a shame," Mickey said.

The six of us rounded the crest of a hill and, stretched out below us, was Bitter Creek. It wasn't much. Maybe it had held four or five thousand at one time, but that was before the bombs fell. Just another drop of a town in the puddle of Nebraska. A little place surrounded by cornfields.

Mickey grabbed my arm as we started down. "Be careful," she said. "We all need to be careful now."

I knew it, too.

The town was just another graveyard, yet I knew it was special. Some how. Some way.

"Where's that facility that Price told you about?" Carl asked me. "The germ warfare place?"

"Probably outside town somewhere. We'll look for it tomorrow," I told him, tuning into the psychic shortwave of the town and feeling its dead immensity settling into me. It was like putting your ear up to the wall of a tomb.

No one said anything as we entered the city limits. There were no signs of anything alive. But there was a smell in the air: death. A putrescent blanket that covered us, suffocating us with its heat and heaviness.

"Mmm, that air," Carl said. "Nothing smells quite like Nebraska."

The streets were lined with rusting cars and debris, the gutters clogged with brown leaves and broken glass. The sun was high in the sky in a hazy, filmy pocket, reflecting off the filthy glass fronts of the main drag. All of which had white crosses painted on them. The military had done that in Youngstown, I remembered, when they cleared houses of plague bodies. But I didn't think that's what this was about. This was something even darker, something pagan at its roots, something more along the line of hex signs.

A police car with flat tires and an imploded windshield stood watch on the outskirts. Behind the wheel there was a skeleton in soiled rags. A silver badge winked on its chest. It was not the only skeleton we saw. There were others sitting on benches, laying in the grass, even parked in chairs behind the windows of businesses. I rather doubt they had died in that state; someone had arranged them that way.

"I smell something," Mickey said.

I was waiting for Texas or Carl to crack a joke about that, but no one spoke. I could smell something, too. Putrescence, surely, but this was something almost worse: the stench of disease and drainage, hospital dressings foul with seepage and gangrene.

We came to something like a village green and it was crowded with people who were sitting or sprawled on the ground, huddled tightly together like beggars. Many of them were dead, but many were not. The living ones saw us, but did not speak.

We kept our distance.

"They're full of the Fevers," Texas said.

There was no doubt of it. Faces were ulcerated, pocked with sores, cracked open like dry earth and running with bile. Eyes were blood-red and glazed. Limbs contorted. Bodies bursting with blood. They were coughing and sucking in rattling breaths. There had to a hundred or more and all of them burning hot with Ebola-X, plague, cholera, anthrax, diseases I could not begin to identify. They gathered in a pool of their own drainage and filth like people at an open air festival waiting for the first band to take the stage.

I had to wonder who or *what* they were waiting for.

"I'm thinking we shouldn't linger," Mickey said.

We moved on.

8

We walked down those empty, leaf-blown streets of Bitter Creek and I knew we weren't alone. We were being watched and it wasn't by The Shape, even though I could feel my significant other getting nearer. It was funny, but I could actually *feel* it, feel The Shape out there—in my guts and along the back of my neck like a hand coming out of the darkness. You didn't need to see it to know it was there. It wasn't time for a selection, not for another week or more.

But The Shape was active.

We were in Bitter Creek.

It had been waiting for this.

But what I felt watching me was not The Shape. It could have been more of the infected like in that park. Because we'd already come across five or six other little communes like that, all of them dying or dead, but waiting. Just waiting.

I didn't think it was them, though. This was something else.

I could feel it just fine. I didn't know if the others could. There was someone out there. I just hoped that whoever it was, was human.

"When are you going to tell us why we're here?" Janie asked me. "When will the grand plan be revealed to the faithful?"

I ignored the sarcasm. "When it's revealed to me, that's when."

The tension between us was almost unbearable now. Everyone was aware of it, but nobody was talking about it. Too much shit to deal with without all that fucking baggage that Janie and I had so carefully packed. Mickey felt the tension and sidled up right next to me, making sure a bare arm or bare leg was in contact with me. Skin to skin. There was alchemy in that and she knew it.

I stood on a street corner, swallowing, feeling the town, sending out fingers of perception in every direction. Where was it? Where was the revelation? I knew it was here. I could feel it going up my spine like fingernails, coiling in my belly, filling my blood with electricity...where was it? When would it show itself?

I reached out to that sphere of darkness in my brain which I acquainted with The Shape's WiFi, but got nothing. The Shape was near, but very much offline.

"Well, Nash?" Janie said. "Are we going to stand here while Mickey dry humps your leg or are we going to get to this already?"

"Fuck you," Mickey told her.

"Wouldn't put it past you," Janie said.

I started walking again.

We came up to something like a town square. Lots of brick-fronted businesses with dusty windows, simple frame houses spread out beyond. The lawns were all yellow and overgrown, the streets plastered with wet leaves. A Mobil station, a video store, a bowling alley, a café...this could have been any of a thousand towns in the country. They were all laid out approximately the same...Main Street or Elm or whatever as a hub, everything else radiating out from it like the spokes of a bike tire. Same old, same old. Just another dismal little town filled with death. You could smell it in the air...a sharp, almost pungent yellow smell of age and decay and memory sucking into itself. The moldering, old smell of a library filled with rotting books...except it wasn't the books that were rotting here.

I saw more white crosses. They seemed to be in the windows of every business and every home.

"What do you make of it?" I asked Texas.

He shrugged. "Damned if I know. The cross, as I understand it, only exists for two purposes: to call something in or ward something else off."

I wondered what Specs would have made of it with that mind of his.

As we walked, sensing the place, letting it fill us like poisoned blood, Janie kept looking at me. I pretended I wasn't aware of it. But, eventually, I looked over at her and those blue eyes of hers were blazing. Hate? Anger? No, maybe something like disappointment. Something *beyond* disappointment. I didn't know what it was. Not then. But it was coming. She was brooding something inside. Something she was going to share with me when the time came.

But not before.

We all had our guns out and we were feeling tense. There was a thickness in the air, the sense that although maybe we were the only ones wading through this particular stream, there were others watching us from the grassy banks, just biding their time, studying us.

About that time, Mickey stopped. Stopped and cocked her head. "I feel...I feel like I'm being watched," she said.

Janie sucked in a breath. Maybe I did, too.

"That's just me," Texas said. "I been watching your ass is all."

"Shut up," she said.

Mickey, as I've said, was intuitive as all hell...she could read people, she could read situations. And she wasn't liking this one at all.

Morse, of course, seeing her standing there looking darkly beautiful and haunted like she did when she was sensing something, snapped a picture of her. Mickey didn't even flinch. She'd had lots of pictures of her taken in the old days and she was a natural at it.

We moved through the streets very slowly, trying to pick up on what was watching us. Outside a little drug store, we found two bodies. Children. They were curled up on the sidewalk, reduced to husks....just wiry and blackened, crumbling. When Carl nudged one with his boot, it fell apart like cigarette ash. I'd seen it before. Sometimes, the Children just decayed like isotopes, burned themselves up from the inside out.

We kept moving.

And still, those eyes watched us.

"Nash," Mickey said, gripping the Browning Hi-Power she carried in both hands like a cop on a shooting range, "I'm getting a real bad feeling here. There's somebody watching us out there."

Even Carl didn't have a smartass response for that.

Morse scanned the streets with his telephoto lens, humming under his breath. Janie looked at me and I looked at her. Maybe I was going to take charge like a true leader, maybe I was about to rally my troops, but something happened.

A door slammed.

Slammed damn hard.

We all jumped.

Then we went after it. We cut down an alley and came out on another tree-lined street. Houses, buildings, and then a little ma and pa lunch counter at the end. I saw movement behind the plate glass windows and went after it. I went in first with my Beretta in my hands, ready to start busting caps. Inside, it was typical...flyspecked windows, a long counter, lots of empty tables. Everything dusty and wreathed with cobwebs. A cross on the glass.

And a girl.

She could have been eleven or twelve, I was thinking. She just sat there in a booth like she'd been waiting for us. She was out in the daytime, so I knew she wasn't one of the Children.

"Hey," I said. "What are you doing here?"

But she wouldn't answer me.

She was dressed in rags that might have been jeans and a sweatshirt once. Her face was grimy, her red hair clotted with filth. And she stank like she hadn't had a bath in months, like she'd been pissing and shitting herself. And judging from those dark stains at her crotch, I think she'd been menstruating, too.

"Take her," I told Carl.

Carl liked that bit. Strictly stormtrooper fantasy. He handed his shotgun to Morse and went over to the girl.

"You got a name, sunshine?"

She just looked up at him with this dull, bovine look. He put the questions to her about who had survived and where they were and what she was doing alone. She just kept staring, though, either an idiot or mad or simply made that way by the world pissing down its own leg and leaving her stranded in a dead town.

He slapped her, just warming up. "Talk, you fucking cunt," he said.

But the girl didn't even make a sound. He might have been striking a rump roast thawing on the counter...this girl wasn't much more than that: animate meat.

"Stop it!" Janie said. "She's just a child! Don't you dare hit her!"

Carl drew back his hand to start again, but I shook my head and he stopped. He shrugged, grabbed the girl by her hair and threw her to the floor. He planted a knee in the center of her back and dug some duct tape from his pack, taped her wrists together behind her back. She did not fight. She did not struggle. When Carl was done, he yanked her to her feet.

"Nash?" he said. "Request permission to piss all over this wench so she at least smells a little better."

Morse took a picture of her.

"Request denied," I said.

"All right," I said to my troops. "Let's take a five."

"I'm all for ten," Texas said.

"Yeah, I need to sit down a minute," Mickey said, dropping into a booth and crossing her long bronze legs, making sure I saw her do it.

I did.

And Janie saw me looking, too.

We ate some MRE spaghetti and pork and beans. Nobody'd had breakfast and we were hungry. I sat there watching the girl and had a smoke, maybe feeling sorry for myself and the shell of the world at the same time. I was looking at the big picture and seeing me and my people, all the other scattered bands, as insects crawling over the rotting cadaver of some dead beast. I think, essentially, the analogy worked.

I closed my eyes for a moment and all I could see was that formless gray pestilence getting closer. The Medusa. I had the shakes. My heart was pounding. I had an overwhelming urge to vomit out everything I had bottled up inside.

"Okay," I finally said. "Break's over. We got shit to do."

We all got to our feet and right away, I was feeling that same old bit again, that we were being watched. I just couldn't shake it. It wasn't The Shape and it wasn't that girl, so then what?

I remember Mickey looking over at me, telling me with her eyes that she was feeling it, too. And then I heard a thudding report out in the streets and it took me almost a split second to realize it was the bark of a rifle.

A hole opened in the plate glass window.

We all dove down, except the girl and Morse. Jesus, stupid harmless Morse. Now he wasn't a fashion photographer doing spreads for *Newport News* and *Spiegels,* no, now he was a combat photographer. For as those rounds kept chewing into the dusty windows and they fell apart like candy glass, shattering amongst us, Morse just stood there with his Nikon to his left eye, working his telephoto and f-stop, trying to get a good shot for *Newsweek* or *Time.*

I yelled for him to get down. I don't remember what I said, but something about getting his fucking head down and then there was another report and a slug caught Morse right in the telephoto. Lucky shot or really good aim, I didn't know. But I saw that camera fly apart and blood and meat blast out the back of Morse's skull. He folded up and died without saying a word. I told everyone to shut the hell up. Somebody out there had a long-range rifle, maybe a .30-30 or a .30.06. I wanted them to get closer so I wouldn't miss.

Silence.

No sound out in the streets and none in the café. After a few moments, I heard a couple voices calling out there. Sounded like kids, teen-agers maybe. We stayed put, drew those bastards in. And they came, muttering amongst themselves. I whispered for the others to just get ready and I rose up behind one of the booths so I could get a look. Sure, maybe a half-dozen kids and some older guy with a rifle. They didn't bother sending out a scout, they came towards the café in a group.

"Get ready," I whispered.

Mickey had her Browning, Texas had his Desert Eagle .50. I had my Savage 30.06 and Carl had his AK.

I watched those peckerwoods converge on the diner. They were quite a crew. They were all long-haired and so filthy that you couldn't tell if they were boys or girls. They carried pipes and axe handles and baseball bats. From the stains on them, I figured they knew how to use them, too. The older guy kept his rifle up, urging the others forward. As they made to climb through the shattered windows, we came up shooting. We drilled three of them before the others even knew what happened. The old guy started shooting and killed one of his ratpack with a wild shot, but did no other damage. We kept shooting and pretty soon they were all down. Even the old guy. Mickey had jacked a couple rounds into his right kneecap and he was done.

Carl hopped out there first, kicking his rifle away.

I followed with Mickey behind me. A couple of those teenagers were still alive, vomiting out blood into the street. They smelled so bad and were so dirty, even Janie wasn't rushing to their rescue. They looked like Neolithic savages, filthy and bruised and pockmarked, their teeth rotting from their mouths. The air stank of gunpowder, violent death, and voided bowels...but I don't think they were infected.

Carl was kicking the old guy when I got there.

I told him to stop. Mickey had done quite a job on his knee. It was blasted to mucilage, one of the bones sticking right through his pant leg like the end of a shattered Pepsi bottle.

"Filth! Trash! Fucking garbage!" he yelled at us. "Y'all ain't nothing but trash and dirt and cunting animals, that's all you is!"

"Shut the fuck up," I told him.

He just stared at me, eyes simmering with hate. "Think you're something all special, eh boy? You ain't shit." To prove that, he spit. "You...you and these animals...y'all don't know what yer in for. No sir, y'all ain't got a clue. But I know. Yes sir, I know."

Texas Slim was kneeling next to him. "So why don't you elaborate, kind sir."

"Hell he say?" the old man wanted to know.

"He wants to know what we're in for," I said.

The old man laughed with a bitter, resentful sound. "Idiots...y'all don't know, do you? Ha! This town ain't gonna be nothing but a boneyard come tonight or tomorrow or the next day! It's coming for all of us! Coming out of the east, yes sir! And there's those here that *want* it to come! You see all them sick ones? They been pouring in for weeks! For weeks! Some have died, but others is hanging in just so they can see it! Look it in the face when it comes home to roost!"

"Look what in the face?" Mickey asked him.

The old man offered her a grin of brown, rotten teeth. "The Devil," he said. "The Devil."

Everyone bristled at this, but none of them were surprised. I had talked with them about it and they had not needed my words. For inside, they knew just as I knew.

Mickey came over and wiped some dirt from my cheek. You should have seen how she did it. She licked her fingertip and then drew it real slow over my skin.

Mickey wanted me and I suppose I wanted her again, too. I mean, really, how could a guy *not* want Mickey? She was a pin-up girl, a centerfold. She had the tits and the ass and the legs, was darkly pretty and seductive. You could just imagine how many guys had whacked off over pictures of her in magazines. Yeah, she was hot. So hot a picture of her in your pocket would have burned a hole in your pants and started a brushfire in your crotch.

But the truth was, she scared me.

She really did.

While Janie turned her head when I called up The Shape and it took its sacrifice, Mickey liked to watch. She *really* liked to watch. Death and violence got her off. Maybe it always had or maybe it was something the end of civilization had unlocked in her. I didn't know, but I did know that she had some seriously scary psychosexual issues. She liked to watch The Shape take its offerings of meat and blood. She liked shooting people. She liked looking at the aftermath of bodies and shattered anatomies. And right then? Looking down at those dead teen-agers? *She was getting off.* If we weren't there, she would probably have masturbated. Her nipples were standing hard against her t-shirt and I was willing to bet that if I slipped my hand down the front of her cut-offs, I could have slid two fingers into her without much trouble.

She was looking from the bodies to me, the hunger all over her. She looked like she wanted to take a bite out of something or have something take a bite out of her.

Janie was watching this, of course.

I caught her eyes once and quickly looked away. Something in them made me wither. I had slept with both girls now, Janie repeatedly.

Trust me, it was no notch on my belt. Because it was always there in the back of my mind, that dread question of what I would have to do if either of them became pregnant. Because if the stories were true, babies *always* became like the Children and usually right away. Monsters. They came right out of the womb like that, literally burning their way out and killing their mothers in the process.

Could I let Janie or Mickey suffer like that?

And better, would I have the balls to put them down if and when it happened?

9

The Hatchet Clans came not thirty minutes later.

Just when you think things can't much worse, they usually do.

I decided to let the old man and the girl go. We didn't need them and I was pretty sure they didn't need us. I didn't know what to do with the old man. I did my best splinting his leg. He looked like he wanted to tear my throat out the entire time.

Carl cut them loose and the girl ran off. The old man looked at us one last time, spit at my feet, and out the door he went, hobbling off with a broken broomstick for a crutch. He looked almost casually at the corpses of his posse and then went on his way. He didn't make it half a block before he screamed.

Carl and I were just dragging Morse's corpse out the door...and I saw three Clansmen hacking on the old guy. Scouts. That meant the main body was coming. I got back inside and told the others to hide. And just in time. For rolling down the streets like a storm, the main body was coming. Screaming, breaking windows, they had arrived.

I watched them storm past the front of the diner in their filthy, ragged olive drab overcoats and gas masks, scalp locks greased, axes and pikes, chains and clubs in their hands. Several carried decapitated human heads. They swung them by the hair. They found the bodies of Morse and the teenagers and set on them in a pack, more pressing in all the time like swarms of insects. They scalped the teenagers. They eviscerated them, dismembered them. They took Morse's head with them.

We were in unbelievable danger.

If it came to it, we could kill quite a few, but I knew that in the end they'd overwhelm us with sheer numbers. They mulled about for about an hour, marching around and hissing to one another through their masks. None of them came into the diner. I figured that was a real spot of luck.

I thought we were going to make it.

Then twenty of them charged. They weren't as stupid as I thought. They knew where we were and they played us, let us relax, let our guard go down slightly—because with the Clans in the street it never went down completely—then they attacked.

We killed at least ten of them, ducked into the back room and went out the rear door into the alley. Right into a nest of those assholes. We started shooting and dropped quite a few, but it was close-quarters combat and they came from every direction.

I saw Carl go down beneath a tangle of five or six of them.

And Texas Slim shouted: "*Nash! On your left!*"

I turned and shot another that was bearing down on me with an axe. And then Texas knocked me to the pavement and took a spear in the belly for it. He'd saved my life but sacrificed his own. They kicked my rifle away and beat me down with clubs. They had Texas down. He was screaming as he was jabbed repeatedly with five or six spears.

I fought to my feet and something collided with the back of my head. The last thing I saw was them hacking on Texas and Janie being dragged away down the alley.

10

I remember coming awake to the sound of my own voice: *"Janie? Janie? Janie...where are you, Janie?"*

I blinked and blinked again. Finally my eyes opened, focused, and I saw the Hatchet Clans. We had been taken to some kind of encampment outside town. In the distance I saw those crucified mummies up on the crosses. There were fires burning, canvas tents pitched. I was tied to a post driven in the ground. Mickey was to one side of me and Janie was to the other. Both of them were unconscious. They were still dressed, so I supposed they hadn't been raped or tortured yet.

But that was coming.

Because that's what the Clans did with women. With men, they generally killed them outright. But maybe they had a special purpose for me. Maybe they would make a grand spectacle of my death.

For the time being, we were of no interest to them.

I watched them sharpen axes and spears, fashion weapons from slats of wood and lengths of iron. If they had voices, real voices, I never heard them, just that indecipherable hissing. Now and again they'd make ratlike squealing sounds as a fight broke out between individuals. And when they fought, trust me, they fought to the death.

I watched a couple of them—women, I thought—threading things onto a length of metal bailing wire. Human heads. Five or six of them. They jabbed the wire into the ear and pushed it right through and out the other ear. Then they tied off the wire between two green tree limbs jabbed into the ground.

One of the heads belonged to Carl.

II

I must have went out cold again because when I awoke, two of the Clansmen were standing right before me and I could smell the hot stink of raw meat, filth, and urine coming from them. One had a knife and he cut me free. Numb, I pitched straight forward like a tree into the grass. Blinking in the hazy sunlight, I looked up at those gas masks on their faces. I knew the subhuman things that were beneath them.

They hissed something at me.

And when I didn't understand, one of them kicked me.

I wanted them to kill me. It was the best I could hope for. I didn't want to see what they did to the girls. Texas and Carl were dead. I was having trouble wrapping my brain around that. Because with their deaths, in a way, everything had died. The core of my posse was gone. My connections were severed. Because Texas and Carl connected me to Sean who connected me to Specs who connected me to Youngstown and Shelly and my life. And now it was gone. I had no center.

"Fuck you," I said at the Clansmen which is what stupid, thick-headed idiots like me always say when we know *we're* the ones who are fucked.

They said something in their garbled voices.

Then I heard thunder. Or what I thought was thunder. But it wasn't thunder at all. Because it came again, a lot closer: a shrieking explosion that vaporized five or six Clansmen, scattering pieces of their anatomy in every direction. Another round hit. Another and another. I could smell fire and smoke and blood.

The encampment was under siege.

The Hatchet Clans were scurrying around madly. I heard the reports of automatic weapons. I saw Clansmen fall beneath volleys of bullets. Through clouds of twisting smoke and around blazing tents I saw the raiders step into view: forms in shiny plastic orange suits with helmets on. There were faces behind the darkened plastic helmet bubbles and air lines leading from the mouthpieces to tanks on their backs. They were completely enclosed. They carried stout, short-bodied submachine guns in their hands.

I remember thinking: *Those are Hazmat suits, biocontainment suits. The kind of suits people like Price wore when they worked with hot agents. Space suits. That's what Price called them.*

This was a fucking biocontainment team.

The Hatchet Clans were outnumbered, out gunned.

They died in numbers. I could hear Janie and Mickey shouting out. I scrambled over the ground, found a dying Clansman and took his machete. He grabbed my leg, snarling at me. I brought the machete down on him again and again. I didn't stop until the blade was gored with blood and he stopped moving.

And when I turned back to race to the girls, two men were standing there in their orange space suits. I could not see their faces through the visors. I could only hear the sound of their respirators hissing in and hissing out. They had their guns aimed right at me—H & K machine pistols, I thought, the kind counterterrorist units used. They did not lower them.

Speaking through an external speaker with a modulated, artificial voice, a man said: "Drop your weapon please."

I was overwrought, I suppose. My life had disintegrated in the last twenty-four hours. I wanted blood. I wanted payback. I wanted some sweet, clean revenge. I suppose I must have looked dangerous with a bloody machete upraised to attack. "But my friends...they fucking killed my friends..." I said.

"They're dead now, the Clans are dead," the voice told me. "They can't hurt you anymore."

I could hear an occasional report of a submachine gun as the Hatchet Clans were mopped up. Soon, I didn't even hear that. There was only silence. The murmuring sound of voices coming through speakers.

I dropped the machete.

They did not lower their weapons. A couple others cut Janie and Mickey loose. They came over to me, eyes despairing and full of questions.

"Come with us," the man said.

"What do you want? We haven't done anything," I told him. "Where are you taking us?"

"To the place you wanted to go," he said. "And tonight...tonight you will meet that which you have been running from."

I felt a chill run up my spine. We had been rescued, yes, but I had a nasty feeling we were about to be given to something far worse. After all the selecting I had done, I had the nastiest feeling that it was *I* who had just been selected.

"What the hell is this?" Mickey said to me.

But I didn't have a fucking clue.

12

Of course, I did. In a way I did.

This is exactly what bathrobe guy had been talking about that day in Gary: *They came in silver buses. I saw 'em. They had orange suits on. They took Reverend Bob and threw him in the bus.* I remembered how intrigued Price had been when we related the story to him after the silver bus hit us in Des Moines. He knew what it meant. Even then he knew exactly what it had meant.

Janie, Mickey, and I were taken in a sliver, windowless bus out to an Army base beyond Bitter Creek. This was *The Creek.* It sat behind a high chainlink fence, actually a series of them with dog runs between, a collection of low white fabricated buildings attached to a larger brick complex. Numerous outbuildings were scattered about. The signs were everywhere: U.S. GOVERNMENT PROPERTY ABSOLUTELY NO ADMITTANCE. And my favorite: DEADLY FORCE AUTHORIZED.

We were taken into one of the buildings at gunpoint. Inside, it was clean with electric lights. I even saw operating computers. It was like going back in time a couple years. For in this complex, the old world was still operating, smoothly, efficiently. We saw other forms in orange space suits mulling about. Many of them stopped what they were doing when they saw us. Several backed away like they were afraid of us.

"I demand to know what this is about," Janie said. "We haven't done a damn thing. What do you want with us?"

Her question went unanswered. This was a military operation, it seemed. We'd get answers if and when they decided to give them to us. We were ushered through a series of hissing airlocks that had to be opened with plastic ID cards. There were guards with guns behind every one. We went through two more airlocks, the signs announced BIOSAFETY LEVEL ZERO and then BIOSAFETY LEVEL 2. Each time the door slid open, I could feel the difference in air pressure. It was like you were being sucked into the room. It was what Price had been talking about: negative air pressure. At Level 2 we were bathed in blue ultraviolet light. Next, we climbed into an elevator and went down quite a ways. When we climbed out a sign said

BIOSAFETY LEVEL 3: STAGING AREA. There were signs around that read: DECON. Which I think referred to the chemical showers you had to go through before going in and particularly when you came out.

We passed through Level 3 and then we reached the big, bad one that price had told me about. There was a stainless steel door before us and just the sight of it made my guts crawl up into my chest:

EXTREME CAUTION

BIOHAZARD

We went through another airlock and into an anteroom with more Decon showers, ultraviolet light sterilizers, and hoses that sprayed chemicals—judging from the signs—on you with the touch of a button.

Janie, Mickey, and I pretty much stuck together. We felt like monkeys going into a test chamber and that's exactly what we were. We were terrified. More figures in orange suits waited for us. Several had blue suits on with airlines hooked to overhead pumps that moved as they did, sliding on tracks. All we could hear was the hissing sounds of respirators.

They echoed and echoed until it sounded like you were living in an iron lung.

The walls were gray, hoses hanging from the ceiling. Every corner and crack and crevice were caulked thickly with some kind of goo, probably to keep anything from slipping out. There was a series of rooms leading off the first as we were led deeper into the maze. I saw labs and animal containment areas lined with cages. We were brought into a small room with three plastic contour chairs against the wall, each separated by about five feet so you could not hold the hand of or touch the person next to you.

We were told to sit and we did.

We didn't even dare move.

Two figures with submachine guns watched over us. Then the third one who'd led us in motioned to them and all three left. A clear plexiglass door slid shut and locked into place.

"What the hell is going on here?" Mickey said, rising to her feet.

Right away there was a beeping alarm. A voice over an intercom said: "Please stay seated."

Mickey sank back down.

Janie and I exchanged looks of absolute dread. We smiled thinly at each other, but there wasn't much hope. We knew we were screwed.

The door slid open and a man in an orange suit came in. He carried a small black metal box with him. The guards had returned.

"All this," I said, "is unnecessary. We are not infected with anything. You don't have to keep us down here. We're not sick."

"Aren't you?" the voice said.

"No we're not!" Janie said. "Please, get us out of here!"

"That's our intention," he said. "Unfortunately, only two can leave. One will join us."

"Fuck this!" Mickey said, jumping up, the alarm going off again. "I'm not a fucking guinea pig."

The man turned to her. "Take the female. She's the one."

"Stop it," I said. "This is insane!"

He was unmoved by anything I said. "You are the one that made the selections."

My face dropped.

"We know about it. We know about your sacrifices to your pagan god. Very well. Make your selection...which of the females goes with you and which stays here?"

I jumped up and a gun was pointed in my face. Janie and I were held at gunpoint.

"Please...don't do this to us," I begged him.

"Make your choice," he said.

"If you'll only listen—"

"Your choice."

It was pointless to argue. I suggested taking me, but that wouldn't do either, I was informed. Only two of us would see the Medusa, the third would stay behind.

"Very well," the man said. He pointed at Janie. "This one—"

"No! No! Get the fuck away from her!" I shouted. "Not her...not Janie..."

"Then this one?" he said.

I swallowed, nodded.

"Nash!" Mickey cried, "Jesus Christ, what are you doing? Are you out of your fucking mind, you sonofabitch? I belong with you! You know I do—"

Two more guards came in, they took hold of Mickey and held her down. She fought. She screamed. She clawed. But in the end, the man took a syringe with a long needle from the black box and jabbed it into her throat, depressing the plunger. Shocked and shaking, Mickey was put back in her seat. Her face was wet with tears.

"This is fucking crazy!" I shouted. "We've done nothing! We're no threat to you! We're not fucking infected! Take us somewhere! Anywhere! Put us in quarantine together! Just get us out of this fucking lab!"

The man was unmoved by anything I said. It meant nothing to him. He stood there like some kind of fucked-up automaton from a B-movie, just staring at me through his visor. Now and then, through the darkened bubble, I could catch a glimpse of a face in there. But I couldn't see it. I couldn't see his eyes and they were what I most wanted to make contact with.

"The effects should begin shortly," he said.

Mickey was curled up in her chair, shaking, her eyes glazed with horror. She looked like she was in shock.

"But she's not infected!" Janie said.

The man and his guards stepped to the door. It slid open behind them. "On the contrary," he said. "Your friend has just been injected with a mutated, lethally hot strain of the Ebola-X virus. As we speak, her system is being flooded with millions of viral particles."

The door slid closed.

This was my hell, my pay-off. All that selecting and sacrificing had led here, down a very dark path to this awful moment of betrayal. I felt dead inside, used-up, hopeless. It took some time before I could even look at Mickey, at the broken deceived thing she now was. Her gaze was enough to make me want to put a gun in my mouth.

"You'll pay for this, Nash," she promised me. "In the end, you'll suffer like I did. You'll die horribly and you'll die alone."

13

Within thirty minutes it began.

Janie and I wanted nothing better than to comfort Mickey, ease her mind somehow, make her realize that she was our friend and we stood by her regardless of what had happened...but we couldn't. She was infected with Ebola-X and we didn't dare come into contact with her. Not that it would have mattered. Mickey hated both of us. She wanted us, and particularly *me,* to know agony.

Within minutes, the real Mickey was...*gone.*

That shocked look in her eyes, she just sat there shaking. She did not respond to anything we said. It was like she had not just been shot up with Ebola, but with some sort of sedative.

We kept calling her name, trying to snap her out of it, but she did not seem to realize we were there.

And then, like I said, within thirty minutes it began.

She went limp in her chair, head lolling to one side, limbs dangling. She was still shaking and as we watched she began to convulse violently, these little broken agonized sounds coming from her throat. Her eyes slid shut. Sweat ran down her face and you could smell the hot stink of it as her fever spiked. Her entire system was under attack. It was devastating.

She sat there, slumped in that chair for a time, not moving or making any sound, then the convulsions began anew. Blood began to run from both nostrils. Her lips peeled back from teeth that were red-stained. A mist of blood came from her mouth. She jerked upright, hands gripping the arms of her chair.

Then her eyes snapped open and they were a brilliant, translucent red.

Janie cried out.

It wasn't so much like Mickey was infected by Ebola-X, but literally *possessed* by it.

She tore at herself, tearing at her skin with her nails. She ripped her shirt open and her breasts and belly were contused with rising sores. She yanked out locks of hair from her head. She screamed with a deranged shrieking sound.

It took her with amazing speed.

Her face—so pretty, so darkly sensual—began to contort like the muscles beneath it were no longer working in conjunction but fighting against one another. The left side began to sag, the right side twisted up in some grim corpse-like rictus. In classic Ebola this was due to brain damage, soft tissue destruction and the dissolution of connective tissues...but with this mutated form of X, I began to suspect it was something even worse.

Her flesh popped with red sores, it went from that lovely olive hue to one that was discolored, mottled, set with livid contusions that seemed to spread out as we watched. Blisters bulged on her face, her legs, from one breast. They popped open, spewing drainage. And as each one popped, dozens more took their place until her face was unrecognizable, just a twisted mask of jellied flesh. Then she began to bleed. It came out of her eyes and mouth, trickled from her ears and bubbled from her pores. She fell to her knees, vomiting out profuse amounts of tarry black blood and poisoned bile.

She let out one last agonized scream.

She gyrated on the floor, head thrashing wildly from side to side and tossing loops of blood over the floor, up the walls, onto the clear plexiglass door where they ran like rain drops. She squirmed face down on the floor, moving with such wild contortions that she seemed practically boneless. Then she rose up on her knees straight as a post and threw herself at the door, striking it with her face and hands, making splatting sounds, and sliding down the glass leaving a greasy smear of blood and macerated tissue.

She trembled and went still, seemed to deflate as if the air was let out of her.

Long before any of that happened, Janie and I were clutching each other, pressed into the corner.

"Why don't they take her away, Nash?" Janie wanted to know. "Why don't they just take her away?"

I didn't know. The room was a slaughterhouse of blood and leaking fluids. The stench of drainage, blood, and infection was hot and nauseating.

Easily a half an hour later, Mickey began to move.

Her corpse began to tremble.

She had to be dead. She had crashed and bled out, the virus burning through her. Then she sat up, her back to us, staring out the plexiglass door through the mess she had made on it.

"Mickey?" I said.

She stood up painfully and turned to look upon us. Her black hair was greasy with blood, filthy plaits of it hanging over her face which was bulging, distorted, like hot wax that had cooled too quickly, settling into all the wrong places. One eye was sealed shut in a web of tissue, the other was huge, bulging from its raw socket like a bleeding, raw egg yolk. Her lips were sealed shut with strings of flesh on the left side of her mouth, but on the right the lips had sunk away, leaving a grin of gums and teeth.

"Nash," she said and it sounded like her throat was filled with wet leaves. "Do you wanna fuck me again?"

Janie cried out and I think I did, too. I held her tight against me as terror filled both of us. I looked upon Mickey, the abomination she had become, and I was literally speechless. It felt like the inside of my mouth had been sprayed with oil. I could not seem to get my tongue to work to form words.

Mickey came forward, pus dribbling from holes in her face. She gripped one breast in her bloody hand and squeezed it. It was the most obscene thing I've ever seen. Because when she squeezed it, it bulged then ruptured open, black juice and liquefied tissue running down her belly.

"What's the matter, Nash? Ain't I good enough to fuck?" she said, getting so close that the heat and stink coming off her made me retch with dry heaves. "Ain't I hot enough? Ain't I? Ain't I? Ain't I?"

God only knows what might have happened next.

But the door slid open and two men in orange suits led her out of the room. She went willingly with them, sensing that she was now part of them and not part of us. They had an orange suit for her. She stepped into it. Rubberized boots went over her feet. A helmet went over her head. The respirator was turned on. I could hear the hollowing hissing of her breathing.

Faceless as the others, she walked off with them.

That was the last I saw of Mickey.

There was no doubt what was going on by that point. There could be no doubt. I could hear Price's voice in the back of my head: *You see, Nash, when a hot virus infects its host, what it's trying to do, essentially, is to convert that host into virus.* But he had said complete, successful conversion was impossible. But he'd been wrong because that's what was happening here...beneath those orange and blue spacesuits there were no people, no healthy organisms of ordinary flesh and blood, but walking, functioning, *thinking* masses of hot virus, viral imitations of human beings and nothing more.

They had nothing to do with Janie or I.

They were in league with The Medusa and they were waiting for it to come, their savior, their prophet, a new god for a seriously warped new world.

Janie and I had not been assimilated yet. That made us dangerous. That's why those figures in the spacesuits had backed away from us when we entered the complex: it had been revulsion and fear. Fear of infection. Fear of contamination. For they feared healthy, normal bodies with their active compliments of antibodies as much as we feared Ebola.

Janie and I were nothing but disease masses now, infections to be eradicated. We were the abnormal ones.

After a time, two forms in orange suits returned. One of them carried the black box.

"It's time," the one with the box said.

"Don't do that to us," I said. "Please. Just kill us. Destroy us. Don't shoot us with that virus."

"We're not going to do anything to you," the man said. "When you are converted, it will be *she* who touches, *she* who welcomes you into the fold."

He was talking about The Medusa.

"Please," Janie, said, tears running down her face. "Don't hurt us. Don't hurt us." She put her hands to her belly. "You can't. I'm pregnant."

14

Three hours later, I was still reeling from that one.

But it all made sense when I finally calmed down and was able to look at it with some kind of perspective. Janie had been strange and moody for some time now, even worse than usual, and that had less to do with me being with Mickey than with something much larger than all that. She told me knew since Gary. When we were in that pharmacy after the Hatchet Clan attack and after those birds fed on the Clans, she had slipped off and gotten a pregnancy test. One of those home jobs where you just read the strip. I remember her disappearing that day. Then coming back with that funny look in her eyes.

"Why didn't you tell me?" I said.

"What would the point have been, Rick? What would it have changed?"

"I had the right to know."

"Maybe you did. Maybe you didn't."

The men in the space suits took us out of the complex by gun point and led us off into the fields and brought us to a hilltop. You could see for miles from our vantage point. And what I saw was a little valley spread beneath us and it was filled with people. The same sort of people we had run into in Bitter Creek: the diseased, the dying, the suffering. That crazy old man had said they had been congregating in the town for some time and for a particular reason.

It's coming for all of us! Coming out of the east, yes sir! And there's those here that want it to come! You see all them sick ones? They been pouring in for weeks! For weeks! Some have died, but others is hanging in just so they can see it! Look it in the face when it comes home to roost!

That's what he had said and now I was seeing them, thousands upon thousands of them crowded together beneath us, a hot wind of pestilence blowing off them as they waited in the seepage of their wastes and drainage. They were moaning and chanting, holding leprous fingers up to the sky, watching for the coming of their god with ulcerated faces and eyes filled with blood.

Dozens of men in spacesuits with submachine guns ringed the bottom of the hill in all directions. Dozens more waited at the fringe of the crowd below. There would be no escape for Janie and I. None whatsoever. At least, that's what they thought. But I had already decided that a swift charge at them would make them open up on us, cut us down out of sheer terror. Because they *were* afraid of us.

Dying beneath a hail of bullets was better than the alternative.

"When will it happen, Rick?" Janie asked.

"Soon," I said.

And it would be soon because there was a spreading stain of gray rising up at the horizon and I knew it was The Medusa, darkening the land as it...or *she*...came.

I sat there, holding Janie's hand like we were a couple lovers waiting for the fireworks to begin on the Fourth of July. I drew off a cigarette, wishing I had a cold beer to go with it. Wishing for a lot of things, I guess. What vexed me was that even though I understood much of what was going on now, I still did not understand my part in it or, more precisely, *The Shape's* part in it. Why did it want us here? What was so fucking important about all this that it kept pushing us west?

What did it want here?

What did it need here?

I had to know, somehow I had to know. I closed my eyes to the mulling crowds below and shut my ears to their fevered cries. I concentrated on that sphere of darkness. This time I did not call it up. I communed with it.

15

Right away a wave of blackness rolled through my brain. My mind was uplinked with that of The Shape and The Shape was letting my mind reach out beyond until I could sense The Medusa out there. I could feel a horrible crawling in my head as if thousands of worms had infested my brain, tunneling, digging deeper, breeding and brooding, their hot, moist eggs bursting with millions of writhing larval young.

I screamed.

In my mind I screamed.

For this was The Medusa, what it was: an invasive life force of infestation and pestilence and charnel horror. Not worms, not really, but exploding particles of virus.

The Medusa's voice was in my head, a dry and snakelike hissing.

I could smell millions of slimy corpses rotting, bursting with gas and worms, greening with putrescence. It was a crypt smell, a stench of fuming corpse ovens, of carrion boiling with maggots, of viral infestation. Of cities heaped with the dead and plucked white bones piled like ramparts up into the sky.

The voice hissed and the worms dug deeper and I felt my mind implode like thunder, as The Medusa enveloped it in a black, pestile cloud of corruption, invading my mind as its children must invade cells: sliding tendrils through membranes, draining them dry, bloating them with a hideous viral pregnancy like millions of eggs hot and juicy that would erupt with seeking death—

16

Janie shook me out of it and I was thankful for that because I don't know if I would ever have come out of it on my own. My eyes opened and I saw that creeping shadow closing in on the valley. I saw the faithful cheer and heard them scream with delight or terror and perhaps both. The Medusa spread across the earth like a fire storm destroying everything in its path.

I had felt it in my mind and I had seen it in my dreams and now I saw its physical reality as everyone in the valley did.

A spreading gray shadow that was blank and formless, as far as the eye could see: lifeless, hollow, a vapor of dead alien plains. Then...fragmenting, swelling and bursting, slitting open like some immense birth canal in an undulant mass of white and worming tendrils that reached for miles, reached right up to stars themselves as the world became carrion threaded by a million-billion hungry corpse worms. The tendrils split apart into more webbing tendrils and filaments and snaking ropes of slime that were viscidly alive.

And beyond it, rising like the cold marble graveyard face of the moon was The Medusa itself: an elongated, mutating, ever-changing firmament of gaseous malevolence. An elongated face like a dead-white moldering corpuscle, flaking and fragmenting in the hot cemetery wind of plague breath and swirling bone dust. A living pestilence of viral matter with a mind of gnawing starvation and immense black tunnels for eyes that reflected the tenebrous glare of shadowy sterile worlds and the dripping voids between the stars.

The faithful began to scream.

They had waited for her, dreamed of her in their bacterial delirium and she had come. Now they sat at her table not as guests but as food and she looked down upon her gathered offerings with a sawtoothed, contorted, cadaverous grin of plague pits, her eyes pulsating with evil color, verminous yellow wastes kissed by cold flames of fever.

Shrouds kissed by stillborn winds, rustling like graveyard rats in subterranean tombs, she unraveled herself, taking what was offered, taking her sacrificial lambs.

I watched them scream as she settled over them, one by one popping like overripe pumpkins and rotten gourds, their blood and tissue and disease meat vaporized and sucked up into the chaotic maelstrom that was The Medusa. She left nothing but smoldering bones in her wake as she moved across the valley taking what was hers and hers alone.

Janie screamed as we felt that hot wind blow up at us like a breath from a crematory oven. She screamed. She fought in my grip. She went absolutely hysterical as I held onto her feeling numb and emptied by the sight of this haunter of the dark.

She grabbed my face. She kissed it again and again. "If you love me," she cried. "Don't let her take me! For the love of our unborn child and the love I have for you, don't let it end this way! Call it! *Nash...call The Shape...*"

Revelation.

This is what made it push us here, prod us ever westward. Yes, it wanted to keep me and mine out of the path of The Medusa. But that was only part of it. The Shape did not love us. It was not some caring, compassionate father figure protecting its children. It did not know love. It did not understand loyalty or devotion or even the need to protect life itself: it knew only hunger and here was the ultimate feast that it had known was coming all the time. This table had been set a long time ago and now it was filled with food just as The Medusa herself was a banquet of life force.

I kissed Janie as that wind grew hotter and held her beautiful face in my hands one last time, then I called up The Shape. I peered into that sphere of darkness, that zone of blackness which was a conduit to it and maybe its own black little beating heart.

I summoned it.

And it came.

Something shifted around us, the air was filled with a thrumming energetic vitality. It went heavy, crackled with static electricity. There was a sudden thrumming sound and an overpowering stink of ozone.

The Shape rose up out of the ether, a whirlwind of shrieking matter, black and buzzing, angry and spinning. A writhing, energized cloud of radioactive dust and debris and force. An elemental field of sentient electrons, wrath and destruction and appetite and I could feel the raw force coming off of it. A stink blew off of it like fused wiring and melting steel, cordite and the breath from foundry ovens.

The Medusa was a relentless, unstoppable machine of death, but The Shape was a sentient, living thermonuclear furnace.

It rose up high as two story building.

It paused there, sparkling with flecks of luminosity and arcs of electricity. Two leering red eyes looked out from that storm of atomic refuse. The noise it created...like screeching metal and hurricane winds and bubbling cauldrons...was so loud you had to shout over the top of it.

"Take them! Take them all! Take everything that's yours!" I screamed at it.

When it moved, that buzzing sound rose and its body envelope began to spin faster. It was doing that now as it came in my direction. At the last moment, I could feel the blazing, cremating heat of the thing and it was like standing too near a smelter full of molten steel. The Shape was still thirty feet from me at the bottom of the hill, but close enough to bake my skin and singe my eyebrows. I collapsed at that very moment. But at least I knew something...I knew what it had been like for those others, I knew the horror they must have felt as they were scalded and incinerated, kissed to ash and embers by that abomination.

The Shape did not want me, of course. It went right for the men in orange suits. They were vacuumed into that living kiln, that living nuclear reactor.

When The Shape takes them, it takes them fast.

They were sucked in, absorbed and leeched and disintegrated, dissolved and vomited out the other side. When they were pulled in, The Shape lit up like phosphorus, like blazing witch-light. You couldn't see much when they were assimilated by the thing, but if you didn't look away, you could catch a few glimpses. Sometimes they flew apart like meat in a vacuum chamber and you saw blood and tissue, limbs and organs and I don't know what spinning into that seething radioactive tornado. I think it actually took them apart at the subatomic level, particulated them, consuming their electromagnetic fields and the very bonds that held their molecules together. When it had what it wanted—and, believe me, this took about ten seconds—it reassembled them, integrated them, and spewed them out the other side...but never the way they went in. Just smoking, blackened heaps that were often anatomically altered. I'd seen arms growing out of backs and heads jutting from bellies, bodied reversed and rearranged from molecular dispersal and realignment. And sometimes, when The Shape took two or more at once, they came out like what we were seeing: a steaming and sparking clot of melted wax with bones thrusting out in every which direction. The figures in the space suits had had their atoms mixed like the fly and the scientist in that old movie. The mass they had been reduced to cooled fairly rapidly and we could see that they had all been fused into one, like plastic army men heated and squished into a whole.

It was sickening and repulsive.

Then The Shape took the faithful that The Medusa had not yet reached.

They were pulled in and disassembled, changed and slapped back together, spit out into a fused and burning mass.

Janie stood up and watched it. I stood by her. We held each other as The Shape moved at The Medusa. I never loved her more than I did at that moment. I loved her so much it squeezed tears from eyes knowing that I had betrayed her in so many ways.

In my ear she said, "Our child can never be born, Rick. You know what it would become. What they all are."

Then she kissed me and ran off down the hill.

I went after her, but not fast enough.

She dove right into that whirlwind of devastation, that thing born of breeder reactors and atomic cremators, that living chain reaction of thermonuclear waste.

I screamed when she came out the other end...smoking and sizzling and mutilated.

There was nothing I could do but dive in myself, but The Shape was moving too fast now, gaining speed for its collision with The Medusa. I scrambled back up the hill and ran as fast as I could, rolling down the other side and into a leaf-filled ditch.

I didn't see The Shape collide with The Medusa, but I heard the explosion. The detonation of two fields of energy colliding. The world went up like an exploding sun, a blinding blue-white flash of light that blinded me and a thundering eruption that shook the earth, leveled the hill and nearly buried me alive in soil, rocks, and debris.

That was it.

When I dug myself free finally, there was no one and there was nothing. The world was a void of steam and smoke and gradually diminishing heat. As it cleared I saw the valley had become part of a greater pit that stretched for miles, blackened and smoldering. Every tree as far as I could see had been blasted to a stump. Hillsides were flattened. Like I said, a void.

I looked into my mind for that sphere of darkness but it was gone. Just gone.

I was alone.

Absolutely alone.

17

Back in high school, as you recall, I read a story in a science fiction anthology and the writer began it by relating the shortest horror story in the world:

The last man on earth sat alone in a room.

There was a knock at the door.

For two weeks now I've been thinking about that story as I sit alone in this room dictating the events that you have just heard on a digital voice recorder I swiped from the complex. For two weeks I've been here in this little house that sits on the edge of the abyss created by the collision of The Shape and The Medusa, which is the borderland between today and tomorrow and perhaps yesterday.

Everyone is dead.

I can't know that for sure, of course, but in my heart I feel that it is true. There are still birds in the sky and things that scurry in the woods. Three nights ago I heard a wolf howl on around midnight and it was the most lonesome, haunting sound I have ever heard. So there is life out there, but none of it is human.

Writing this down has been a great joy for me, a greater horror, and the greatest pain I have ever known.

I've had to admit things about myself, look at my life from a bird's eye view and what I saw has not been pleasant. I only relate what happened and now, as they say, my tale is told.

Two days ago red spots started popping on my skin. I am weak. My joints ache. This morning my nose began to bleed.

Mickey has her revenge.

Her curse is complete.

It will be done in twenty-four hours, I think, as I can feel it escalating. Speech begins to get difficult. How I contracted Ebola-X two weeks after the last vectors were destroyed in that atomic firestorm of the collision, I do not know. My Geiger Counter told me that the area was saturated with radiation for three days before dropping back to the high end of near-normal. Radiation sickness I could understand...but this, well, it makes me believe in Karma, it makes me believe that I'm paying for the lives I took.

It makes me believe that Mickey's curse was the real thing.

I'm ending this recording now. I doubt if anyone will ever listen to it because, let's face it, there's no one left *to* listen to it. I will lay down now in my deathbed and wait for it while I dream of my beautiful wife and remember my friends, remember Sean and Carl and Specs and Texas and Mickey. And particularly Janie and the love we shared, the child we made that was never to be born.

The last man on earth sat alone in a room.

There was a knock at the door.

It was Death...

THE END

CPSIA information can be obtained
at www.ICGtesting.com
Printed in the USA
LVHW040121200123
737519LV00002B/203